Howard Hill

The Creighton Family Saga

Book Two

by

Betty Larosa

authorHOUSE®

AuthorHouse™
1663 Liberty Drive, Suite 200
Bloomington, IN 47403
www.authorhouse.com
Phone: 1-800-839-8640

First published by AuthorHouse 6/12/2008

ISBN: 978-1-4343-8275-7 (sc)
ISBN: 978-1-4343-8276-4 (hc)

Library of Congress Control Number: 2008903376

Printed in the United States of America
Bloomington, Indiana

This book is printed on acid-free paper.

ACKNOWLEDGEMENTS

First of all, I want to acknowledge and thank all those who created such a demand for *Creighton's Crossroads*, the first book in this four-part series, and asked how soon this second book *Howard Hill* would be available. The overwhelming response was gratifying.

Now I really have to search for adequate words to thank my dear husband Gene who supported me throughout this long process, offered advice, and supplied answers to my many questions. He then took up the unenviable task of acting as my business manager/cheerleader when the first books were delivered to our home. He is a dear and a real keeper.

Once again, thanks must go to my friend and mentor, Gerald Swick. Without your help and encouragement, Gerald, I would not be writing these words of praise about you for my second book. Thanks. It's such a small word, isn't it? But it carries heart-felt gratitude.

Several years ago during my research, I made several inquires and was led to Professor William D. Henderson at Richard Bland College, the College of William and Mary, in Petersburg, Virginia. He not only responded to my inquiry, he shared a wealth of information about wartime Petersburg from his own research. Words cannot convey my thanks to him for giving me so many invaluable insights into the plight of that besieged city.

I cannot neglect to thank Christopher Calkins, Chief of Interpretation at the Petersburg National Battlefield. He answered my questions with genuine interest and offered encouragement with my work. Many thanks, Chris.

And, of course, all those who were mentioned in the acknowledgments in *Creighton's Crossroads* may consider themselves thanked once again for their interest and support. To the many readers across the country whose response to my feeble efforts gave me the lift I needed to carry on. Thanks to each and every one of you.

Betty Larosa

He may be surprised when he reads this, but I dedicate this book to my amazing grandson Ryan who also loves history.

'I am my beloved's and my beloved is mine.'

Solomon's Song of Songs
Chapter 6, Verse 3

CAROLINE
1864 - 1865

Chapter 1

SINCE ITS FOUNDING 153 years ago, the mistresses of Howard Hill had never given a thought to doing laundry—or any other menial task, for that matter. It had never been necessary before. Before Fort Sumter. Before the food shortages. Before the slaves ran off. Before the Yankees.

Caroline Howard, current mistress of Howard Hill, straightened up and arched her aching back. Since early this hot June morning, she had been bent over the laundry tub washing the bed sheets. Several times, she'd become light-headed in the oppressive Tidewater Virginia heat, but managed to overcome it.

How delicious it would be, she moaned to herself, to bathe my face in cool water, sit in the shade of the gazebo and rest my back. But there was no time for that. Cassie and Mina, the remaining house slaves, had already aired the mattresses and carried them upstairs. The sheets had to be taken in, ironed and put away after she finished washing the last of her undergarments.

Later that afternoon, while ironing the sheets at the back door to catch the cross breeze from the front door through the entry hall, Caroline cocked an anxious ear. "What is that commotion down on the main road?" she wondered aloud to Cassie who had just come downstairs.

"Don't know, Miz Caroline," Cassie said. "Me and Mina was wonderin' that ourselves. Sounds like the whole Confederate army down there."

"Haven't we had enough to deal with," Caroline grumped, and spit on the iron to test it.

As she folded the last of the sheets, Caroline heard her mother-in-law Dorothea call from the front porch, "Caroline, please come and tend to these people. They have no business on our property and are creating such a furor."

"How I hate this war," Caroline muttered to herself. "It can't end soon enough for me." Picking up the sheets, she started toward the porch.

At the front door, she gasped in disbelief at a sight she had never seen in all of her twenty five years. A huge cloud of dust hovered above the City Point Road nearly a quarter mile away. The cloud appeared to be moving toward the plantation, and within that awful disturbance, she could see animals and wagons.

As the mass of dust, animals and humanity moved closer up the driveway and spilled out into the meadow, she saw scores of soldiers on horseback, others in wagons or on foot, covered with dust and sweat and blood, dropping to the ground from exhaustion and the deadly heat. But they are not our boys, she thought with panic. They are Yankees!

"Caroline, tell those Yankees they will have to move on," Dorothea Howard commanded with a wave of her fan at the intruders. "I cannot permit those people on the place while Morgan is off fighting for the Glorious Cause."

Caroline stared at her mother-in-law as she rocked languidly in her wicker chair and watched the approaching blue-clad intruders through narrowed eyes. Mother Howard truly is losing her mind if she expects me—a woman alone, armed only with freshly ironed sheets—to tell the Union army to move on. She stood on the top step of the porch, one hand shading her eyes from the sun, and watched as a Union officer approached her on horseback.

"Good afternoon, ma'am. I am Major John Wesley Madison, at your service." Removing his hat with a gallant flourish, he bowed in the saddle to her. "In the name of the United States Army, we are hereby confiscating your property."

"What did you say?" she shouted back at him. "I cannot hear you above all this noise. Did you say you were confiscating our property? No, Major," Caroline shook her head, "I am afraid you will have to move along. We simply cannot allow Yankees on the place. Goodness, what would people think?"

"I am sorry about this, ma'am," Major Madison shouted back, his tone polite, "but we cannot concern ourselves with that. As you can see, my men and their mounts are exhausted."

At this point, an officer with a scruffy beard appeared out of the swirling dust and noise. "What is the problem here, Major?"

"Sir, I am having trouble convincing this lady that we are confiscating her property for a few days."

"I see." The Colonel fixed his intense black eyes on her. "What is your name, madam?"

She shrunk away from those eyes that were at once intimidating and pain-filled. "Mrs. Morgan Howard," she managed to say loud enough to be heard, before breaking into a fit of coughing from the dust. "And this is my mother-in-law, Mrs. Justin Howard."

The Colonel touched the brim of his hat to acknowledge Dorothea before turning back to Caroline. "Colonel Philip Creighton of the Strickland Pennsylvania Volunteers, at your service, and we are indeed confiscating your property."

"If you have come looking for food, Colonel, our own quartermaster department has already picked us clean. In case you haven't noticed," she added, pointing toward the empty fields in the distance, "we are in the midst of a drought. And now, you descend upon us like the plague and disturb the tranquility of our home with all this dirt and commotion, and expect me to greet you as welcome guests."

Colonel Creighton removed his dusty hat and slapped it several times against his thigh. "Madam, we are fully aware of the conditions hereabouts. We have been strangling on this damned dust for weeks. But I promise you, we will be here just long enough to rest and feed the men and animals then be on our way."

Stiffening at the Colonel's course language, Caroline informed him in clipped tones, "In that case, Colonel, I must ask you to mind your language."

The Colonel placed his hat over his heart and shouted, "My deepest apologies for my offensive language, Mrs. Howard. Allow me to assure you that no harm will come to you or your property during our brief stay. I will issue orders to that effect." After clapping his hat on his head, he barked over his shoulder, "Lieutenant Southall!"

"Sir?" Another officer rode forward and favored Caroline with a dazzling smile before looking to Colonel Creighton for orders.

At the handsome Yankee's smile, Caroline suddenly became aware of her disheveled appearance and tried frantically to tuck in the loose hair that straggled about her face.

"Lieutenant," the Colonel was saying, "secure this area. Find water for the men and horses. There should be a well at the back of the house. And see if there is a stream nearby. Ask First Sergeant Powell to send a trooper up and down that main road to find someone who can tell us where the hell our provisions are. Let headquarters know that we are encamped here for the time being.

"Then, after posting pickets and looking over the grounds, give me your recommendations at a staff meeting," the Colonel glanced at his pocket watch, "in about an hour. Meanwhile, I need to lie down. This damned leg is still killing me. I beg your pardon again, ma'am," he offered by way of a perfunctory apology to Caroline.

"Yes, sir." Lieutenant Southall saluted and rode off, calling for Sergeant Powell.

Caroline watched the Colonel dismount with a tightlipped grimace, and limp up the porch steps. As he passed by her, she wrinkled her nose at the odors emanating from his person. It has been quite a long time since the Colonel has come in contact with soap and water, she thought, and lowered her eyes. Just then, she spied a bandage on his left leg that was spotted with fresh blood and wondered if he had recently been wounded, which would account for his foul mood.

At this point, Dorothea rose from her chair to confront the Yankee intruders. Her thin frame was clad in a blue flowered dress worn thin by years of washing and ironing, her gray hair pulled back into a severe knot. With blue eyes that showed no fear, she said with authority, "Sir,

I cannot permit this invasion of my home. I must ask you to remove yourself and those—" she pointed her fan toward the front meadow, "—those ruffians with you."

Giving her a chilling smile that crinkled the dust on his face, Colonel Creighton bowed. "I appreciate your sentiments, madam. You have my word as a gentleman—"

Jerking her chin, Dorothea sniffed in disdain.

"—I repeat, as a gentleman, that I have already given assurances to the other lady that no harm will come to anyone on the premises. Nor will any of your property be molested. Now, if you ladies will excuse me, I must see to my men. After the staff meeting, you will be apprised of the rules you must observe during our stay here, which I assure you again, will be of short duration."

"Rules? In my own home?" Dorothea waved her fan under his nose. "I simply will not tolerate this. Caroline, tell this reprobate that we cannot abide such effrontery."

"Save your breath, Mrs. Howard," Colonel Creighton said to Caroline. "The matter has been decided." Reaching suddenly for the porch rail to support himself, he turned to the other officer, "Come with me into the house, Major Madison. We will select a room best suited for my needs. And be away from all this noise."

"Yes, sir. Ladies." Major Madison bowed to Caroline and Dorothea before following Colonel Creighton into the house.

Caroline stood, as though rooted to the porch floor, and watched the two Yankee officers disappear into the entry hall, unmindful of the frantic activity all around her. Teamsters swore at the balking, weary mules pulling supply wagons, mounted cavalry pounded up the driveway toward the back of the house, officers shouted orders. But she was unaware of it all.

Yankees had invaded her home.

Chapter 2

COLONEL PHILIP CREIGHTON collapsed into a straight-backed chair inside the entry hall. "Ah, it's much better in here." He surveyed their surroundings with a critical eye. "The house should suit our purposes quite nicely for no longer than we will be here."

Hardly of grand proportions, but built to accommodate a large family, the house appeared well kept. In the Southern tradition for good ventilation, the back door was situated opposite the front door in the wide entry hall. The stairs rose to the second floor on the left side of the hall. The ironing board, abandoned by Caroline moments earlier, stood at the open back door.

Through the door, Philip could see that chaos reigned. Dr. Cook barked orders about where he wanted his medical tent set up. Corpsmen scurried at his commands. Barely audible within the confusion, Philip could hear the feeble moaning of wounded men, and he shuddered.

Turning his attention to the room on the left of the front door, he observed that it served as the company parlor and music room. A small pianoforte sat in the bow windows. A tapestry sofa with gracefully curved legs placed before the fireplace was flanked by lamp tables. Two brown horsehair chairs faced the sofa. On the wall directly opposite the door hung two black silhouette portraits. Undoubtedly, Philip thought, Howard ancestors from the previous century.

The large family parlor across the hall revealed dust covers on the furniture, now layered with fresh dust. Hobbling down the hall beside Wes, he glanced into the dining room on the right, which boasted a table capable of seating twelve people comfortably. A breakfront sat on the back wall. On the opposite wall, over a mahogany sideboard, hung a beveled mirror flanked by empty candle sconces. Two large windows faced west, their lace curtains hanging limp in the stifling heat. Through the windows, Philip could see his company of men riding up the driveway toward rest and, hopefully, water.

Across the hall from the dining room, Wes pointed out a good-sized room that had obviously been used as the plantation office. A large desk sat perpendicular to the window with a red leather chair facing it. Behind the desk stood a tall bookcase containing almanacs, farm ledgers, and books relating to animals and agriculture.

Philip jerked a thumb toward the empty gun cabinet in the corner. "All the guns are gone."

Wes grinned. "No doubt carried off by the Howard men to fight for the Glorious Cause."

"Yes, leaving these poor women defenseless," Philip said with disgust, and limped back to the front of the house. "I will use this room as my office, Major," he said, and entered the room with the silhouette portraits. "It will afford me some degree of privacy as well as an unobstructed view of the driveway. Have someone bring my field desk in here, but only after the men have rested and seen to their mounts."

"Yes, sir. I'll see to it. By the way, how are you feeling now?"

"I'm all right," Philip said, not happy about being reminded that he'd passed out from the heat and loss of blood before his men out on City Point Road. "How is your hand?"

Wes inspected his right hand. "The swelling has gone down and it doesn't ache as much."

Philip cracked a half-smile. "It looks a hell of a lot better than my leg."

After Wes' departure, and while making mental notes about rearranging the room, Philip was startled to see the younger lady standing in the doorway, still holding her folded sheets.

Moved by the panic in her eyes, he limped toward her and said in a gentle voice, "I regret that our sudden and rather chaotic appearance has disturbed the tranquility of the household, Mrs. Howard. I assure you that we are not wild beasts on the prowl to ravage unprotected ladies. May I inquire how many are presently in the house?"

"Just Mother Howard, Aunt Emmaline and myself. Aunt Emmaline is bedfast. I believe she is dying," Caroline added in a barely audible voice.

"I am sorry to hear that. Where are your men folks? The darkies?"

She paused before answering, "My father-in-law passed on several years ago. My husband and his brother Justin were with General Armistead. Justin was killed at Gettysburg last year. I have not had any word at all from my husband since that time, or heard anything about his fate. I have been living with the uncertainty of not knowing if I am a widow. The darkies ran off, some to join the army. As for the others, I don't know. Now," she said, lifting her chin, "you know exactly how vulnerable we are."

"I am sorry about your husband and his brother, ma'am. Do you mind if I inquire as to the nature of your aunt's illness?"

"The poor thing hasn't been able to cope with the war and all the shortages. After losing her nephews and so many other family members and friends, she has taken to her room. She keeps Father Howard's sword at her bedside to thwart any Yankee who might try to molest her."

Philip suppressed a smile at the image of the elderly lady defending her honor with a sword. "I admire your aunt's spirit, but she has nothing to fear from us. She is safe in her bed. But I will ask Dr. Cook to look in on her when he has a moment."

"That is kind of you, Colonel, but I doubt that my aunt will allow him in her room." Caroline blushed and suddenly appeared flustered. "I must go now. Cassie and Mina are waiting for these." She tapped the freshly-ironed sheets and, turning, started toward the stairs.

"Wait," Philip called out. "Who are these other two women? You did not mention them earlier."

"Cassie and Mina are the only house darkies who did not run off."

"But you said there were only three of you." As he limped toward the stairs, his frown deepened. "Why didn't you mention these women before?"

Caroline cringed against the banister. "I thought you meant only white folks."

"I meant anyone living on the premises," he said in an exasperated tone, unwilling at this point to engage in a discourse about the evils of slavery. "Oh, by the way," he waited until she paused on the second stair tread and turned to face him, "I would take it kindly if you ladies stayed close to the house while we are here. We would not want anyone else learning of our presence during the next two or three days."

Caroline gave him a measured look. "In that case, Colonel, we shall pray most earnestly for your imminent departure."

During the staff meeting an hour later, Philip's men sprawled on various pieces of furniture in the room now used as his office. They all agreed that the shady meadow at the rear of the house was the ideal location for the hospital tents, due to its proximity to the well. Sergeant Powell suggested placing the mess tent on the east side of the house, nearest the stream.

"What about the horses?" Major Madison asked.

"There's a small stream on the other side of the orchard. The water is running pretty low but it's real shady down there."

"Sounds good," Philip nodded. "Now, Major Madison, what are your recommendations for quartering the officers?"

Wes Madison assigned sleeping quarters in the parlor across the hall to the other officers, with Father O'Boyle opting to sleep outside with the enlisted men. Dr. Cook was assigned the plantation office near the back door, providing him easy access to the hospital area. Picket duties were already assigned and the blacksmith found a suitable location for his fire and forge.

"As for the ladies," Wes continued, "in order to ensure their safety, I suggest that the upstairs rooms be declared off limits to all military personnel."

"My thinking exactly," Philip said. "I might add that anyone violating that order will face severe penalties. The officers must emphasize that to the enlisted men, and remind them that all personal property, including the gardens and stock, must be respected. Is that clear?"

"Yes, sir," the officers replied in unison.

"Well," Philip said, standing to indicate that the meeting was over, "now that the horses have had their fill at the stream, I say it is our turn to do something about our own disreputable conditions, with a bar of soap in hand."

Once he was alone, Philip allowed himself the luxury of propping his throbbing leg on the sofa. Closing his eyes, he savored the relative calm after the horrendous weeks they had just endured. Finding it impossible to unwind, he looked around for something to read.

He spotted several newspapers on the lamp table and before long was engrossed in the early March editions of the *Richmond Whig* relating the details of the ill-fated Dahlgren Raid, whose mission was to free the Union soldiers being held in Libby Prison and Belle Island in Richmond. But because the Union raiders' movements had been monitored from the time of their departure at Culpeper until the two columns reached Richmond, the Rebels were ready and waiting for them.

How sad, Philip thought. This plan could have been successfully executed by a strategist such as General Sheridan instead of Dahlgren, that pompous child in a colonel's uniform.

Philip was jarred into the present by the entrance of Joseph Dawson, the young corpsman sent by Dr. Cook to treat Philip's leg. Dawson, whose fair complexion had been freckled by the sun, placed his bag on the floor beside the sofa and, removing the freshly soiled bandage, studied Philip's wound. "It's seeping again," he said, then cleaned the leg with deft, experienced hands before applying the moldy bread poultice and wrapping it with fresh bandages.

"I imagine you have done this more times than you care to count," Philip said. "What you corpsmen do is so essential, yet few of us ever thank you for what you do." He winced as Dawson pulled the bandage tightly around his leg.

"Thank you, sir. That's the nicest thing I've heard in quite a while. By the way, sir, you look a might peaked. You should take it easy and drink lots of water."

Philip waved off his suggestion. "A few minutes off my feet and I will be fit again."

Dawson gathered up his medical supplies. "If you'll excuse me, sir, I better be gettin' back before old Doc commences to yellin' for me. He can get right testy sometimes."

Philip chuckled. "It's part of his charming bedside manner."

"Yes, sir. I'll look in on you tomorrow to check that dressing," Dawson said, backing out of the room. "And remember what I said about takin' it easy and drinkin' lots of water."

Philip grinned to himself when he overheard Dawson confide to Sergeant Powell on the front porch, "You know, Sarge, the Colonel ain't so bad. Right cordial in fact. For an officer."

Chapter 3

"NO, NO, NO!" Dr. Cook shouted. "Let me repeat that, Colonel Creighton—no!" Dr. Franklin Cook, the company surgeon and admitted curmudgeon, had joined the Strickland Volunteers two years earlier during their deployment in Washington.

"But, Doc," Philip pleaded, "my duty is with my men. Can't you hear the battle?" He indicated the sound of rifle fire drifting eastward on the wind from Battery Five.

"I am fully aware of what's going on, Colonel, and from what I am told by the incoming wounded these last two days, a crippled colonel isn't going to turn the tide." He wagged his finger under Philip's nose. "Don't you realize how close you came to getting gangrene in that damned leg? I would have had to amputate it if that had become the case. Now stop pestering me. I'm sure there's plenty of paper work you can attend to."

Discouraged, Philip hobbled up the back stairs into the hall that felt relatively cool after standing in the searing heat. Sitting at his field desk with a reluctant sigh, he busied himself by reading Wes' first draft of an

After Action Report, scanned the daily reports, and Captain Hanford's notes about compliance with the Sanitary Commission's regulations.

Leaning back after a while and stretching his taut shoulder muscles, he went outside to find First Sergeant Powell. He and the First Sergeant were on the front porch engaged in an animated conversation when Captain Hanford approached and asked to see him privately.

"Certainly, Captain. Please wait in my office." Philip turned back to Sergeant Powell and said, "I have seen Private Smith's name on the daily report for one infraction or another nearly every day since we left Washington. Warn that scoundrel that if this continues, I will put him on picket duty for one of the Rebs to use as target practice."

Removing his hat with a wry smile, Sergeant Powell scratched his sweat-matted hair. "Now, Colonel, you know Smith would laugh at that 'cause he knows bounty jumpers can't be trusted on picket duty. Too many of them just disappear."

"Be that as it may, he has had his last warning. If he continues stealing from the troops, he's liable to wake up some morning with his throat slit. While it wouldn't break my heart, I shudder at the paperwork involved." Philip waved his hand with finality. "Just do something with him."

"Yes, sir." The First Sergeant saluted and walked away, grumbling to himself.

Captain Hanford jumped to attention as Philip strode into his office, growling, "If it's not one damned thing, it's another." He slumped into a chair. "Now the criminal element has crept into the army." Taking a deep breath, he calmed himself. "So, Captain, what can I do for you?"

"Sir, I don't know if this is appropriate on my part to mention, but I noticed as soon as we arrived that these ladies were needy, and low on food staples. I wondered if you might be agreeable to our giving them something to tide them over after we leave."

"What did you have in mind?" Philip asked after some thought.

"I was talking to the younger Mrs. Howard yesterday and she remarked that she would give anything for a cup of real coffee. I gave her some from the mess tent, but I thought it would be nice if they had some coffee, canned milk, flour. Things like that. With your permission, of course, sir."

Stroking his newly-grown beard, Philip digested the request. "That's an excellent idea. On the other hand, headquarters might construe our generosity as giving aid to the enemy. But what the hell." Taking several green backs from his pocket, he gave them to the Captain. "Here, put these in the proper hands and get the items you mentioned and whatever else they might need. And see if the old lady upstairs needs anything special. The way Mrs. Howard talks, she could die at any time."

"Yes, sir." Smiling broadly, Captain Hanford accepted the money. "I'll see what I can do."

As Captain Hanford turned to leave, Philip added with a grin, "By the way, Captain, if you mention a word of this conversation to anyone, I will deny it ever took place."

"Yes, sir. I understand. Thank you, sir." At the door, Captain Hanford paused. "I just remembered. We are leaving on that scouting mission in the morning."

"Damn, it slipped my mind at the moment. Oh well, you can get the supplies for the ladies when you get back. Hopefully by then, I will have this damned poultice off my leg and can get back in the saddle myself."

The Strickland Volunteers, led by Major Madison, returned four days later from scouting the Confederates' western defenses.

About to expire in the 110-degree heat, Wes watered his horse before going inside to report to Philip. In the hall, he passed Dr. Cook coming out of Philip's office. "Is Colonel Creighton all right?" Wes asked.

"He's fine, and smiling for a change. Good to have you back safely from your expedition, Major," the doctor added as he hurried away.

Wes knocked on the half-open door to Philip's office. "Are you busy, sir?"

"Come in, Wes. I have something to show you." Smiling, Philip pulled up his left trouser leg. "Look, no more poultice. Just a nice clean bandage. Dr. Cook says the wound is nearly healed, and he has finally liberated me."

"That's great news, sir. I know you have been chomping at the bit to get back into action."

"Speaking of action, how was your mission?"

Wes collapsed into a chair. "Just as we thought, the Confederates are stretched pretty thin at that point around the Weldon Railroad. As for the latest assault on Petersburg, I haven't heard any casualty figures yet, but I hear the news is grim."

Philip slapped the arm of his chair. "Damn. How can a badly out-fitted and out-numbered Confederate army hold our superior numbers at bay? From the time we crossed the James until now, nothing has gone right. If only the promised food had been delivered. If only General Baldy Smith hadn't hesitated attacking Petersburg the first night. If only we'd had proper communications. If only—If only. By God, we should have taken the day instead of allowing Beauregard time to pull troops in from Bermuda Hundred and Richmond."

Wes did not respond to Philip's tirade.

Philip regarded him intently across the room. "Are you all right?"

"Yes, just disappointed. I thought the war would have been over by now." Wes rested his head against the back of the chair. "Oh God, Philip, I'm tired down to my bones. It seems more like two years since we left Washington, instead of two months."

"Seems longer sometimes." Philip winced at the screams and moans of the wounded drifting into the house from the medical tent. "As long as I live, I will never get that sound out of my mind." Sitting up, he grumbled, "I can't remain here in comfort while those poor devils are out there suffering."

Wes forced himself out of the chair. "I had better get started on my After Action Report. But first, I need a cup of coffee. Even bad army coffee would taste good now."

Pulling on his boots, Philip followed Wes out the back door toward the medical tents, his limp hardly noticeable. Philip found that the medical tents were filled to over-flowing. Amputated legs and arms were piled chest high outside the tent. The corpsmen scurried about in an effort to stabilize the wounded before moving them to the massive new hospital being built adjacent to City Point.

Philip watched Dr. Cook in the midst of the confusion, barking orders. Father O'Boyle worked feverishly alongside him, his auburn head bent over the mangled bodies, offering words of comfort, or administering the Last Rites to the dead and dying.

Staggered by the number of wounded, Philip's stomach revolted at seeing them lying about, awaiting treatment, with no protection from the swarms of flies and the relentless sun.

Feeling helpless, he returned to the house, wondering how he would ever get the sights and sounds of all this misery out of his mind.

Or the stench.

Chapter 4

AS CAROLINE HELPED Cassie roll the last of the linens to be used as bandages, she looked up at the sound of a wagon pulling up to the back door. Glancing out the kitchen window, she saw a Yankee captain jump down from the army wagon. With an indifferent shrug, she went back to rolling the bandages.

Captain Hanford knocked tentatively before stepping into the steamy kitchen. "Excuse me, Mrs. Howard. May I come in?"

Caroline stood up, her hand at her throat. "What is it, Captain? Is something wrong?"

"No, ma'am. We have something for you. Bring those things in here, Private." Smiling, he stood aside as several enlisted men carried in the 'requisitioned' items.

Gasping in disbelief when she saw all the food staples, Cassie said, "Glory be, Miz Caroline, look at all that food. And oil for the lamps."

Flustered, Caroline asked, "Captain, what is all this?"

"Begging your pardon, ma'am, I bring Colonel Creighton's compliments. The Colonel thought, well, that is, we all thought you could use a few things." Bowing, he backed out of the kitchen, leaving the two women gaping in amazement.

Caroline rummaged through the boxes and cans. "Oh dear," she fretted, "I'm not sure I should accept all this."

"Why not?" Cassie asked, frowning. "We need them things real bad."

"I know we do, but they came from Yankees, and you know what Mother Howard would say if she found out." She had watched Dorothea become increasingly difficult since the Yankees' arrival last week. She stayed in her room day and night, watching the endless activity from her bedroom window. She had even accused Caroline of stealing their food and had begun locking the root cellar and the smokehouse, even though they had long since been empty.

"She don't need to find out about where all this come from," Cassie said with a wink. "I'll put everything away in my hidey-hole. She won't never know a thing."

"No, prudence dictates that I decline the Yankees' generosity," Caroline said without conviction. "Don't put anything away until I speak to Colonel Creighton."

"Excuse me, Colonel," Caroline called from behind Philip in the entry hall later that day. "May I speak with you a moment?"

Turning toward her, Philip heaved an exasperated sigh. "What is it, Mrs. Howard? I'm rather busy."

"I will only be a moment," she said, her voice firm.

"Very well." He stood aside, allowing her to enter his office ahead of him. Caroline had just taken a seat when he asked abruptly, "Now, madam, what may I do for you?"

"To get to the point," Caroline began, her eyes meeting his steadily, "I want to thank you for the food and supplies Captain Hanford delivered earlier. It was quite a pleasant surprise."

Philip shrugged. "We could see that you folks haven't had much for a while."

"I appreciate the gesture but I'm afraid I cannot accept."

"May I ask why not?" he asked with a cocked eyebrow.

"That should be obvious to both of us, Colonel."

Philip chuckled. "You mean about our being enemies? Nonsense. I would like to think that we are still civilized."

"You and your men have behaved in a most civilized manner. And while it is true that we are in dire need, I feel duty-bound to make my position known to you. On the other hand," she avoided his intense gaze, "my mother-in-law and aunt desperately need sustenance. You don't know how long it has been since we have had flour for bread. You would not believe what flour sells for in Petersburg these days."

Puffing on his cheroot, he regarded her through the smoke. "Mrs. Howard, Captain Hanford gave you those supplies out of concern for you and your family's welfare. You would not want to hurt his feelings by rejecting his kind offer, would you?"

"Of course not," she stammered. "But I hope you can appreciate the dilemma it presents for me. I felt at first that I should reject the offer, but since you put it that way, I cannot deny the others the benefits of this unexpected boon. I'm just not sure how my mother-in-law will react when she learns of it."

A smile crinkled the corners of Philip's eyes. "I won't tell if you won't."

Flushing, Caroline lowered her gaze. "Thank you, Colonel. Your thoughtfulness is much appreciated." She stood, then said tentatively, "I hope you don't mind if I make a personal observation."

"What's that?" he asked absently, looking up from a report he had already begun reading.

"You don't like women very much, do you?"

Philip yanked the cheroot from his mouth. "Why do you think that?"

"The way you look at me and my mother-in-law, the way you treat us. I get the distinct impression that you don't have much use for women."

"I'm sorry, Mrs. Howard, if my manner makes you uncomfortable. Call it a peculiar quirk in my nature, but I find it disagreeable engaging in war with civilian ladies in harm's way."

"I didn't mean that, Colonel. It's something more personal."

"I don't know what the hell you're talking about." Jumping up from his seat, he turned away from her and stared through the lace curtains, recalling the people and events that had brought him to this sorry state, the betrayal by his own mother, and the treachery of his greedy, faithless wife.

After a moment, he faced her and said softly, "I beg your pardon, ma'am. I have been too long in this man's army. As a consequence, my language leaves something to be desired."

"It is not so much your language that I find offensive as your attitude. What have I, or any of us, done to annoy you?"

Philip waved off her question. "No one has done anything. As I said before, I do not like waging war near defenseless women."

Caroline faced him squarely. "Colonel Creighton, you cannot think that we are overjoyed by your occupation of our home. We have all endured quite enough already. Although, I must admit that you and your men have made every effort to be respectful."

He bowed in response to her remark. "We felt it was the Christian thing to do." After a moment's pause, he stepped closer to her. "While we are being honest, Mrs. Howard, I must say frankly that I am surprised by your own attitude. Your mother-in-law's reaction to our sudden intrusion is more in line with what I had expected."

"Colonel," Caroline said in a voice tinged with hot feelings, "I am not about to make things any more difficult for myself and my family for a cause I no longer believe in. I don't care who wins this war, so long as it is over soon."

Philip raised his eyebrows. "I admire your courage, ma'am, and the fierce practicality of your answer. So," he asked as she turned to leave, "have I satisfied your curiosity on that one point?"

Caroline paused at the door. Keeping her back to him to hide a suppressed smile, she said, "Colonel, you have told me more than you know."

"Mrs. Howard, before you go." He stammered and cleared his throat. "We, that is, the, uh, Strickland Volunteers did not anticipate being here more than a week. To demonstrate our good will, my officers and I would deem it an honor if you would join us for dinner before we vacate the premises. Say, tomorrow evening? I assure you, we will be on our best behavior. Perhaps it will compensate in some small way for disturbing your tranquility. And for my own personal shortcomings," he added with a gentle smile.

"I would be happy to join your officers. It has been too long since we entertained at Howard Hill. Although, the circumstances are hardly conducive for entertaining, are they?"

"Hardly." Philip bowed with a smile. "Thank you, ma'am. I will inform my staff of your decision. I'm sure they will be very pleased."

"Shall we say tomorrow at six o'clock?'

"Six o'clock, it is," he nodded, trying not to gaze too intently into those soft, brown eyes that captured his attention for the first time. Silently, he cursed her—and all women. They have a disconcerting way about them, swishing their skirts and smelling sweet when they are near.

But, he reminded himself, I have learned my lesson all too well where the ladies are concerned. I will be on my guard with this one.

Chapter 5

NEXT DAY, PHILIP reined in his horse at the Union army's headquarters in City Point, four miles to the east of Howard Hill. Leaning forward in the saddle, he stopped a young lieutenant passing by. "Excuse me, can you direct me to the General's briefing?"

The young officer shook his head. "Sorry, sir, it concluded some time ago."

"Damn," Philip swore under his breath. After returning the lieutenant's salute, he wondered if he should return to Howard Hill or seek out his friend Col. Austin Graves to get the details of the briefing. Glancing around, he saw Colonel Graves approaching him from the Eppes plantation house.

"Creighton," Colonel Graves smiled, and waved at him. "It's good to see you again."

"You too, Colonel." Philip dismounted and shook his hand. "I came to sit in on the briefing but I got held up by a heated argument with the company surgeon about my being here at all."

"Too bad. It has been over for nearly an hour. Come, we'll have some coffee and I'll give you the details."

They relaxed on the grounds of the Eppes plantation house overlooking the confluence of the Appomattox and James Rivers, and sipped the coffee from the mess tent.

After catching up on the latest army rumors, Colonel Graves related the details of General Grant's briefing. "I suppose you've heard that Lee sent reinforcements to Beauregard to counter Meade's latest attempt against the Confederate defense lines."

"Yes, I heard. The Confederates are proving as stubborn as hell."

Graves squinted against the sunlight reflecting off the river. "Unfortunately, the action was all for naught. Neither army gained ground while the casualties mounted."

Philip leaned back in the field chair and puffed on his cheroot. "What's the next plan of action?"

"I believe the general staff has finally discovered that the usual methods of warfare cannot dislodge an entrenched enemy," Graves said in a facetious tone. "And now, after accomplishing the greatest sleight of hand in military history by sneaking more than one hundred thousand men across the James undetected, we can't even take a city guarded by a few thousand troops.

"But," Austin added, "you are, no doubt, familiar with Grant's bulldog attitude. He won't give up until he takes the city, as well as the railroads supplying Petersburg and Richmond. He will simply wait the Rebels out, just as he did at Vicksburg."

"Siege," Philip groaned. "That could last for weeks. Or months. Are you sure about this?"

"Grant is determined to end it here."

Philip spilled the remains of his coffee onto the ground and asked, "What is our next target?"

"The Weldon Railroad."

"Our most recent reconnaissance has shown that the Rebel defenses are stretched pretty thin at that point," Philip said. "When will this mission take place?"

"Next Wednesday. But first, the General has ordered that the men and horses be rested. He feels they deserve that much after the hell they have been through."

Standing, Philip gazed at the slow moving Appomattox River. "At least I will have some good news for my men. They can certainly use a respite."

"Can you stay for lunch, Colonel? I hear General Smith is providing one of his famous spreads in his tent, with servants to wait on us, wine, the works."

"How can I refuse the opportunity to have servants wait on me in grand style?" Philip replied, and followed Austin to General Baldy Smith's tent.

Still glowing from the wine he'd enjoyed at General Smith's sumptuous repast, Philip returned to Howard Hill and informed his staff that their attempts to take Petersburg had now become a siege.

"Also, gentlemen, you may inform your sections to take their ease. General Grant has ordered the troops to rest for several days. After that," he concluded with a sardonic grin, "we are going into the railroad business. That's all. I will see you gentlemen this evening at the dinner with Mrs. Howard."

During this much-needed lull in the action, the mail packets caught up with the army, bringing the best medicine for the sagging spirits of the troops—letters from sweethearts, wives, and families. If a prize had been given for the most letters received, David Southall would have won, hands down. Laughing at the good-natured jibes about his volume of mail from broken-hearted belles in Washington, David sauntered off to savor them in private.

Not far away, Wes settled in the shade of a tree to revel in Jane's letters. From his window, Philip watched Wes and David with envy. There are no love letters from my dear wife, he thought with a grim smile, only newsy letters from my sister Jessica, Rachel Strickland, Denton Cobb, as well as the ones from Matthew.

While absorbed in one of Matthew's letters about the army's action in Georgia, Philip heard a sound at the door and glanced up. Wes was leaning against the doorjamb with an anguished look on his face, a letter dangling from his hand. Philip's heart leapt into his throat. "What's wrong, Wes?"

"It's Jane," Wes said in a strangled voice. "In her letter written," he glanced at the date, "the middle of May, she wrote that she was, well, that we were expecting again. In this letter dated just one week later. . ." His voice broke and trailed off. Regaining his composure, he said, "She—she lost the baby."

Philip stood up slowly. "I'm so sorry to hear that. Is she all right?"

"The doctor told her she can have more children. But she went through this alone, without my help or comfort." He covered his face. "What will become of my babies if I don't survive?"

Philip gripped Wes' shoulder. "I wish I could let you go home, but you know the situation right now. Why don't you write her a nice long love letter? Let her know you are all right. And give her my warmest regards for her health."

Wes walked out of Philip's office without a word, closing the door softly behind him.

Philip stood in the center of his office, grinding his teeth in helpless frustration, knowing there was nothing either of them could do. In the face of the overwhelming casualties they'd witnessed, it appeared highly unlikely that either of them would live to see the end of the war.

But, he thought, unlike Wes, I have nothing to lose.

Chapter 6

FOR THEIR DINNER with the lady of the house, Philip had asked Lieutenant Hasselbeck to secure several chickens, a ham, rice and other items from the City Point depot. Cassie even promised to bake a berry pie, now that she had flour and sugar. The officers declared that they hadn't enjoyed such luxury since leaving Washington.

Another luxury Philip's officers hadn't enjoyed since leaving Washington was a real bath. Life in the saddle did not allow for the refinements of life, much less basic cleanliness. They all agreed that a trip to the stream would improve their appearances considerably. Not to mention their spirits.

"In our present disreputable condition," Captain Hanford laughed, "our own mothers would deny us."

Promptly at six o'clock, the officers set aside their whiskey glasses and snuffed out their cigars. Lounging off to one side and sipping his drink, Philip grinned at his hard-bitten officers who appeared as nervous as schoolboys before their first dance. Comic proof, he concluded, that women have the strangest effect on men, even the most battle-hardened.

Red-faced from the heat and humidity, Lieutenant Hasselbeck and Captain Hanford tugged at their freshly brushed tunics. David Southall, apparently not bothered by the heat, presented a striking appearance in his dark blue tunic.

"How refreshing," Wes confided to Captain Hanford, "to be civilized again. I've nearly forgotten how to use table manners. By the way, gentlemen, remember your language in the lady's presence."

Upon hearing Caroline's footsteps on the stairs, each officer gave his tunic one final tug. Philip bit his lip to keep from laughing out loud.

With a shy smile, Caroline entered the dining room to gallant bows from the officers. They each took turns telling her how pleased they were that she had consented to join them.

"Thank you, gentlemen. Please, be seated." She took her customary place at the foot of the table. The officers seated themselves, two on either side of the table. Philip was left with no choice but to sit at the head of the table opposite Caroline. Once they were seated, she asked David to pour the wine.

Cassie and Mina served the fried chicken and rice, ham, biscuits and gravy, along with fried ochre and stewed tomatoes from the puny remnants of the scorched kitchen garden.

Caroline glanced around the table. "It seems that Dr. Cook is not present. Did he have an emergency?"

"No, ma'am," David answered from his seat on her right. "The doctor begs to be excused. He was too tired to join us. It is not often that he gets a chance to rest. And Father O'Boyle had made other plans."

"In that case, I shall have Cassie fix a plate for the doctor and the Reverend. If that is all right, Colonel."

Philip looked up with a tomato slice on his fork. "I'm sorry, ma'am. Is what all right?"

"I suggested that Cassie prepare a plate for the other gentlemen who were unable to join us."

A quick frown flitted across Philip's brow, replaced by a half-smile. "That's very thoughtful of you, Mrs. Howard. I am sure they will be appreciative."

"Very well." Caroline turned her attention to the other officers. "What about you gentlemen? What did you do before the war?"

Peter Hanford spoke up. "I taught school on the upper level. I was about to go into private tutoring for wealthy students when the war broke out and duty called."

Wes informed Caroline that he had been a textbook editor. "But I must admit that I miss my wife and daughters desperately. There were times when I considered deserting, but my sense of honor prevailed," he added, and ducked his head at this admission.

The other officers squirmed in their seats and cleared their throats before nodding agreement about being homesick.

Not I, thought Philip. Remembering the agony and embarrassment of his encounters with Elizabeth in Washington and Crossroads, the knife slid from his hand with a clatter against his plate. All heads turned in his direction. Scarlet crept above his collar. "Sorry," he mumbled.

Wes forced a smile and quickly intervened, "What about you, Mrs. Howard?"

"There is really not much to tell," Caroline murmured.

"Were you born in Petersburg, ma'am?" Peter Hanford asked.

"No, I was born in Surry County, down river. I came to Petersburg one Christmas nine years ago to visit friends. It was then I met Mr. Howard. After a brief courtship, it was arranged that we marry the following spring."

Conversation between Caroline and the other officers continued until Cassie brought in the pies. As the officers exclaimed their delight, a sudden movement in the doorway behind Caroline's chair caught Philip's eye.

Dorothea Howard stood in the doorway, her eyes wild, her hair flying. "Harlot!" she screamed at Caroline.

Startled by the violent outburst behind her, Caroline jumped from her chair and spun around to face the source.

"Scarlet Jezebel! Whore!" Dorothea hissed. "Is this how you keep Morgan's memory while he is away fighting for the Cause?"

White-faced, Caroline swayed a moment before slumping back into her chair.

Squinting at Philip, Dorothea poked a bony finger at him. "I saw you. Both of you. Meeting by the well and talking. You think I don't know, but I saw you." She glared at each of the officers in turn, then back to Caroline, who was, by now, overcome.

Philip reacted before the others. "Lieutenant Hasselbeck, escort that woman out of here. Captain Hanford, call Dr. Cook to attend to Mrs. Howard here."

Taking Dorothea by the arm, Lieutenant Hasselbeck led her, protesting, from the room.

David knelt beside Caroline's chair, holding her hand and whispering consolation. With her hand on his sleeve, Caroline thanked him absently but looked to Philip for support.

Philip stood behind David, dark-faced, clenching his fists. "Gentlemen, I believe we have been adjourned." Ignoring the pleading look in Caroline's teary eyes, he bowed stiffly and said, "Good evening, ma'am," and stalked from the room. Wes followed him.

In his office, Philip paced and swore. "What the hell does that crazy woman mean by making those wild accusations?"

"She is obviously demented, sir," Wes said. "It is my guess that she and the younger lady have had their problems all along."

Philip ripped off his tunic. "Perhaps, but it's damned galling. A pleasant diversion for the staff has been ruined by that crazy old woman."

Captain Hanford poked his head in the door. "Dr. Cook is on his way, sir."

"If you will excuse me, sir," Wes said, "I have some paperwork I must attend to."

Philip threw himself onto the sofa and stared into the empty fireplace. *She was speaking for my benefit during dinner,* he thought. *Looking at me with those innocent brown eyes. What does she mean by doing that?* He ripped off his left boot and tossed it behind him. *Sorry, Mrs. Howard, but I am no longer easy prey to those feminine tricks.*

Dr. Cook strolled into Philip's office just as he tossed his other boot aside. "I have given the old woman a sedative," he said. "Young Mrs. Howard is all right. Just a bit shaken and, I might add, mightily embarrassed. For some strange reason, Colonel, she was quite concerned about your reaction."

Philip gave him a puzzled look. "Why the hell should she care about my feelings? I mean nothing to her."

"Perhaps it was your charming manner."

Turning on Dr. Cook, ready to take him to task for his presumption, Philip paused and thought better of it. Feeling suddenly drained, he said, "Perhaps you're right. I have been a bit brusque with her. But I have a lot on my mind. I cannot be bothered with the sensitivities of these women."

Dr. Cook yawned. "I appreciate your position, Colonel, but have you ever considered that this young woman has been engaged in her own life and death struggle these past few years?" Without waiting for a response, he shuffled out of the room.

Philip stared after him. Indeed, he was perfectly aware of the desperate struggle of all the civilians in this war. He knew that prices were outrageous in Petersburg. Flour was selling for $240.00 a barrel. Through all the privations, rampant inflation, loneliness, illness and imminent death, young Mrs. Howard had struggled alone on this farm with a crazed mother-in-law, a dying aunt and two frightened darkies.

Even so, Philip thought with grudging respect, it doesn't alter the fact that I will continue to maintain my distance from her.

To settle his nerves, Philip pulled on his boots and walked onto the front porch for a breath of air. The sky was clear and every once in a while, the sharp report of sniper fire could be heard in the distance. The acrid smell of smoke from campfires hung low in the humid night air. Somewhere amid the campfires, someone strummed a guitar as several men sang *Lorena*, a soulful song especially popular with the Southerners.

Breathing deeply of the soft evening air, Philip smoked a while, listening to the music and small talk around the fires. Throwing away the stub of his cheroot, he went back into the house. He was startled to find Caroline in his office, pouring coffee.

"I thought you might like your pie and coffee now, Colonel," she said in a shaky voice.

"If you will recall, madam," he said, taking care to soften the edge in his voice, "this area is now off limits to civilian personnel."

"Yes, I know." Lifting misty eyes, she said, "I cannot begin to tell you how sorry I am about what happened this evening. It was quite disconcerting."

"To say the least. What about you?" he asked with concern. "How are you feeling?"

Handing Philip the coffee cup with an unsteady hand, she murmured, "Better, thank you," and dropped her eyes under his penetrating gaze. "I believe you take milk in your coffee, no sugar. And I thought you might like a slice of Cassie's pie."

So, he thought, casting a rueful glance at her, she knows how I drink my coffee. "Thank you," he muttered. After taking a few bites of the pie, he asked, not bothering to hide the suspicion in his voice, "Is there something in particular you wanted to talk about, Mrs. Howard?"

"No, just a continuation of what we discussed yesterday."

"I didn't mean to appear rude then, but I assure you that whatever I had on my mind at the time had nothing to do with you." He sat his pie plate forcefully on the lamp table. "Is that all?"

"Yes." Standing, her chin quivering, Caroline picked up the tray.

"Wait." He reached out to detain her. "I—I'm sorry for sounding so abrupt."

"I realize our situation is unique, Colonel, but we must make the best of it. Don't you agree?"

"Yes, I do. That was the reason for the dinner this evening. It's just that, well, never mind. It's not important. Thank you for the pie and coffee, Miss Caroline. That was a thoughtful gesture on your part."

"You're welcome."

"Good night," he added with a gentle smile.

Stopping at the door, Caroline regarded him with a wry smile. "Good night, Philip."

Long after he had closed the door and pulled off his boots, it struck him that he had called her Miss Caroline for the first time. And, he realized with alarm, she had called him Philip.

Damn!

Chapter 7

JUST AFTER DAWN on June 22, Union cavalry skirted the western Confederate defenses around Petersburg, intent upon capturing the Weldon Railroad. To counter this action, General Lee sent A. P. Hill's Corps to ward off the Union advances. Fighting was fierce, with the out-manned and out-gunned Confederates forcing the Union troops back.

During the furious skirmish, Philip found himself in a withering cross fire and wheeled his horse about. A moment later, he felt a searing sensation rip through his right side. The scream of pain that escaped his throat was lost in the din of battle. Falling from his horse, his face slammed against the ground with tremendous force. Fighting continued all around him.

Next day, the Army of the Potomac regained some of the hotly contested ground west of the Jerusalem Plank Road but did not gain control of the Weldon Railroad. They were ultimately forced to withdraw, losing 1,700 men to wounds, death or as prisoners, and again failed to accomplish their mission.

In the grim aftermath, the medical corpsmen on both sides began making their way through the mangled bodies to locate the wounded. The burial detail followed, picking up the bodies of the dead and throwing them into the backs of wagons.

Grumbling to himself about this unsavory job, a Union private in the burial detail picked his way through the bodies. Even with the kerchief tied over his nose to ward off the stench of dead humans and animals, he still gagged. He abhorred this duty but, he reminded himself, that is the price one must pay for stealing. The army no longer drummed thieves out of the service or shot them. Instead, they are given the most unsavory details as punishment. It was almost enough to make a man give up stealing, he decided.

Still cursing at his fate, he stumbled over the body of a Union colonel. With help from a comrade, he lifted the body under the armpits and was ready to sling him into a wagon with the other corpses when he heard a groan. Terrified, the private dropped the body and backed away. Good Lord, he gulped to himself, after seeing the colonel's hand twitch, this man is still alive.

"Got me a live one here," he called to the ambulance driver in an unsteady voice. Shaken and pale-faced, he returned to his grisly work.

David Southall was on his way to the rear of the action for orders, and to see if Philip was there. Wes had warned him earlier to be on the lookout for the Colonel, who hadn't been seen since yesterday. Seeing the burial detail, David reigned in his horse and asked the sergeant in charge if they had seen Colonel Creighton.

"Can't say, sir," the sergeant said, deliberately spitting tobacco juice near the head of a dead Confederate captain. "Some of these here men don't have no faces."

Increasingly concerned, David rode from ambulance to ambulance, asking about Philip. At the fourth ambulance, the blood-splattered driver said, "Come to think of it, sir, we did pick up one colonel." He jerked his thumb toward the rear of his wagon. "Have a look."

Scrambling into the back of the wagon, he was nearly overcome by the stench of dried blood and filthy bodies. Holding his breath, he searched each man frantically before finding someone who resembled

Philip. But, with so much dried blood, dust and sweat that obliterated the badly swollen face, he couldn't be certain it was Philip.

David examined the body closely for something familiar. The colonel's right hand lay inert across his chest and, on the little finger was a familiar signet ring. Reaching under the shattered tunic, he found the pocket watch bearing the initials PJC. Thank God, he thought, the Colonel's watch hadn't been stolen by the burial detail, as so many valuables usually were.

He called forward to the driver, "Take this man to Howard Hill on City Point Road. Our company surgeon will take care of him there."

Several hours later, the ambulance wagon lumbered up the crushed shell driveway of Howard Hill to the waiting Dr. Franklin Cook. "Here's the Colonel, Doc. He's pretty bad."

After a hasty examination of Philip's unconscious body, Dr. Cook said, "I have already run out of room in the hospital tent. Take him into his office."

The doctor ran ahead to Philip's office to clear a place for the litter, barking orders to those around him. "Tell Father O'Boyle to get started out back. He knows what to do. Dawson, see if you can locate Mrs. Howard. I may need her help with the nursing duties. And tell her to bring some bandages. The Colonel's dressings will have to be changed regularly."

Gazing down at Philip's shattered torso, he muttered under his breath, "If I can pull him through."

Corpsman Dawson found Caroline in the family cemetery beside the fresh grave of her Aunt Emmaline who had died in her sleep the day before.

"Pardon me, ma'am," Dawson said, removing his hat, "I don't mean to intrude on your grief, but Dr. Cook sent me to ask if you would help him with Colonel Creighton. He's been hurt pretty bad."

Her hand flew to her throat. "Colonel Creighton is wounded?"

"Yes, ma'am. He lost a lot of blood. The Doc says. . ." But before Dawson could finish his sentence, Caroline lifted her skirts and ran across the meadow, unmindful that the corpsman was enjoying a glimpse of her ankles.

Running into the hall past several enlisted men who looked concerned, Caroline stopped at the door to Philip's office. She let out an audible gasp at the frantic scene before her. Philip lay face-down on a door that had been taken down and placed over the piano, his hands dangling over the edge. Someone tore off his blood-soaked blouse while Sergeant Powell yanked off his boots. When one of them moved aside, Caroline saw that the right side of his back was fouled with blood and dirt. She covered her mouth with both hands to keep her stomach down.

Dr. Cook looked up at the sound of her gasp. "Ah, Mrs. Howard, there you are. Did you bring the bandages? For God's sake, woman, don't just stand there gaping. Hurry! And bring some hot water."

The doctor worked feverishly on Philip, washing away blood and dirt before probing the wound. "Looks like the bullet went clear through," he mumbled, mostly to himself, "judging by the size of the exit wound in his back. Look, here's a bit of bone, likely from a rib." He held up the splinter in his probe before tossing it aside. "I pray the bullet didn't hit his liver or a lung. Mrs. Howard," he called over his shoulder, "bring that lamp over here. I need to suture the wound, provided I can stop this damned bleeding."

During Dr. Cook's frantic suturing efforts, Philip roused from his chloroform stupor and cried out in agony. He thrashed about and tried to raise his head but was too weak. "Let me die," he mumbled.

"Like hell I will," the doctor growled, while trying to restrain Philip's flailing arms. He jerked his head to the corpsman assisting him. "The chloroform's worn off. Quick."

"No, let me. . ." As Caroline helped in the struggle to hold Philip's arms, the corpsman's swift reaction silenced his feeble protests.

More than an hour later, Dr. Cook fell back onto the sofa, removed his spectacles and rubbed his eyes. "I have done all I can. Thank you for your help, Mrs. Howard. Because we are overwhelmed with wounded, I will require your further assistance in changing the Colonel's dressing every few hours until the wound stops seeping."

He stood up and stretched. "Now, I'd better do what I can to prolong the lives of those other poor devils, so they can live to die another day."

Blinking back hot tears, Caroline nodded. She waited in the hall as Captain Southall and the corpsman lifted Philip's inert body onto his cot, then removed the door that had served as an operating table. They also carried away his filthy uniform and the blood-soaked cloths used during surgery.

Once she was alone with Philip, she adjusted the sheet on his naked body then sat in a chair near his cot to begin her vigil.

As she lit a lamp at dusk, Caroline heard a noise at the door. Turning, she saw Dorothea outlined in the door opening. The light from the hall lamp behind her made her face a grotesque mask.

"So, he's dying, is he?" she asked in a croaking voice. "He killed Emmaline. It is only fitting that he pay for his sins. As the Lord God Jehovah will make you pay for yours, harlot," she added, pointing an accusing finger.

Realizing it was useless to reason with her, Caroline led the poor woman up the stairs to her room. Before long, she thought with a shiver, I will be left alone with this addled old woman.

Caroline spent the night on the sofa with one eye open. At sunup, she was at Philip's side, checking his bandage. Cutting away the soiled wrapping, she gently lifted his shoulders to re-wrap the wound. When she had finished, she covered him with a clean sheet then slid the soiled one out from beneath the clean one to preserve Philip's privacy, and her own sense of modesty.

Leaning over him, she whispered in his ear, "Please, don't die, Philip."

Dr. Cook dragged in just then, looking haggard. "Here," he thrust a cup of coffee in her direction, "I reckon you can use this. How did he pass the night?"

"Quietly," she said, accepting the cup with a grateful smile.

"You have done a fine job, Mrs. Howard. I appreciate your help more than I can say. Well, I'm off to bed," he yawned. "Call me if you see any change in the Colonel's condition."

At sunset on the second day, Philip began to stir. In an instant, Caroline was at his side. He moaned and winced with every movement, then tried to open his eyes. Before slipping back into unconsciousness, he mumbled something.

Later, while dozing, Caroline heard him talking out loud. Sitting up, she saw him thrashing about, mumbling incoherently. She knelt beside the cot and tried to calm him. He raised his head off the pillow and glared at her with glazed eyes. "You think you will be rich now, don't you? But you will get nothing from me, you whore. I have seen to that."

Alarmed by his delirious ranting, Caroline ran for Dr. Cook.

When the doctor came into the room, Philip was sleeping peacefully. After a cursory exam, Dr. Cook said, "He's burning with fever. Bathe him with cool water. I will look in on him later."

Caroline bathed Philip's fevered face and arms with clean cloths dipped in water. After an hour, she sat back and placed a cloth over her own eyes. Even with her eyes covered, she sensed that she was being watched. Dear God, she thought with panic, is Mother Howard prowling again?

Removing the cloth, she saw Philip staring at her again, his swollen eyes filled with hate. "Don't care any more. Want to die. You will get nothing. Neither will that damned poltroon." He mumbled something else before falling back onto the pillow.

"Shh," she whispered in his ear. "I will take care of you, Philip. You just get well."

There it is again. That soothing voice imploring me to get well. Who is it? Elizabeth? No, she doesn't give a damn if I live or die. Whose voice is it? Whose lips brushed my ear? Whose gentle hands touched my forehead? Not Elizabeth's. Her hands, like her heart, were always cold as ice.

What is this dreadful pain in my back? Am I dead?

The painless fog closed in again, enveloping the gentle voice and hands.

Chapter 8

AT NOON ON the third day, Philip awoke, blinking and confused. Once he got his bearings, he was surprised to see Caroline sitting on the sofa, her sewing in her lap.

"Hello," she said, smiling. "Welcome back." She hurried to his side and placed a gentle hand on his forehead. "Now that your temperature has broken, I believe you will be all right."

Her touch felt vaguely familiar. *Was it she who whispered to me? No, it must have been a dream.* He ran his tongue over his parched lips before trying to speak.

"What is it?" she asked. "May I get you something?"

He struggled to say, "Water." While drinking from the glass she held to his lips, he studied her carefully. *Could it have been her hands I felt? Her words I heard?* Thanking Caroline, he lay back on the pillow.

"You gave me quite a start last night, Colonel. You were delirious and called me all sorts of names that I cannot repeat."

Still too groggy to understand what she meant, Philip drifted off into restful sleep. At sundown, he awoke and asked for more water just as Dr. Cook stopped by to look in on them.

After examining Philip, Dr. Cook heaved a sigh of relief. "Mrs. Howard, I never believed in miracles, but this is indeed a miracle. The Colonel has no business being alive." He smiled at her through his white beard. "I don't know how to thank you."

Caroline blushed. "I was happy to help."

After the doctor left, Philip motioned for Caroline to come closer and asked in a raspy voice, "How long have I been here?"

"They brought you in three days ago."

"Have you been here the entire time? While they cleaned me and fixed my wound?" When she nodded assent, he gasped, "My God, madam, you had no business being in here."

"Dr. Cook asked me to help because he was deluged with injured. I only did what I could. And," she added with a quivering chin, "to repay you for your kindness to me."

At her wounded look, he said, "I thank you for that, Mrs. Howard, but you must be replaced by a corpsman or an enlisted man. Please call Lieutenant Hasselbeck in here for me."

"The doctor doesn't want you to do anything but rest just now."

"Madam," he said, struggling to make his voice sound authoritative, "I give the orders here. Call Lieutenant Hasselbeck."

Smiling now, she bent over the cot and straightened his sheet. "Colonel, I do not wear a Yankee uniform so your orders mean nothing to me. You just rest while I fetch some water from the well. Cassie is preparing you some broth."

Philip ground his teeth at her boldness. Then, fuming at his own helplessness, he watched as she exited the room, so sure of herself.

Caroline returned a short time later with a tray. When she tried to feed him, he clamped his mouth shut. "Are you going to be difficult, Colonel? I have lost too much sleep to have you act like a petulant child, so I would appreciate some cooperation."

"Someone else should be assigned to do this. It is unseemly that you are here."

"Have no fear, Colonel. I am not about to take over your command. Now open up."

"Damn it, Mrs. Howard, I will not be patronized. Call Dr. Cook. Get one of my officers. Do something, but just get the hell out of here!"

Stricken by his outburst, she stumbled from the room and bumped into the doctor in the hall.

Dr. Cook stood in the doorway with his hands on his hips, his apron splattered with blood and matter. "What the hell is going on?"

Trying not to wince at the renewed pain in his side, Philip lay back on his pillow. "I don't want Mrs. Howard in here. It is indecent," he said, jiggling the sheets to indicate his nakedness beneath. "Where are my officers? I want a casualty report."

"I can give you an up-date, Colonel. We did not take the Weldon Railroad and the army lost nearly two thousand men to death, injury or as prisoners. At present, the General's staff is more than likely huddled around their maps at City Point, formulating another useless plan of action. As for Mrs. Howard, she was here at my request. And, I might add," he bent a baleful eye on Philip, "you owe that lady a great deal of thanks. She saw to your care at great sacrifice to her personal feelings."

"What do you mean?" Philip asked in a subdued voice.

"Her Aunt Emmaline died the first day you were gone. The poor woman expired from complications of malnutrition and age. Given the circumstances, I would say that Mrs. Howard has been extremely generous."

Contrite, Philip mumbled, "I didn't know."

"Of course, you didn't, but you can show the lady some semblance of gratitude instead of swearing at her like a stevedore. As for your officers, I gave them strict orders that you were not to be disturbed. As soon as you are well enough, you will be moved to City Point, then on to Washington to recuperate."

Alarmed, Philip struggled to prop himself up on one elbow. "No, I won't go to Washington. I cannot leave my men. Please, Doc, I won't be swayed on that point. I must stay here."

Dr. Cook considered a moment then said, "All right, Colonel. You can remain here. I wouldn't want those damned jostling ambulances breaking open my beautiful needlework on your back. But for the time being, you are out of business. End of discussion."

Philip lay back on the cot, a small smile playing in his eyes. "You forget, Doctor Cook, that I outrank you."

"We will talk about military rank when you are back to your old self," Dr. Cook grinned.

On his way out, he paused at the door and said with a wink, "Oh, and by the way, Mrs. Howard stays."

Philip awoke and blinked several times to clear his head from the fog of sleep. Glancing out the windows, he judged by the light filtering through the curtains that it must be about six o'clock in the evening. Surveying the room, he saw that his boots had been cleaned, polished and placed next to the field desk, along with his personal belongings. A fresh uniform and hat hung on the back of the door. A quick look at his desk told him that Lieutenant Hasselbeck had taken care of business in his usual efficient manner.

Well, he decided, I believe it's time to sit up. After several feeble attempts, he fell back against the pillow. How humiliating, he groaned inwardly, to lie here and endure having someone hover over me.

"Now do you believe the doctor?" Caroline asked from the doorway. "Colonel, you are weak because you lost a great deal of blood." She placed a pitcher of water on a lamp table. "Also, I feel it is only fair to inform you that the doctor has prevailed upon me to continue my duties here. I agreed, but only as a favor to him."

"Mrs. Howard," Philip cleared his throat, "I cannot tell you how sorry I am about the way I spoke to you earlier. I—I didn't know about your aunt, but it was no excuse for my rude behavior. I am truly sorry, especially after all you have done for me. Will you forgive me?"

She considered a moment before saying, "There is nothing to forgive, Colonel. I realize you did not know about Aunt Emmaline's passing. I chose to overlook your behavior because of the fever."

"Henceforth, I promise to conduct myself in a more civilized manner." A smile curved his lips as he fidgeted with the sheet then added, "Which is something I have not done these past few years."

"I got that impression," she replied, fighting back her own smile as she placed a napkin under his chin.

Tearing at the napkin, he grumped, "What's this for?"

"The doctor wants you to eat something to regain your strength."

"I will feed myself, thank you."

"All right, Colonel, let me see you do that."

Philip heaved a helpless sigh and allowed her to help him sit up. After a few spoons of broth, he took a sip of water then pushed her arm away.

"Enough," he whispered.

"Very well. You have had enough activity for today." She picked up the tray and started toward the door.

"Mrs., uh, Miss Caroline," he corrected, and continued with feeling, "I have a great many things in my life which I regret, but none as egregious as treating you so shabbily. It is certainly no way to repay you for your patience and kindness."

"You don't have to explain, Colonel. I realize that under normal circumstances, I would not have been permitted in your room, feeding you and changing your bandages. But these unique times call for drastic measures. And some understanding."

"I just wanted you to know," he muttered.

A smile of understanding passed between them.

Over the next few days, Philip's condition—and his relationship with Caroline—improved. His bandages had to be changed less often now that his wound had nearly healed over. It was at those times that he felt the most uncomfortable. As she wound the cloth around him, the motion required her to pull the bandage over his chest then, with her other hand, reach under him to pull it around. During this process, both of her arms were around his torso, her face inches from his. At times, her soft brown eyes met his and held.

At other times, the touch of her fingers on his chest, a touch that seemed to linger a bit too long, caused him to catch his breath in exquisite agony. His head spun with the scent of her lilac water, and he scolded himself for enjoying the intimacy of those moments.

During the long nights when he couldn't sleep, he thought about her. No, his logical voice reminded him, it can only lead to complications. But, oh, he groaned, how can I resist those soft brown eyes of hers with that unmistakable look of longing?

After two weeks, Dr. Cook allowed Philip out of bed, with the added privilege of walking briefly outside his room. Leaning heavily on Lieutenant Hasselbeck's arm, and guided by Caroline, he walked on unsteady legs to the front porch to have lunch with his officers. Afterward, he shuffled back to his room for a much-needed nap.

With Caroline's assistance, and Dr. Cook's approval, Philip visited the other wounded, once he was able to negotiate the back steps.

By mid-July, the two of them became a familiar sight, strolling in the orchard, reading to each other, or sitting on the porch at sunset.

Chapter 9

"I MUST SAY, Colonel," Dr. Cook pronounced after examining Philip's partially-healed scar, "considering the seriousness of your wound, your recuperation has progressed more rapidly than I anticipated."

Philip thrust his arm into the sleeve of his blouse. "Since you're grinning like a damned fool, I assume I am going to live."

The doctor regarded Philip over the top of the spectacles that always rested halfway down his nose. "I suspect that the reason for your rapid recovery has nothing whatsoever to do with my skills as a surgeon."

"What do you mean?" Philip asked with a sudden frown.

"Your nurse deserves a great deal of the credit, not I. Only she could have coaxed you into relinquishing your duties and getting proper rest until you had recovered your strength. You can shake your head and deny it all you want, Colonel, but that miracle could never have been accomplished by a host of army corpsman."

"You have been inhaling too much chloroform, Doctor. Granted, Miss Caroline did an admirable job, but she accomplished it mostly by running over me without so much as a by-your-leave," he said with a twitch at the corner of his lips.

"If you say so." Grinning, Dr. Cook packed away his stethoscope. "However, you must continue taking it easy a while longer. Rest when your body tells you to, or I will report you to your nurse."

Suppressing a grin, Philip gave the doctor a dismissive wave. "Get the hell out of here, you old sawbones, before I have you arrested for impersonating a doctor."

That evening, Philip strolled onto the front porch. He sat on the top step beside Father Brendan O'Boyle who was resting his back against a column, gazing at the sunset.

Philip studied Brendan in the dim light, with his rusty red hair, blue eyes full of feeling and innocence, and strong chin. He worked assiduously beside Dr. Cook, doing the distasteful tasks of disposing of amputated limbs or discarding soiled bandages. Just a few years older than Philip, he'd had an athletic build but his once sturdy frame had been slowly decimated by over-work and missed meals.

"Rough day, Brendan?" Philip asked.

"Umm," Father O'Boyle replied without moving. "It's good to see you up and about, Colonel, and looking so well."

"Thank you. However, I am concerned about you. You look worn down, Brendan. You must have a care for yourself."

"I do care, but not for myself. I must see to the needs of others."

After sharing small talk about the day's activities, Brendan stifled a yawn. "Well now, I have enjoyed our little chat but I had best catch a few winks of sleep and then it's back to work. I promised one of the men that I would write a letter to let his family know he's alive." He patted Philip's knee as he stood. "Good night, sir. We must get together like this more often."

"I agree." Philip rose when Brendan did, and stretched. "I think I will turn in, too."

Returning to his room, Philip left the door slightly ajar, allowing the night breeze to flow in from the windows into the hall. Settling down by the lamp, he opened the latest edition of the *Crossroads Herald* and scanned the familiar names in the wedding announcements, obituaries and betrothals. At a muffled sound, he cocked his head toward the door. One of the officers must have dropped a boot, he decided with a shrug, and continued reading.

There it was again, only this time it was followed by the sound of running and what sounded like scuffling. He walked to the door and listened. Something fell but this time, the sound was directly overhead. Philip shook his head in sympathy at the thought that old Mrs. Howard must be on the rampage again.

Alarmed by what now sounded like a desperate struggle, with furniture scraping across a bare floor and the sound of more than one person running, Philip dropped the newspaper, grabbed his sidearm and headed for the stairs.

David and Wes met him in the hall, looking concerned. "What's going on?" Wes asked.

"I don't know. Old Mrs. Howard must be acting up again. Miss Caroline may need our help." Philip charged up the stairs, followed by Wes and David.

At the top of the stairs, Philip motioned for Wes to check inside the old woman's room. Wes opened the door a crack, peered in, and saw her sitting in a rocking chair, staring out the back window into the dark. Wes inched the door shut without a sound.

"If she's here," Philip whispered, "who the hell is in there with Miss Caroline?"

More crashing sounds and a woman's cry sent the three men scrambling across the hall to Caroline's room. Forcing the locked door open, they found the room in disarray, with a shattered water pitcher lying just inside the door. Caroline was sprawled across her bed, pinned down between the legs of the troublesome bounty jumper Private Smith. With one hand clamped over her mouth, Smith's other hand fumbled with the buttons on the front of his trousers.

To Philip, Smith bore the look of a feral animal anticipating a bloody feast. His greasy black hair hung down over his eyes, his leering grin revealed rotten teeth. Unfazed by the sudden intrusion of the three officers, he continued on with his purpose.

The entire scenario flashed before Philip's eyes, creating the eerie sensation of being transported to another time, another place. He wasn't in Caroline Howard's bedroom in Virginia. No, this was a hotel room in Washington City where his damned cousin Julian was taunting him, daring him to act.

"You gentlemen are just going to have to wait your turn," the arrogant smiling face was saying, bringing Philip back to the present situation.

During the brief instant that Smith was distracted, Caroline managed to free a hand and rake her nails across his face. "Bitch!" he hissed, and brought the back of his hand across her face with a resounding crack.

Hearing Caroline's cry of pain, Philip rushed forward, yanked Smith away from her and hurled him against the wall. "By God, you will get the firing squad for this."

"Now, Colonel," Smith held up his hands in a defensive gesture, "you ain't gonna begrudge a man a bit of enjoyment, are you? She's just a Reb bitch. You can have her when I'm finished. Hell, you can all—"

Before Smith could finish his obscene offer, Philip drew his side arm and fired point blank into Smith's head. Smith flew backward, his brain matter and blood splattering against the wall. Philip took a step forward and fired three more shots into the prone man's head and body, rendering him unrecognizable.

Screaming and hysterical, Caroline ran to a corner across the room as Wes yanked at Philip's arm. "For God's sake, Colonel, enough. The man is dead."

He shrugged off Wes' hand. "Lieutenant Southall, get a detail up here to remove this slime." Regaining his senses at last, Philip glanced around the room. "Where is Miss Caroline?"

Wes indicated the shadowy corner where Caroline cringed with her face to the wall.

In a rush of tenderness, Philip reached out to console her. At the touch of his hand on her shoulder, Caroline threw her arms around him and cried into his chest. The force of her embrace made him catch his breath as a sting of fresh pain shot through his side. Caught off guard by her reaction, he held his arms away from her at an awkward angle.

Then, without willing it, he lowered his arms and embraced her. As he did so, he could feel her body trembling with each sob. "It's all right, Miss Caroline," he whispered. "My men will take care of everything."

"Stay with me, Philip," she pleaded in a muffled voice. "Please."

Turning to shield her from the sight of Smith's blood, he whispered in her ear, "You know I can't do that. But I promise you, no one will ever try to harm you again."

David, waiting at the door, cleared his throat before saying, "Excuse me, sir. I sent for the darkies to look after Mrs. Howard."

Philip nodded silent acknowledgment.

When Cassie and Mina appeared moments later, clearly terrified by the horrific scene, Philip said, "Take Miss Caroline to the room across the hall and stay with her. And see that this room is cleaned up before she enters it again. My men will give you any help you might need."

As the two women led Caroline across the hall to Emmaline's room, the full effect of all that had just occurred struck Philip like a blow. He slumped against the wall and watched as several enlisted men removed Smith's body on a stretcher.

Satisfied that matters were well in hand, Philip ran down the stairs to his room, poured a drink with an unsteady hand and downed it in one gulp. He dropped onto the sofa, acutely aware of the ache in his side.

Wes slipped into the room and sank into a chair across from Philip. Handing Wes a glass, he asked, "Why wouldn't he stop, Wes? It was as if he was daring me to enforce my order."

"He left you no choice, sir. If you'll allow me an observation, I have never seen you so out of control. Not even in Washington. You looked almost possessed."

"I'm sorry. I don't know what came over me. For some reason, I couldn't help myself." Draining his glass, he reached for the bottle before asking, "Is Miss Caroline all right? He—he didn't have his way with her?"

Wes shook his head. "I'm sure he didn't. By the way, when the men carried Smith away, I saw old Mrs. Howard standing at her door with a wild look in her eye. It was almost as if she was gloating. She made a comment I found unnerving, something about the whore wreaking her havoc."

Philip looked up sharply from pouring another drink. "How could that old woman possibly believe that Miss Caroline brought this on herself?"

"We may never know." Standing, Wes yawned. "I believe we have all had more than enough excitement tonight, so I will take my leave."

Philip thanked Wes for his help before gulping down the remnants of his drink. Still wincing, he lay on his cot with every muscle in his body tensed. Unbidden, he relived the moment he'd held Caroline in his arms and realized that he'd had felt something he hadn't felt in a long while—tenderness toward a woman.

He shifted positions to get comfortable but the ache in his healing sutures only reminded him of Caroline's tearful embrace. *No, I mustn't think about her. I have done just fine without any female entanglements.*

But, he realized with trepidation, *if I hadn't been awake to intervene,* Smith may have done his deed and been gone with no one the wiser— or to identify him later if he left no living witness. Squeezing his eyes shut, he visualized himself standing over Smith's body, pumping bullet after bullet into the bloody pulp that had once been his face but seeing Julian's face instead. *Dear God,* he groaned, *I don't regret killing the bastard but why did I react in such an appalling manner? Civilized men don't act like that.*

Then, from the deepest recesses of his mind, he recalled something Samantha had said the first night they met: 'With sufficient provocation, even you could kill.' He shuddered at its ominous prescience, given that he had also been willing to kill Julian in that Washington hotel room.

He thrashed about on his cot in a vain attempt to erase the horrors of tonight's events. His logical voice reminded him of other practical matters, such as submitting a written report of this incident to headquarters. *With Smith's previous record,* he thought, *I'm sure they will concur with my actions.*

Dozing at last, the vision of a woman in a flowing white gown danced in his dream, reached out to him. A floating specter, with long brown hair cascading over her shoulders, she gazed at him with longing. In her loveliness, she seemed real, as real as the dream of her tender kisses in his delirium last month. It was almost as if he could reach out and touch that diaphanous figure. As if. . .

"Hold me," the vision whispered against his ear.

Wakefulness came slowly. Using the dim light threading through his half-open door, he focused bleary eyes on the nightgown-clad figure kneeling beside his cot. Her hair did indeed cascade around her shoulders.

He sat up with a start. "My God, what are you doing in here?"

"I'm frightened, Philip."

Careful, his logical voice warned, choose your words carefully. Don't upset her any more than she already has been. "You have had a harrowing experience, Miss Caroline," he said in a gentle voice, "but you needn't be afraid any longer."

"I can't stop shaking." She gripped his wrist. "Please, let me stay a while."

"It wouldn't do for you to be seen in my room," he whispered, conveying his sense of urgency. "It could lead to things neither of us would be able to control. While I don't want to compromise your reputation, I cannot guarantee what might happen if you stayed. Please," he prodded gently, "you must go."

"But I want to be with you," she insisted.

With great tenderness, he held her away from him. "Please, go now."

Caroline slumped to a sitting position onto the floor, rested her head on the edge of the cot and covered her face. "I have been frightened and alone for so long. I want to feel safe again."

Gazing down at her helpless state, his heart went out to her. "I am aware of the heavy burden you have borne these last few years, caring for everyone, doing the work of dozens of people. You have every right to feel frightened and weary." He touched the soft hair that hid her face. "Let me reassure you, Miss Caroline, I will personally see to your safety during the remainder of our brief stay here."

She lifted her head, bringing her face within inches of his, and whispered, "Thank you." Then, slowly, with deliberate care, she slipped her arms around his neck and drew him closer.

That damned logical voice interfered again and warned him to beware. But, he groaned inwardly in reply, her lips are so close, and she smells so good. And those eyes, eyes so full of innocence and fear—and longing. Eyes that can make a man disregard every vow he ever made.

Steeling himself to the moment, he drew back and, with gentle reluctance, pulled himself free of her embrace. "No, I cannot and I will not take advantage of the situation. For God's sake—for both our sakes—please go."

Neither moved for several moments, their faces so close he could feel her warm breath on his cheek. Presently, she nodded, touched his lips with the tip of her index finger, and slipped away as silently as she arrived.

With a deep sigh of relief, Philip fell back onto his cot, uncomfortably aware of the lilac scent that lingered in her wake.

Sleep was long in coming that night.

Chapter 10

EXHAUSTED, HIS BACK aching with fresh pain, Philip rode to City Point early the next morning with a written report of the shooting incident in his tunic pocket, along with a request for a commendation to reward Father O'Boyle for his tireless service. Even the most outspoken anti-Catholics in the company had nothing but kind words for the priest.

The four-mile ride also allowed Philip time to clear his head. *Dear God*, he marveled, *I shot a man's brains out last night. But even more unbelievably, Caroline came to my room. She wanted me to hold her, and to. . .*

No! his logical voice warned him, *I cannot allow it to happen. I must avoid her at all costs.*

As he rode toward the General Grant's headquarters, he noticed how completely the Army of the Potomac had taken over the little town of City Point. Riding past St. John's Episcopal Church, he observed that the wounded had filled the little church and even spilled out onto the lawn. Further along, he saw a group of men playing baseball. Judging by the cat-calls and raised voices, they were having a good time.

At headquarters, Philip tossed his reins to a private and asked to see Colonel Graves as soon as he was free. As he waited, Philip roamed about the Eppes Plantation in the hope of driving last night's disturbing memories from his mind. Maybe, he told himself, if I crowd enough work into my days and nights, maybe, just maybe, I can forget how Caroline felt in my arms. How she—

"Hello there, Colonel Creighton," Colonel Graves' voice interrupted his thoughts. "Say, didn't I hear that you had sustained a serious injury? How are you feeling?"

"Fine, sir. Still a bit sore but, given the circumstances, I consider myself fortunate."

"Come, let's sit under the trees. This damned heat is abominable." Once they were seated at a small table in the shade, Colonel Graves asked, "Now, what can I do for you?"

"I came to hand deliver a report about an incident that occurred at my headquarters last evening, and to explain in person some pertinent details that I felt were better left off paper."

Colonel Graves scanned the report. "So, you shot one of your own men. You state here that the man disobeyed your orders in front of others, leaving you no alternative. Is that the essence of it?"

"Yes, sir, on the surface. You see, to protect the ladies who live on the property, I declared the second floor of the house off limits to military personnel. Smith, if that is his real name, was aware of my order but went to Mrs. Howard's room for the purpose of," he paused and cleared his throat, "well, no gentleman likes to speak of it. He taunted me after I ordered him at gun-point to cease and desist, so I shot him. I could not allow this unspeakable thing to happen to the lady. I'm sure you will agree that we are not here to violate the civilian ladies."

Nodding agreement, Colonel Graves kept his hazel eyes fixed on Philip as he related the details of his story.

"As for Smith," Philip added, "it is my personal opinion that the man was a bounty jumper."

"What have you done with the body?"

"I asked my officers to look through his belongings to determine his true name and where he came from. Once that's done, we will ship his body home. If not, we will bury him nearby."

Colonel Graves placed the report on the table. "I see nothing untoward in your actions. I agree that we cannot allow those under our command to run rampant, raping women and the land with impunity. I must warn you, however, that there will be an inquiry."

"Yes, sir, I understand that. I, and my men, will cooperate fully with the investigation."

"But, based on what you have described, and based on Smith's unsavory background, I expect no action will be taken against you. Now," Graves leaned back in his chair, "if you have nothing else, perhaps you will allow me to buy you a drink. You look perfectly wretched, man."

"I'm surprised I look that well," Philip replied with a wry smile. "I could use a drink, but first, I have one more matter to discuss." He slid his commendation request across the table. "We have an excellent chaplain in our company whom I believe deserves a citation for his devotion to duty."

Colonel Graves read the commendation. "Father Brendan O'Boyle. A tough Irishman?"

"And very dedicated, sir. That dedication should not go unrewarded."

"And so it shall not, Colonel. Is there anything else?"

"Yes," Philip smiled, "I believe I heard something about a drink."

"Done. We will have a drink or two, then see what's going on down at the wharves. With any luck at all, we should be back in time for Colonel Pleasants' briefing about the tunnel your fellow Pennsylvanians are digging over by Elliott's Salient."

"Sounds interesting. I believe I will stay for that." Anything, Philip thought, to delay my return to Howard Hill.

They walked to the edge of the bluff overlooking the mile-long stretch of wharves lining the riverbank. Colonel Graves pointed down the slope at the various activities. "They have a new engine workhouse down there. Supplies are shipped in daily to build our own narrow-gauge railroad that will allow us to transport supplies directly to the battle lines. There are two steam engines pumping in our own water supply."

Philip shook his head. "This whole operation amazes me."

"Take a deep breath, Colonel."

Even over the smell of horse dung baking in the sun, sweaty, unwashed bodies, and myriad other smells rising from the wharves, Philip caught the unmistakable aroma of fresh bread. "Where is it coming from?"

Graves pointed southeastward. "From our bakery over there, not far from our defensive entrenchment. At the commissary, you can buy just about anything your heart desires. General Grant believes that the army must be well supplied if they are to succeed. We have our own city within a city here." He tipped his hat to a passing Quaker nurse. "Ma'am."

Philip tipped his cavalry hat as well. "You seem to have everything any army would need."

"Hell, we have barracks and an enormous hospital, while you and your men live the Spartan life of an army in the field."

"Well, not quite," Philip grinned, choosing not to reveal his own comfortable accommodations.

"Ah, here we are," Colonel Graves exclaimed. "This saloon may not be Harvey's Oyster Bar or the Willard, but at times, it looks pretty damned good." They seated themselves in the dingy, make-shift saloon on Prince Henry Avenue and ordered drinks.

"I haven't received a letter from my brother lately," Philip said, and made a face at his drink. "What's the latest news about Sherman?"

"From what I understand, good and bad." Graves lifted his glass to his lips. "Sherman is still advancing against Johnston, but it is slow going and very costly. Those damned Confederates are firmly entrenched but our boys continue to flank them and advance, inch by inch, mile by bloody mile, forcing Johnston to fall back toward Atlanta. If Atlanta falls, we will control the deep South as well as the rail lines." His eyes grew dark as he finished off his drink. "It has all been hell, hasn't it, Philip?"

"Hell, and then some," Philip agreed, as the grim news intensified his fears for Matthew's safety.

After more small talk, Colonel Graves swallowed the last of his whiskey and said, "Let's start back to headquarters. We don't want to miss Colonel Pleasants' briefing." He tossed a few coins onto the table.

Outside the dim saloon, Philip blinked to adjust his eyes to the glaring sunlight.

"We're in luck," Austin said. "There is the afternoon sprinkling cart. We can fall in behind it while they water down the roads. That way we won't choke on this damned eternal dust."

Chapter 11

WHEN CAROLINE AWOKE that same morning, she was immediately aware of the sore muscles and bruises on her body where Smith had thrown her against the wall. Her left jaw was swollen where he backhanded her. She lay quietly for a few moments, focusing on last night's events. Recalling her brazenness in Philip's room, she blushed and stuck her head under the pillow.

Rising a few moments later, she put on a freshly ironed dress and went to the kitchen for a breakfast of coffee and leftover biscuits, compliments of the Union army. She remembered the time when breakfast was as big a meal as dinner. But that was when Morgan and Justin ran the farm, and Father Howard presided from his wicker chair on the porch.

Yes, it was all so different during those carefree days, she sighed into her cup. They are all gone now, except for Mother Howard and me. Four frightened women are all that is left of this once proud plantation. But, she wondered, as she had wondered for well over a year, is Morgan still alive?

Thoughts of their tumultuous eight-year marriage revived mixed emotions—and her anguish after learning of his many mistresses. Her inability to conceive had driven Morgan to prove his manhood with a frenzy that went beyond obsession. But, she thought, her eyes hardening, he cannot say that I did not do my duty to him. Yes, I did my duty with no emotion and certainly not love.

Until last month.

For all his gruffness and the fierceness in those intense black eyes, Philip has become a safe haven for me. His voice soothes away my fears. Blushing again, she covered her face. Why am I having these shameful thoughts?

Tempered by the hardships of the last few years, Caroline had discovered that she could make decisions on her own, something she had never had to do in the past. Well-bred young ladies were not expected to make decisions or have serious thoughts about the condition of their world. That was man's business.

Dear Lord, I pray this horrid war ends soon. I want to sleep at night without jumping at every sound. If things don't change soon, I will become as mad as Mother Howard. I need the security Philip's presence has brought me, despite the haunted look in his eyes. And the dark need that seems to be driving him.

Caroline started out the back door to check on the scant kitchen garden that had been scorched in the two-month drought. At the well, David Southall greeted her with his most charming smile. "Good morning, Mrs. Howard." His expression changed abruptly to one of concern. "I hope you passed a restful night."

Caroline lowered her gaze, recalling her indelicate predicament when the officers burst into her room last night. "Yes, thank you. I cannot begin to say how much I appreciate all you did for me."

"No need, ma'am. I am grateful that we were able to protect your honor." David flashed his smile again. "If I may be so bold, I would be honored if you would consider riding with me this afternoon. Perhaps it will help you to forget—everything."

Caroline turned away from his insistent blue eyes so she could think clearly.

"I will be on my best behavior," he swore, with his hand over his heart.

She smiled in return. "All right, Lieutenant. It will be fun riding with a gentleman again. But, alas," she indicated the empty stables, "I have no horses left."

"I will borrow one from our corral. Shall we meet after lunch at about one o'clock?"

"That will be fine." Lowering her eyes again under his devastating smile, she wondered if Philip would ever look at her that way.

Dorothea stood at her bedroom window overlooking the back yard. She watched David smile at Caroline. Observed Caroline's reaction, nodding her head at something he said. Dorothea's eyes narrowed. Jezebel! Doing her sinful deeds out there for everyone to see. Violating her husband's memory with her evil ways. She thinks I don't see, but I am armed with the Lord's might. The Lord will visit His wrath upon her. His justice will prevail!

Philip rode back to Howard Hill, still uneasy about Colonel Pleasants' briefing on the tunnel project. Perhaps the tunnel could be dug according to the Colonel's specifications, but he didn't have much confidence in the proposed plan following the explosion. There were too many differing opinions, and too many loose ends.

Turning his horse into the main gate, he rode past the huts his men had constructed from scrap wood and mud to protect them from the brutal sun. They acknowledged his passing with salutes before going back to their card games, letter-writing, laundry, or reading the newspapers purchased from the vendor's wagon.

As he dismounted at the corral, movement in the orchard caught his eye. Turning in that direction, he was surprised to see David and Caroline walking side by side, leading their horses, and completely engrossed in conversation. An unfamiliar twinge flared inside him.

Nonsense, he snorted to himself. Why the hell should I care if David squires Mrs. Howard on an afternoon ride? It is better that she is otherwise occupied.

On the way to his office, Philip called to Lieutenant Hasselbeck who appeared out of nowhere. "Lieutenant, please inform the staff and

First Sergeant Powell that we will have a meeting in one hour. And see if the cook has any coffee that is fit to drink."

"Yes, sir. Right away."

Philip had just settled down at his desk when Cassie appeared at his door. She was tall and erect in her bearing, her white head wrap adding to her dignity. A handsome woman, Philip had thought upon meeting her, with a good mind and eyes that missed nothing. "Here you is, Colonel Philip. I seen you come in and figured you'd need a cup of good coffee."

"Thank you, Cassie," he smiled. "I must admit that your coffee is infinitely better than army coffee and I don't need a knife to cut it. Uh, how is Mrs. Howard today?" he asked in an off-hand manner, knowing damned well that she was just fine, judging by the tender scene he had witnessed in the orchard.

"She's some better today. That Lieutenant took her ridin'. He's a mighty nice man. For a Yankee," she added with a grin. "He looked after her almost all day."

Philip shifted in his chair. "I am happy to hear that she is well." Thanking Cassie again for the coffee, he turned to his desk and wondered with apprehension if she was aware of Caroline's visit to his room last night.

At four o'clock, the officers and First Sergeant Powell entered Philip's office. Once everyone was seated, Philip began, "Gentlemen, digging of the tunnel at Elliott's Salient is progressing nicely. Colonel Pleasants' company has many Pennsylvania coal miners who have already dug about half way toward their goal. I have drawn a rough diagram of the project from memory. They are now at this point," he indicated the spot on his diagram.

The staff gathered around the diagram to get a better view.

"Right about here," Philip continued, "they were forced to slope the tunnel upward to avoid some heavy clay. Barring unforeseen delays, they should reach their destination by late July. Colonel Pleasants feels that the Confederates must suspect something as they have begun digging their own tunnels to intercept ours, but their attempts have failed.

"Once our tunnel is complete, charges with long fuses will be planted under the Confederate position here," he pointed again to the diagram. "The explosion should catch the enemy off guard, resulting in panic and chaos. Any questions so far?"

Captain Hanford spoke first. "Sir, what about the debris they would have to carry out?"

"And wouldn't there be a problem with ventilation?" Sergeant Powell asked.

"They have taken care of both contingencies," Philip assured them. "Remember, these are coal miners who know their business. Several plans were discussed, however, regarding action after the explosion, such as a charge by our troops directly through the affected area immediately after the blast, or a two-pronged attack to surround the area. I personally feel the latter has merit because it allows us to contain the enemy within the blasted area.

"Someone at the meeting asked about using colored troops in the first charge, but that was dismissed. They did not want it to appear that the colored troops would be considered expendable while the white soldiers were held in reserve."

Wes nodded. "We wouldn't want to be accused of sacrificing the lives of black soldiers to save those of white men."

"Exactly," Philip said. "We have made enough blunders already. Of course, you are not to breathe a word of this, especially to the newspaper reporters. General Grant wouldn't like reading the exact date and time of the explosion in a Washington or New York newspaper." As he spoke, Philip noticed that David was staring out the window with a faraway look in his eyes.

Standing abruptly, Philip indicated that the meeting was over. After his officers departed, he stared out the window himself and thought of Caroline, as he surmised David had earlier. *What the hell does it matter,* he thought with a shrug, *if David adds Miss Caroline to his list of conquests? I certainly don't need another female complication in my life.*

Chapter 12

AFTER SIX WEEKS in the saddle, bloody battles and a long recuperative period from his wound, Philip was now so gaunt that his uniforms, or what was left of them, hung in shapeless folds on his frame. He assessed his shabby appearance in the entry hall mirror as Wes looked on.

"Wes, have you ever seen anything as disreputable as this uniform? Except, of course, the wearer. I look like a damned scarecrow."

"We could all use new uniforms. Yours, however," Wes added with a wry smile, "does look the worse for wear."

"In that case, why not accompany me to City Point to buy some new ones?"

"Fine," Wes said. "I will meet you in about an hour."

Philip and Wes returned from City Point later that afternoon wearing new uniforms and boots, and still grinning from a side trip to a saloon. After purchasing two uniforms for himself, Philip treated Wes and himself to new cavalry hats.

He approached Cassie before supper with his new tunics slung over his arm. "Cassie, I hesitate to impose upon you again, but I would appreciate it if you'd alter these uniforms for me. I will pay you handsomely."

"Colonel Philip, after all you done for Mina and me and Miz Caroline, I be happy to do that for you. But I want to know how you get these uniforms made so fast?" she asked, fingering the fabric.

"They were made on Mr. Howe's new sewing machine."

"I heard about a machine that sews clothes. How does it work?"

"The machine that does the stitching is run by people in garment factories. They can turn out thousands of uniforms a year. I am not an engineer, so I cannot explain it very well."

"Glory be. What won't they think of next?" After listening to Philip's instructions and taking his measurements, Cassie took the tunics and the new insignia to her room off the kitchen.

Philip then led his horse to the corral to have her watered and rubbed down. After visiting the wounded, he walked toward the house and had just stepped in the back door deep in thought when Caroline came around the corner from the dining room and bumped into him head-on.

He jumped back at the unexpected collision. "Miss Caroline," he stammered, "I—I'm sorry. I didn't see you. My mind was elsewhere."

Blushing, she murmured, "I confess, Colonel, that I too was preoccupied."

He tried not to stare at her too closely. "Uh, how have you been?"

"Fine, thank you," she replied, and lowered her gaze.

Despite her statement, he could see that she appeared wan from her traumatic experience with Smith, and yet, so inviting.

"Is Cassie still staying with you?" When she raised her eyes, he saw the bruise on her face, bringing back memories of that awful night— and her visit to his room

"Yes."

"That's good," he said with a nod. The urge to reach out and caress her bruised face rose up inside him. No, his logical self warned him again, stop it. I will bid her good day and go about my business. I just wish she wouldn't look at me that way.

The slow tick-tick of the hall clock accentuated the awkward silence between them. Distracted by its sound, but never taking his eyes off her, Philip wondered if the clock had always ticked that loudly.

"And you, Colonel?" she asked. "How are you doing?"

"Um, feeling stronger each day. As a matter of fact, Major Madison and I just acquired some much-needed uniforms." He pulled on his baggy old tunic to demonstrate. "Now I won't live in fear of being strung up on a fence to scare the crows away from the corn."

Laughing, she said, "Cassie told me you asked her to alter your new tunics. She also told me about the sewing machine that made them. Amazing, isn't it?"

"Yes." Moved by the vulnerability in her eyes, Philip shuffled his feet. Then, with stunning force, came the renewed awareness of the deep void in his life. The void only a woman can fill. Perhaps, this woman? No. Walk away, damn it. Now.

"Well, if you'll excuse me," she said with a sigh, and turned to leave.

Ignoring the logical voice inside him and pushing all reason aside, he called out, "Miss Caroline?"

She turned toward him with an expectant smile. "Yes?"

"May I have a moment more of your time?" He hesitated, thinking, Why in the hell am I doing this? "I—I was just wondering if you would have supper with me this evening?" Logic regained control and he stammered, "I'm sorry, I don't mean to intrude. Perhaps you have other plans."

She thrust her hands into her apron pockets. "After what happened the last time, don't you think your officers might object if I had dinner with them again?"

"I, uh, I was not thinking of including them." At her startled reaction, Philip felt himself flush. "Would seven o'clock be agreeable? I will ask Cassie to cook for us."

"Yes, seven o'clock would be fine," she said in a barely audible whisper.

He walked with her to the bottom of the stairs and watched as she went up to her room. Once she was out of sight, he pounded his fist on the finial. Damn it, something is happening and I can't stop it. I don't want to stop it.

***

In the parlor that served as the officer's quarters, David Southall regarded himself before the great pier mirror. Looking remarkably fit, his tanned face accentuated his blue eyes and white teeth to great advantage. His blonde hair was streaked by constant exposure to the sun. Not bad, he thought. *Perhaps Mrs. Howard will think so too. That lovely lady was a most pleasant companion on our ride the other day, so tonight I will call on her for an evening of diversion we will both remember.*

Wes poked his head into Philip's office at five thirty that afternoon. "Say, Philip, the sutler said some fellow brought in some fighting cocks. Pete, David and I are going down after supper to place a few bets. Want to come along?"

"What about Lieutenant Hasselbeck?" Philip asked, not daring to believe that he would be alone in the house with Caroline this evening.

"He has a card game over by Battery Five. They have some fancy card games over there. How about it?"

"No, thanks. Maybe we can plan a card game or play some baseball later in the week. Don't lose all your money tonight," he added, "or I will write to Jane and tell her everything."

Dorothea sat by the window, as she had for the past week, marking certain passages in her bible—and watching. She watched Caroline stop by the well and speak to the wounded Union soldiers, confer with Dr. Cook, and turn at the sound of that Yankee colonel's voice.

She watched every move, unaware of her personal distressed condition. It didn't matter that the armpits of her dresses were stained with dried perspiration. Or that her oily hair was matted to her head from lack of care.

The darkies can plead and nag all they want, she thought with a jerk of her chin. *Nothing matters except exacting the Lord's justice on that harlot.* Squinting, she watched the Yankee officers laughing and talking as they mounted their horses. "They think I don't know," she muttered. "But I know. And the Lord knows. Yes, even in the Book of Jeremiah, He knew how to deal with faithless people."

Dorothea pursed her lips and read again from the Sixth Chapter of the prophet: 'They were confounded, because they committed abomination: yea, rather they were not confounded with confusion, and they knew not how to blush: wherefore they shall fall among them that fall: in the time of their visitation they shall fall down, saith the Lord.'

"There," Dorothea said aloud, and tapped her bony finger on the fifteenth verse, "is proof from the Lord. He knows of their abomination and will repay them. And I shall be His instrument." Her eyes glowed with the fire of righteousness now that her mission had become clear.

Chapter 13

CHECKING HIS APPEARANCE again in the shaving mirror, Philip chuckled to himself. *Preening is something David usually does. Oh well, I might not be as handsome as David but I look passable in this new uniform.*

Pausing, he frowned at his reflection. *What the hell is wrong with me? Why am I doing this? Especially after what took place the other night right here in this room? Nothing happened,* he assured himself, *and nothing more than dinner and conversation will take place this evening. I do not intend becoming emotionally involved with her. This is nothing more than reciprocation for Caroline's kindness during my illness.*

Just as he stepped into the entry hall from his office, he and Caroline met at the bottom step. Laughing, he said, "Isn't this the second time today that we have literally bumped into each other?"

She returned his smile. "Yes, we seemed destined to be at the same place at the same time."

"Well, um," he stammered, and cleared his throat to disguise his sudden nervousness, "I thought we might have a glass of wine in my office while we wait for Cassie to call us."

"That sounds nice."

Allowing her to pass through the door ahead of him, he became keenly aware of the lilac scent that usually surrounded her. Careful, he warned himself again.

"I must tell you," he said, pouring two glasses of wine, "about the great hazards this bottle endured on its journey south from Washington City. But, as you can see," he held the bottle up, "it came through every peril unscathed."

Caroline accepted a glass from him. "Thank you, Colonel."

"I like it better when you call me Philip. It is less military and formal."

Cassie appeared at the door just then and announced that dinner was ready.

"Thank you, Cassie." He turned to Caroline. "Shall we go in? I will bring the wine and the glasses to the table." He followed her to the dining room, his senses assailed by her sweet aroma. This time, he told the warning voice in his head to mind its own damned business.

Cassie had set the table as best she could with the remaining pieces of the family china. Candles flickered in mismatched holders. The sun, low in the western sky, cast deep shadows in the dusky light. The lace curtains on the tall windows billowed in the westerly breeze.

Dinner consisted of a small portion of ham, mysteriously procured by Philip, boiled greens, baked sweet potatoes, and cornbread still warm from the oven. Philip held the dish of ham for Caroline as she helped herself then took several slices for himself. Instead of passing her the dish of potatoes, he spooned a large helping onto her plate.

"Enough," she protested. "I can't eat that much. Please remember, sir, I am not a man."

"I noticed that," he teased. At her questioning look, he added, "I have also noticed that you don't eat much."

She laughed out loud. "Oh, really, Colonel? I'm sorry. We did agree to dispense with titles, didn't we—Philip?"

Yes, he thought, we dispensed with formal titles the other night when I wanted to pull you into my cot.

Now that the banter and laughter had dissipated their initial awkwardness, they relaxed and chatted about many things, but nothing that touched on the war.

"What did you do in Pennsylvania?" she asked, as she picked at her food.

"I helped my father run the family businesses. And I traveled a good bit. Nothing very interesting."

"Travel is always interesting. Where did you go?"

"After college, I took the obligatory Grand Tour of Europe. I rode a barge down the Nile. Saw the pyramids. The coliseum in Rome. The Matterhorn in Switzerland. Castles on the Rhine. But, even after all that, I was happy to get back home."

"That sounds fascinating. I didn't realize you came from a wealthy family. Did you visit Florence, Italy, during your travels? My favorite poetess lives there."

"You mean Elizabeth Browning? Yes, I stayed in Florence, but I was more intrigued with Michaelangelo's statue of David. And the cafes," he added with a grin.

"And the beautiful Italian ladies?"

Suppressing a smile, he reached for his wineglass. "The historic buildings and art works were the only objects of beauty I observed in Italy."

"Liar," she teased, and reached for her own wineglass.

Philip took a moment to study her in the flickering candlelight. Something was different about her tonight. Was it the way the candles lit her eyes? No, it was something more than that. She looked strangely confident, like a woman who had come to a difficult decision.

"I must admit, Caroline, how much I admire your courage. You have survived this war, despite overwhelming odds. You have also made our situation here more agreeable." He took her hand in his. "Thank you," he whispered, and squeezed her hand.

"You flatter me, sir," she murmured, but did not move her hand. "I am not all that courageous. I have lived in constant fear these last few years that we would lose everything. Or starve."

"I could not stand by and let that happen." His dark eyes grew gentle. "Caroline, let me say again how much I appreciate what you did for me when I was wounded. I deeply regret my abominable behavior toward you. I can never make that up to you, and simply to say I'm sorry seems so inadequate." He pressed her fingers to his lips.

Reaching out with her free hand, Caroline caressed his face. "No, it is I who can never thank you. Philip," she began tentatively, "I want to thank you for something else—for not taking advantage of the situation the other night."

The touch of her hand on his face had the sensation of a branding iron, but he controlled his reaction enough to say in a hoarse whisper, "Believe me, asking you to leave was pure torture."

She lowered her gaze to her napkin. "I can't imagine what you must have thought of me."

"I thought nothing except that you were frightened. I am thankful that we were able to prevent anything more serious from happening."

"You saved my life, Philip. I can never thank you for that."

He leaned closer. "No need."

They regarded one another for a moment before Caroline rose abruptly and fussed at the sideboard. "Would you like your coffee now?" she asked in a quavering voice.

He stood, took her hands and held them fast. "What's wrong, Caroline? I thought we were having a pleasant conversation."

"We are, but being with you like this," she looked up directly into his eyes, "I—I realized suddenly that you have awakened feelings in me that I have never felt before."

His eyes held hers a moment longer, his mind racing. Is she sincere? Or is she merely playing a role to get what she can from me? Is she a predator? Or merely a frightened, lonely woman?

He leaned closer to her, still unsure of her motives. Their lips met, tentatively, tenderly, at first. As the long-suppressed yearning rose up within him, his arms were around her in one swift motion, crushing her against him. Between their fevered kisses, she whispered his name in a way that made his knees go weak. The urge for her grew stronger.

After a few moments, she stepped back from his embrace and, without a word, took his hand. Hesitating a moment, Philip pondered the ramifications if he proceeded beyond this point. What the hell, he decided. Who knows where I'll be tomorrow? Or next week?

He picked up the glasses and wine bottle and followed her up the stairs. At least this time, he assured himself, I will have my eyes open. I won't be caught unaware this time.

Not this time.

"So much left-over food," Cassie grumbled, as she cleared the table later. "I ain't never seen the like. First, the Colonel wants me to cook for them then they don't eat nothin'."

Mina shook her head. "What a shame, leaving all that food in these hard times."

"I seen the Colonel carryin' a bottle of wine when they come in to eat. They was both carryin' their glasses with them. Now where you suppose them glasses and that bottle got to?"

Mina raised her eyes to the second floor.

"No," Cassie protested with a shake of her head.

"Now, Cassie, I know you don't wanna think nothin' bad about Miz Caroline, but where else would they be?"

"You reckon they is up there together, him and her?" Cassie gasped.

Mina's troubled eyes confirmed Cassie's suspicion.

When they returned to the kitchen carrying the dishes, a blue-clad form crouching near the big fireplace startled them. Stepping closer, Mina asked warily, "Who's there?"

The figure stood and held out his arms to her. "It's only me, Daniel. I don't mean to scare you none. You got any food for a hungry man?"

Mina threw herself into her husband's arms and, tiny as she was, became lost in his embrace, laughing and crying at the same time.

"Woman," he complained with a smile, "you is gonna drowned me in your tears. Now hush up and gimme a kiss." After sharing several desperate kisses, he sighed, "Lord, it sure is good to be home. Where's everybody at?"

"Dead mostly," Cassie answered in a cryptic tone. "All the other darkies done run off and young Mr. Justin, he got hisself killed up north some place. Ain't heard nothin' about Mister Morgan since then. Miss Emmaline, she died a couple of weeks back. Ole Missy," she indicated the bedroom overhead, "she done gone clean outa her head. Me and

Mina, we has to lead her round and feed her like a chile. Ain't nothin' round here been the same."

"Why, Miz Caroline even took up with a Yankee colonel," Mina added with emphasis.

Daniel's jaw dropped. "The devil, you say. My, how times is changed."

Sitting at the place Mina set for him, Daniel devoured most of the leftover food. When he finished the meal and drained the last of the coffee from his cup, he leaned back with a contented sigh. "That was the best meal I had since I joined the army. Ain't no cookin' like home cookin'," he said, and gave Mina a significant smile.

Shyly, she reached for Daniel's hand and said good night to Cassie.

Cassie shooed them out of the kitchen. "You two go on and get outta here. I don't mind cleaning up the kitchen."

From her bedroom window, Dorothea watched Daniel and Mina make their way across the back yard toward their cabin. Compressing her lips, she thought, they have all turned to evil. She has even infected the darkies with her adulterous ways. Such evil shall not go unpunished. She will know the Lord's wrath. This very day the Lord's judgment shall be visited on them.

Chapter 14

IN THE COURSE of an hour, David Southall lost fifteen dollars on the cockfights. "At this rate," he groaned, "how can I afford to buy paper for my letters to the lovely ladies in Washington? I'm going back to Howard Hill."

Sauntering away, he waved his hat in a jaunty salute to the officers' ribald remarks. Laugh, if you will, he thought. I have a better game in mind. Tonight, I will add one more broken heart to my list of conquests.

In his quarters at Howard Hill, David ran a silver brush through his hair and brushed the road dust from his tunic. Humming lightheartedly, he retrieved a bottle of brandy from the bottom of his travel bag. Holding it up to the lamp, he thought with a smile, Mrs. Howard and I will put this to good use this evening.

One last check of his appearance assured him that he looked quite irresistible.

He treaded lightly up the stairs past Dorothea's door. She seems to hear and see everything, he thought, with a shake of his head. Pausing at Caroline's door, he took a deep breath before knocking.

After a long pause, he heard the startled reply, "Who is it, please?"
"Lieutenant Southall, ma'am."

Caroline opened the door a crack. "Yes, Lieutenant? Is something wrong?"

"No, ma'am. I brought you this bottle of brandy." He held the bottle out to her. "I have always felt that fine liquor should be shared with a lovely lady. I hope you like brandy." Smiling his most disarming smile, he waited for the invitation to step into her room.

But, before Caroline could reply, Philip moved from behind the door into David's line of vision. "Bring it in, Lieutenant. Brandy is much better after dinner than wine." He held up his empty wineglass.

The sight of Philip in Mrs. Howard's room obviously at ease, with the collar of his military blouse undone, left David momentarily speechless. Flustered by his awkward predicament, he took a step back.

Philip lit a cheroot and blew the smoke above his head. "I hope you remember, Lieutenant, that the last man who came to this room was shot."

David looked him squarely in the eye. "Yes, sir, and I hope the next man does not suffer the same fate."

At David's pointed retort, Philip's face darkened but he held his tongue.

"Your servant, ma'am," David mumbled to Caroline with an elaborate bow before turning on his heel.

Caroline leaned against the closed door, her hand at her throat. Philip stood across the room in the front of the fireplace, keeping his back to her. He chewed on his lip and thought, damn, why did David have to come to her room tonight, of all nights?

"Now everyone will know," he heard her say behind him.

"You needn't worry about David." He turned to face her. "He has never tasted defeat with a lady before so he is not about to admit to his fellow officers, or to anyone, that he had been turned away from your door."

"But what must he think?" she cried. "I mean, seeing you here. Us, together like this."

Hurrying across the room to her, he held her at arm's length. "Look at me, Caroline." He peered intently into her eyes. "We both knew it would come to this sooner or later, didn't we? It has been there between us from the beginning. But tonight, I could resist you no longer. To tell the truth, I didn't want to. Maybe I should be sorry for what happened between us, but I'm not."

"But we sinned. We are adulterers!" she cried through her sobs.

He kissed the top of her bowed head. "I know you are upset over David's surprise visit. So am I. And I feel like a cad for putting you in this situation." He glanced over her shoulder to the corner where he had shot Smith. Even though all traces of his blood had been removed, the reverberations from the shots he'd fired into Smith still rang in his ears.

Averting his gaze, he asked, "Are you sure you are all right staying in here so soon after—?"

"I'm not afraid," Caroline assured him with a sniff into her handkerchief. "Mina did an excellent job of cleaning up. She even destroyed the sheets. Several of your men whitewashed the wall after she cleaned it."

"I am relieved to hear that." Philip retrieved the tunic he'd draped over a chair. "I must leave before the others return. I won't subject you to another scene like the one with David."

As he approached the door, her imploring eyes held his. Philip held out his arms to her. "Come here, Caroline, let me hold you before I go."

Without a word, she slid into Philip's arms.

"Caroline, I—I . . ." He tightened his embrace. "I won't forget what passed between us tonight." He took her hand. "Come, walk down the hall with me."

After sharing a tender kiss, they walked in silence to the top of the stairs, his arm around her shoulders. On the landing, he kissed her again, descended halfway to the bottom of the steps, turned and smiled at her.

The officers entered the back door just then, all talking and laughing at the same time. As Caroline smiled down at Philip, the door to Dorothea's room flew open. An ear-piercing shriek filled the air. Wild-eyed, Dorothea screamed at Caroline, who remained frozen on the landing. "Harlot!" she cried down to her. "You have incurred the Lord's wrath! Today, you who have sinned in the eyes of God shall know justice."

She swooped down on Caroline, fists flying, and landed several sharp blows. Momentarily immobilized, Philip recovered himself and started up the stairs to defend Caroline. Wes darted past him and grabbed Dorothea's arms. Peter Hanford followed Wes, telling Caroline to run as they struggled to subdue Dorothea.

Seconds later, Cassie appeared, followed by Mina and Daniel, who was carrying his army pistol. Seeing the desperate struggle, Daniel fired a warning shot in the air. The sharp report resounded in the hall, bringing the frantic activity to an abrupt halt.

Everyone, except Dorothea who continued ranting, looked toward the source of the shot. Peter Hanford finally succeeded in securing Dorothea around the waist and carrying her bodily to her room. Cassie rushed past Philip up the stairs to care for Dorothea.

Shielding Caroline, Philip said to Daniel, "By God, man, put that weapon away before someone gets hurt. Who the hell are you anyway?"

Mina spoke up. "That's my man, Daniel. We jumped the broom before he left to fight in the Yankee army. He come home for a visit."

Peeking over Philip's shoulder, Caroline breathed a sigh of relief. "Daniel, why on earth are you shooting at us like that?"

"Miz Caroline, I wasn't shooting at nobody. I thought them Yankees was doin' ole Missy harm, what with the ruckus and all."

Still leaning on Philip to support her shaky knees, she said to him, "Daniel is Mina's husband. He left about two years ago to join the army."

Philip relaxed. "Very well, Private. But put that gun away before someone gets hurt."

Sheepishly, Daniel slipped the gun into his belt as Mina crept up the stairs to help Cassie.

Assisting Caroline down to his room, Philip said, "It's over now, Caroline. You rest here a moment and collect yourself."

Wes knocked on the half-open door and peered inside. "May I come in, sir?"

"Yes, Major, come in. Can you see bruises on Caroline's face where the old woman struck her? Perhaps I should send for Dr. Cook. What do you think?"

Wes examined Caroline's face. "I agree that Dr. Cook should look at her. She seems traumatized by it all."

"I will get the doctor myself," Philip said. Holding her hand, he fought the urge to kiss her. Instead, he motioned for Wes to follow him into the hall.

"We have a situation here," he said once they were alone. "That old woman could go berserk again at any time and do Caroline real harm. With our present set-up, it is impossible to keep a constant eye on her. Do you have any suggestions?"

Wes thought a moment before saying, "I can't see how we can do anything differently, other than ask Miss Caroline to lock her door or have Cassie sleep in the aunt's empty bedroom across the hall. That way she can hear if the old woman starts prowling."

Philip nodded in agreement. "Both are good suggestions. And since Cassie is the only one who can handle the old lady, tell her to move up there tonight."

"Yes, sir. You should go back to Miss Caroline now. I will ask Dr. Cook to look in on old Mrs. Howard after he checks on Miss Caroline."

Philip nodded agreement before hurrying back to his room.

Wes stopped part way to the back door and, frowning thoughtfully, said, "I can't help wondering what set the older woman off in the first place."

Philip paused at the door, his eyes evasive. "I guess she just reached her breaking point. Could you understand anything she said?"

"No, there was too much noise and confusion."

Relieved by Wes' response, Philip nodded and returned to his room to find Caroline in tears. "What's all this?"

"Oh, Philip, she knows. She must have seen us, or heard us."

"Nonsense. She just chose this particular moment to snap."

"No, she said I had sinned in the eyes of God. She called me a, well, you know."

"What's all the fuss?" Dr. Cook asked from the door.

"Old Mrs. Howard went berserk tonight. She attacked Miss Caroline and nearly knocked her down the stairs. She has some pretty nasty bruises here." Philip pointed to the bluish marks appearing on Caroline's face. "Major Madison and Captain Hanford subdued the old lady and took her to her room. I wonder if you could give her a sedative. She could be dangerous."

Dr. Cook made a face. "She's just a crazy old woman. She can't harm anyone." He moved the lamp closer to Caroline to get a better look. "Hmm. You did sustain a bruise or two. Should be a beauty tomorrow. Are you all right otherwise, Mrs. Howard?"

"Yes. I suppose so."

"I will give you a mild dose of laudanum then you get to bed, young lady. If you have any problems, let me know."

"Thank you." She swallowed the thick liquid then leaned against the pillow Philip had placed behind her head.

The doctor motioned for Philip to follow him out to the hall. "See that she gets to her room before the laudanum takes effect. I will look in on the other lady now."

Philip watched him go upstairs to Dorothea's room before returning to Caroline's side.

Still lying against the pillow with her eyes closed, she whispered, "Mother Howard knows about us, Philip. This must be God's way of telling us that what we did was wrong."

"Nonsense. Put those ideas out of your head. Come, put your arms around my neck."

"What are you doing?" she asked when Philip scooped her up in his arms.

"I am taking you to your room as the doctor ordered."

"I can walk."

"Hardly," he whispered, his voice thick with emotion. "Besides, I can tell that the laudanum has already taken effect by the way you slur your words. Put your arms around my neck." When she did so, Philip bent to kiss her.

"Not now." She placed a finger against his lips. "Someone may come in."

"All right. I will wait until we get upstairs. Hush now, and put your head on my shoulder."

In Caroline's room, he placed her on the bed and sat on the edge beside her. Holding her hand, he recalled the short but intense interlude a few hours ago on this very bed. A knock at the door interrupted his reverie.

"May I come in?" David asked, before pushing the door open.

Caroline motioned to him. "Yes, Lieutenant. Come in."

Philip did not move from his place beside Caroline.

David took a few steps toward her bed. "I heard about the altercation. Are you all right, ma'am?"

"She's fine, thank you, Lieutenant," Philip said curtly.

Caroline squeezed Philip's hand to silence him. "Thank you for coming, Lieutenant," she said, maintaining her grip on Philip's hand, despite the effects of the laudanum. "I appreciate your concern."

"I can't help wondering why old Mrs. Howard would do such a horrific thing."

"Why indeed?" Philip asked, jumping to his feet and facing David.

David turned on him. "Are you insinuating, sir, that I had something to do with this?"

"No, Lieutenant, I am asking you directly."

The two men stood face to face, glaring at one another.

"Philip," Caroline broke into their staring contest, "you cannot believe that Lieutenant Southall had anything to do with this."

David's eyes did not waver under Philip's. "I appreciate your confidence in me, ma'am, but I can answer for myself. I would never do anything to harm you, and I believe the Colonel knows it."

"You have paid your respects to Miss Caroline," Philip said, his jaw muscles flexing.

David turned his gaze to Caroline. "I am relieved to see that you are unharmed, ma'am. If at any time I may be of assistance, I am your most humble servant." Bowing over her, he brushed his lips against the back of her hand.

Philip remained at the foot of the bed until David left without glancing in his direction.

A few moments passed before she broke the tense silence. "Philip, how could you have made such an unfounded accusation against him?"

"Think for a moment, Caroline. All this took place after you rejected his advances. Doesn't that strike you as an odd coincidence?"

"No, it does not. David is a gentleman who would do nothing untoward." Suddenly alarmed, she tried to sit up. "Philip, what is it?" she asked, again slurring her words. "You look so strange."

He avoided her questioning eyes. "It's nothing, Caroline. I will let you get some rest. Good night." He exited before she could question him further.

In his room, Philip leaned against the door with his eyes closed. How could I have made such a fool of myself by accusing David like that? And why did I ignore my resolve not to become involved with Caroline? It has been nothing but disaster since she and I. . .

"Dear God," he muttered to himself, and ran a trembling hand over his sweaty face.

Dimming the lamps, he threw himself onto his cot and scrutinized his reaction to David's concern for Caroline. Her reaction to him had been kind and appreciative, as usual. So why did I act like some damned fool who was—what? Possessive? Or worse yet, jealous?

No, it wasn't jealousy. It was resentment that David planned to add Caroline to his list of conquests.

Chapter 15

TWO DAYS AFTER Dorothea's attack on Caroline, Philip left the mess tent carrying his coffee cup, intent on finding Caroline and perhaps arranging another rendezvous. Poking his head in the kitchen door, he saw her putting away the breakfast dishes.

"Good morning, Caroline. I thought I would find you here."

Caroline gave him a shy smile. "Good morning."

"I looked for you yesterday, but Mina said you decided to stay in bed and rest. How are you feeling today?"

Her smile faded, her look became evasive. "Better." Pausing, she bit her lip. "If you have a moment, Philip, I would like to speak with you."

"Of course." He approached her with a look of concern.

"Could we talk somewhere away from prying eyes?" She lifted her eyes upward, indicating Dorothea's window above them. "In the grove by the stream perhaps? I will meet you there in a few minutes."

Philip nodded understanding and watched her hurry away, past the blacksmith's wagon and beyond, through the meadow leading down to the stream. Along the way, the wounded, the corpsmen, even the blacksmith acknowledged her passing with respect.

Tossing the remains of his coffee onto the ground, Philip entered the back door of the main house and set his cup on the entry hall table. Continuing out the front door, he turned right off the porch and started toward the stream through the orchard, away from Dorothea's prying eyes.

Once he and Caroline were settled in the shade next to the stream, Philip swatted at a swarm of gnats. "Damn this heat and these annoying insects. Excuse my language. It must be ninety degrees and it's not even nine o'clock. How on earth do you tolerate this ungodly heat?"

"I suppose you get used to it," she replied with a distracted shrug. "Philip. . ."

"Caroline, if you don't mind, I would like to speak first. I doubt that I will have the courage if I don't do it now."

"If you like." Smoothing her skirts, she waited for him to begin.

He gazed intently into her eyes. "First of all, are you truly feeling better this morning?"

"I have a few sore muscles and this bruise still hurts, but I am all right."

Philip leaned closer, so close he could smell her clean soap scent and touched her bruised cheek. "I'm sorry about this and I am sorry about my boorish behavior with David that night."

"The vehemence of your reaction did surprise me. It was a drastic change from—earlier." She caressed his face with gentle fingers. "I wondered how you could have been so warm and passionate earlier in the evening then, in an instant, turn so dark and cold."

He pulled back from her touch. "Suffice it to say that I made too much of what I perceived as my unique standing at the time. Upon reflection, I realized that what I felt toward David was resentment because he came to your room hoping to seduce you. He may have misread your kindness to him, as well as your reasons for going horseback riding with him."

"How can that be? It meant nothing more to me than a pleasant diversion. I thought he wanted to distract me from the unpleasantness after that awful man tried to. . . Anyway, I feel sorry for David."

Philip turned an incredulous look on her. "Sorry for him? Women fall all over him. Many times, I have seen him work his charms on them, only to break their hearts later. I feared that he planned on making you his next victim."

She kissed his cheek. "That is very gallant of you, sir, but it really wasn't necessary."

He reciprocated by placing a gentle kiss on her lips. "I should have known you were too intelligent to be taken in by his roguish ways. Can you forgive my stupid behavior? I had no right to think or say what I did—about either of you. As a result, however, I may have damaged my relationship with him."

"Oh no," she cried, and clutched at his hand, "that makes me feel even worse. When I said I wanted to talk with you, it was to tell you that, well. . ." Her voice trailed off and she lowered her eyes. "Oh, Philip, I can't help thinking that Mother Howard knew what we did. Why else would she call me those awful names and attack me like that? All that night I suffered fits of guilt about—about what we had done."

Philip withdrew his hand from her grasp and rose to his feet. He jammed his hands in his pockets, stared at the low-running stream and thought, Well, I have done it again, allowed myself to be used, and made a fool of myself with David into the bargain. But what the hell, she and I both knew what we were doing. That it wouldn't last. I will be gone soon and it will be over.

Caroline's pleas broke into his thoughts. "Philip, I beg you not to be angry with me."

Still staring at the dappled sunlight dancing on the water, he answered in a flat voice, "I am not angry with you, Caroline. I understand perfectly, and I agree with you." Turning, he regarded her with sad eyes. "It is well that we are of like mind on this matter. But you must not blame yourself. I should not have taken advantage of the situation."

"You didn't take advantage. I could have stopped it at any time, but I didn't." She looked beyond him at a passing butterfly and said in a soft voice, "I could not."

Startled by her admission, Philip sank to the ground beside her.

"Yes, it's true," she nodded. "Oh, Philip, I have never felt this way before. Never, not even in my wildest dreams, could I have imagined anything like those moments I shared with you. You were so gentle, so considerate. But please," she placed a hand on his chest, "don't think that I have done this before. I mean not with anyone except Morgan, and even then. . ."

Philip took her hands into his. "Caroline, I have never thought of you as anything but a lady. I assure you, however, that it will never happen again."

Accepting the handkerchief Philip offered her, she dried her eyes. "It is a relief to know you feel the same way. My only excuse for this moral lapse is that I have been frightened and alone for so long. As a consequence, I turned to you in my need. After you left the other night, I realized how selfish I had been. With so much responsibility on your shoulders already, you do not need the added burden of a hysterical female."

Again, her gaze faltered. "Also hounding me is the uncertainty that Morgan may still be alive. Not knowing anything for certain is worse than reconciling myself to the reality of his death."

At the mention of Morgan's name, Philip swallowed the bile rising at the back of his throat. "I'm sure it has been difficult for you."

Caroline rested her back against a tree, covered her face, and released the tears that had been building within her for years. "I have tried to carry on as best I can. With the slaves gone, I have had to manage the farm and Mother Howard, and I am so weary of it all."

"Of course you are. You have done the work of dozens of men. That takes a great deal of courage." Philip remained quiet for a few moments, allowing her to cry out her fears and emotions.

"Oh dear," she fussed as she dried her eyes, "I have bungled this so badly when the last thing I want is to hurt you. After all you have done for me I cannot repay you with rebuffs or recriminations." She ran the back of her hand along his scruffy jaw line. "There is so much goodness in you, Philip. Don't look at me like that. It's true. I cannot imagine what happened to darken your soul but I feel that I have come to know the real Philip Creighton. I shall always treasure our brief time together."

Philip kissed the back of her hand that rested on his shoulder. "As will I." Standing, he exhaled a long, weary sigh. "Now that we have come to an agreement, we must be mindful that the next few days may prove awkward. It is inevitable that we will run into each other. And," he said in a significant but gentle tone, "what occurred the other night will always be there between us."

"I am fully aware of that." Caroline blinked back more tears. "This may sound strange, but I cannot bear to lose your friendship entirely. I have been so lonely, and I like being with you, talking with you. I would like very much for us to remain friends."

Philip considered then shook his head. "After all that has happened, do you truly believe that we can remain nothing more than just friends?"

"Can't we try?"

After a thoughtful pause, he relented. "I suppose so. After all, it is for only a few more days."

"Thank you for being so understanding."

Smiling, Philip helped her to her feet. "We had better get back before we are missed." He did not release her hand or relinquish her eyes.

"A favor, please?" she whispered. "Kiss me, one last time."

As he bent to oblige her, he jerked his head back with a frown. "What are these blotches?" He touched the red areas on her cheeks and chin. "I noticed them earlier. Does it hurt?"

"It burns a little."

As the reason for the mysterious rash dawned on him, Philip rolled his eyes. "Oh, Lord, Caroline, did my beard do that to you? Perhaps I shouldn't kiss you now. I don't want to exacerbate your condition."

Slipping her arms around his waist, she smiled up at him. "It won't hurt."

He kissed her, tenderly at first, trying not to irritate her face. Then, to his surprise, her arms crept around his neck. As her fingers curled the unruly hair at the nape of his neck, he tightened his embrace.

After several long moments, she drew away from him. "Well, Colonel," she said breathlessly, "shall we go back?"

Weak-kneed and flushed, Philip followed her back to the house, trying with all his might to convince himself that he would have no problem keeping his distance from her.

No problem at all.

Chapter 16

BY LATE JULY, the air was electric with excitement. The flurry of activity at Elliott's Salient helped Philip keep his bargain with Caroline. When his curiosity about digging the tunnel got the better of him, he and Wes rode over to the project, taking in the details of this fascinating work and asking the miners of the 48th Pennsylvania about their progress.

He also buried himself in his endless paperwork, and found reasons to be at City Point more often. He even moved his field desk to the front porch to do his work, thereby avoiding a chance encounter with Caroline in the hall or back yard. When they did meet, he would smile and tip his hat, inquire politely after her health then walk away quickly.

Caroline likewise found ways to keep her hands busy, but her mind kept wandering back to that night in Philip's arms. No matter how hard she tried, she couldn't erase the memory of his kisses, or the look of desire in his dark eyes.

But she was determined to keep her part of their agreement. In the mornings, she would stand in her bedroom window, waiting for him to appear in the front yard for morning formation. Only then would she hurry down the steps to the kitchen or the well.

Her emotional state made the task of caring for Dorothea increasingly difficult. No amount of coaxing on her part could convince Dorothea to eat. She would simply squint at Caroline and call her a whore.

"Miz Caroline, be careful," Cassie called out one afternoon several days later, bringing Caroline back to the moment, and took the flat iron away from her. "You gonna burn that dress just like you burnt the pillowcases. You all right, chile? You been lookin' right peaked. Set down a spell and let me finish that ironin'. Then I'm gonna put you to bed with some hot Borage tea," she pronounced with a nod that settled the matter.

"I'm all right," Caroline protested, and shrugged off Cassie's hand. "I don't need tea, and I don't need to go to bed."

During her turmoil the last four days, Caroline felt an increasing need for spiritual guidance, and considered attending church services. But getting a ride into Petersburg, even with a pass, was difficult. Besides, she groaned to herself, I dread facing that horrid Reverend Parsons.

She recalled his last visit when he had kissed her on the cheek and leered at her in a loathsome way that unsettled her. He had even hinted broadly that he was more than willing to keep her from becoming lonely during Morgan's absence. At the time, she refused to believe that his motives were prompted by anything other than his Christian duty. After all, she had reasoned, he was a minister offering pastoral solace.

She had convinced herself of this when, on a Sunday not long after that, he assisted her into the buggy and run his hand over her back in a suggestive manner. This time, his meaning had been unmistakable. If I were of that turn, she thought with a shudder, I certainly would not look to him. He is totally unattractive, and evil-looking. Not the sort to turn a woman's head.

Philip, on the other hand, with his haunted eyes and tender lips. . . Stop it! she scolded herself. I must not think about him. Or how it was with him.

***

Sitting in her room, Dorothea gripped the arms of her rocking chair with hands that had lost most of their flesh. She compressed her lips with righteous indignation. *They have incurred His wrath. The Day of the Lord is coming. No longer will He countenance their waywardness. I am His willing instrument of Justice. He has spoken to me. Told me what I must do.*

The Union artillery bombardment of Petersburg increased. The relentless pounding by the Dictator, an artillery piece so large that it was mounted on its own railroad flat car, frayed Caroline's nerves beyond the breaking point. With each day, her headaches worsened. *I wish I could speak to Philip*, she thought. *Be reassured by his presence.*

Each night, she massaged her temples, longing for relief from the bombardment, the unremitting heat, and her blasted headache. After suffering for days, she decided to speak to Dr. Cook about getting something to assuage her torment.

Next morning, drenched with perspiration, Caroline felt as though she had not closed her eyes all night. She bathed in cool water, powdered liberally, and slipped into her last clean dress, thinking, *I must remind Cassie to wash clothes today.* On her way down the stairs, the smell of freshly-brewed coffee was so sickening she decided to have the tea Philip had provided for her.

Starting out the kitchen door with the water pitcher, she bumped into a Union officer. "Good morning," she said without looking up, and proceeded toward the well.

"Good morning, Caroline," the officer replied.

She stopped and turned at the sound of the familiar voice. "Philip?" She walked toward him for closer inspection then, noticing the two-toned facial skin, she said, "My word, you have shaved off your beard."

"Yes, it's much too hot for a beard. Besides, I only grew it after we left Washington because I had no time to shave."

"No other reason?" she prodded with a sly smile.

"None that I can think of," he replied, returning her smile. Then his expression turned serious. Pulling her into the kitchen, he motioned for Cassie to leave them alone.

Something desperate in his eyes made her grasp the edge of the dry sink for support. "What's wrong?"

"I must tell you something." He peered intently into her face. "My God, Caroline, you are as pale as a ghost. Are you feeling unwell again?"

"I didn't sleep very well last night. It must be the heat and that infernal bombardment." She shook her head. "I'm sorry, what did you want to tell me?"

He drew in a deep, hesitant breath and said bluntly, "We are leaving today. I doubt that we will be back. I have ordered that a sufficient amount of food staples, supplies, and kerosene for the lamps be left behind. You should have enough for several weeks." Pulling his side arm from its holster, he handed it to her. "Take this, and don't let anyone into the house, under any circumstances. Do you understand?"

"Should you be giving this to me?" she asked, holding the gun away from her.

"Probably not, but I cannot leave you defenseless. I have a spare in my saddle bag."

Paralyzed by his sense of urgency, she thought, Dear God, he's leaving. He may not return. After placing the gun on the dry sink, she tugged at his sleeve to draw his attention away from the window and the frenzied activity outside. "You can't go. You haven't regained your full strength yet. I have seen. . ." She bit her lip before admitting that she had seen his bare torso when they lay together. "Your wound is barely healed," she corrected herself.

He gripped her shoulders. "Caroline, something is about to happen that may end the war. I just came to say good-bye and to thank you for, well, for being so kind—to all of us."

She slumped against the wall. "Thank you? Good-bye?" she said in a voice crackling with emotion. "Just like that?"

"No, not just like that. But we did agree. Besides, we both knew this day would come." He stepped closer and whispered, "I will never forget you, Caroline. As for what has passed between us, what can I say? What is there to say?" He gave her a sad smile. "I will cherish my memories of you and all that we have been through together."

With his hands braced against the wall on either side of her, literally surrounding her, she reveled in the power of his presence. Looking into his pained eyes, it was as though she could see deep inside him, into that place where memories are stored. She recalled the first moment they saw one another, their struggle to pull him through his serious illness, the bond that formed out of that struggle. His protective arms around her. That night of passion in her room.

"I never thought I would feel this way again," he whispered, and reached for her.

"Colonel Creighton," Lieutenant Hasselbeck called through the back door, "the men are mounted and ready, sir,"

Philip huffed in disgust at the untimely interruption. "This is one time I wish he weren't so damned efficient." Turning back to Caroline, his eyes were tender once again. "There is so much I want to say. So much I need to say, but there is no time. Just knowing you changed me for the better." He kissed her on the cheek and hurried out the door.

With her fingers touching the cheek he'd kissed, Caroline heard him mumble good-bye. She listened as he mounted his horse, ordered his men to form up their columns and un-case the colors, as they thundered down the driveway. Out of her life.

No! her mind screamed.

She charged up the steps to the dining room and into the front hall, tears blurring her vision. Outside, on the top step of the porch, she waved and called to him but her voice was lost in the din of horses' hooves, jingling spurs, and wagons rumbling behind them.

She saw Wes turn in his saddle as she waved her arms. He reined in his horse abreast of Philip's and motioned toward the house. Philip looked over his shoulder to where Wes pointed. At the sight of her, he wheeled his roan mare about and rode toward her. Sliding off the wrong side of the saddle, he swept her into his arms and, before the entire company of officers and enlisted men, he kissed her soundly.

"Does this mean that we are no longer just friends?" he asked with a twinkle in his eye.

She pressed her lips against his ear and whispered, "Come back to me, Philip."

His quick response was a deep, possessive kiss. Then, untying the ribbon at the throat of her dress, he stuffed it into his pocket. He remounted and saluted her with a smile and a wave of his hat before joining his column.

Teary-eyed, Caroline watched him wave to her at the gate before the column turned right and headed east toward the James River. Please, Lord, she prayed in her heart, watch over him and bring him back to me.

Chapter 17

LATE THE NEXT day, Dorothea left her room and crept across the hall. Pressing her ear to the door of Caroline's bedroom, she heard no sound within. Only the occasional distant report of sniper fire disturbed the silence. Trying the knob, she found the door locked. Strange, she thought with a grim smile, but no matter. The Lord has told me that this is the Day of Judgment. With all those Yankees gone and out of the way, I can do the deed with no one the wiser. Caroline will pay for her sins. She cannot forsake her marriage vows then smile sweetly upon her husband's return from war as though she had remained faithful to him.

Caroline raised her throbbing head from the pillow, disturbed by the sounds of movement in the otherwise silent house. She heard footsteps and a door open and close somewhere, heard the protesting scrapes of drawers being pulled open. Who can be rummaging about?

Cassie? Mina? Lying back on her pillow, she thought, thank God I still
have Philip's gun with me.

Presently, without warning, a sharp abdominal cramp struck,
forcing her to draw her knees up. It became excruciatingly clear in the
next few moments why she had been in so much distress. It was time
for her monthly. This is going to be a difficult one, she thought with
dread. Cassie will insist on a brew of Bagwort, her cure-all for female
disorders, instead of Borage tea for what she called my melancholy. At
the moment, I would drink Hemlock if it afforded me relief from this
misery.

Caroline got out of bed with some difficulty and, stumbling to
the bureau, found the clean rags Cassie kept there for this purpose.
Stripping off her soiled, sweaty nightgown, she bathed her face and
arms and put on a clean nightgown. Weak and trembling, she reached
for the cool cloth to assuage the pounding in her head before crawling
back into bed.

Dorothea slipped out the back door and kept close to the out-
buildings in the early evening shadows. She made her way into the barn
unnoticed by the few remaining wounded and corpsmen. Barring the
barn door behind her, she felt her way around by memory, rummaging
through the tack equipment, unmindful of the bits of hay and dust
motes swirling about her.

Before long, she found the proper instrument to exact justice on
Caroline and held it up, smiling. "Yes, this will do very nicely. I will
avenge you, son, for your wife's infidelity. Let the name of the Lord be
praised."

As light filled Dorothea's eyes, she turned resolutely to fulfill her
mission.

Cassie left the main house to console Mina after Daniel's recent
departure. Approaching the cabin, she saw Mina sitting on the porch,

staring disconsolately at the sunset. "Here, honey, I brought you some Borage tea. You drink this and you'll feel fine again."

"Me and Daniel didn't have hardly no time together," Mina sniffed. "It hurt so much to let him go again."

After talking the evening away, Cassie left Mina and strode along the familiar dark path to the back door of the main house. She climbed the stairs to sleep across the hall from Caroline in accordance with Philip's stern instructions, despite her uneasy feelings about sleeping in a white woman's bed, especially Miss Emmaline who had always looked down her nose at the darkies.

But before going to bed, she unlocked Caroline's door and peeked in at the sleeping figure with her back to the door. Poor chile, she thought, she missin' that Yankee Colonel somethin' fierce, just like Mina missin' her man.

With a sigh, Cassie recalled her love for the blacksmith Silas. But, she remembered with the stirring of those painful memories, that once old Massah Justin discovered that she and Silas had eyes for each other, he sold Silas off to a cotton exporter in Mississippi.

Cassie closed the door to Caroline's room and tiptoed across the hall, nursing the revived ache in her heart. Throwing herself fully clothed onto the bed, she fumed with renewed anger. Ole Massah Justin intended to breed me himself but I risked anything, even death rather than lay with him. No man but Silas has ever possessed my body. Or my heart.

She slept fitfully the rest of the night, filled with longing for Silas.

All was quiet at Howard Hill.

After crossing the James River, General Hancock's Second Corps and Sheridan's cavalry began their diversionary trek to probe and harass, with the purpose of drawing Lee's attention away from Petersburg. Lee, believing a new assault against Richmond was underway, responded by transferring troops to the south and east of the capitol city.

On Thursday, the second day of the operation, Philip's Pennsylvanians moved on orders from General Sheridan to reconnoiter around Four Mile Creek. Reining in his horse, Philip scanned the landscape through his field glasses. "The diversion worked," he exclaimed with glee. "Lee is still sending in reinforcements."

"He's in for a hell of a surprise come Saturday," Lieutenant Hasselbeck grinned.

Most of the skirmishes before Richmond occurred around a place called Deep Bottom, with stiff resistance from the firmly entrenched Confederates who drove back the Federals. Ending the expedition on the third day, the Union force was ordered back across the pontoon bridge to the south shore of the James and their next mission—the impending action on Saturday.

Late Friday evening, the Strickland Volunteers rode up the driveway of Howard Hill, weary and eager for food and water, and a brief rest for men and horses. Beside the corral, Philip dunked his head into the water trough to rid himself of road dust and sweat. Rising up with a great gasp for air, he shook the water from his hair.

"Ah, much better," he sputtered. Removing his blouse, he dried his face on it and rubbed the dampness from his hair. During the process, he remembered the ribbon he'd taken from Caroline on Wednesday. He pulled it from the breast pocket, wondering how many times he had reached for it, or smelled its lilac scent before falling asleep. Or felt her lips against his ear in his dreams?

He glanced up at the windows at the back of the house, intent upon saying hello to her before leaving again in a few hours. But the upstairs rooms were dark. Disappointed, he removed his saber belt and went inside to get some sleep.

Rising from their three-hour nap, the officers and troopers gathered in formation in the front meadow. Once the columns were formed and the colors un-cased, the Strickland Volunteers left Howard Hill, this time riding west toward Petersburg, and the action that, please God, Philip prayed, would end this damned war.

Chapter 18

NEAR ELLIOTT'S SALIENT, Philip's command was placed in reserve in a ravine nearly a mile away. Tension and anticipation filled the air all around them. Unable to contain their curiosity any longer, Philip and Wes rode to the higher ground overlooking the tunnel's opening.

At three fifteen that morning, Colonel Pleasants himself lit the fuse that would ignite hundreds of pounds of explosives. He scrambled onto a parapet, anticipating the results of his regiment's work for the past month that was timed to go off at three thirty.

Everyone waited, tense and impatient. The time came and went.

Philip fidgeted in the saddle. "It must be nearly four o'clock," he whispered to Wes. "Why hasn't the damned thing gone off?"

"It will be dawn soon," Wes reminded him with a yawn.

"I wonder how long they'll wait before doing something."

At four thirty, they saw two men, apparently from the 48th Pennsylvania, crawl into the tunnel to locate the problem. When they came out, word quickly spread that the fuse had gone out at the splice.

The two men had re-lit the fuse and now everyone anxiously awaited the explosion, expected to go off in approximately fifteen minutes.

Riding back down the ravine where the Strickland Volunteers waited, Philip informed them of what had happened. Taking out his watch, he had just flipped the cover open when a muffled rumbling like summer thunder shook the earth. The explosives erupted with a deafening roar, spewing earth, equipment, animals and sleeping men nearly one hundred feet into the air, leaving a crater sixty feet wide and thirty feet deep.

The dazed Confederates, however, did not lose control of the situation. In short order, they rallied under General Mahone and re-formed their position. The first wave of the attack by the Ninth Corps was a disaster. By mid-morning, approximately 15,000 Union troops were contained within the damaged area, little more than unprotected targets for the irate Confederates.

The deafening explosion nearly knocked Caroline from her bed. When she came to her senses, she thought the end of the world was at hand. Throwing her wrapper around her shoulders, she unlocked the door with her own key and ran across the hall to Aunt Emmaline's bedroom.

Cassie was sitting up in bed, terrified, clutching the sheet to her throat. "What was that?" she asked in a trembling voice. "This here the Day of Judgment?"

"It would seem so." Wide-eyed, Caroline pointed out the west-facing window at the huge column of smoke rising in the early dawn sky. "That must be the something big that Philip mentioned before he left the other day. It does indeed look like the end of the world."

After several minutes of straining to see what was happening, she glanced around with concern. "Where is Mother Howard? Surely, she cannot have slept through that monstrous noise. Go and see if she's all right."

Cassie hurried to Dorothea's room and, finding it empty, reported this to Caroline.

Caroline bit her lip and considered. "Maybe she became confused or frightened and ran downstairs. She has to be here somewhere, but I don't have the energy to look for her."

"You do look right peaked," Cassie observed. "You get back in that bed."

"I am feeling a bit nauseous too." In her room, Caroline changed her soiled rags, asked Cassie to fix some tea, and crawled into bed, still trembling with fear and pain. By mid-morning, her cramps had intensified, as did her flow. And the tea did nothing to assuage her discomfort. Surely, she prayed, this will pass in a few hours.

Shortly before noon, Cassie entered Caroline's room, carrying a tray. "Here's some more tea, Miz Caroline. I brought a hot flannel sheet to put on your belly. It might help with them cramps."

Before long, the discomfort and headache that plagued Caroline these past two days slowly dissipated. When Cassie looked in on her later, she was deep in sleep, the first she'd had in days.

Philip and Wes rode to the top of the ravine and beheld a spectacle of awesome magnitude. The hundreds of dead and wounded lay in the rubble amid equipment and dead or dying horses. Acrid smoke from the explosion and incessant rifle fire assailed their nostrils and hovered over the battlefield, making for poor visibility. The Confederates pounded their attackers mercilessly, and those Union soldiers who were still alive, clung to the sides of the crater for protection.

Philip adjusted his field glasses. "My God, it looks as if hell itself has opened up out there. Why is Burnside ordering more men in there? They are being slaughtered like cattle in a charnel house. Look," he pointed, "the Confederates have flanked our men. They don't stand a chance. Damn."

Wes stared in awe through his own field glasses. "It's Fredericksburg all over again."

The rising sun beat down on the melee, its throbbing heat affecting the men's brains. Many simply collapsed from heat exhaustion. The dead and wounded lay in the unforgiving sun, the stench of bloody wounds and rotting flesh filled the air already heavy with smoke. Green flies swarmed over the scene, torturing those still alive and adding to their misery. Horses screamed in agony.

Sickened by the scene, Philip trained his field glasses on the gun parapet where Colonel Pleasants stood watching the action. He saw the colonel storming about and waving his arms, obviously swearing at the disastrous results of his month's work.

"At least, Pleasants can say that he carried off his assignment with precision," he told Wes. "I would be just as furious as he is, now that these incompetents have botched their part."

Believing the operation a failure, General Grant ordered Meade to halt the attack. Burnside, on the other hand, argued that organization could be restored and so, ignored the order. As a result, many more men died needlessly. The affair ended shortly past noon.

Caroline awoke in the mid-afternoon heat, groggy after just a few hours' sleep. Recalling the events of earlier that morning, she slipped down the hall to check on Dorothea. Still no sign of her. She stood in the center of the upstairs hall, fretting. How strange that Mother Howard would disappear for so long without a word. *I must find her before she does harm to herself, or to someone else. I swear, she has become as helpless as a child, needing constant supervision.*

A search of the rooms on the first floor, including Philip's office, revealed nothing. She checked the kitchen, the laundry shed and the smokehouse. Still nothing.

Frantic by now, she stood in the back yard, hands on hips, wondering where Mother Howard could be. Moving from one outbuilding to the next, she checked the loom house, she even rapped on the door to the necessary. Considering a moment, Caroline decided that, in her addled state, Dorothea may have wanted to be near her husband.

"Dear Lord," she prayed aloud, as she hurried toward the burying ground, "please, let me find her unharmed."

Along the way, Caroline remembered that she hadn't checked the barn. As she approached, she thought it strange that the big door was barred from the inside. Who would do that? The Yankees? No, they were forbidden to go into the barn. Whoever barred the door must still be inside.

Maneuvering her fingers through a crack in the door, she knocked the bar free and pushed the door open. The stench of something rotting instantly assailed her senses. No doubt, a small animal had been trapped and died inside. Squinting, she allowed her eyes time to adjust to the deep shadows. It was then that the horror came into full view. Gasping for air, she staggered backward and fell against an empty feed barrel.

Slowly, slowly, she twisted, suspended from the rope, her eyes bulging, her flesh already dark and putrefying in the devastating heat.

Caroline inched her way toward the door, unable to take her eyes off the corpse of Dorothea Howard.

Chapter 19

SHORTLY AFTER THREE o'clock that afternoon, the Strickland Volunteers returned to Howard Hill. Drained by the blistering heat and the horrors they had just witnessed at the Crater, the bone-weary men dropped to the ground, wanting nothing but sleep.

Philip slid from his mare, holding his right side. Reaching down to loosen his saddle cinch, he grimaced and hissed with pain.

"What's wrong, sir?" Wes asked, rushing to Philip's aide.

Philip clung to the saddle horn and whispered, "I hate to admit it, Wes, but my side is killing me. I don't think I can remove this saddle."

"I'll see to your horse, sir. You go inside and lie down. Perhaps you should have waited a while longer before getting back into action," he added with concern.

With his head buzzing from exhaustion, Philip climbed the three stone steps to the back door, planning to throw himself onto his cot and sleep for days. The commotion from the returning troopers, the ambulance drivers cursing, and the screams from the hospital tents seeped into his consciousness but this time, he paid no heed.

Inside the entry hall, it suddenly became clear to him that one of those cries was a woman's.

Looking up toward the sound, he saw Caroline, barefoot and clad only in her nightgown, running down the stairs toward him. Her hair straggled about her face and shoulders, her eyes were wild and frightened. Dark circles accentuated her extreme pallor.

She threw herself into his arms with a cry, "Oh, Philip, I can't stand any more."

Stung with even more pain as her body slammed against his, he caught his breath but managed to croon soothing words to her and stroke her disheveled hair. Cassie appeared on the landing just then, looking apprehensive. Philip questioned her with his eyes.

Placing a finger to her lips, Cassie shook her head. Philip nodded but wondered what could have happened during his absence that left Caroline in this hysterical state. "Send for Dr. Cook," he told Cassie, as he lifted Caroline into his arms. Wincing, he carried her into his room and laid her on the sofa.

She grasped the front of his filthy tunic with both hands, holding him fast, and said in an exhausted voice, "You must never leave me again. I have tried being strong, but this is too much."

"It's all right, Caroline, I am here now." Holding her close, he rocked her until Dr. Cook appeared, looking frazzled, and annoyed at being summoned away from his duties.

After a cursory examination, the doctor pronounced, "A mild dose of laudanum should take care of the hysterics. Although, after what she experienced today, it's no wonder she collapsed," he added, and returned to his more pressing duties, leaving a bewildered Philip wondering what the hell had happened during his absence.

Presently, when he could see that the laudanum had taken effect, he gritted his teeth against the ache in his side and carried Caroline to her room. Once he was satisfied that she was comfortable, he whispered to Cassie on his way out of the room, "Come with me."

Downstairs, Philip closed his office door and turned to face Cassie. "What in the world happened to leave Caroline in this shocking state? Did someone come into the house and attack her again?"

Cassie shook her head. "No, sir. They was real nice and helpful."

Curious, he took a step toward her. "Who was helpful'?"

"Well, sir," she stammered and wrung her hands, "after that big explosion early this mornin', Miz Caroline commenced to wonderin' why ole Missy didn't come round asking what happened. So Miz Caroline went lookin' for her."

"I thought you and Mina were keeping a close eye on her."

"We was, but the last few days, she started actin' real nice, like her ole self. Not sayin' mean things or nuthin. She ate when we put food in front of her, and went to bed when we tole her. She even tole me to wash her hair. She cleaned herself up every mornin' and night. We thought her bad spell passed. Anyways," Cassie said, taking a deep breath, "like I said, Miz Caroline went lookin' for her this mornin'. Later, I mean, after she was feelin' better."

Alarmed now, Philip gripped Cassie's arm. "Has Caroline been ill in my absence?"

"Just the heat and all that noise with those big Yankee guns," Cassie said vaguely, and pulled free of Philip's grasp. "She took to her bed with a, uh, you know—a headache."

Taking Cassie's meaning that the problem was that female thing, he asked, "Did anyone ever find the old woman?"

Cassie shook her head. "That's the thing. Miz Caroline thought ole Missy, being scared by that explosion and all, might be hidin' in the buryin' ground with old mister. So, on her way out there, Miz Caroline stopped by the barn." Hesitating, she turned away from Philip.

"Please, come to the point," he pleaded. "You are driving me mad with all this mystery. Was the old lady hiding out there in the family cemetery?"

Cassie turned to face him again, tears streaming down her cheeks. "Oh, Colonel Philip, that poor chile found ole missy hangin' from a rope in the barn, all black and swole up. I took out runnin' when I heard her screamin' like she seen the devil hisself. Ole Missy, she was, well," she swallowed hard, "she musta done it last evening after we all went to sleep."

Philip fell into a chair and stared at her, stupefied. "My God. Where is the body now?"

"Dr. Cook wrapped her in a gunny sack after some of them nurse men cut her down. Then, when Miz Caroline come to, I had a awful time gettin' her to her room."

"I don't wonder, after witnessing a scene like that." He jumped up and paced. Opening his door, he called, "Lieutenant Hasselbeck!"

The poor weary lieutenant appeared immediately. "Yes, sir?"

"I know everyone is exhausted, Lieutenant, but I need a coffin immediately. I just learned that old Mrs. Howard passed away, so it is imperative that we bury her as soon as possible. Detail some men to dig a grave next to her husband's and ask Father O'Boyle to say a few words over her. I'm afraid that's the best we can do, given the circumstances."

"I will see to it right away, sir." Lieutenant Hasselbeck saluted and disappeared.

After Cassie left him, Philip fell into his chair and stared into space, trying to comprehend this latest calamity.

"Sorry to disturb you, sir," Wes said, knocking on Philip's door. "I just heard about the old lady. I understand Mrs. Howard found her."

"Don't call her that."

"What?"

"Don't call her Mrs. Howard. I don't need to be reminded that she is another man's wife."

"She is, you know, and our peculiar circumstances make any involvement unwise."

Standing, Philip looked Wes directly in the eye. "I don't need sermonizing from you, Major Madison."

"I am merely offering my objective view, sir," Wes answered in a cold, clipped voice.

Philip paused, sighed, then shook his head. "I'm sorry, Wes. I am so damned tired I don't know what the hell I am saying."

"Do you love her?" Wes asked.

"I don't know." Philip threw up his hands in despair. "I just don't know."

"One thing is certain, Mrs.—Miss Caroline has grown dependent upon you. I don't mean to sermonize, Philip, but you must consider the consequences."

"I am well aware of the consequences. But if she needs me, I will be here for her."

"Do you really believe that? I have seen how you are with her. How you kissed her when we left the other day. It is only a matter of time before something serious happens between you."

"If she needs me, I am here. That's all I can say."

"And whatever happens, happens, no matter who gets hurt?"

Philip walked behind his desk, putting distance between him and Wes. "I do not intend for anyone to get hurt."

"What about Washington?"

"There is nothing in Washington to concern me."

"Saying it doesn't make it so. You have a wife, and Miss Caroline may still have a husband out there," Wes pointed northward, "waiting to come home to her."

"He fell with his brother last year at Gettysburg."

Wes regarded him evenly. "Are you willing to risk everything, not knowing for certain that he is dead? As your friend, I am merely pointing out possible consequences."

"And as your friend, I am warning you not to say any more. Now, if you will excuse me, Major, I would like to get some sleep."

Chapter 20

WAKING AT TWILIGHT with a start, Philip sat straight up in his cot, listening. The only sounds he heard were the ones of army routine. Fully awake now, he remembered Caroline. And old Mrs. Howard.

Lying back with a weary sigh, he stared at the ceiling, recalling this morning's explosion and ensuing battle, and the men who had fought so valiantly and the many who died needlessly. Sitting up again, he reached for his tunic, thinking, I must put all those thoughts aside. Tonight, I must look to Caroline.

On his way up to her room, he stopped at the window on the landing overlooking the back yard, his thoughts turning bitter at the futility of this senseless war. He watched the wagon bearing Dorothea's coffin wind its way toward the burying ground, the lantern swaying from the rear bumper in the dim light. That old woman is surely another casualty of this war, he thought, driven to extremes by circumstances beyond her understanding or control.

He watched until the wagon disappeared beyond the tree line before plodding up the stairs toward Caroline's room. The unnerving sounds emanating from the surgery tent floated on the night air, setting his teeth on edge. I have to steel myself to all that, he told himself. My first concern must be for Caroline. But I can't let her know about my back or she will threaten to call Dr. Cook down on me.

Opening her door without a sound, he saw that she was still asleep. He lit the lamp and sat in a chair, watching her. How lovely she is, he thought. Even more so in repose. Moved by her fragility, he rose and kissed her forehead.

Stirring, she opened her eyes and reached for his hand. "Are you back?"

"It would seem so."

"Please, don't leave me again," she pleaded, her tortured eyes revealing the strain of the last few days. "I need you too much."

"I am here for as long as you need me." He kissed her hand.

After a few quiet moments, Caroline asked, "Did Cassie tell you what happened?"

He remained silent.

Her face contorted with the anguish that had been mounting within her over the past two years. "Dear God, it was so awful, seeing her hanging there like that. And her eyes . . ."

"Hush." Philip pressed a finger to her lips. "Don't talk about it. Or even think about it."

Throwing her arms around him, Caroline clung to him, crying uncontrollably for several minutes. When her sobbing subsided, she snuggled against his chest. "I need you so much, Philip. Yesterday, when I heard that awful explosion and heard all the shooting and thought you might be gone forever, I couldn't bear it. I cried for you, and prayed for you. Oh, Philip, don't you know what I am trying to say? I have tried but, heaven help me, I cannot deny it any longer. I love you."

Philip caught his breath. Her declaration of love immobilized him, leaving his defenses shattered in the face of her sincerity. All the reserves he had erected so carefully around his heart the last few years disintegrated in an instant. "Oh, Caroline," he whispered in a husky voice.

Standing, he walked to the windows, not seeing the last faint streaks of pink lingering in the western sky. Do I dare risk the vulnerability that love requires? No, I can't go through that again. Not this soon.

And how can I be sure Caroline hasn't confused love with her need to be protected? When I look into her eyes, I see no duplicity. Unlike Elizabeth, she has never demanded anything from me, except to be protected. Am I ready to trust again? What do I say to her?

"I have thought long and hard about what we discussed by the stream last week," Caroline was saying, interrupting his turmoil. "I am sorry we sinned but I cannot deny what I feel for you. For the first time in my life, I know what love is. I don't want to lose that. Or you."

Turning back to her, he admitted softly, "Caroline, I'm not sure I can be all you want me to be." His expression darkened. "Besides, there are things about me that you don't know. Dark, unpleasant things."

She held out her arms to him. "We can work them out together." Once he'd come to her and sat on the edge of the bed, she enveloped him in her embrace. "I love you, Philip. I have never been so sure of anything in my life. Nor have I said that to any other man." She kissed him several times before pulling him down on the bed beside her, still holding him close. Absently, she ran her fingers over the rough scar on his back. "Is this still tender?"

"A little," he said, and fought the urge to flinch. As she snuggled against him, Philip was conscious of her lilac scent, and her soft body pressed against his. Dear God, he thought, I want her again. But is the price too high?

"Tomorrow," Caroline was saying into the warm hollow of his neck, "I must make arrangements for the burial."

"No need for that. I took it upon myself to spare you that ordeal. She is being buried now."

"Right now?" She sat up, facing him. "But I should be there."

"Absolutely not. You stay here and rest for the next few days. I will be your doctor," he said, and managed a wan smile, "but only if you promise not to be as difficult a patient as I was."

"Very well," she agreed with a reluctant sigh, and sank back onto her pillow. "Besides, I don't have the strength to do anything just now." She reached for his hand. "I will tell you a secret, Colonel darling. I knew the first time I met you that you weren't nearly as menacing as you appeared."

He cocked a wary eyebrow at her. "Oh really? And how did you arrive at that conclusion?"

"By the haunted look in your eyes. I could tell you were hurting. Not just your wounded leg, but here," she tapped the place over his heart. "Inside."

Sitting up abruptly on the edge of the bed, Philip turned his back to her and thought, Why does it always come back to that? To the past and the betrayals of those I trusted. Why does it come back to haunt me?

"Philip, dear, what is it?" She placed a gentle hand against his back. "Did I say something wrong?"

"No, of course not. Get some rest, Caroline. I will see you in the morning." Bending over her, he kissed her cheek and left before she could ask more questions that he was unwilling—or unable—to answer.

Chapter 21

ON AUGUST 18, General Warren's Fifth Corps moved westward around Petersburg to destroy that part of the Weldon Railroad used by General Beauregard to ship supplies to the city.

The Strickland Volunteers were ordered in the other direction across the James River with General Hancock's Second Corps to create a diversion for Warren. Philip soon discovered that the two additional weeks of rest had done his aching wound a world of good. Spending that time in Caroline's company, and seeing to her healing process after Dorothea's death, hadn't done him any harm either. But he was still struggling with his own feelings about Caroline's declaration of love.

After scouting the Confederate fortifications near Fussell's Mill, Philip pulled his troopers back behind a blind of trees to consult their map. "This damned map is worthless," he said, slapping his dusty hat against his thigh. "Nothing is where it's supposed to be."

Sergeant Powell mopped the sweat from his face with his kerchief. "Do you want to send a runner to the General, sir?"

"Right away. Meanwhile," Philip added, surveying the action through his field glasses, "it is imperative that we draw fire away from our infantry or they will get slaughtered. Captain Hanford, take your men further east. Harass the Confederates. Make them think our whole damned company is there. Captain Southall, take your men toward the northeast and do the same thing. Hopefully, we can salvage something today."

"Yes, sir," the captains answered in unison, and rode away shouting for their sergeants.

The five-day diversionary action ended in yet another debacle. The Strickland Volunteers, after crossing the river in the driving rain, headed back toward Howard Hill, grumbling about accomplishing nothing—again.

Philip let his poor limping mare follow her nose to the water trough in back of the house. Sliding from the saddle, he let the mare drink her fill before leading her to the blacksmith's wagon. "See what you can do for my mount, Sergeant. She's thrown a shoe. Also, please have someone brush her down for me and feed her."

Turning from the blacksmith, he tilted his head to let the collected rain fall from the brim of his hat. "Has anyone heard anything yet about General Warren?" he asked Sergeant Powell.

"Yes, sir. One of the wounded over there," he pointed toward the medical tent, "said A. P. Hill hit Warren pretty hard on Friday. We lost nearly four hundred men. Crawford's whole bunch got captured. Over twenty-five hundred of them."

Grimacing at the staggering figures, Philip ambled to the well for a drink of water.

"By the way, sir," Sergeant Powell began.

"Philip!"

Both heads turned at the sound of Caroline's voice.

Seeing her in the kitchen door, Philip's weariness fell away. He hurried into the kitchen, closed the door and leaned against it, mud-splattered and weary, a four-day old stubble bristling on his face. "I want desperately to kiss you right now, but," he ran a dirty hand over his chin, "I don't want to give you another beard burn."

Backing away from the overpowering smell of horse, mud and sweat emanating from him, she demurred. "I have missed you terribly too, but I can wait a while longer for my kiss. What would you like for dinner?" she asked, watching the corners of his eyes crinkle when he smiled at her.

"Anything but beans and beef jerky," came his quick reply. "All the way back across the river, I could think of nothing but a nice home-cooked meal at a table with candles and wine."

"I will tell Cassie to start cooking while you bathe."

"Sounds wonderful. I'm going down to the stream where I plan to have a good long bath." He leaned closer and whispered, "After that, I am all yours."

After lingering over their meal in the candlelit dining room, Philip and Caroline repaired to her room to say hello properly. Catching her in his arms, he swung her around, squeezing her until she complained that he was hurting her ribs.

"I am so happy to see you, Carrie, I could break all your ribs." He nuzzled her on the neck. "God, you smell good."

"I am relieved to say that you do too," she laughed, "now that you have shaved your scruffy face and left your malodorous self in the stream."

"I've wanted to hold you like this for days," he whispered between kisses. "I missed you so much. I could not get you out of my mind."

She studied him closely for a moment. "Philip, dear," she paused, as though choosing her words carefully, "you appeared somewhat distracted during dinner. Anything you care to talk about?"

Disengaging himself from her embrace, Philip removed his tunic, hung it on the back of the door and walked to the front windows. Staring into the twilight, he thought, how do I tell her that we have again been ordered to take the Weldon Railroad? In light of the wound I sustained there the last time, she is bound to worry.

After a long silence, he said, "I received a dispatch shortly after our return this afternoon. We've been ordered back into action as soon as the horses and men are rested."

Her hand flew to her throat. "Where?" she asked in a hoarse whisper.

Keeping his back to her, he said softly, "You know I can't tell you that, sweetheart. Suffice it to say, we are heading west."

General Hancock's Second Corps joined General Warren's Fifth Corps south of Petersburg at the Weldon Railroad line. On August 23, Hancock's Corps helped destroy the rail line west of the Union siege lines.

Confederate General A. P. Hill, on the other hand, had his own plans for Hancock. While Warren's infantry struck hard at the rail line the next day, Hill's Corps defeated the Second Corps in a surprise attack at Reams' Station. On the Federal flank, the Strickland Volunteers barely beat back a charge by a determined Confederate cavalry.

During the engagement, Philip's mount wheeled around in a desperate attempt to avoid a run-away horse that was dragging its dead rider by the stirrup. Unseated by his frightened mare, Philip hit the ground, head first.

At sundown on Sunday, Caroline settled down in her room to read. Presently, she heard far-off rumbling. Thunder, she thought. She cocked an anxious ear. No, that isn't thunder. Rushing to the windows, she saw the Strickland Volunteers turning into the main gate.

"Thank God," she whispered, as she looked for Philip stride his mare. But he was nowhere in sight. Wes was riding at the head of the column. "Oh, no," she gasped, and tore down the stairs.

Practically dragging Wes from his horse, she demanded, "Where is Philip?"

"In one of the ambulance wagons," Wes replied, barely masking his own concern. "He and his horse went down and he sustained a head injury."

Before Wes could say another word, she ran to meet the wagons and asked each driver about his passengers. When she found Philip in the next to the last wagon, she asked to be helped inside so she could ride the rest of the way with him.

At her touch, he stirred and whispered, "I'm back," before slipping into unconsciousness.

Waiting until Dr. Cook finished examining Philip was pure torture for Caroline as she sat on the bottom stair tread in the entry hall and prayed.

At last, the doctor came out of Philip's office and gave her a smile. "You can go in now, Mrs. Howard. But first, a few instructions. Colonel Creighton sustained a severe concussion. He must not sleep just now or he could lapse into a coma. Talk to him, give him coffee, do anything, but do not let him fall asleep. Understood?"

He chewed on his lip a moment, considering, before adding, "I think it is only fair to warn you that because of this concussion, the Colonel is blind. I'm sure it is temporary so . . . Mrs. Howard, are you all right?" He caught her as she slumped against the wall.

Recovering herself, Caroline leaned heavily on the doctor's arm. "I'm sorry. It was so unexpected to hear you say that."

"Forgive me for being so blunt. I did not mean to startle you. I don't know how the Colonel is going to handle this, but I am sure it won't be with much grace. You know how independent and headstrong he is. However, if anyone can help him through this difficult time, it is you. Now," he added, gently nudging her toward the door, "go in there and work your magic."

Still trembling from the devastating news, Caroline watched as the doctor hurried out the back door to see about the other wounded. Work my magic? she thought. How can I help Philip through something I cannot grasp myself?

Taking a deep breath and squaring her shoulders, she peered into Philip's room. He was seated on the sofa with his head resting against the back pillows, his eyes closed. She slipped into the room and stood beside the sofa. "How do you feel?" she asked.

Reaching out for her, he said in a quavering voice, "Come closer, Carrie. I can't see you."

She sat beside him on the sofa and slid her arm through his. "I'm so sorry, Philip."

Leaning close, he pressed his forehead against hers in an attitude of intimacy and said, "I'm scared, Carrie. I have been shot twice already, but I have never felt panic like this. Dear God, if I am blind, how will I care for you?"

Struggling to remain calm, she said without conviction, "Let's not worry about that just now. Let's think about getting you better. I'll ask Cassie to bring us some coffee."

Leaning back with a sigh, he said, "No, I'd rather sleep for a while."

"Dr. Cook feels that you should not sleep just now." She took his arm to prevent him from lying down. "Please, sit up while I get the coffee."

Returning a few moments later with a tray, she placed it on Philip's field desk and poured two cups for them. "You must not lose hope. Dr. Cook believes your blindness is temporary. Something about swelling in the brain." She placed a cup in Philip's right hand.

"What if it isn't temporary?" he asked before taking a sip. Reaching in the direction of the lamp table, he set his cup on the edge. It teetered then crashed to the floor. He slammed both fists against the seat cushions and swore, "Damn it, I can't live like this. Please leave, Caroline." He waved her away. "I need to be alone."

"It was just an accident," she offered in a consoling tone, and bent to retrieve the shattered cup. "I do it all the time."

"The hell you do," he yelled back, and jumped up. A step away from the sofa, he bumped into a chair and muttered a profane oath.

Caroline led him back toward the sofa. "You are understandably distraught. I will stay with you a while."

His back stiffened. "No, I prefer that you leave."

She slid her arms around his torso. "That sounds familiar, Colonel darling. Didn't you order me out of here just a few months ago? Be patient a while longer."

He shrugged off her embrace. "I am in no mood to be humored. Please leave."

She backed away, hot tears stinging her eyes. "Very well." On her way out, she bumped into Wes.

"Excuse me, ma'am," Wes mumbled. He stared after her retreating figure before asking, "Did I hear the two of you arguing?"

Philip reached for the back of the sofa. "We weren't arguing. I just told her I wanted to be left alone."

Wes watched him feel and stumble his way along the sofa and lie on the seat. "Are you feeling dizzy, sir? Do you want me to leave?"

"No, please stay. I'm not just dizzy. It's this damned concussion. It has left me blind. That's why I asked Caroline to leave. I cannot bear having her see me this way."

Stunned, Wes fell into the chair opposite Philip and watched his eyes radiate from side to side, as though searching to see something. Anything. "Is there anything I can do? Write a letter to your family? Or to Matthew?"

"No, absolutely not." Exasperated, Philip sighed. "I'm sorry, Wes. I didn't mean to shout, but I do not want my family to know about this yet. Besides, there is nothing anyone can do except worry needlessly."

"If you say so." Wes considered a moment before asking, "Are you up to seeing your officers?"

Philip shook his head. "I couldn't bear their pity."

"As you wish. I will wait until tomorrow."

After Wes' departure, Philip reflected on his harsh treatment of Caroline, but this only worsened his mood. Damn it, he swore to himself, how could I have railed at her that way? She is my one hold on sanity and I pushed her away when I needed her most.

Damn.

Chapter 22

THROUGHOUT DR. COOK'S examination early the next morning, Philip remained impatient. "Any change?" he asked.

"Looks the same as yesterday," the doctor replied as he waved an unnoticed hand before Philip's face. "Can you distinguish between dark and light?"

"No."

"You are going to experience some dizziness, Colonel. Maybe some nausea. I want you to rest, but do not sleep during the day. You will feel better as time goes along."

"How much time?"

"There is no way of knowing that."

"Thanks for the words of hope," Philip snorted.

"I believe in telling my patients the truth." Dr. Cook placed his hand on Philip's shoulder. "You have come through much worse, Colonel. You will come through this too. Be patient. By the way, I asked Mrs. Howard to look in on you from time to time."

"And I asked her to stay away."

"Are we going through that again? I still have a lot of wounded men waiting for me out there." He jerked a thumb toward the back yard. "Consider yourself fortunate that you are not losing a limb. Or your life. Of course, it is up to Mrs. Howard if she wants to subject herself again to your abuses.

"Now sit still, damn it, while I wrap your eyes. I don't want you straining them by trying so hard to focus." Once Philip's eyes were bandaged, Dr. Cook snapped his bag shut. "Remember, no sleeping during the day," he admonished again before leaving.

Philip drained the last drop of cold coffee from his cup and, feeling carefully along the edge of the lamp table, he set it aside, making certain that it was firmly secure. *Now what do I do?* he fumed. *Go to Washington and vegetate in some damned hospital until they send me home to be pitied and cared for by strangers?*

Pounding the arm of the sofa, he said aloud, "Why didn't I just die?"

"Sir," Lieutenant Hasselbeck said from the door, "the staff would like to see you. Is this a bad time?"

Composing himself, Philip shifted his attention toward the sound of the voice. "It's all right, Lieutenant. Tell them to come in." He heard the shuffling of feet and inaudible mumbling. "I can hear perfectly well, gentlemen. Only my eyes were affected, not my ears."

"Good morning, sir," Wes said, "Lieutenant Hasselbeck and Sergeant Powell are with me."

"Where are Captains Hanford and Southall?"

The three men exchanged glances as they took their seats.

"Captain Hanford is dead," Wes said in a strangled voice.

Philip exhaled a great gush of air as though he had been punched in the abdomen. "Pete's gone? How did it happen?"

"Shot through the throat," Sergeant Powell's voice broke, "when Wade Hampton's cavalry attacked us from the left. They brought his body back this morning."

"If you wish, sir," Wes said, "I will write his family a letter and return his belongings to them."

Philip gripped the arm of the sofa, his face completely drained of color. "Thank you, Major. I will sign the letter when it's ready. What about the three of you?"

"We are fine, sir," Wes assured him, "except the Lieutenant here got a pretty bad saber slash on his left arm. He's got it sutured and dressed, in a sling, and ready to continue his duties."

Philip sat up sharply. "I'm sorry to hear that, Lieutenant. I won't ask how you managed to convince the Doc to let you stay, but I'm glad you are still with us. This company, or what's left of it, would collapse without you and Sergeant Powell."

"Thank you, sir," Jesse Hasselbeck replied.

"What about you, Major?"

"Not a scratch, sir," Wes replied. "Thanks, I am sure, to Jane's prayers. Once the good Lord gets His orders from her, I doubt that even He dare not comply."

Philip chuckled with the others at Wes' remark, helping to lighten the somber mood in the room. "If Jane's prayers are that effective, have her include all the rest of us. What about Captain Southall?"

Sergeant Powell shot a glance at Wes before clearing his throat. "He took a minie ball in the leg, sir. It's pretty bad."

"Damn," Philip muttered. "Major, do you have enough information to write the After Action Report?"

"Not yet, sir. However, there is one bright spot, despite the high casualties. We are still in control of the Weldon Railroad." Shuffling the papers in his hand, Wes asked in a hesitant voice, "What did Dr. Cook say about your injury, sir?"

"He doesn't know how long this damned blindness will last." Philip rose unsteadily. "Thank you, gentlemen, for coming. Advise your men to take their ease. They have earned it."

Caroline sat by her window, still feeling the sting of Philip's rejection after two days. *Does he really mean for me to stay away? Should I present myself in his room and say that I am doing what Dr. Cook asked, or honor Philip's demand that I leave him alone?*

On the other hand, I understand his fear and frustration. He is used to being in charge, taking command of any situation. But why can't he realize how much he needs me now? Or how much I need him? Will he hate me for seeing him this way? Will he think he has failed me? Heaven forbid, that he would not want me any more because of this affliction.

Caroline sat up with a start. *Or worse yet, could this be God's punishment for our sins? It isn't fair. Why should Philip be punished when it was I who wanted this to happen?*

Overcome by guilt and shame, she covered her face and cried, *dear God, what have I done to him?*

Philip passed two lonely days in his office. The officers sought his advice, Dr. Cook checked him regularly, and he ate as best he could, while berating anyone who offered to help.

As acting commander, Wes kept Philip abreast of all activity. "Not much going on at the moment. I wrote a letter to Pete Hanford's family. You can sign it here." He guided Philip's hand to the bottom of the page where Philip scrawled his name. "Are you feeling better, sir?"

"Somewhat. The thumping in my head has subsided, but I still feel dizzy and nauseous when I turn my head too quickly." Handing the pen back to Wes, he said, "Thanks for doing all this. I have every confidence that you will do a fine job."

"Not without Lieutenant Hasselbeck's help. I have discovered, as I'm sure you have, that he really runs this outfit. Well," Wes backed toward the door, "I will check on you tomorrow, sir."

With Wes' departure, Philip found himself overwhelmed by a strange new sensation, one he'd never experienced in his life—complete loneliness. To combat it, he reverted to his newly acquired habit of listening for Caroline's footsteps on the stairs.

On the third day, Philip had an unnerving thought. *Will she ever come back? Thanks to my inexcusable behavior the other day, I wouldn't blame her if she doesn't.*

Nearly mad with boredom, he sat by the window, listening to the raucous swearing of his men in the front yard, their arguments over card games, or reading letters aloud to lonely comrades. Smoke from their campfires wafted through the open windows, triggering memories of the nightly campfires on their long, bloody trek from Washington.

Subtly, slowly, his awareness shifted from the outside activity to another, closer presence behind him. The aroma of lilac water suddenly surrounded him, and he grinned. "It's about time."

Caroline touched his hand resting on the arm of the chair. "I had to come back. I knew you could not go on without me."

Philip brought her hand to his lips and kissed it. "If the last three days are any indication, truer words were never spoken." He allowed her to lead him to the sofa. "Caroline," he began, after they were seated, "I cannot tell you how sorry I am for speaking to you so harshly the other day. In my frustration, I didn't want you to see me that way. Can you forgive me?"

"I have to," she replied in a teasing voice. "It occurred to me during my exile that you were not in your right mind—as usual. But, more importantly, you need me now more than ever." She planted a kiss on his cheek. "Don't you?"

Philip caressed her face and touched her hair. "I thought I would go mad without you."

"How are your eyes? Can you see anything yet?"

"I'm not sure. Each day, when Doc removes the bandage, I think I see light. But I wonder if it isn't just wishful thinking. Thank God, my head no longer aches. Each passing day only increases my fear that this blindness will be permanent, and I wonder what will happen to us."

"Nothing will happen to us, so don't let those thoughts affect your healing. I love you, Philip. We will be together, no matter what. You must believe that."

He squeezed the hand she'd slipped into his. "I am happy to hear that. However," he added with a silly grin, "in my own defense, I must confess that I momentarily lost sight of who is really in command around here."

Chapter 23

SLEEP BECAME DIFFICULT for Philip. Each night, he struggled with the fear of living a life of dependence. Each new dawn brought fading hope that he would ever see again. Most mornings, he would sit by his window, listening to his staff out on the front porch as they shaved, or talked about letters from home, or discussed the latest dispatch from headquarters. Feeling a part of this routine by just listening to them became a necessary element of maintaining his sanity.

On this particular morning, he sat on the edge of his cot wondering if he would see today. Corpsman Dawson entered Philip's room just then, carrying his breakfast tray. Dawson had been assigned the unenviable task of helping Philip dress and shave.

"Morning, sir. Major Madison sends his compliments and says he will be in to see you after morning formation."

An hour later, Wes entered Philip's room and said in a brisk voice, "Good morning, Colonel. Are you ready for the morning briefing?"

"What I am ready for is to be out and about, doing my duty," Philip said, and set his coffee cup aside with a harsh rattle. "Wes, I have been thinking. If this blindness is permanent, I'll have a difficult time adjusting to it."

"Dr. Cook never indicated that it's permanent. So until you are better and declared ready to resume your duties, I will be happy to assist you any way I can. Now," Wes said, rustling his papers, "are you ready for business?"

"No, but let's get to it anyway. Have you had any word about when our replacements will arrive?"

"A few enlisted men are being processed through headquarters right now, but no word yet about the officers. By the way, as your brother is with Sherman, I thought you would be interested in the latest report from Georgia. Our boys have cut the last two rail lines into Atlanta. There has also been fighting around a place called Jonesborough. Atlanta is as good as ours."

"At last, some good news," Philip said with a trace of a smile. "Any word on casualties?"

"No," Wes replied before consulting his notes. "Closer to home, there have been no recent deaths from sniper fire or new injuries. There are ten or twelve men on sick call, mostly bad cases of chafing, dysentery, and the usual malingerers. By the way, you may have heard the men cheering earlier. The paymaster finally arrived."

"Thank goodness, the boys will finally be paid. See that they pay the washerwomen first. It has been months since they've been paid." Philip lowered his voice. "I need to ask a favor, Wes. Each payday, I usually check with First Sergeant Powell about the needs of the enlisted men, problems at home, illness and the like. He keeps track of those things and distributes my pay among those in need. Of course, gambling debts aren't considered.

"I also slip the washerwomen a few extra dollars to make their lot a little easier. I would take it as a personal favor if you would continue this with Sergeant Powell until I am able to resume my duties. And please do not mention this conversation to anyone else," he added.

"Certainly, sir. I will see to it right away." Wes looked over his notes again. "Oh, yes, one more thing. A photographer is roaming the area taking pictures of anyone willing to sit for him. What would you say to his taking a picture of our staff?"

"Capital idea," Philip nodded. "Make the arrangements."

"Yes, sir. And now," Wes added, "I have saved the best for last, sir. Headquarters sent this letter officially exonerating you in the Private Smith shooting."

"That's a relief," Philip said with obvious satisfaction.

"Well, after the officers and enlisted men testified on your behalf, the inquiry board confirmed that you had no other choice." Wes gathered up his writing pad and pencil. "Is there anything you need?"

"Yes. I am about to go mad cooped up in this damned room. Will you please help me down to the stream? I need to get away for at least an hour."

"Of course, but I will have to sneak you past Dr. Cook."

"To hell with him." Philip stood and waited for Wes to take his arm. "We'll go out the front door so Doc won't see us."

Wes led Philip to a level place by the stream and helped find him a place to sit. Thanking Wes, Philip asked him to return in an hour.

He removed his tunic and sat with his back against a tree, breathing deeply of the cool air. Sounds of busy birds overhead in the trees and the murmuring stream filled his senses. Aware of the sounds of bees and horseflies close by, the scents from wildflowers, he reveled in his first freedom in over a week.

"I can hear you," he said to the birds, "but will I ever see you again?" On a whim, he unwound the bandage covering his eyes. The sudden exposure to light made them tear up but he noticed that the pain was not as severe as a few days ago. He closed his eyes and prayed before opening them again, Please God, let me see something, anything. A shaft of light or movement.

Gathering his courage, he opened his eyes slowly. Is that light I see filtering through the darkness? He stood, keeping his hand on the tree as a reference point. He blinked. Yes, I see movement. What is it? It's too blurry to make out. But I can see light. Thank you, God.

Sitting again, he re-wrapped his eyes then listened to the sounds all around him. I can't expect too much too soon, he thought, but at least there is some improvement.

Wes returned more than an hour later, full of apologies. "Sorry to be so long, sir. I lost track of time."

"It doesn't matter. I sat here listening to the myriad sounds around me. It's amazing how many different sounds there are in nature." He stood up, using the tree as an aid. "I am ready to go but first, I would like to stop by the surgery tent and visit the wounded."

"Good idea. They have been inquiring about your progress."

Wes led Philip up the slope toward the surgery tent where they stopped to chat with some men waiting to be treated. A sudden commotion inside the tent interrupted their conversation.

Father O'Boyle's calm voice was drowned out by a distraught man's objections. "No! I won't let you do it."

"You will die for sure if I don't take that damned leg off," Dr. Cook's voice boomed.

"I don't care. Let me die!"

Philip nudged Wes toward the sound of the argument. "See what's going on in there."

Entering the tent, Wes found Dr. Cook and Father O'Boyle struggling with a patient on a blood-drenched operating table. The patient, thrashing his head from side to side, strained to break free of their grip. When he turned toward Wes, the sight of David Southall's contorted face made Wes grip the tent flap for support.

"Do you need some help, Doctor?" Wes asked in a shaky voice.

"This is none of your concern, Major," David shouted at him.

"Listen here, Captain," Dr. Cook shook a bloody finger at David, "I don't need your permission to save your life. Now lie still so Father O'Boyle can administer the chloroform."

David knocked the cloth from the priest's hand. "Get the hell away from me. I won't spend the rest of my life as a helpless cripple. What would I be then?"

"A hero, you goddamned idiot," the doctor growled. "The ladies love a hero who has been wounded for the glory of his country. It's better than an aphrodisiac. Now lie still, damn it. I haven't got all day to fool with you. Father O'Boyle, put this man under, even if you have to use a gun to do it." He leaned closer to Wes and whispered, "Bad wound. Shattered the bone. I knew it would have to come off eventually."

Wes watched David's eyes roll back as he succumbed to the chloroform. "What are his chances?"

"Of recovering? Excellent, once I take this gangrened leg off."

Satisfied that David was sedated, Dr. Cook reached for the surgical saw. At this point, Wes beat a hasty retreat from the tent.

"What was that all about?" Philip inquired when Wes reappeared.

"Doc has to take off David's leg."

Pale and shaken, Wes led Philip toward the house.

Chapter 24

AFTER HIS SURGERY, David refused to eat or see anyone. He lay, uncommunicative, with his face to the tent wall. As he pleaded with Dr. Cook to increase his morphine, the doctor considered before saying, "Son, I can't bear to see you like this. So, to ease your obvious discomfort, I will increase it, but only a little."

Several days later, when Father O'Boyle looked in on him, David roused himself from his morphine fog and greeted the priest with a pathetic smile. "Good afternoon, Father. Forgive me for saying so, but you don't look well."

Father O'Boyle admitted that he was a bit tired and, leaning closer, whispered as if to a co-conspirator, "Dr. Cook has promised that when this war is over, we will get gloriously, roaring drunk and stay that way for days. Perhaps you would like to join us."

"A good binge is what we all need," David agreed in a slurred voice.

"That's the ticket. Now is there anything I can do for you, my boy?"

"No, thank you. Oh, by the way," David said, catching hold of the priest's sleeve, "I know Doc is busy, but he seems to have forgotten my morphine. Could you take care of it for me?"

With a sympathetic smile, Father O'Boyle patted David's arm. "Of course, Captain. I will see to it right away."

Crossing the back yard, Dr. Cook approached Caroline as she drew water from the well. "Excuse me, Mrs. Howard, I must beg another favor of you. If memory serves, you proved an excellent nurse on a previous and rather difficult occasion. Could I impose upon your good graces to help me again by coaxing Captain Southall out of his melancholy? I figure if you can handle that black-hearted Colonel, you can handle anyone.

"The Captain hasn't been eating well since his surgery," he continued. "I suspect he has become dependent on morphine, which isn't uncommon after drastic surgery. If I learn that he is addicted, I have no choice but to ship him to Washington." Dr. Cook shook his head. "See if you can coax some common sense into him."

"I'll see what I can do," she assured Dr. Cook with a smile.

A short time later, Caroline stood at the opening of David's tent, holding a wash basin. She blinked back tears at the drastic change in his appearance. His blue eyes, once confident and bright, were now glazed and sunken into dark sockets. His blonde hair was dirty and unkempt.

"Good morning, Captain," she said with a forced smile. "I hope you don't mind the intrusion. It is time for your bath."

"I don't wish to be disturbed," he said in a barely audible voice.

"I'm afraid that places me in an awkward position, as Dr. Cook has asked me to perform certain duties, and he is not a man to be crossed. Besides," she placed the basin on a table next to his cot, "it will give us time to visit. I might even arrange for us to have lunch under the trees. Wouldn't you like to get out of this stuffy old tent?"

David turned away from her. "Please, don't patronize me."

"I am not patronizing you, Captain. Dr. Cook asked me to bathe you and several other men. He didn't say anything about socializing." Caroline looked stricken. "Oh, please, sir, do not be ungallant to me."

"I do not wish to appear ungallant, but I am not feeling sociable."

"I won't be long, then. Meanwhile, you can tell me the latest news from Washington. I hear you receive a great deal of mail. Are you still breaking the ladies' hearts?"

"I'm afraid that is a thing of the past. Besides, who would want a one-legged, good for nothing?"

Ignoring his self-pity, Caroline toweled his arms dry. "Had you a profession before joining the army?"

"I considered the stage but," he indicated his missing limb, "the Confederacy put a quick end to that."

"With your good looks, Mr. Booth will be forced to leave the stage."

"Please, Mrs. Howard," he groaned, "you must not be so obvious. J. Wilkes Booth plies his profession on two good legs. At present, I am a rival to no man. Here, or in Washington."

Caroline bit her lip at his obvious reference to Philip, and her feelings of pity for David increased. "Have you considered writing for the stage?"

David paused to summon his waning strength. "No, but I have tried my hand at poetry."

"You must show me some of your works." Straightening his sheets, Caroline regarded her handiwork. "There, you look quite presentable, if I do say so myself."

David turned dull eyes on her. "If you don't mind, I haven't the strength to maintain a conversation, much less be sociable."

She feigned a pout. "You cannot deny me the pleasure of your company at lunch."

"I am not fit company for anyone, least of all a pretty lady."

"Then have pity on me, sir, and let Dr. Cook think I am doing as he asked."

"Very well," he sighed. "We will see how I feel tomorrow. But you must promise not to patronize me."

Over the next four days, Dr. Cook observed that under Caroline's diligent care, David's outlook brightened and his overall condition showed extraordinary improvement.

On a steamy day early in September, as Dr. Cook walked by David's tent, he overheard something that fired his temper. Throwing back the tent flap, he demanded, "What the hell is going on here?"

"I am giving Captain Southall his morphine," Father O'Boyle replied, startled by the doctor's tone.

Dr. Cook glared at David. "You charmed this man into giving you additional doses, didn't you?"

David turned away from the doctor's accusing eyes.

Father O'Boyle cleared his throat and muttered, "I'm sorry, Doctor. I had no idea. I thought I was helping him."

Dr. Cook patted the priest's shoulder. "I know you did, Brendan. It's not your fault. Now, if you will excuse us."

"Yes, of course," Father O'Boyle nodded, and hurried from the tent.

Dr. Cook leveled sad eyes on David. "I have suspected for some time that you have been getting additional doses but I couldn't prove it. I should have known that not even Mrs. Howard's best efforts could have affected such a miraculous recovery."

He sat on the cot across from David's and leaned toward him. "Look, son, I cannot, in all conscience, allow you to continue this foolishness. You aren't the first soldier this has happened to and you won't be the last. I regret having to do this, but I decided several days ago that the time has come to ship you to Washington. I will send instructions to cut back on the morphine until you are no longer dependent on it."

David sat up, his hollow eyes wide with fear. "No, I can't make it without morphine."

"Don't worry, David," Dr. Cook patted his shoulder, "it will be all right. Now, have someone get your gear together. You leave for City Point later this afternoon. I will see you before you go."

The doctor rose and started for the tent opening. Pausing, he turned and frowned at David. "I think you owe Father O'Boyle an apology for abusing his trust and his kindness."

"I will take care of it," David said, then turned his face to the wall.

Caroline had just taken her bed sheets off the clothes line and started toward the kitchen door as someone called to her from behind. Turning, she saw Father O'Boyle coming toward her.

"May I speak with you a moment, Mrs. Howard?" he asked, removing his hat.

"Certainly." She placed the laundry basket on the stoop. "What can I do for you, sir?" Even after all these months, she still could not bring herself to call him Father or Reverend.

"Captain Southall asked me to inform you that he is leaving for Washington City on the evening packet. Before he goes, he would like to speak to you."

Caroline thanked him, and headed for David's tent. "You wanted to see me?" she asked, standing at the tent's opening.

"Come in, please." Leaning against the center post, he resumed folding his military blouse. "As you can see, packing requires that I do a clumsy balancing act. Dr. Cook assures me that I will be fitted for a wooden leg in Washington. Maybe then," he stuffed the blouse into his travel bag with a frustrated gesture, "I can dance the jig."

"May I help you with that?" She reached for the socks on his cot.

"No, thank you," he said in a clipped voice, and jammed the socks on top of the blouse. "I hope you don't mind that I asked to see you before I go. I wanted to thank you for all you have done for me."

"Will you write to me?"

"Miss Caroline, you know as well as I. . ." He paused, his eyes clouded and shifted away from hers.

"Yes, of course," she murmured, and looked down at her dusty shoes. "What will you do after you leave the hospital in Washington?"

"Stay in the army, if they will have me. I'm sure the War Department has plenty of jobs for a needy cripple," he said with bitterness. Reaching into his tunic pocket, he said in a gentler tone, "I wrote this for you. But, please, do not read it until after I am gone."

She took the sealed envelope. "As you wish."

"Miss Caroline," he stammered, swallowed hard then shook his head.

She stood on tiptoe and kissed his cheek. "No need to say anything. I understand. Be happy, David. I will never forget you."

He leaned into her kiss. "Thank you. I wish you and the Colonel all the best."

"Are you ready, sir?" Corpsman Dawson asked from the tent opening.

Neither David nor Caroline responded immediately to Dawson's question. She simply stared at him with a shocked expression at his comment about Philip.

"Yes, Corpsman," David said, still gazing intently at her. "Take my bag, please. I will be along in a moment." He touched her cheek with his free hand and, keeping his back to the corpsman, he whispered, "You will never know the difference you have made in my life."

Blinking back hot tears, Caroline moved her lips, forming the words 'thank you' and stood aside as the corpsman helped David out of the tent.

Following David's departure, Caroline sat in the gazebo and stared at his sealed note. What could be so important that he did not want me to read it until after he had gone? With trembling fingers, she broke the seal and unfolded the paper.

"If you will recall," the brief note began, "I once spoke of my feeble attempts at poetry. I feel certain you will agree with my assessment once you read this.

> She came so fair that summer's day
> And stood there, drenched in light.
> She tore my heart and wrenched my soul
> And reveled in my plight.

What say I when she comes into view?
My heart is but her slave.
Dawns fair the day she smiles on me
And sees my love, not his.

When you think of me, dear Miss Caroline, please think kindly.
Your ob't servant, David"

Poor dear, lonely David, Caroline thought, and with tears misting her eyes, pressed the poem to her heart.

Chapter 25

"THANKS, WES." PHILIP sat at the now familiar spot by the stream. "This isn't the first time you have acted as nursemaid for me, is it?" he asked, referring to those dark times after discovering that Elizabeth and Julian's affair was the scandal of Washington society.

"No, and I'm getting tired of it," Wes teased.

"No more than I am. I dislike being looked after." Philip paused before asking, "Would you mind asking Caroline to come down later. She can help me back."

After Wes left, Philip leaned against the tree and took a deep breath. The peace of the place settled over him but still could not penetrate his inner turmoil. His hearing, always sharp, was now acute, and he delighted in the myriad songs of a mocking bird, the buzz of bees going from flower to flower, and the racket of the cicadas. Inside this haven of trees, the war did not exist.

As he had done the previous days, he unwound his bandages and laid them aside, keeping his eyes closed. Taking a deep breath, he opened them, slowly, hesitantly, fearful of the results. The harsh light offended his sensitive eyes, so he closed them again and waited.

When he opened them, he waited until they adjusted to his surroundings before glancing around. Yes, I can see light and forms. It wasn't my imagination this morning when I saw Dr. Cook's silhouette against the windows. Can it be true? Is my vision returning?

Movement to his right caught his attention. Philip stood up and, cocking his head, he focused his mind toward the sound of the nearby stream. Blurred shafts of sunlight danced on the water's surface. Slightly to his left, a small object moved. Even though it was dim, he could discern a rabbit nibbling on clover. A butterfly flitted by on its way to a clump of wildflowers. "My God," he whispered in awe, "I can see that it's yellow."

Dropping to the ground, he wept with joy. "Thank you, Lord. Thank you."

A footfall sounded behind him. Reaching for his handkerchief, he dried his eyes and composed himself.

"Hello there," Caroline called.

"Ah, Nurse Caroline, I believe." Smiling, he reached for her hand. "It is so nice to enjoy your full attention now that your other patient has departed."

She sat next to him on the ground and kissed his cheek. "Why, Colonel, I do believe you are jealous of David."

"Hardly." He pulled her into his arms and kissed her with uncharacteristic ardor.

"Philip, please," she freed herself from his embrace, "you take my breath away." She leaned closer to inspect his eyes. "Philip, dear, should you have removed your bandages? Your eyes look as though they are watering."

Unwilling to admit that what she observed were actually tears of joy, he said, "I have been removing them for several days. But only when I am alone."

She studied his eyes intently before asking in a wary voice, "Philip, can you see?"

"Yes, I can," he replied with a smile. "Not clearly, but I can discern outlines. I just saw a rabbit. And a yellow butterfly." Tears re-appeared in his eyes. "It was a beautiful sight."

"Oh, darling, I am so happy for you."

"Yesterday, I noticed light and shadows and again this morning when Dr. Cook checked my eyes. I was hesitant to say anything to him for fear that it was only wishful thinking. Before long," he said, tracing a finger across the bridge of her nose, "I'll be able to see those adorable freckles."

Reacting to his teasing about unwanted freckles, she smacked at his shoulder. "Freckles? Why didn't you tell me before that I had those awful things?"

"I can't believe you had not noticed them," he laughed. "Frankly, I find them endearing."

"Endearing?" she sputtered. "You are laughing at me, aren't you?"

He reached for her hand still balled into a fist and kissed it. "Why would I do that? You know how I feel about you."

Caroline's facial expression became sober. "No, I don't," she said, her tone no longer teasing. "Tell me."

Averting his face from the challenge in her voice, he muttered, "Damn it, Caroline."

She yanked his chin around to face her squarely. "No, you are not turning away from me this time, Philip. Or changing the subject, as you usually do. Say what you mean."

Their eyes met and held for several long moments.

Philip's gaze wavered first, as the last of his defenses crumbled within him. He stole a glance at her and saw that her eyes were still fixed on him, waiting for his reply.

"All right," he said at last. "I'll say it." He forced her back onto the trampled grass and, with his face inches above hers, he whispered, "I love you, Caroline Chandler. Is that what you want to hear? I'll say it again—I love you."

She wrapped her arms around his neck and surrendered to his kisses.

"You have known all along, haven't you?" he asked with his lips pressed against her cheek.

"Of course. Only love could have prompted all the wonderful, thoughtful things you have done for me. Despite your constant state of denial, your feelings for me showed through."

His crooked grin betrayed his discomfort at being found out. "I would have seen to your safety and given you food in any event, because it was the right thing to do."

"Philip, if you don't mind," Caroline toyed with the button on his tunic, "I would like to ask a question about something that has bothered me for a while."

"I would not want to be responsible for worry lines on that pretty face. What is it?"

"Were you reticent to say you loved me because there was someone else?"

"No," he answered without hesitation, "there is no one else."

She kissed him again. "Thank goodness. I don't think I could endure it if there were. When I learned you were wounded that first time, my heart stopped. I knew right then that you meant more to me than anyone ever has. Or ever could."

"I must confess that I likewise had a moment of truth. It was after I drove you away because of this blindness. It was pure torture not hearing your voice or having you near me. I realized then how much I needed you but was too cowardly to admit that it was because I loved you."

He lay beside her on the ground. "While we are admitting the truth, there is something that has always bothered me. That is, how you could have been attracted to me in the first place? Or even loved me?" He regarded her with wonder. "I was nothing but rude to you at first."

"I suppose you want a truthful answer rather than a philosophical discussion about the mystery of why one person loves another." Without waiting for his response, she continued with a wry smile, "When you first limped onto my front porch all dusty and smelly with sweat, and barking orders, I could see that you were hurting, down deep in your soul. When I sat with you during your delirium, Wes would come in and keep me company. He told me things about you, about your suicidal indifference during battles, as though you didn't care if you lived or died."

"At the time, I didn't care. Life held no meaning for me. Then you came along, hell-bent on saving me with your unconditional love. Caroline, when this war is over, I intend taking you away with me. We can live somewhere far from everyone we know. Perhaps Europe for a while." He lifted his eyes, now tender and hopeful. "What I am trying to say is that I want to marry you."

"Oh, yes," she whispered before being engulfed in his arms. "Yes, yes, yes, I will marry you."

Chapter 26

"YOU SAY IT started earlier this week?" Dr. Cook asked, regarding Philip with suspicion.

Philip sat on a high stool outside the medical tent, patient and smiling. "Yes, it began gradually over the course of this past week. With each day, I began seeing more clearly. It's not completely normal, but a definite improvement."

"Amazing." Dr. Cook scratched his head. "It's nothing short of a miracle. I didn't think the swelling would subside so quickly. Well, Colonel," he announced as he put his instruments away, "you should be able to resume some of your duties in a few days."

"A few days? What's wrong with tomorrow morning? I am tired of sitting around listening to my hair grow. I want to go back to work in the morning."

"All right, you damned stubborn mule, if you feel up to it," Dr. Cook agreed with a reluctant sigh. "But mind you, only on the condition that you take it slow at first. And don't even think of riding. You don't need to jostle your already addled brain just yet. I expect you to let me know when the haziness has completely dissipated. Or if the dizziness recurs. Agreed?"

"Agreed," Philip said with a broad smile. He stood up and shook the doctor's hand. "Thanks, Doc." He paused before adding, "I don't mind admitting that I have learned an important lesson from this experience."

"Oh?" Dr. Cook asked with a sly grin. "And what, pray tell, would that be?"

"I will never again take anything for granted."

That evening, Philip and Caroline smiled at one another across the dinner table. They became even closer with Philip's admission that he loved her. They laughed, shared secrets, teased one another, made plans for their future together, but there was never a hint of going to her bed again. He remained faithful to his promise, difficult though it was at times.

"What did the doctor say about your eyes?" she asked, as she held his hand across the table.

Philip twirled his wineglass by the stem with his free hand. "He was amazed that I had recovered so quickly. If three weeks is what he calls quickly. I even bullied him into allowing me to return to my duties now that my vision improves with each passing day. As a matter of fact, I can even see something there."

"If you dare mention my freckles again," she threatened, "I will throw a biscuit at you."

He feigned enormous innocence. "I? Never. Fear of retribution prevents that word from ever escaping my lips. I was referring to those big brown eyes of yours. All you have to do is look at me, my love, and I am putty in your hands."

"Why, Colonel, you will turn a girl's head with remarks like that." She rose and held out her hand. "Shall we repair to your office?"

Standing, Philip gave her a deep bow. "I am your most humble servant, madam."

In his office, he poured two glasses of wine and handed her one before sitting in a chair opposite the sofa. "How have you been sleeping?"

"Not very well. Lately, I have been having nightmares."

He leaned forward, his interest piqued. "What kind of nightmares?"

"It's awful. I hear a gagging sound that awakens me. It frightens me so that I want to run down the stairs to the safety of your arms." She put her wineglass on the lamp table beside her. "Oh, Philip, I am so tired of it all. At times, when I feel overwhelmed, I want to unburden my fears onto you. You seem so sure of yourself, capable of handling any situation."

"I am not nearly as confident as I appear. But I am certain of one thing—nothing or no one will ever harm you again. I will see to it personally."

Caroline smiled her thanks. "It is such a lovely evening and the crepe myrtle is in full bloom. Why don't we go for a walk?"

Standing, he arched his eyebrows in surprise. "Young lady, are you trying to seduce me?"

"Why, sir," she teased in her best Tidewater drawl, "how can you even think such a thing?"

Laughing, he bent to set his wineglass on the table beside hers just as she started to rise. His face brushed close to hers. Neither of them moved. Keeping his eyes focused on her, he circled her waist with his right arm and drew her close. His left hand reached for the lamp and turned the wick, plunging the room into darkness.

The sound of screams, high-pitched and keening, broke through Philip's sleep. A woman's cry. Far off in the distance. He tried to rouse himself from his sleepy stupor just as something sharp struck him in his ribs. Then something that felt like a fist glanced off his cheek. He bolted upright, ready to defend himself from an attacker as he'd been trained to do. But there was no uniformed attacker hovering over him.

In that brief instant of uncertainty as he glanced around his dark surroundings, he realized that this was not his office. No, he was in

Caroline's room and it was her cries that woke him. Fully aware now that she was sobbing uncontrollably beside him, he turned toward her and caught her flailing arms. In an attempt to calm her, he drew her close to him and crooned, "It's all right, sweetheart. I'm here."

Burying her face in his chest, she pointed frantically toward the ceiling. "Can't you see her? It's Mother Howard. There—hanging from the ceiling?" She snuggled tight against him, taking his breath away. "Dear God, Philip, make her go away."

"Hush, sweetheart. I'll take care of it." After laying her back onto her pillow and kissing her damp cheek, Philip lit the bedside lamp and held it high. "Look, there is no one here." He moved the lamp to every dark corner of the room. "It must have been one of those bad dreams you told me about." Returning to the bed, he gathered her into his arms again. "It's all right, Carrie. There is no one here but us."

"But I saw her, watching us. Calling me names."

"It was just a dream," he whispered. "Let me hold you while you try to get some sleep."

She lay in his arms for a long time, not moving or speaking. Finally, she stirred and shifted around to face him. "Are you asleep?"

Philip stretched and grinned at her. "Not any longer." He rolled over away from her to check his pocket watch on the bedside table. "It's after four o'clock. The sun will be up before long." Sitting up on the edge of the bed, he put a cheroot between his lips and reached for a lucifer.

Caroline propped her pillows up against the headboard and sat up behind him. "Oh, Philip, please don't smoke that foul thing now."

Over his shoulder, he gave her a surprised look. "I'm sorry, Carrie. Why didn't you tell me before that it offended you?" Standing abruptly, he tossed the cheroot onto the table. "There, I simply will not smoke any more." He grabbed his trousers off the rocker and pulled them on.

Caroline picked at the sheet thoughtfully. "Philip, there is something I would like to show you. I have worried and fretted about it, but decided that I do not want to have any secrets from you." She got out of bed, ran to her dressing table and rummaged through a drawer.

"Secrets?" he asked, while pulling up his suspenders. "That sounds serious."

She returned with David's note but hesitated a moment before handing it to Philip. After reading the note and the poem, he handed it back to her with a perplexed look. "Well?"

"I did not want you to think that my feelings for David were more than friendship."

"Sweetheart, it never entered my mind. Besides, I knew Dr. Cook had asked you to look in on David."

"I—I never dreamed that David's feelings for me ran this deep." Caroline shook her head in wonder. "It escapes my comprehension why he should want me when he might have his pick of so many belles in Washington City."

"Because you were unattainable," Philip answered with a smile. "And perhaps like me, he came to admire you and your strength. Dire necessity forced you into some critical decision-making. Something, I am sure that was previously unheard of for a Southern lady."

"Yes, and something I would have gladly relinquished." She gave him a quizzical look. "But I had the impression you didn't like David."

"Not so. David is a fine officer, despite his being a scamp. His romantic escapades amused me. Until he turned his sights on you, this is. The night he came to your room, I knew what he intended to do. That was the only reason I made my presence known to him. My intention at the time was not to compromise you, or embarrass you. But I could not allow him to charm his way into your room in order to seduce you."

Throwing her arms around him, she rested her head on his chest. "My hero. I love you so much."

He savored her embrace before responding in a husky voice, "I love you too, sweetheart."

Caroline lifted her gaze to meet his. "Yes, I know. Even David knew it."

Philip gave her a sheepish grin. "It seems that I was the only one unable—or unwilling—to see the obvious. But I see it now, and I do adore you, Carrie."

"There is something else, isn't there? I can see it in your eyes."

Freeing himself of her embrace, Philip walked to the east-facing window. He stared unseeing at the first hint of light on the horizon.

Through force of will, he quelled the damned logical voice that plagued him at the most inopportune times.

He turned to face her with a forced smile. "I—I don't, oh hell, Carrie, at this moment, I am too happy to think about anything that happened before I met you. My sight is restored, and I am madly, joyously in love."

Caroline returned his smile. "I have never felt like this before either. However," she chewed on her lower lip, "I have been thinking."

"Uh, oh, that's sounds dangerous."

"Don't be such a grump. It occurs to me that you know everything about my life, where I live, my family and background, but I know nothing about you."

He hunched his shoulders in a helpless gesture. "What is there to know? I come from a small town in eastern Pennsylvania called Creighton's Crossroads, named for the first Philip Creighton, who also founded the town."

"Really?" Caroline sat in the center of the bed, crossed-legged. "I imagine you were considered quite a catch. Did all the girls set their caps for you?"

"I'm sure my name and money were irresistible to some," he mumbled. "However," his smile returned, "I must hasten to add that none of the ladies I met were anything at all like you."

"What a noble, not to mention appropriate, thing to say. What are you looking at?" she asked, cocking her head.

"At how adorable you look, sitting there like that."

"Don't change the subject," she commanded, and waved her hand for him to continue.

"Yes, ma'am." He bowed in deference to her order. "To continue, both my parents are still living. I have an older brother George, who is married to a shrew named Ellen. She is, unhappily for the rest of us, begetting little baby shrews."

Caroline covered her mouth to keep from laughing out loud. "What a nasty thing to say."

Philip's lips twitched. "But true, nonetheless. You already know about my younger brother Matthew. My sister Jessica is nineteen and still unmarried. I fear that if she does not change her waspish ways, she may never marry. There," he spread his hands, "you know all there is to know about me."

"Not quite. Now, the all-important question," she said, smiling at his discomfort, "have you ever been in love? Before meeting me, that is."

Philip whirled around to face the window again.

"What was her name?" Caroline asked quietly after a long pause, the smile now faded from her eyes.

Unable to withstand her insistent silence, he turned to face her. "Samantha. We had planned to marry but events intervened. I have not seen her or heard from her in nearly five years. That is all I am going to say about it."

"Oh, sweetheart, I'm sorry," she said with feeling. "I knew something had affected you deeply." She opened her arms to him.

Philip crawled onto the bed and, taking her into his arms, said against her ear, "I love you, Carrie. I cannot imagine my life without you."

She held him closer. "Oh, my sweet Philip, I have waited so long for you."

The gesture, her words, all spoke of her trust in him, and he panicked. *She's right. There must be no secrets between us. Tell her. Tell her now, you fool, before the moment passes. Tell her about Elizabeth, and how she drove me to the edge of madness.*

Tell Caroline that I am not yet free to marry her.

Chapter 27

STILL AGLOW FROM Philip's ardent proof of his love these past weeks, Caroline strolled onto the front porch. It promised to be another hot day, even this late in September. Humming to herself as she sat in the wicker chair, she noticed Wes seated on the bottom porch step, his head bent over something.

"Good morning, Major. Reading something interesting?"

Wes glanced up with a start. "Yes, ma'am. The mail just arrived. I have four letters from Jane. Even my girls have written to me." He held up the scribbling of his two little ones.

"How adorable," she smiled. "Did Philip receive mail too?"

"Yes, ma'am. Right here." He indicated several editions of the *Crossroads Herald* bound together on the step beside him.

"I will take it in for him. You go on with your reading."

Smiling his gratitude, he handed her the packet. "Thank you, Mrs. Howard."

Caroline carried the packet to Philip's office and, in the process of placing it on his desk, an envelope slid from the folds of the newspapers to the floor. As she bent to retrieve it, the return address to a Washington hotel caught her eye. Above the hotel's address, obviously written in a woman's hand, was the name—Mrs. P. J. Creighton. Caroline caught her breath. Mrs. P. J. Creighton? Mrs. Philip Jonathan Creighton?

Dropping the envelope, she let out a cry and ran up the stairs, tripping part way up and bruising her knees. In her room she started to throw herself onto her bed but, seeing the place where she and Philip had been together, lying in each other's arms, she hesitated.

Overwhelmed by shame, she ran across the hall and fell onto Aunt Emmaline's bed.

Several hours later, she sat up, her eyes red and swollen, her sore knees thumping with pain. Rising, she studied her disheveled image in the foggy mirror over the washstand. "You filthy whore!" she cried in disgust as she pounded the mirror with her fists.

Frozen by humiliation and anger, she spent the rest of the afternoon in the rocking chair, the curtains drawn, and staring straight ahead, thinking all those things a devastated woman thinks. Philip will return soon, she thought, and as usual, he will expect me to be ready for him, all fresh and sweet smelling. She wrinkled her nose. I am certainly not sweet smelling today.

She smacked the arms of the rocking chair with her palms. How could I have been such a fool? I should have known. I should have known!

Hearing his voice in the entry hall just before six thirty, Caroline shifted in the chair. He never varies his routine. First, he will go to his room, remove his dirty uniform and freshen up. Then he will expect me to have dinner with him. He takes so much for granted. He makes all the rules of our romance. Our romance, she sniffed in disgust. It's nothing but a farce, like the hundreds of other wartime dalliances. In a few years, he will have trouble recalling my name—if he thinks of me at all.

She covered her face with hands icy from nerves and, somewhere deep inside her, a fresh reservoir of tears broke free. Mother Howard was right about what I have become. Even Cassie predicted dire consequences if I became involved with Philip. But no, I was headstrong, believing I knew what I wanted.

Philip's voice sounded again in the lower hall. Answering questions. Giving orders. Her head came up at the sound of his boots on the stairs. A moment later, he called to her in her room, called again in the hallway.

She made no effort to respond.

He called into Emmaline's room. "Caroline? There you are, sweetheart. I have some news that I cannot wait to share with you."

Entering the room, he stopped short and caught his breath. "My God, it's like an oven in here." He threw back the curtains and opened the west-facing windows, letting in the evening breeze. "That's better. I ran into Colonel Graves at headquarters today and he. . ." Turning to face her, he stopped in mid-sentence. Her ravaged appearance changed his expression from an easy smile to startled surprise.

He fell to his knees beside her chair. "Sweetheart, what's wrong?"

"Don't touch me," she said in a strangled voice, and jerked her arm away from his touch. "You needn't look so puzzled, Colonel. Or lie to me any longer. I know everything now."

"You know what?" Expelling an exasperated sound, he stood up. "What the hell is going on, Caroline?"

"I must ask you to remember your language, Colonel."

"Stop calling me Colonel in that tone of voice and tell me what happened."

She turned cold eyes on him. "All right, I will tell you. I know about your wife—Mrs. Philip J. Creighton. I saw her letter in the morning mail."

Even under his tan, she could see that he blanched, but said nothing.

After several moments, she asked, "Why did you tell me, while looking me straight in the eye, that you were not in love with someone else? Several weeks ago when you told me about Samantha, why did you conveniently neglect to mention that you have a wife?"

He slumped to the floor beside her chair. "I did not intend to lie to you." He sat for a long time with his head down, staring at the back of his weathered hands.

At any other time, her heart would have gone out to him but, at this moment, she wanted to hurt him as badly as she had been hurt. "Please, do not compound the matter with more lies and half truths."

Jumping to his feet, he paced back and forth before the windows. Shaking his head finally, he threw up his hands in a helpless gesture. "I don't know what to say. I have no excuses to offer. Very simply put, I was too much of a coward to tell you about her when I had the opportunity. I did not want to destroy what we have."

"Correction, Colonel, what we *had*."

Hurrying to her side, he held her wrist in a desperate grip. "Please, Carrie, don't say that."

"Take your hands off me," she said through her teeth.

For a moment, he didn't move. His eyes searched her face. Then, reluctantly, he let her go.

She regarded him through her tears. "I am curious, Philip. When you leave here, did you intend to shake my hand and say 'thank you, ma'am, for the use of the hall'? A few years from now, will you laugh over your after-dinner cigar and talk about the hardships of the war, and that little fling you had with what's-her-name in Virginia?"

Philip rose and walked to the window, keeping his back to her. "Is that what you think of me?"

"I don't know what to think about anything. Oh, Philip," her voice cracked, "how could you do this to me?"

He swung around to face her, his expression stark with pain. "All right, if you want to know the truth, I will tell you about that damned letter. It contained the same old thing—another demand for more money in the divorce settlement. You see, for the past year, I have been corresponding with my attorney about divorcing Elizabeth. I had asked for the divorce when I enlisted in the army but she continues to forestall the inevitable by dreaming up more unreasonable demands, undoubtedly, in the hope that I will be killed and make her a rich widow.

"But I took care of that possibility. If I die, she inherits nothing. The bulk of my estate goes to my brother Matthew." His voice rose to a fevered pitch as his anger grew, his dark eyes flashed. "She's a fool if she thinks I will finance her affair with my own cousin. She is nothing but a damned whore."

Caroline broke into violent sobs. "Then you must think no better of me, for I am guilty of the same thing with you."

Philip reached to console her. "No, sweetheart, there isn't the remotest similarity between the two of you." Gently, he brushed an errant strand of hair from her face.

Reacting to his touch, she wanted to kiss away his haunted look, the look that always tore at her heart. Instead, she pressed her handkerchief hard against her eyes.

Philip sat on the floor again, rested his back against the side of the bed and considered for several moments before saying in a soft voice, "Elizabeth has not been a part of my life since shortly after our marriage. She made it abundantly clear from the start that she hated the sight of me, and married me solely for my money. We can't even be in the same room without going at each other's throats. My life with her was a living hell.

"So, when President Lincoln called for volunteers after Fort Sumter, I joined the cavalry company in Crossroads. I felt no particular surge of patriotic fervor at the time. I viewed the war as a way to escape my marriage with some shred of honor. My hope was that I would be killed. In fact, I wanted to die," he added, his voice breaking and fading.

Caroline caught her breath and again fought the urge to reach for him.

After a moment, he continued in a hard-edged voice, "The last time I saw that wanton bitch, she was in bed with her paramour and I was holding a gun to his head. I had every intention of sending that unholy pair straight to hell."

"Why did you marry her?" she asked in a strangled voice.

He shrugged in a helpless gesture. "I have asked myself that question many times. Looking back, I can see that I never loved her. I suppose I needed to assuage my wounded pride after," he swallowed hard before saying, "after Samantha left me."

He stood and stared at nothing beyond the open bedroom door. "I have seen Samantha only once since then and, as implausible as it sounds, it was during my wedding trip. I saw her at one of those resorts in what is now West Virginia and asked her why she left me. When I learned that it was my own mother who told her that I intended not to marry her but to make her my mistress, I realized what a blind fool I had been. But there was nothing to be done about it then. I have not seen Samantha since, and have driven all thoughts of her from my mind."

He gazed down at Caroline. "I hope you understand now why I was such a lout when we first met. My experience with the ladies has been less than inspiring, and I vowed never to risk that again." He reached down and touched her hair in a tentative gesture. "But you taught me to trust and to love again."

Not wanting to react to the thrill of his touch, Caroline dried her tears.

Philip watched her for a few seconds before walking to the window again and stared at the flickering campfires on the front lawn. "I swear to you on my honor, Carrie, I did not play you false. Do you believe me?"

She lowered the handkerchief from her eyes. "I—I'm not sure. At least not as certain as I was a short time ago."

"Would it have made a difference if you had known this from the beginning?"

She thought a long time before answering, "It would have made a difference. Yes. But I'm not certain about that either."

"And now that you know the truth?"

"Honestly, Philip," she cried out, "don't you think I have a right to feel dirty and betrayed? I gave you several opportunities to tell me all this. I even asked you if there was someone else and you said 'no'."

Philip slammed his fist against the wall and swore under his breath. Calming himself, he said in a controlled voice, "As I recall, you asked if I was in love with someone else. The answer to that question was then, and still is, a resounding no. For the last three years, I have not considered myself married. She was never a wife to me. I believe marriage is about more than physical intimacy. It is also about sharing and emotional intimacy."

"And trust," Caroline said in a soft voice.

Hanging his head low, he mumbled, "Yes, and being deserving of that trust." He hesitated during the ensuing silence before going to her and kneeling beside the chair. "Sweetheart, you must believe that I never intended to hurt you. I would die before I ever harmed you. My only thought is to love and protect you."

Clearing his throat, he continued, "There is something else I have not told you. I tried on several occasions to learn something about Morgan's whereabouts, but there was no record of him in Washington or in Richmond. I thought that once we knew something definite, we could continue planning our future together." He placed a tentative hand on her arm. "Does that sound as though my intentions were less than honorable?"

Caroline felt the trembling in his fingers as they rested on her arm. After regarding him for several moments, she stood. "If you will excuse me, I have a great deal of thinking to do."

"Sweetheart, wait. Please." Rising, he hurried across the room and stood close behind her. "I have something more to say."

She stopped in the doorway and waited. His warm breath made the skin on the nape of her neck tingle.

"First of all," he said in a husky voice, "I want to assure you again that I did not set out to deceive you. Haven't I proven many times how much I love you? Haven't I provided you with food and necessities, even at the risk of being arrested for giving aid to the enemy? Didn't I shoot one of my own men to protect your honor?"

He caressed a lock of her hair. "I can't bear the thought of losing you, Carrie. I love you. I still want to marry you. And I will continue seeing to your welfare as long as I have the power to do so."

Trembling and uncertain, Caroline tried not to respond to his caress, or to the desperation in his voice. Instead of throwing herself into his arms, she said in an unsteady voice, "Thank you, Philip, but that will no longer be necessary," and strode across the hall to her own room.

Chapter 28

SLEEPLESS AND FRUSTRATED, Philip paced around his room
and swore at himself for failing to act when he had the opportunity to
tell Caroline about Elizabeth. Stupid, stupid! he muttered to himself.
And now Caroline is suffering because of my cowardice.

When he threw himself onto his cot sometime around two o'clock,
he heard Caroline pacing overhead and thought, she must be as
miserable as I am. He lay on the cot, his arms folded behind his head,
picturing her in a flowing nightgown as she walked around her room.

He sat up on the edge of the cot. Damn it, I'm going up there right
now and end this once and for all. I will tell her—what? Hell, if she
doesn't want me, I cannot force myself on her.

He lay back on the cot and prayed that by morning, she had decided
to forgive him, and not end it between them.

Caroline wrung her hands in torment. Several times, she walked
to the door and gripped the knob. I will go down there and tell Philip
that it doesn't matter. Nothing matters as long as we are together. I

want him to hold me and assure me that nothing exists but our love. Unbidden, she recalled his surprised expression when she mentioned his wife.

Sighing in resignation, she crawled into bed.

Shortly before dawn, a familiar gagging sound awakened her. She sat up with a start. Floating before her horrified eyes was the spectral figure of Dorothea, dangling from a rope attached to nothing, staring at her with glazed, unseeing eyes.

Philip had just pulled his suspenders onto his shoulders when he heard Caroline's cry and running footsteps. Remembering her nightmare, he realized that in her present state of mind, it was bound to recur.

He ran out of his room, up the stairs two at a time and rapped softly on her door. "Carrie, are you all right?"

"Yes," she whispered.

"Open the door, please, so I can see you."

After a long pause, she opened the door a crack and peered out, her eyes dark and sunken from exhaustion. "It was the nightmare again," she said in a feeble voice.

Philip felt his heart melt within him. "Let me come in, sweetheart, and hold you until you feel better."

"No. I have to think with my head, not my heart. If I let you in, I won't be able to do that."

"Sweetheart, you cannot expect me to leave you like this, knowing how distressed you are."

Tears welled in her eyes. "Oh, Philip, if we go on with it, I will be a marked woman. With your being divorced and who knows what my status is, we will not be received in polite society."

He struck his fist against the doorjamb and swore, "Damn polite society! And damn what people think."

Caroline recoiled from his outburst. "I'm sorry, Philip."

She started to close the door, hesitated, then called to him after he had started down the hall. "Philip, wait. You mentioned last evening that you had good news you wanted to share with me. What was it?"

He stopped halfway down to the landing and looked up at her. He thought a moment then shrugged. "Nothing important. Colonel Graves informed me that I am in line for promotion to brigadier general."

A smile started across her lips. "I would hardly call that nothing."

"It doesn't matter," he answered in a flat voice. "I declined the promotion. I have no ambitions for a military career. I want to stay with the men I joined up with." He raised his eyes to her as she leaned over the stair railing, listening. "But mostly I wanted to stay here with you," he finished in a soft voice before continuing down the steps.

Wes, barefoot and clad only in his long johns, met Philip at the foot of the stairs. "I heard a commotion. What happened?"

"One of Caroline's recurring nightmares," Philip replied. As he started past Wes toward his room, it occurred to him that here might be the source of his trouble. Turning, he said in an icy voice, "Well, my friend, I hope you are satisfied."

Wes gave him a baffled frown. "What are you talking about?"

"You know damned well what I'm talking about. You never did approve of my involvement with Caroline so yesterday you saw an opportunity to do something about it. Well, your plan worked beautifully, Major. She saw Elizabeth's letter." Philip brought his face close to Wes'. "Why, I wonder, would Caroline go through my mail when she has never done that before? It is my guess that someone guided her to it."

"Wait a minute. Are you telling me that Miss Caroline did not know you were married?" Wes rolled his eyes in disbelief. After reflecting a moment, he said, "As I recall the events of yesterday morning, I was reading my own mail when she came onto the porch. She asked if you received any mail and offered to take it to your office. I had no idea there was anything else in that packet besides your newspapers. I assure you, that was all I said or did. What you do is your own damned business and, as far as I'm concerned, you can go to hell."

Wes slammed into his room, leaving Philip standing in the hall with a wedge between him and his friend, and a widening gap between himself and the woman he loved so dearly.

He checked the hall clock. Nearly six o'clock. "I have to get away," he muttered. "Go somewhere. Anywhere."

After dressing and shaving quickly, he tossed down a cup of coffee in the mess tent, left hasty instructions with Lieutenant Hasselbeck, and tore off on his horse toward City Point.

Chapter 29

INSIDE ONE OF the many dingy saloons serving the military in City Point, Philip elbowed his way to the bar and ordered a bottle. He paid no heed to the other officers standing at the plank bar, imbibing and gossiping, or to those who sat at the rough-hewn tables. The place smelled of sweat—human and animal. A cloud of cigar and pipe smoke hung in the stagnant air. Several camp followers approached Philip but he rejected them with a surly reply and returned to his bottle.

By mid-afternoon, the effects of hard drinking overtook him. Bleary-eyed and disheveled, he staggered out of the saloon and down the dusty road toward Union headquarters on the Eppes plantation. Reeling, he stumbled to the tent of a very surprised Colonel Austin Graves who caught Philip before he collapsed.

"My God, man," Colonel Graves said, "you look as if you've been drinking with a vengeance. You'd better come inside and sleep it off."

"My intentions 'xactly," Philip slurred.

"I have never seen you so blind drunk. What the hell happened?"

"I needed a few drinks to forget," Philip mumbled before crumpling mindlessly onto the cot.

Austin looked in on Philip later that evening, and again before retiring himself. Once during the night, Philip bolted from the cot and vomited into the pail outside the tent flap. The rest of the night, he spent perspiring, moaning, and muttering in his sleep.

The next day, Austin shook Philip's shoulder to rouse him. "Philip, wake up. It's already past noon."

Philip struggled to sit up on the edge of his cot and moaned about his throbbing head.

"You look wretched, man. I'll have my orderly bring a tub of water for a bath and suggest that you make use of my razor." Austin indicated the wash stand and mirror. "By the way, do you have any recollection of paying a visit to the bucket outside?"

Philip gave him a blank look. "Was I sick?" he managed to ask, despite his dry, raspy throat. "I don't remember a thing."

"You also mumbled a lot in your sleep."

Philip kept his bloodshot eyes fixed on the tent floor. "Sorry. I hope I didn't keep you awake."

"Not much. You just babbled about all of them being alike."

Philip rubbed his eyes with his knuckles but offered no response to Austin's remark. After bathing gingerly in cold water, he scraped the stubble from his face. Studying the age lines around his blood-shot eyes in the shaving mirror, he thought, *Good grief, I look older than my thirty two years. Women certainly have a way of aging a man.*

In his uniform, freshly brushed by Austin's orderly, with his boots shined, Colonel Philip Creighton appeared a bit more presentable. Very carefully, and while trying not to disturb his throbbing head, he made his way to the mess tent for several cups of coffee. *Even army coffee will be welcome,* he decided. He took a seat in the mess tent with his back to the river to protect his eyes from the sun's offending glare. A hand on the shoulder roused him from his stupor.

"Are you back among the living?" Colonel Graves asked.

"For God's sake, Austin," Philip groaned, "speak softly."

Austin sat on the bench beside him, concern etched on his face. "What happened?"

Philip hitched his shoulders. "What always happens—a woman."

"Did you get a Dear John letter?"

"I don't want to talk about it," Philip said, and stared into his empty tin cup.

Austin motioned for a private to pour them more coffee. "Why don't you stay here for another day? Perhaps you will feel better by then, and hopefully you'll look a hell of a lot better."

"Do I look that bad?" he croaked before gulping down more hot coffee.

"Let's just say that more strong coffee and a good night's sleep will do wonders for you. By the way, have you changed your mind about that promotion to brigadier?"

"No, I want to stay with my company. Besides, I don't deserve a general's star."

Next morning, Philip approached Austin in the mess tent, still looking haggard. "Thanks for taking me in, Austin. Sorry about," he shrugged, "well, about everything."

Austin studied him closely. Dark sagging bags were evident beneath Philip's eyes. His hair was still wet from bathing. "Will you be all right?"

Philip waved his hand in dismissal. "Forget everything I said yesterday. I'll handle it." Shaking Austin's hand, he added, "I don't know how I will ever thank you, my friend."

"No need to try. I hope you get everything straightened out."

So do I, Philip thought.

Half an hour later, Philip arrived at Howard Hill and thought with wonder, I never dreamed that riding up this driveway would be so difficult. He glanced up toward Caroline's bedroom windows but saw no movement of curtains. No smiling face peered out at him.

After watering his horse, he entered the back door and found two unfamiliar officers seated in the entry hall near the front door. He nodded first to the one who had had his head in a book, then to the other who smiled languidly in return.

Lieutenant Hassselbeck followed Philip into his office and informed him that the two replacement officers arrived yesterday afternoon. "Do you want to see them now?" he asked.

Jesse's question, that seemed so loud, intensified his headache, and he winced. "Might as well." At least, he mused, it will occupy my mind for a while. "Have the enlisted replacements arrived yet?" he asked.

"No, sir, but I heard their paperwork arrived at headquarters. They should be here any day."

"Very well. Give me a few minutes before sending these two in." He ignored his aide's not so discreet scrutiny of his haggard appearance.

Philip brushed his teeth and threw more cold water on his face before sorting through the paperwork that had accumulated during his two-day absence. At the two officers' approach, he returned their salute and advised them to be at ease.

"Good afternoon, gentlemen. I am Colonel Creighton." Or what is left of me, he thought, and ran a furry tongue over his lips. "Welcome to the Strickland Volunteers."

The first man, with dark serious eyes, was rumpled and pudgy, giving the appearance of a ripe pear. Philip doubted that even the finest tailored suit would improve this man's appearance. His thinning, dull brown hair exposed most of his shiny scalp. "Sir, Lieutenant Francis Warden, from Michigan," he said crisply. "My orders, sir."

Philip winced again. Why does everyone have to talk so damned loud? After accepting Warden's orders, he turned his attention to the other officer, who was taller than Warden and thinner, with graying hair. His light blue eyes were merry and mocking.

"Sir, Captain John Chapman, formerly of the One Hundred Seventh New York Volunteers." Chapman handed his orders across the desk.

Philip detected an air of the drinker about him, but thought with an indifferent shrug, I am no better and intend getting worse. After giving their orders a perfunctory glance, he said, "Major Madison will acquaint you with your specific duties. Are there any questions?" He squeezed the bridge of his nose between his thumb and forefinger, hoping to ease the throbbing in his head.

"Not at this time, sir," Warden responded, and snapped to attention.

"Very well. Dismissed." Philip returned their salutes, and took up the chore of wading through the mound of paperwork awaiting his attention.

Chapter 30

AFTER FOUR LONG, lonely days and nights, the realization was inescapable—Caroline missed Philip desperately, and longed to see him again. She had repeatedly gone over everything he had recounted to her. But, she decided finally, *the more I think about it, the more confused I become. Should I seek him out and admit I had over-reacted? Or just. . .*

This is nonsense, she chided herself. *I must do something to occupy myself. I need a walk to clear my head, and if my path should happen to cross his, who is to say it was not an accident?*

Shortly before supper, she bathed and dusted liberally with lilac powder and donned a freshly ironed dress. She descended the stairs and, stopping at the mirror in the front hall, smoothed her hair.

"Well, what have we here?" a voice said behind her. "The mistress of the hall, I presume."

Whirling around with a start, Caroline came face to face with a tall Yankee captain ambling toward her with a drink in his hand. He smiled at her, mischief danced in his eyes.

"How do you do, my dear lady? Captain John Chapman, your most humble servant." He gave her a mocking bow. "And who might you be?"

In the face of his forward manner and the strong smell of liquor, she lifted her chin. "I, sir, am Mrs. Morgan Howard, mistress of Howard Hill."

"Are you under house arrest or anything as romantic as that?" He reached out to touch her. When she jerked her arm away, he chuckled. "My, my, a lady with spirit. May I offer you a drink, my dear?" He saluted her with his glass.

"No, thank you," she replied in her iciest voice.

"Is there anything else I might offer you? I am at your service, day or night."

"I find your conduct offensive, sir." As she spoke to him, she kept backing into Philip's room, hoping against hope that he would be there.

Undaunted, Chapman followed her. "Come now, my dear lady, can't we be friends?" He reached for her again but she sidestepped his grasp. She started to protest again when the other officers spilled through the front door, laughing and talking. Chapman gave her a leering smile and sauntered away.

Wes walked into Philip's office with a concerned frown. "Are you all right, Mrs. Howard?"

"Yes," she said, blinking back tears.

"Were you going in to supper?"

Squaring her shoulders, Caroline said with tears in her eyes, "Yes, I was."

Wes offered his arm. "In that case, allow me to escort you to the dining room."

After that encounter, Caroline did her best to avoid the obnoxious captain but he seemed to make it his business to watch for her and torment her with his indecent suggestions. Alone and frightened, she wondered what she would do now that she no longer enjoyed Philip's protection.

***

While reading the latest dispatches from headquarters, Philip heard someone clear his throat. He looked up and saw Wes stepping into the shade of the octagon-shaped gazebo.

"May I speak to you a moment, sir?" Wes asked with studied formality.

Philip indicated a seat across from him. "Certainly, Major."

Taking a seat, Wes said in a low voice, "Sir, a situation has arisen concerning the lady of the house, and I feel it is my duty to advise you of my intentions before taking action."

Philip put the dispatches aside and leaned forward, suddenly interested. "What about her?"

"Captain Chapman has been making unwelcome advances to the lady. He's made improper suggestions, and has even put his hands on her which causes her much distress. Because of my regard for her, I cannot tolerate such behavior from one of our own men. It is my intention to confront him. My request is that you support me, should the matter become ugly."

Philip's expression turned dark. "Your regard for the lady in question is exceeded only by my own. Thank you for bringing this to my attention. However, you needn't worry about it. I will see to the matter personally." His mind raced to form the outline of a plan. "Isn't there a dinner planned by the officers this evening?"

"Yes, sir," Wes answered with a questioning expression.

"See that Caroline is invited. Do or say whatever you must to ensure her presence."

"Yes, sir." Wes rose to leave.

Philip held up his hand. "Wes, wait a moment, please. I need to speak to you." He paused, searching for the right words. "I cannot begin to say how sorry I am about the way I lashed out at you the other morning. I was upset because I had just had words with Caroline. You were handy so I vented my anger on you." He shook his head. "Had I been sensible at the time, I would have realized that you are too good a friend to have done anything so petty. Hell, the truth is, I miss our talks in the evening over drinks."

With a bemused expression, Wes said, "Hell, I can do better than that—I miss you too. I am relieved you brought this up, Philip. If you had not said something soon, I would have. When I calmed down and thought about it, I realized that you must have been reacting out of anguish."

"I know you don't approve of my involvement with Caroline, but this is not just a wartime fling. I love her and I intend to marry her."

"I'm glad." Wes offered his hand. "She is obviously good for you and no one knows better than I how much you deserve this happiness."

The friends shook hands and clapped each other on the shoulder.

"I don't know how you tolerate me," Philip said with a crooked smile.

"Somebody has too."

Chapter 31

AT SUNSET THAT evening, Philip stood in the door to his office, rubbing his sweaty palms on his trousers. Taking a deep breath, he marched down the hall toward the dining room, praying that his little plan would not blow up in his face, as everything else seemed to.

Upon entering the dining room, Philip saw Chapman at Caroline's side, offering to escort her to a place at the table. When he took her arm, her immediate reaction was to jerk it away. Red-hot anger flashed before Philip's eyes, making him want to shoot Chapman between his shoulder blades right then and have done with it.

Instead, he said in a controlled voice, "Gentlemen, forgive my tardiness," and walked straight to Caroline. With his heart in his throat, he took her hand and said in his most ardent voice, "My dear, you look lovely this evening." Brushing his lips near her cheek, he whispered, "Smile and act as if you are happy to see me."

"Thank you, Philip," she murmured, and squeezed his hand.

Philip assisted Caroline to her chair and took his seat opposite her at the head of the table. Jesse Hasselbeck and Wes sat on one side of the table, with Lieutenant Warden and Captain Chapman across from them.

"So, gentlemen, have I interrupted anything of interest?" Philip asked, casting an inquiring gaze on each officer before coming to rest on the errant captain.

Wes spoke up. "Not really, sir. Captain Chapman and I were just discussing sound military procedure, like surveying a situation before moving into an unknown area, to see how the land lays, so to speak."

The other officers exchanged puzzled glances at this curious remark.

Philip lifted an eyebrow to acknowledge Wes' meaning. To Chapman, he said, "That is very wise of you, Captain. One cannot go wrong following sound military procedure."

Chapman flushed, but said nothing. Message received—stay away from the Colonel's lady.

Philip stole a hesitant glance at Caroline and was relieved to see a smile that expressed her gratitude to him for putting Chapman in his place. Feeling the tension of the last five days ebb from his shoulders, he said, smiling at last, "So, my dear, what has Cassie prepared for our dinner?"

"Chicken and dumplings, I believe."

"Good. I'm starving." Their eyes met and held for a brief moment. "Hungrier than I've been in days."

After dinner, Philip excused himself and went directly to his office. He felt he should no longer presume upon Caroline's good graces, now that his confidence in her ability to discern what he was about with Chapman had been confirmed. With the latest edition of The Crossroads Herald in his lap, he pondered the evening's events and decided that Caroline seemed a willing accomplice in his plot to rescue her from Chapman's advances. But, he couldn't help wondering as he picked up the newspaper, how willing was she otherwise? And, more importantly, how would they proceed from here?

After an hour or more, the hall clock striking eleven roused him from sleep. The newspaper lay crumpled on his lap and the uneasy feeling that he was not alone made him sit up with a start. She was standing in the shadows near the door.

"I'm sorry. Did I disturb you?" Caroline asked in a hesitant voice.

"Never. I must have dozed off while reading. Please, come in," he said, offering her a chair.

"No, I can't. I just came to thank you for your gallantry this evening."

Is thanking me all she has on her mind, he wondered, coming here at this hour, with her hair down around her shoulders? And her wrapper tied up tight to show off her tiny waist?

Delighting in her scent, he clasped her hand in his. "Wes told me about Chapman, and how he had been harassing you. That's why I concocted that little charade at dinner. When I walked into the dining room and saw him put his hands on you, I wanted to shoot the bastard."

With a sheepish grin, he added, "I must also admit that when I approached you, I expected you to slap me and tell me to go to hell."

She returned his smile. "Oh, no, I wouldn't have done that, even though I too was nervous about having dinner with you. Oh, Philip," she whispered, "how can I ever thank you for rescuing me from that horrible man?"

"Just say that you forgive me and that it's not over between us." He leaned closer, kissed her lightly on the cheek and slid his lips down onto her neck.

Leaning into his caress, she said, "It is I who beg your forgiveness. After all you shared with me the other day, I understand your reticence about trusting your heart to another woman, especially to one you hardly know. I can now appreciate the difficulty you must have felt in admitting that you love me."

He shook his head. "No, I was wrong not to have told you the truth from the beginning. Our love cannot be based on lies or secrets. Carrie, I can't tell you how sorry I am for the pain it caused you."

"That's all behind us now." Caroline slid her arms around his waist, lifted her face and looked him in the eye. "I love you, Philip Creighton. You belong to me. You always have."

A smile curled his lips. "Yes, ma'am, I certainly do. But that is mostly because you are so damned persistent." He kissed the tip of her nose. "And so irresistible."

"Seriously, Philip, I am sorry for doubting you." Narrowing her eyes, she regarded him intently. "That reminds me. I saw you briefly the other day when you returned from wherever you went. You looked so haggard, as though you had been drinking heavily. I felt even more guilt because I knew that I had brought it on."

She held up her hand to silence him. "No, let me finish. I know you felt that I doubted your intentions toward me, and your honor. I vow that will never happen again. As for your offer to tell me about your life before we met, you don't have to say a word. As far as we are concerned, there is no past. Besides, how can I doubt the love of someone who refused a general's star just to remain near me?"

"A general's star is a mere trifle compared to what I would have lost by obtaining it."

"I love you, Philip. Nothing or no one will ever come between us."

He bent and kissed her more tenderly than he ever had before.

As they stood locked in an intensely intimate embrace that went beyond the physical, Philip thought with sudden panic, yes, we will put the past behind us and look to our future together.

Provided I survive this damned war.

Chapter 32

BY LATE SEPTEMBER, hostilities had diminished along the Petersburg defense line. With the calm, came boredom, and the soldiers soon grew weary of the endless daily training. A few landed in the stockade for fighting or other infractions. Many followed more relaxing pursuits, such as swimming in the Appomattox River, doing their laundry, writing letters, sewing missing buttons on their blouses, or playing baseball games with other companies.

The Strickland Volunteers decided to try their hand at the new game of baseball with a Pennsylvania infantry regiment. Philip arrived after the game had started at an improvised field off City Point Road southeast of Howard Hill. Lounging under a tree, he laughed as the teams exchanged cat-calls and taunts at the bumbling play from both teams.

What he found even more amusing were the antics of Lt. Jesse Hasselbeck. Acting as the coach, he stormed around the field, offering advice here or berating a mistake there. Philip marveled at the change in his usually quiet demeanor, and wondered if this really was the taciturn lieutenant he had known for nearly four years.

Col. Austin Graves dropped down onto the ground beside Philip and thrust a bottle of root beer into his hand. "How is the game going?"

Philip accepted the cool drink with thanks. "I don't know a damned thing about this game and wonder if anyone out there does. The most enjoyable part is watching Jesse Hasselbeck. Since I've known him, Jesse has never connected four words together at the same time. Today, he's acting like a madman." He took a long pull on the root beer. "Thanks for this. It tastes good in this heat."

"I thought you would enjoy it." Austin leaned against the tree trunk and drew up his knees. "What do you hear from Matthew?"

"I got a letter about a week ago saying that Sherman has taken Atlanta and ordered the civilian population to evacuate. Our troops now occupy the city and are finally able to rest. I pray Matt is safe and well."

"I'm sure he is, or—"

A sudden burst of activity on the field of play distracted Philip and Austin from their conversation. Standing, they gazed intently at the group of men gathered at one of the bases. Jesse Hasselbeck rose up out of the huddle and motioned frantically for Philip.

Throwing down his bottle, Philip ran across the field, leaving a trail of dust in his wake. "What's wrong?" he called.

"It's the Major," Jesse said. "His arm is hurt pretty bad."

Philip knelt beside Wes. "What happened?"

Dazed, and obviously embarrassed, Wes presented a comic figure, sitting there on the ground with blood trickling down his right cheek. "I don't know," he muttered, and stared at his right wrist that had already begun to swell.

"We'd better get you to a doctor," Philip said, laughing, and helped Wes to his feet.

Hearing the sound of approaching horses on the driveway, Caroline peered out through the curtains of her bedroom windows. She saw Philip and Wes riding slowly toward the rear of the house. It appeared that Wes' arm was wrapped in something like a bandage or a sling.

She checked her appearance in the mirror before hurrying down the stairs to inquire about Wes' condition. At the foot of the stairs, she heard a buggy pull up in front of the house. Peering through the glass panel beside the front door, her heart leapt into her throat at the sight of Reverend Jedediah Parsons alighting from his buggy.

"Oh, damn," she said aloud, mimicking Philip's army language, "what is he doing here? And without his sister?"

Recalling his unsettling actions toward her on previous occasions, she decided that the old lecher was not going to intimidate her in her own house. Squaring her shoulders, she walked resolutely to the front door that stood open, as it usually did during warm weather. "Good afternoon, Reverend," she greeted him with a forced smile.

The squat little minister removed his hat and drawled, "Good day, my dear Miz Caroline."

The redness of his face, quite obvious today, confirmed what she had always suspected—that he was a secret drinker. His left eye, cocked at an odd angle, combined with a constant leer that made him even more repugnant.

"Where is Miss Lucille?" she asked, looking beyond his shoulder.

"My sister was unable to accompany me today." He strolled into the front hall, appearing to Caroline like a man with a purpose. "After hearing about the loss of our beloved sister Dorothea, I felt it my Christian duty to call on you to offer my condolences."

Backing away, she offered her hand to discourage any attempt to kiss her. "I appreciate your concern, but it was not necessary to travel all this way. May I offer you some tea?"

"Tea? My dear, how did you acquire such a luxury?"

"It was a gift."

"Oh? Well, in that case," he said, leering again, "shall we go into the parlor?"

"It is no longer the company parlor. The Yankee officers use it for their quarters."

He turned an incredulous look on her. "Yankees? Right here in the house with you? My dear, how can you permit such a thing? To have them out there in front of your home and on the grounds is outrageous enough, but in your own house."

"The Union army did not require my permission. I can assure you that I am quite safe. My rooms upstairs are off limits to the soldiers." And, she thought with a twinge, there is a dead Yankee to prove it.

"Well, I suppose that arrangement is acceptable. Although, I cannot imagine how you can abide having those bluebellies in the house."

"They have been very kind, even offering us their protection. They have also provided us with food that we would never have been able to afford, had it been available. Shall we go in?" she asked, indicating the way to the dining room.

"Perhaps we should retire to your rooms upstairs, then."

"No," she responded more sharply than intended, "the dining room is more convenient." Upon entering, she said to Cassie, "Reverend Parsons has come to call. Please bring in some refreshments."

Nodding, Cassie stopped setting the table and hurried to the kitchen. A few moments later, she appeared bearing a tea tray, complete with small squares of warm corn bread.

"My, my, such luxury," Reverend Parson commented, and proceeded to gorge himself.

Just as he was about to make another comment, Caroline heard Philip's voice at the back door. Oh no, she thought, he can't come in now, of all times.

"Carrie," he said, laughing, before he reached the dining room door, "you should see poor Wes. He's. . ." Philip stopped in mid-sentence at the sight of a man in black minister's garb, about to put a bite of cornbread into this mouth.

A quick glance at Reverend Parsons' crimson face assured Caroline that he'd heard Philip address her in a familiar manner. Mortified, she rose slowly and made the awkward introduction. "Colonel Creighton, may I introduce my pastor, Reverend Parsons. Reverend, this is Colonel Creighton, the Union commander here."

"Reverend," Philip said halfheartedly, and gave Caroline a penitent look.

Parsons inclined his head ever so slightly to acknowledge Philip's presence.

"I will not intrude upon you and your visitor, Miss Caroline. If you will excuse me," Philip mumbled, and backed out of the room.

"It seems it is I who has intruded upon your assignation, Miz Caroline." Reverend Parsons indicated the table setting for two. Summoning all the ecclesiastical dignity his five foot two inch frame afforded him, he continued in his holier-than-thou voice, "As your pastor, it is my duty to remind you of the dangers of consorting with the enemy, even if that enemy does provide you with the niceties of life. I cannot bring myself to think how you must repay him."

Livid now with anger, Caroline gripped the edge of the table to support her wobbly knees. "Reverend Parsons," she began in a strained voice, "I must ask you to leave my house." Gaining courage, she continued, "I have not forgotten the indecent overtures you have made to me in the past and I suspect that you came here today believing I would be alone and vulnerable."

"Now, Miz Caroline," he offered in a conciliatory tone, "you are incorrect when you say that I have made indecent overtures to you."

"No, sir, I am not," she replied, raising her voice. "I must ask you again to leave."

Philip reappeared in the doorway, his face dark as a thundercloud. "Miss Caroline, are you having a problem?"

Trembling, she swallowed her rage. "No, Colonel. Reverend Parsons was just leaving."

Parsons assessed Philip's threatening presence, with his hand dangerously close to his side arm. "Yes, Colonel, I'm afraid a minor disagreement has arisen. However, I will require a safe conduct pass back through the Yankee lines."

"See my orderly on the front porch. Good day to you, sir," Philip said in an icy voice.

As the minister began his hasty retreat, Philip remained in the door way, forcing the man to squeeze his way past him. Safely in the hall, Parsons turned a malevolent eye on Caroline. "This episode is not over, Miz Caroline." Claiming his hat from the hall table, he scurried away.

"What the hell was that all about?" Philip demanded after hearing the front door slam.

"He made remarks about—about us," she said with a quivering chin. "He even had the temerity to preach at me."

"What gives him the right to judge you?"

Caroline waved her hands before her as if to clear the air. "Please, don't. It's over." Slumping against the wall, she covered her eyes with a trembling hand. "Oh, Philip, that man's filthy mind has dirtied what we share. Will it always be like this for us?"

"No, I will not allow it," he assured her as he took her into his arms.

Leaning against his chest, she dabbed at her tears then looked up into the tender concern in his eyes. "What on earth prompted you to come back into the house just when I needed you?"

"I was talking to Wes in the gazebo when Cassie came running out to tell me that she heard the two of you arguing. She asked me to intervene. I gather that Cassie has no use for the Reverend either. Why is that?"

Caroline hesitated before answering honestly about the minister's prior improper advances. "He denied it, of course, and said that I had misunderstood his intentions. But I saw something in his eyes back then that disturbed me. I have tried to recall when I may have given him the slightest indication that I desired a romantic encounter with him, but can recall none."

"Do you think that was his intention today?"

Still teary-eyed, she nodded. "He even suggested that we go up to my room after I told him we could not use the parlor." She reached for his hand. "I nearly died when you called out to me before you knew he was here."

Philip flushed. "I am so sorry. I didn't notice that you had a visitor when Wes and I returned. "

"I doubt you would have. He must have followed you and Wes up the driveway. That reminds me, was that a sling I saw on Wes' arm?"

Philip nodded with a smile. "He sustained some minor injuries on the field of sport." At her quizzical look, he added, "It occurred during a baseball game. I was telling him that he qualifies for a medical furlough when Cassie came for me."

"I'm so glad she did," Caroline said with relief. "I don't know how much longer I could have stood up to him. Look at me, I am still trembling."

He took both her hands to steady them. "Sweetheart, I cannot tell you how sorry I am for causing you this distress and embarrassment. I swear to you, if that ugly bastard ever shows up again, I will shoot him on sight."

Caroline smiled, despite being distressed. "That is gallant of you, Colonel darling, but I don't think I'll be bothered by him again."

Chapter 33

A QUIET, HUMID pall hung over Howard Hill on this lazy early October afternoon. Caroline sat by her bedroom window, watching the activity in the front yard, and realized with a start that she no longer thought of these men as the enemy. A few of them reclined under shade trees reading letters from home, or were writing to loved ones. An enterprising sergeant was doing a brisk business giving haircuts, after a terse comment from Philip about seeing to their appearances. For his part, Philip had joined his staff for a swim in the Appomattox River, while Wes was still enjoying his medical furlough at his home in Pennsylvania.

Caroline decided to use this rare opportunity from her never-ending chores to wash her hair. But Philip's absence, even during this much-deserved respite on his part, left her feeling alone and bored. *I never realized until now,* she thought, *how safe I feel now that there is so much activity on the place, especially after the isolation and loneliness of these last few years.*

With a sigh, she ran the brush through her freshly washed hair and complained to Cassie, "There is no breeze today. The air is so heavy I will never get my hair dry before Philip gets back."

"Gimme that brush, Miz Caroline. I'll see what I can do. You sure do have pretty hair," Cassie said as she pulled the brush through Caroline's damp tresses. "So soft and curly."

The sound of carriage wheels on the crushed shell driveway drew Casssie's attention from Caroline's hair. Squinting through the curtains, she gasped, "Glory be, if it ain't young Willie Matheny and his ma, Miz Alice. And they got that Miz Lucille Parsons with 'em. What you suppose they want, comin' all the way out here?"

Caroline clutched at her throat. "Quick, pin my hair up, then go down and let them in. Bring up a tray later."

Cassie pinned Caroline's hair with fumbling fingers before hurrying to answer the door.

Presently, a heavily perspiring Miss Lucille Parsons entered Caroline's bedroom, clad in a dark threadbare afternoon dress. Sweat-soaked tendrils of black hair escaped from under her straw bonnet. Removing her lace gloves, she took in her surroundings with one sweep of her beady black eyes. Her chin was drawn down into her scrawny turkey neck in the familiar attitude of disapproval of all she surveyed.

Alice Matheny, cousin to Morgan Howard, followed behind her. Painfully thin as a result of deprivation and stress from the bombardments, she too was clad in a dress that had seen better days. Her mended lace gloves did nothing to hide her freckled hands, no strangers to hard work. An old straw gardening hat sat askew on her dull brown hair.

"Caroline, my poor dear," Alice said, and embraced her cousin warmly. Her guileless hazel eyes brimmed over with emotion. "I have been so wretched thinking about you out here all alone in this big house. And when I heard about poor Aunt Dorothea, I was nearly overcome."

"Thank you, Alice." Still holding Alice's hand, Caroline accepted a peck on the cheek and a murmur of condolence from Miss Lucille. "But as you could see when you arrived, I am hardly alone."

"I declare," Miss Lucille huffed, still out of breath from her climb up the stairs, "I will never get used to the sight of Yankee uniforms so near Petersburg. I was frightened out of my wits with them all around us on the porch until Cassie answered the door."

"They won't harm you," Caroline assured her. "Please, have a seat. You don't know how happy I am to see family and friends again."

Alice dabbed the perspiration that shone on her upper lip. "I was so desperate to see you again that I begged Willie to drive us out here. He left us out front and said he would return in an hour." She leaned closer and confided, "He did not want to stay around all these Yankees."

"I hope to see him when he comes back for you. Tell me, is it as bad in town as I have heard?"

"Oh, Caroline," Alice moaned, "I cannot begin to recount the horrors. Thank goodness, we live on the west side of town. It is not so bad there, but the east side has been severely damaged by the shelling. The town is nearly deserted. Folks are leaving in droves, taking what few possessions they can carry."

"That's right," Miss Lucille agreed and, not to be outdone, added with pride, "but by some miracle, the gas works has been spared. Most of the tobacco warehouses have been damaged, and one of the iron works has had to close because of severe damage."

Alice nodded. "Then there was that nasty business in July over by Blandford Church when those awful Yankees blew up our boys in their sleep." She waved her fan furiously. "It has been such a nightmare."

"Yes," Caroline said, "I remember that explosion quite vividly. It nearly knocked me out of my bed."

"And if that weren't bad enough," Miss Lucille picked up the narrative, "this drought has withered our kitchen gardens away. We have nothing to eat ourselves, much less have anything to tithe when the quartermaster comes round to collect food for our boys."

"How dreadful," Caroline whispered, distressed by their revelations.

"Willie pesters me every day to join up," Alice said, her voice wavering, "but I cannot let him go. What with losing his father two years ago, Willie is all I have left."

"Why should you sacrifice your only son?" Caroline said, patting Alice's hand. "Who will take care of you when this awful war is over?"

Miss Lucille bent an indignant gaze on Caroline. "Caroline Howard, do you realize that you are advocating disloyalty to the Glorious Cause by telling Alice to keep Willie at home?"

Caroline lifted her chin. "I know perfectly well what I am saying. If we can spare one mother the agony of losing a son, then I say spare her."

"Well!" Miss Lucille sputtered.

"I am reluctant to let him go," Alice drawled in an apologetic voice, "but my conscience bothers me for being so selfish."

"You are not selfish. Far from it. Willie is your only son." Caroline brushed away a tear. "I feel justified in offering that opinion because I—I have no one left." Turning to direct a comment to Miss Lucille, she noticed the spinster's eyes radiating about the room. So, her evil brother told her about Philip and now she is looking for tangible evidence.

Miss Lucille pursed her lips and said in a wheedling voice, "Caroline dear, we will need a safe conduct pass back through the lines. Perhaps that Yankee colonel of yours that my brother spoke of will oblige us."

"Any of the officers will sign a pass for you," she answered calmly. "You need only ask."

"Me? Ask a Yankee for a favor? I think not. You, on the other hand, seem on intimate terms with them. Why don't you ask?"

Caroline was casting about for a tart response just as Cassie brought in the tray. "Thank you, Cassie. Will you pour for us?" she said, not trusting herself to refrain from throwing hot tea into Miss Lucille's smirking face.

"Tea?" Alice exclaimed, staring wide-eyed at the goodies on the tray.

"I couldn't believe it when Jed told me that you served him tea," Miss Lucille chimed in. "And fresh cornbread."

"The Yankee commander has provided us with some necessities. I suppose he feels he owes us that much for having confiscated our home."

Alice frowned thoughtfully as she accepted a cup from Cassie. "I would say he owes you more than a tin of tea for all they have put you through. How can you abide having them around the place?"

"No need to worry. The commander has given strict orders that we are not to be bothered, or any of our property destroyed." She closed her eyes against the memory of gunshots reverberating off these very walls when he shot that horrid man for defying his orders.

"Well, I suppose you are fortunate to have a humane Yankee in charge," Alice conceded.

"I have heard so many horror stories about them, it makes my blood run cold," Miss Lucille said with a shudder. "So, Caroline," she continued, smiling into her tea cup, "tell us more about this dashing Yankee commander of yours. Is he very handsome?"

"Miss Lucille!" Alice gasped. "I am sure Caroline does not look upon that Yankee with any more interest than she does one of her field hands."

"Colonel Creighton has proven himself a gentleman in every regard," Caroline answered in a firm voice. Then couldn't help adding, "By the way, this is Yankee tea, and the cake you are eating was made with Yankee flour. Think what you will of it, I am grateful for all he has done for this family."

"It is certainly obvious that you are not making the necessary sacrifices for the Cause," Miss Lucille declared with a self-righteous sniff.

Caroline sat her cup and saucer aside with a clatter. "How is my starving going to win this war? There are enough people starving as it is, but it does not seem to help. Nothing helps, not even your Starvation Balls I've heard so much about. Or living behind all those bales of cotton you have stacked at the doors and windows of your homes. We cannot withstand their might any longer. They have so much and can assault us with more," she ended in a quivering voice.

"Well!" Miss Lucille jerked her head in disapproval of Caroline's outburst, and placed her own cup on the tray, but not before finishing every last drop of tea and consuming the last cake crumb. "Not only are you eating Yankee food, you are spouting Yankee propaganda. This colonel has obviously brainwashed you." Rising with great ceremony, she announced, "Alice, I believe it is time we take our leave."

Caroline glared at her, hot tears stung her eyelids.

"I am so sorry, dear," Alice said. "Would you like to come into town to live with me?"

"Thank you, no," Caroline said in a strangled voice. "I feel safer here."

"Alice Matheny, you are a fool," Miss Lucille hissed, and looked pointedly at the bed. "Why should Caroline leave the protection of her Yankee colonel and all this Yankee food? If she lived in town, she would have to starve like the rest of us loyal Confederates."

Alice embraced Caroline. "I am so sorry."

"I cannot bear the thought of you and Willie going hungry," Caroline said, distressed. "Let me give you some food. I have so much."

"I appreciate the offer, but anything I'd take would be confiscated by our own boys who have so little themselves. Thank you anyway," Alice added with a hug.

Frowning, Caroline chewed on her lip and considered. "There must be a way."

"What a dolt you are, Alice. If you must accept Caroline's charity, at least use the method our brave Southern ladies employ so successfully. They are able to smuggle food and medicines into their homes, and right under the noses of both armies."

Alice and Caroline looked at her with bewildered expressions.

Miss Lucille pointed to their skirts. "Your hoops, of course. You can secure whatever you want under your skirts. No gentleman would even consider asking a lady to lift her skirts. Including a Yankee, I dare say."

Caroline smiled. "Of course." Taking Alice's hand, she led both ladies downstairs. Miss Lucille remained behind in the entry hall as Caroline and Alice hurried out to the pantry, where they tied cans of beef, small bags of coffee and flour to her hoops.

"If the Yankees catch me," Alice moaned, "they'll surely shoot me."

"No, they won't." Caroline patted Alice's skirts. "There. No one will ever guess."

"Thank you, Caroline. God bless you for your kindness." After kissing Caroline's cheek, Alice walked with deliberate care to the front door where Miss Lucille tapped her foot impatiently.

"Caroline," Miss Lucille demanded through pursed lips, "will you please see to our safe conduct passes? Willie just pulled up in the buggy."

Caroline glared through her tears and thought, you damned hateful witch. How I would love to tell you to go to hell. Instead, she stepped out onto the porch and said in a strained voice, "Lieutenant, will you please see about getting safe conduct passes for these ladies."

"Certainly, ma'am." Lieutenant Hasselbeck tipped his hat to her visitors.

Caroline stood aside, her teary eyes cast down, as he wrote out the passes.

With her safe conduct pass clutched in her gloved hand, Alice walked gingerly toward the waiting buggy. Jumping down from the seat, Willie glowered at the Yankee soldiers on the porch and in the front yard before waving a greeting to Caroline. As he offered to assist his mother up to her seat, she let out a small cry and shook off his hand. He turned to Caroline, hunched his shoulders and spread his hands in a helpless gesture.

Lieutenant Hasselbeck gave Caroline and quizzical look. "Is something wrong with that lady, Mrs. Howard? She walks kind of funny."

"She—she is having back trouble."

Before their buggy reached the main gate, Caroline turned and ran inside, stumbled up the stairs and threw herself onto the bed.

Relaxed and refreshed after his swim, Philip watered his mare and asked a private to rub her down and feed her. Taking a drink from the dipper at the well, his protesting stomach reminded him that he hadn't eaten much today and it was already well past six o'clock.

Before grabbing a bite in the mess tent, he looked into the kitchen to see if Caroline might be there. Instead, he saw Cassie at the worktable, grumbling, and punching her bread dough before setting it out for the morning baking. "I don't know what that dough ever did to you but I must remember never to make you angry at me."

Startled at the sound of his voice, Cassie growled even louder, "She ain't got no right comin' here like that, makin' her cry."

Philip's smile faded. "What are you talking about? Who made who cry?"

"That Miz Lucille Parsons. She come here today with Massah Morgan's cousin Miz Alice Matheny, all talk and meanness, sayin' things to Miz Caroline."

"What kind of things?" he asked, frowning.

"Things 'bout all the food we has to eat and where it come from," she muttered.

He felt hot blood rise to his face. "This Miss Lucille Parsons you mentioned, is she related to that sorry excuse for a preacher who was here about a week ago?"

"Yes, sir. And they is the two evilest people I ever knew. And her tellin' Miz Caroline she ain't no proper Confederate, starvin' like the rest of them."

"Caroline will never starve as long as I am here. Where is she now?"

"Upstairs, cryin' her eyes out since they left." Cassie returned to taking out her anger on the bread dough.

Taking the stairs two at a time, Philip found Caroline sprawled across the bed, sobbing quietly. His anger changed to sympathy at the sight of her distress.

"What happened, sweetheart," he asked with tender concern as he sat on the bed beside her. "Cassie told me your cousin Alice and that Parsons woman were here. What did Miss Parsons say to leave you in this state?"

Caroline sat up and dried her swollen eyes. "Oh, Philip, it must be all over Petersburg by now that I am a scarlet woman."

"I don't ever want to hear you say that again. Besides, what makes her think she is righteous enough to pass judgment on you? That dried up old bitty would mostly likely lift her skirt for the first man who looked at her."

Suppressing a smile at that unlikely event, Caroline pressed her forehead against his shoulder. "You are so naughty to say that. But I have always suspected that she was jealous of me because, at one time, she wanted to marry Morgan herself. I don't think she has ever forgiven me for that."

"There, you see. She is just jealous because you married the man she wanted. And if that weren't enough, you have another adoring man at your feet, hopelessly in love with you. Come now, sweetheart, dry your eyes. And promise me that you will never cry over the likes of her again."

"But she will tell everyone in town about us."

Sensing her torment, he asked, "Does it really matter what they think?"

"A little," she sniffed, and a single tear trickled down her cheek.

Anguished by the heartache represented in that solitary tear, he realized the full import of her situation. Dear God, he thought, what have I done to her?

Drawing her closer, he whispered, "Oh, Carrie, I am so sorry."

Chapter 34

LIEUTENANT HASSELBECK RAPPED on Philip's door and announced, "You have a visitor, sir."

Philip looked up from his desk and saw Col. Austin Graves grinning at him over the Lieutenant's shoulder. Standing with a smile, Philip extended his hand. "Colonel, what a pleasant surprise. It's good to see you, sir. Have a seat."

"Thank you, Colonel." Austin shook Philip's hand before seating himself on the sofa.

"May I offer you a drink?" At Austin's nod, Philip poured two drinks and handed one to him. "Now," he said, sitting in a chair across from his visitor, "what brings you out this way?"

"Nothing much," Austin said between sips. "There's not much going on right now, so I thought I would drop by and say hello. As I was riding up the driveway," he observed, looking around the room, "I couldn't help noticing that you are not exactly living a Spartan existence."

"Hardly," Philip smiled. "But I didn't want to brag about it. I was afraid others might try to move in on us and enjoy the pleasures of plantation life."

"Undoubtedly," Austin agreed. "What's that you have in your hand?"

"Photographs of my staff that were taken last month. I still wasn't seeing very well at that time."

Austin reached for the photograph and studied it carefully. It showed Philip's staff arranged on the front steps, looking sharp in their tunics, polished boots and shiny swords. Philip was seated on the middle step, Wes beside him, Lieutenants Hasselbeck and Warden directly behind him. Captain Chapman sat on the bottom step with First Sergeant Powell and Father O'Boyle.

"Mighty impressive. One would think you could actually win a war with a determined-looking group like that."

"That's a sobering thought," Philip replied with a grin.

After returning the photograph to Philip, Austin held out his glass for a refill. "I thought you might be interested in a bit of information that reached headquarters yesterday. We learned through our sources that the Confederate spy, Rose Greenhow, is dead. Apparently, she had been on a mission to England for Jeff Davis and returned aboard the blockade runner Condor. The ship must have run aground during a storm off the North Carolina coast near Fort Fisher. When her body was recovered, they found that not only was the lady carrying dispatches for Jeff Davis, she also had about two thousand dollars in gold hidden in her clothing."

Philip shook his head. "What a hell of a way to go. When did this happen?"

"More than three weeks ago, around the first of October." Austin lifted his glass in a toast. "Here's to the Rebel Rose."

"And to General Sheridan's continued success in the Shenandoah Valley," Philip added.

"To Sheridan." Austin drained his glass. "His success in the valley will certainly increase Lincoln's chances for defeating McClellan in the election next week."

"Lincoln is sure to get the army vote. All my men have been reading his campaign pamphlets and, I believe, planning to return him to office."

"Yes, Lincoln is very popular with the army. Now," Austin set his glass aside and reached in his tunic pocket, "to a more pleasant subject. I'll wager you thought that we'd forgotten about the commendation you requested for your chaplain back in July."

Philip threw up his hands in mock dismay. "Would I question anything headquarters does?" Chuckling, he added, the bourbon mellowing his expression, "I assumed the request had gotten lost in the monumental paperwork this army is famous for."

"We have been somewhat pre-occupied, what with the war and all," Austin replied with a facetious grin. "During this much-appreciated lull in the action, we managed to catch up on some of our paperwork." He handed the commendation to Philip.

"Thanks, Austin, I appreciate this. I will present it to Brendan during afternoon formation."

During small talk, Philip noticed that Austin's eyes were now evasive and said, "All right, Austin, what's the real reason for your visit?"

Austin cleared his throat, hesitated, then said, "Well, uh, to get right to the point, your name has been mentioned again for promotion to brigadier."

Philip swirled the bourbon in his glass. "My feelings about leaving this company have not changed. Thanks anyway."

"My God, man, this is the second time you have turned down a general's star. Think of your future."

"Commanding a brigade, not to mention the politics of high command, has never appealed to me. Nor do I have plans for a military career. I started the war with these men and I intend to see it through to the end with them."

"Very well," Austin conceded with a shrug. "If you feel that strongly about it, I will inform headquarters that you have not changed your mind." His eyes grew troubled once more. "Philip, I'm afraid there is something else. Some disturbing reports have filtered back to headquarters about your giving aid and comfort to the enemy. To be more precise, that you are providing supplies and food to certain ladies."

"Guilty as charged. But it is not what it seems. The truth is, when we confiscated this place in June, I found five women alone and in desperate need. Two of them are former slaves. I merely provided them with the basics of life to alleviate their misery."

Austin bolted from his chair. "Good grief, don't you realize what headquarters could make of that? There is even talk of an investigation."

"I am fully cognizant that my actions could be considered disloyalty to my oath," Philip replied. "But tell me, Austin, could you ignore a dying old woman? Or another lady who was rail thin from hunger and overwork?"

Austin resumed his seat and muttered, "I suppose I would have found it difficult."

"Of course, you would have. Any gentleman would. The one older lady died from want and starvation just weeks after our arrival. The other lady eventually went mad when her world fell apart and every member of her immediate family died." Philip considered mentioning that Dorothea had actually committed suicide, but decided against it.

"As for the younger lady," he continued, "Dr. Cook is particularly fond of her. To her credit, she has nursed many of our wounded before they were transferred to City Point. My entire staff holds her in high regard. I felt that the very least I could do was repay her kindness by alleviating some of their hardship. After all, she was under no obligation to give comfort or aid to us, the enemy."

"That brings up another point," Austin began tentatively.

"Don't say it, Austin," Philip said, his face suddenly dark. He took a deep breath before continuing in a softer tone, "This is my personal life. Not open to scrutiny. My association with the lady in question does not interfere with my duties. Nor is information passed along. In fact, we do not discuss the war at all.

"I realize my actions may be construed as aiding the enemy, but I am willing to accept the consequences for those actions. If it means a court martial, you can put me in chains right now, but I will continue providing for her welfare."

"I am certain that won't be necessary. Is she the lady who— "

"Caused me to drink myself senseless?" Philip finished the question for him.

Giving Philip an abashed grin, Austin nodded. "I would not have worded it quite that way."

Philip responded with a curt nod. "Those issues have been resolved and all is well again." He stood abruptly and stared out the window facing the front yard. "I can hazard a guess as to who is responsible for this gossip."

Turning back to Austin, he placed his hands on the top of his desk and leaned forward. "Last month, Major Madison informed me that Captain Chapman made indecent advances to the lady in question from the first day he arrived. The Major felt compelled to intervene on several occasions to protect her honor, as well as her safety."

Regarding Austin steadily, he added, "I put that bastard Chapman in his place by letting him know how things stood between Caroline and me. Apparently, he is trying to get back at me by insinuating that I am guilty of nefarious or even treasonous activity."

He reached for the photograph of his staff and handed it to Austin. "This is Chapman," he tapped his finger on Chapman's image, "who I believe started this nonsense."

"Yes," Austin nodded, "I have seen him around headquarters many times. Likes his drinks, and the ladies too, as I recall. I try not to judge people before getting to know them but, in his case, I disliked him at first sight."

"Your instincts were accurate. The man is a poltroon, and to my mind, is certainly not fit to replace Peter Hanford."

Austin leaned back in his seat with a great sigh. "This sounds like an internal matter to me. I hope you understand that I had to ask."

"Of course, and I realize how awkward this must have been for you, given our friendship. You may assure the General, and anyone else who cares to listen, that this matter is not what was represented to them." He retrieved a framed photograph from his desk and held it up for Austin's inspection. "This is Caroline. I love her, and I intend to marry her. And, as you well know, I am not the first Yankee officer to fall under the spell of a southern lady."

Austin studied the image of the smiling young woman with dark, luminous eyes gazing just beyond the camera's lens. "She's lovely. I wish you happiness.

"I think it's only fair to mention," Austin continued, "that when this matter first reached Headquarters, everyone questioned its validity because of your reputation for leadership and honor. I volunteered to make inquiries before any action was taken, especially since you had been nominated for promotion. As for Chapman's rumor mongering, I will take care of that."

"I appreciate your trust—and your loyalty," Philip said with feeling.

"Well," Austin smiled, "now that those issues have been resolved, aren't you going to offer me another drink before afternoon formation?"

Chapter 35

WITH THE PASSING of October into November, the trees were now ablaze with color. A soft golden haze settled over the landscape. The days became shorter, the night air more chill. And Lincoln had been re-elected by a landslide, with the help of his loyal troops in the field.

On this particular evening in late November, Caroline sat by the kitchen fire sipping tea, smiling to herself. The sound of an approaching horse outside the kitchen door caught her ear. She perked up, alert and listening. "I hope that's Philip," she said to Cassie, who bustled about the kitchen. "He said he would return this evening or early in the morning."

"Hello in there. Anybody at home?"

Caroline flew out the kitchen door and into Philip's arms. He held her tight as he kissed her. "I have been counting the hours till your return," she said, returning his kisses. After a few moments, she pointed to his bulging saddlebags. "What have you got in there?"

"You will see soon enough." To Cassie, standing in the doorway smiling at them, he said, "Get your Dutch oven going. I have a job for you." He held up a fat hen and a bag of groceries. "We are celebrating Thanksgiving tomorrow with a chicken, if not a turkey, and all the trimmings I could confiscate. There is some beef in that sack, fresh fruit and coffee, cornmeal and lots of other things. Right now, I would appreciate it if you would make sandwiches and coffee. I am starving."

"I got some soup on the fire. And tomorrow, I'm gonna fix that hen like no hen ever been fixed before." Smiling, Cassie carried the groceries into the kitchen.

"Thanksgiving?" Caroline asked with a puzzled frown.

"Yes. President Lincoln proclaimed the fourth Thursday in November as a national day of Thanksgiving, even for the Southern states. You can thank the editor of Godey's Lady's Book—what's her name?—for convincing him to make the proclamation."

"Mrs. Sarah Hale is her name," Caroline replied with a smug jerk of her chin. "But a celebration in the middle of a war? What have we got to be thankful for?"

"What have we got to be thankful for? My dear, we have each other." Taking her by the hand, he led her inside to his office where he tossed his saddlebag aside and stoked the low-burning fire. Once the fire was burning brightly again, he settled on the sofa with his arms wrapped around her. He gazed at the framed pictures of them now prominently displayed on the mantle. After he had warmed himself, he rose and rummaged through his saddlebags.

Caroline watched with unabashed interest. "What have you got in there?"

"Be patient," he grumped good-naturedly, and continued groping in the bottom of the bag. "All right, Miss Nosy, close your eyes. I have something for you."

"Oh, Philip, thank you," she squealed with delight as he held up the latest copy of Godey's Lady's Book, and absently kissed the air near his cheek. "Do you mind if I look through the magazine now? I am dying of curiosity."

"Of course not. You go ahead and enjoy it while I read this letter from Matthew. I haven't heard from him for several weeks."

The letter, dated Nov. 17, was written somewhere between Atlanta and Savannah. 'Although, there wasn't much left of Atlanta,' he wrote, 'my last view of the city was a huge column of black smoke. During our occupation of the town, Gen. Sherman became incensed in the extreme when he saw the shocking condition of our men who had escaped from the prisons. They were nothing but skeletons. But this army keeps moving. I am tired but fine. Cannot wait to get this damned thing over,' he finished.

Me too, Philip thought, troubled by the dark tone of the letter.

Glancing up, he watched Caroline as she leafed through the magazine. "I must say, Carrie, I have never seen you looking so well. Do you suppose that being in love is good for one's health?"

"What do you mean?" she asked, a small smile playing on her lips.

"Turn around. Let me look at you." After she'd complied, he said, "What I mean is that you look wonderful. So content." He traced his fingers over her cheeks that had filled out recently, and ran his hands over her breasts and down her arms. "You look fuller and decidedly healthier than you did several months ago."

"Well, the credit—or blame—for my condition is entirely yours."

"My, that sounds ominous. Are you blaming your well-being on all the Yankee food you have been consuming?"

"It has nothing to do with Yankee food. Think, Philip. Can't you guess why I look so different?"

He studied her closely. After a moment, a smile of comprehension spread across his face. "Are you sure?"

"Yes. I suspected something last month but when another month passed, I was certain."

He was still kissing her, telling her how happy he was, when she gently nudged him away from her. "Philip dear, I have been thinking about something. A baby is not exactly a blessing in our situation."

"I know, sweetheart, but there is nothing we can do until we learn something definite about Morgan and my divorce becomes final."

"No, that's not it." She turned away from him and, drawing a deep breath, she stammered, "I had considered asking Cassie if she could do something about this. She told me some time ago that she learned how to take care of this sort of thing from her grandmother. She said there were herbs and other ways a woman could. . ."

Before she could finish her sentence, he gripped her by the shoulders and said, "Are you saying what I think you are saying? No, I do not want you to even think about that. I have heard horrific stories about what happens to desperate women who do that. Sweetheart, you could bleed to death. Anything could happen. No, it's too dangerous."

At the sight of tears welling in her eyes, he gathered her into his arms. "Oh, Carrie, honey, I'm sorry for speaking to you like that. I appreciate your apprehension about this baby but for me, this is wonderful news. I love you and I want our baby." He gave her a tender kiss. "I'm sorry about my outburst. I became fearful at the thought of losing you. You are so very precious to me."

Suppressing his own emotions and fears, he held her closer and said, "There, we will never speak of it again. Agreed?"

With her moist cheek pressed against his chest, she said, "Forgive me. I feel ashamed for even considering it."

"Hush, sweetheart. Come and sit here with me." He pulled her onto his lap and whispered endearments to her. After a few quiet moments, he asked, "When?"

"By my count, early June."

"Early June," he repeated, his mind racing into the future.

"Philip, are you truly pleased?"

"Yes, sweetheart, I am. I must confess, however, that it never occurred to me that this could have happened since you'd never. . ." He bit his lip to keep from making reference to her marriage. "Oh, my dear, now I have more reason than ever to be grateful on this Thanksgiving Day."

With a joyous smile, Philip pushed her back onto the sofa and was kissing her soundly when Cassie appeared at the door to announce that supper was ready. They both peered at her over the back of the sofa, looking sheepish at being caught during this intimate moment.

Holding hands and smiling, they followed Cassie to the dining room where a supper of soup and sandwiches awaited them.

"Did Caroline tell you the happy news?" Philip asked Cassie with a broad smile.

Cassie stopped pouring his coffee. "Humph. She didn't have to tell me nothin'. I knew it before she did." Holding the coffee pot above Philip's cup, she asked, "You happy 'bout this?"

"I am delirious with joy." Patting her hand, he added, "You must help me take care of the two most precious people in my life."

"Colonel Philip, don't you worry none about that."

Philip sipped his coffee with Caroline's hand clasped tightly in his. "Just think, sweetheart, in the spring, I will have a son. And maybe as a bonus, this damned war will be over and I can begin making a home for you and our baby."

"What makes you so sure it will be a son?" Caroline asked with a teasing grin.

"Because I said so," he replied with a nod that settled the matter.

"There's gonna be two babies come spring," Cassie announced.

"Two?" Caroline and Philip asked in unison.

Cassie nodded, looking quite pleased with her announcement. "Mina, she's carryin' Daniel's chile. Due most likely before Miz Caroline's time." She gazed heavenward. "Praise the Lord for new life in this here house instead of death."

"The ladies hereabouts will be blooming come spring," Philip said with a wink.

Caroline's heart leapt with sudden terror. Dear Lord, she thought, squeezing Philip's hand, the armies will resume fighting in the spring.

And spring comes early in this part of the country.

Chapter 36

HUNCHING HIS SHOULDERS against the late January chill, Philip yanked the collar of his greatcoat up around his neck and glanced around the Calvert Street station in Baltimore to get his bearings. It was difficult for him to realize that only 24 hours ago, he had received a telegraph message from his brother George, informing him of their father's sudden death. It still didn't seem real, what with the frantic packing, travel arrangements, and saying goodbye to Caroline.

Real or not, he thought, here I am, in response to George's urgent pleas for assistance.

A cab driver appeared out of nowhere and picked up Philip's travel bag. "Where to?" he asked, a cigar stub clenched between his yellowed teeth. Philip gave him the name of the hotel and climbed into the cab, grateful to be sheltered from the cutting wind.

Arriving at the downtown hotel where Henry kept a standing reservation, he went directly to the room number George had given him. His knuckles had barely touched the door before it flew open. George stood outlined against the gaslights in the room, his appearance disheveled, his eyes red.

"Philip," George sighed with relief, "thank God, you are here at last."

After shaking George's hand, Philip tossed his greatcoat aside. "I still can't believe this has happened. Were you able to get in touch with Matthew in Savannah?"

"We sent telegraphs but, as yet, have received no reply."

"Damn. I should have contacted Sherman myself. Now, very calmly, George, tell me what has been done so far and what needs to be done."

George fell into a chair and reached for his handkerchief. "When I arrived early yesterday, the hotel staff was sympathetic and helpful, but extremely vague. Even when I questioned them about particulars, no one had any answers."

"Where—where is Pa's body?" Philip asked in an unsteady voice.

"At the embalmers," George replied, trembling visibly. "The hotel manager had them take him last night. He suggested it might be best."

"Very good," Philip nodded. "What did you mean when you said that the hotel staff seemed vague? Was there some question about the circumstances of Pa's death?"

George sat up, his eyes wide and serious. "I may be wrong, but I have the unsettling feeling that Pa didn't die here in his room. I can't explain why I feel this way. Perhaps it was all those furtive looks from some of the staff, their strange silence. The manager was helpful but too much so, as though trying to keep me from asking too many questions." George's eyes misted again. "It's all so mysterious."

Turning in disgust from George's blubbering, Philip stared out the window toward the harbor. "Did the embalmer say when he would be finished?"

"Tonight," George sniffed before returning his kerchief to his pocket. "Forgive my manners, Philip. Do you want me to have something sent up to eat or drink?"

"No, I'm not hungry, but I would like a drink. I would also like to meet with the manager so we can get some answers," he added, as George yanked on the bell pull to summon a waiter. "Perhaps I can get some sense of why you suspect that Pa did not die here. By the way, who packed Pa's things?" he asked, pointing to the bags sitting at the foot of the bed.

"I don't know," George shrugged. "They were packed when I arrived. It's all very odd." A knock at the door broke into their exchange. "That must be the waiter." Opening the door, he found not a waiter but a lady clad in black. A veil concealed her face. "May I help you, madam?" he asked in a sharp tone.

"I hope so, Mr. Creighton," came the reply from the beneath the veil.

"Do you know me?"

Philip came forward to intercede. "Come in, please."

"Thank you." Taking a seat, the lady lifted her veil to reveal the face of a lovely, dark-haired woman. Her sad hazel eyes betrayed arduous crying. "Allow me to introduce myself. My name is Rosamund Farley. I am a longtime friend of your father's. I wish to convey my condolences to you on his passing. He spoke of you both quite often."

George stared at her, silent and dumbfounded.

"How do you do, Mrs. Farley," Philip said. "Is there something my brother and I can do for you?"

Twisting the handle of her reticule, she lowered her gaze. When she looked up again, tears glistened in her eyes. "I came to ask a favor. If it is agreeable with you, I would like to see Henry again before you take him home."

"By what right?" George demanded.

"I am sure you feel that I have no rights," she replied in a calm voice, "but Henry and I meant so much to each other."

"Was my father with you when he passed away?" Philip asked gently, pointedly ignoring George's astonished glare.

She nodded.

"I'm very sorry for you, Mrs. Farley."

"Philip," George interrupted in a tone suggestive of a reprimand.

Philip exhaled an impatient sigh, and motioned for George to be silent. Damn, of all times for him to become assertive, and so damned judgmental. Just like Mother. He poured a glass of sherry for Mrs. Farley and said, "George tells me the embalming will be finished this evening. If you like, we can go there together."

"Thank you, Philip. I would like that very much. And thank you, George."

George stood silent for a moment, his lips compressed. "This revelation has caught me by surprise," he replied tersely.

"I understand perfectly," she murmured. "I can see that you disapprove of my connection to your father. I'm grateful that you agreed to see me."

Philip sat on the sofa beside her and took her hand. "Mrs. Farley, George also informed me that the hotel staff has been very helpful but somewhat secretive about the circumstances surrounding Pa's passing. Can you tell us what happened?"

Her eyes grew cloudy with pain. "I am sorry about that. The hotel manager and employees were only following my instructions. You see, Henry had been with me that evening. We had just finished dinner and he settled down to read, as was his habit. I had seen to a few things myself before playing the piano for a while. It soothed him when I played Beethoven. I thought he had dozed off so, after a while, I shook him to awaken him.

"When he didn't respond, I became alarmed. I sent for my personal physician, who came at once. After examining Henry, he determined that it must have been his heart. Needless to say, I was stunned." Her voice faltered. "Forgive me," she said with a sad smile, "I am still not quite myself."

She looked from one brother to the other. "It is my wish that scandal not touch Henry or his family. That is why I asked my doctor and a servant to bring Henry here to his room. I spoke with the hotel manager and begged his discretion in this matter. He understood fully, once I paid Henry's bill, with a good deal extra as an incentive for his silence."

George raised an eyebrow. "So that's why they were so secretive."

"I didn't know what else to do," she said in a quivering voice. "My only thought was to spare your family any undue awkwardness if the truth ever became known."

"That is most considerate of you, Mrs. Farley," Philip said. "Isn't it, George?"

His lips still compressed, George muttered, "I suppose so. No one wants a scandal."

A sudden rap at the door interrupted the debate. George answered the door and found a waiter bearing a tray with a light supper, drinks, and a pot of tea.

"I hope you don't mind," Mrs. Farley said by way of explanation. "I took the liberty of ordering the tray when I arrived. I thought you and George might need some refreshment after your long journey. I also asked the manager to confer with us. He should be here shortly."

"Thank you," Philip said with a smile. "That is very considerate of you. Isn't it, George?"

"Yes, very."

Good, Philip thought. Perhaps now we can lift some of this burden from Mrs. Farley's shoulders, as Pa would have expected.

Chapter 37

SHORTLY AFTER DARK, the Creighton brothers escorted a heavily veiled Rosamund Farley into the embalmer's establishment in an old section of town. Following the emotional private viewing, George returned to the hotel, while Philip escorted Mrs. Farley to her home.

They arrived at her cottage in a quiet old neighborhood. "You don't mind if I lean on you, do you?" she asked, with her arm linked through his. "I need your strength just now. Please, come in for a moment."

"I would like that very much. Thank you."

Before a cozy fire in the parlor, they drank brandy-laced tea in silence for several moments. Philip had the uncomfortable feeling that Mrs. Farley was studying him.

"You favor Henry in looks," she said. "And from what I have observed so far, in temperament too. I have heard so much about you that I feel I know you already. "

"My father and I enjoyed a special relationship. My brother Matthew is very much like him too." He gazed at her and mused, Pa was right when he said that she was a lady of singular qualities. "You cared for my father very much, didn't you?"

"Oh, yes. He had been an associate of my late husband's, and assisted me during all those confusing business matters after his death. Our friendship grew gradually. We would sit right here and talk the hours away. I may know more about your family than you do. But you can be sure of one thing—your father loved you very much."

Philip leaned forward into the soft glow from the fire and whispered, "Knowing that gives me great consolation. But you must forgive George, Mrs. Farley. I'm afraid he is a bit judgmental. His view of the world tends to be limited, and quite rigid."

"You needn't explain. Now that I have met George, everything Henry told me about him makes sense. He indicated that George and Jessica are a good deal like their mother. He worried about Jessica."

"With good reason." Taking a sip of tea, he smiled. "A long time ago, when Pa and I were sharing confidences, he made reference to you, though not by name. I see now why he was so taken with you. I hope you don't mind that I mention this. You may rest assured that no one else knows about this."

"That explains why you weren't as shocked as George when you learned who I was." She reached over and patted the back of his hand. "You don't know how much your support means to me during this difficult time."

Averting his face, Philip stared into the fire. "I have no right to judge you and Pa. Or anyone else. I too made a bad marriage so I left my wife to join the army." Caroline came to mind just then. Her adorable freckles. Those eyes that never failed to weaken his defenses. "Happily," he went on, "I met a lovely lady in Virginia who fills my life with a joy I never dreamed was possible. We plan to marry as soon as my divorce becomes final."

A smile brightened Rosamund's face. "I'm sure you will be very happy with your lady."

"Thank you. In about five months, everything will be perfect. We are expecting a child at that time. Hopefully, this war will be over and I can begin life with my new family." He set his teacup aside and stood up. "I really must go now, Mrs. Farley. I appreciate this opportunity to talk with you. Thank you for being Pa's friend, and for making him happy."

"We both loved Henry, didn't we? We will miss him very much."

"Yes, we will." He bent over her hand. "Good night."

"Goodbye, Philip."

Philip returned to the hotel suite to find George sitting before the fire, his chin resting on his chest, drink in hand. He did not look up at Philip's entrance.

"It's getting colder," Philip remarked, shrugging off his greatcoat. "How about pouring me one of those?"

Without comment, George rose and did as Philip asked, resumed his seat and stared silently into the flames.

"What's bothering you?" Philip asked.

George turned on him with uncharacteristic fury. "Can't you guess? It's the way you catered to that woman." He took a gulp of bourbon. "And I never thought our father could be capable of such reprehensible conduct."

Philip gave him a wry smile. "Disillusioned? Well, I'm afraid that is the way of the world."

"Pa was too old for that nonsense."

"Love is not nonsense," Philip retorted, "at any age." He took a seat opposite George and continued, "Think for moment. Have you ever noticed any affection pass between our parents? Have you ever known Mother to show him the least bit of kindness or consideration? No, she drove Pa away with her cold, imperious ways. That is the reason he turned to Mrs. Farley."

"That's a convenient rationalization. People their age do not engage in sexual activity."

"Even if that is true, they can at least exhibit the affection that binds people together and eventually builds over years of living together, weathering emotional crises, and raising a family. They should respect one another. Mother respects nothing but her position and Pa's money. Just like Elizabeth," he added in disgust.

George sat up, suddenly interested. "What do you mean?"

"Why in the hell do you think I joined the army? For patriotic reasons?" Philip took a long drink of his bourbon. "It may shock you to learn that, at this very moment, I am madly in love with a lady in

Virginia and plan to marry her." At George's bewildered expression, he shrugged. "Think what you will of me. I don't give a damn. Not any more."

He continued with a bitter edge in his voice, "It wasn't long after our marriage that it became clear to me that Elizabeth was just like Mother, selfish and grasping. So, I cut her out of my will before I left. Denton Cobb is presently negotiating a divorce settlement on my behalf. Remaining true to character, Elizabeth is delaying the inevitable with every tactic she and that goddamned Julian can think of."

George slumped against the back of his chair, too startled to speak.

"Sorry to shock you with these revelations, but your dear sister-in-law had carnal knowledge of our cousin long before I ever met my lady. So you see, I have perfect grounds for divorce." He took another sip. "Like a damned fool, I let the issue of divorce slide during the early part of the war, believing I would be killed. No such luck," he added with a dark smile.

George shook his head. "I don't know what to say. This doesn't sound like you, Philip."

"That's because I am a different man, thanks to a lovely, brown-eyed lady who taught me what love truly means. I am not saying it is moral or right, but every man needs to be loved. And every woman."

"You are rationalizing again."

"Don't judge me—or Pa—too harshly until you know all the facts." Philip's eyes narrowed. "Not until you understand all the plotting and scheming that went on within the family. And the betrayals. All I ask is that you reserve judgment."

George considered for several moments before responding, "That's asking a lot."

"I realize that." Philip leaned forward and gripped George's wrist. "Can I trust you never to mention this conversation to anyone? Especially to Ellen. She shares everything with Jessica and Mother. This is important to me, George. Besides, it would serve no good purpose for anyone else to know the true circumstances of Pa's passing. As for my divorce," he released his grip on George's arm, "they will learn about that soon enough."

George agreed with great reluctance.

"Thank you. I appreciate your discretion." Philip finished off his bourbon. "Let's get some sleep. Tomorrow, we take Pa home."

Chapter 38

LATE THE NEXT afternoon, Mr. Hornsby, owner of the mortuary in Crossroads, met Philip and George at the train. Philip instructed him to take the casket directly to the family mansion and prepare everything for the viewing the next day.

After reminding George of his vow of silence, he said, "We are both exhausted and there is nothing left to do tonight. Why don't you go home? I will see you in the morning at Mother's."

"I don't know how much longer I can bear up," he sniffled, and reached for his handkerchief.

Suppressing the urge to shake his brother and tell him to brace up like a man, Philip gripped his shoulder instead. "A good night's sleep is what we both need." He watched George plod toward the waiting cab, his shoulders slumped.

In his own home, Philip ordered a hot bath drawn. Slipping down into the tub, he relished his first bath in a real tub for longer than he cared to remember. After a leisurely soak, his bed beckoned him to lay down his burdens for the night.

Lying on the pillows, he stared into the darkness and thought, now it begins—the strain of pretending. The grieving First Family of Creighton's Crossroads presents a united front to the community. He turned over and pounded his pillow. Was there ever a family in more disarray?

Arriving at the family home the next day, Philip went directly to the formal parlors already crowded with dozens of floral arrangements and notes of condolence. The family sat en masse for a private viewing before the other mourners arrived. Ursula sat in a straight-backed chair next to the brass-trimmed mahogany casket, her face a mask. All regal bearing, she was properly clad in her black silk widow's weeds, trimmed with fine French lace, her icy blue eyes downcast.

The perfect image of a bereaved widow, Philip thought with disgust.

Jessica stood behind their mother, crying into her black handkerchief. The depth of her grief struck him as uncharacteristic.

Teary-eyed and shaken, Uncle Ben came forward to shake Philip's hand and exchange a few words. Philip bent to kiss his Aunt Helen, her usually cheery countenance now drawn and pale. Crouching before his cousin Maggie's chair, he kissed her cheek. "Hello, my little darling."

Maggie took his hand. "I cannot tell you how sorry I am about Uncle Henry's passing. I was very fond of him."

Philip's eyes misted. "I know you were, Maggie. Thank you. Now, if you will excuse me," he kissed her slender hand, "I must see to my duties."

Breathing in a resolute sigh, he stood and turned toward Ursula. Setting aside his personal animosity for the duration of this difficult time, he touched her shoulder tentatively.

Ursula was on her feet in an instant, pressing her flushed, dry cheek against Philip's. "Thank God, you are here at last, my son. My strength."

He stood rigid and unyielding, wondering, When did I become all this to you? Or is this simply a show for the benefit of those watching?

Philip turned to view his father's body. He fingered Henry's sleeve, unable to touch his cold flesh. The thought struck him that it seemed such a short time since he had been home to attend Robert Strickland's funeral. Was it last year, in February? So many things had happened during this past year that it seemed just a few months ago. Or an eternity ago.

George appeared at Philip's shoulder and whispered, "Prepare yourself."

"For what?" Philip asked, turning. As he did so, his gaze fell on Elizabeth's fur-clad figure in the doorway to the parlor. "My God, what is she doing here?"

"She arrived this morning with Julian." He leaned closer and said, "After what you told me about them, it is obvious that they are involved. I'm surprised that Mother hasn't sensed it. You know what a nose she has for those things."

Philip's bloodshot eyes narrowed. Yes, why hasn't Mother noticed that her precious Elizabeth is nothing but a damned whore? Or does she prefer to overlook it for the sake of appearances? After all, Elizabeth was her imperial choice and Mother doesn't like to be wrong.

Elizabeth approached him, her arms outstretched. "Philip, dear, I was just devastated when I learned of your father's passing."

"What the hell are you doing here?" he growled in a low voice into her ear. Grabbing her by the arm, he yanked her back into the entry hall.

"Let go of me or I will make a scene you won't soon forget. Aren't you going to speak to your cousin?" She indicated Julian standing in the dining room doorway, smirking at them over his coffee cup.

Cold anger rose in Philip equal to the rage that nearly drove him to murder in Washington. "Goddamn you both," he hissed. "How dare you show up like this? Have you no decency?" Then drawing in several deep breaths to control himself, he said in a measured tone, "I want you both to mind your manners during my father's funeral. Do I make myself clear?"

Julian's lips twitched in amusement. "Still giving orders, Colonel?"

"Once this is over, I don't ever want to lay eyes on either of you again."

"We wouldn't want to cause any talk, would we, darling?" Julian said with a mocking bow.

"Heavens no," she cooed, "although everyone else seemed thrilled to see us, especially your mother."

"Everyone else doesn't know you the way I do," Philip snorted, and stalked away.

Throughout the rest of the day, Elizabeth played the perfect daughter-in-law, seeing to Ursula's needs and coaxing her to drink some brandy, and commiserating with Henry's friends and associates. Nor did Aunt Helen suffer from lack of attention. Elizabeth ordered Julian to fetch and carry for his mother, and to see to his dear sister Maggie's comfort.

At nine o'clock that evening, after the guests had departed, Jessica suggested that the family withdraw to the dining room where the maids had laid out light refreshments. George indicated that he and Ellen must leave to see to their small children who had been left in their nanny's care.

Philip took advantage of the moment to freshen up and to relieve himself, and to enjoy a brief moment of quiet. When he returned to the dining room, his head was thumping with a headache brought on by the pressures of the day.

He was in the process of removing his tunic when Ursula gasped, "Philip, dear, you are even thinner than last year. Isn't the army feeding you properly?"

"I eat very well," he answered. "I lost a few pounds last summer when I was wounded."

"Wounded?" the ladies cried in unison.

"Yes," he said matter-of-factly before taking a bite of Gerta's cinnamon cake. "As you can see, I have made a complete recovery and returned to my duties."

Ursula turned on Elizabeth. "You should have told me about this, you naughty girl."

Philip caught Elizabeth's eye and gave her a look that dared her to misspeak.

"Now, Mother Creighton," Elizabeth replied smoothly, "Philip was right not to say anything. You and the entire family would have worried needlessly, had you known."

He saluted her quick thinking with his coffee cup. Turning to Maggie seated next to him, he engaged her in conversation as the others ate and talked among themselves.

Presently, Helen stifled a yawn. "Ben, are you ready to retire?"

"My goodness," Ursula declared before Benjamin could respond, "it is nearly ten thirty. I cannot imagine where the time has gone."

Philip stood and grabbed his tunic off the back of his chair. "If you all will excuse me, I will be on my way too. Good night, everyone."

"You are right, Philip, it is time we left," Elizabeth said in a syrupy voice.

"You and Elizabeth will join us for breakfast," Ursula said, following them to the front door.

"I will be here," he answered flatly, and glared at Elizabeth's smug smile. He made no move to kiss Ursula good night, or make contact with her in any way.

Ursula regarded him with astonishment before presenting her cheek to Elizabeth. "Good night, dear. See that Philip gets a good night's rest."

In the process of buttoning his greatcoat, Philip glanced at Elizabeth. Their eyes met and held, almost as a challenge. Grief, and the strain of pretending all day, had taken its toll of his nerves. When the maid opened the door for them, the sudden blast of the cold night air only increased his headache.

Inside the carriage, he rubbed his throbbing temples and thought, I can't think about tomorrow, or this family of mine. This family of strangers.

Sitting across from him, Elizabeth asked, "What's wrong, Philip? Tired?"

He stared out the window in silence.

"You needn't worry about my sleeping with you tonight, if that is what has you on edge. I left my luggage at Mother's. I told her I would stay with her. Isn't that a cozy arrangement?"

"It's a damned good arrangement," he muttered, and continued massaging his temples.

Undaunted, Elizabeth continued, "I must say, you look quite well, despite your weight loss. No," she said, thoughtfully assessing his appearance, "I think it is more than that. You look—I don't know—content somehow, as though you may have a mistress hidden away somewhere."

Philip kept his eyes closed for fear of betraying the accuracy of her well-placed jab. "Why would any woman want someone as repulsive as I?"

She shrugged. "I'm sure some women might find you attractive. Well, here we are at Mother's. Good night, Philip. I do hope your headache goes away."

Smiling to himself, he thought, it is going away right now, but not far enough.

Chapter 39

SHORTLY BEFORE EIGHT o'clock the next morning, Philip arrived at Ursula's home. Alighting at the side entrance, he let himself in and was welcomed by the aromas of Gerta's cinnamon rolls and freshly brewed coffee. In the dining room, already set for breakfast, he poured himself a cup of coffee. As an afterthought, he poured another cup and went in search of his Uncle Benjamin. He found his uncle in the back parlor, reading the family-owned newspaper.

Benjamin looked up with a smile at Philip's entrance. "Morning, Philip."

"Good morning. Here, I thought you might like a cup of coffee."

"Thank you," Ben said, reaching for the cup. "This is just what I need. I have been reading this article about the fall of Fort Fisher. Another article said that Sherman was moving northward from Savannah, Georgia. I guess that means Matthew will be heading in the right direction again. And the House of Representatives is about to vote on the Thirteenth Amendment, abolishing slavery. I also saw a notice that Senator Everett died in Boston. Lots of things are going on in the world, but what does any of it mean in the end?" He looked at the closed doors to the front parlor where Henry's body lay.

"Are you being fatalistic, Uncle Ben? Most of what happens in this country has a direct bearing on our lives in one way or another. We are in a desperate struggle to preserve the Union. If we fail, a hell of a lot of good men will have died in vain. I would like to think that these last few hellish years of my own life have been spent for something worth while."

"Now who is being fatalistic?" Benjamin asked. "Once the war is over, you will return home to tremendous responsibilities."

"I'm sure I will, but Pa prepared me for that. At the moment, I am formulating several plans of my own, depending, of course, on the outcome of the war."

"Everything depends on the outcome of the war," Benjamin sighed. "What a disgrace this war is—kind fighting kind. In some instances, brother against brother."

"Sometimes nothing makes sense." Placing his coffee cup on the lamp table, Philip rested a hand on his uncle's shoulder. "Would you care to join me in the other parlor for some private time with Pa?"

"I went in earlier for a prayer and some remembering. It's hard to comprehend that he is gone." Benjamin stared off into the past. "I remember as boys how we would detour on the way home from school and take a dip in the creek. We'd fib to Mama and tell her that we had to stay after school. I remember bobsledding in the winter, building snowmen. It was all so carefree then. At that age, we were completely oblivious to our position."

Ben finished his coffee before saying with a sigh, "I suppose I should have felt slighted when our father practically cut me out of the family fortune and left me to fend for myself. But, hell, I wasn't cut out for high finance. I guess he knew me better than I knew myself."

He stood up and stretched fully. "I must admit that I have a happy life. I have a woman I love and who loves me. I am also doing what I want with my life. There aren't many men who can make that claim. What about you, Philip? Are you happy?"

Caught unaware by the question, Philip hesitated a moment, then realized, Yes, for the first time in my adult life, I am truly happy. But I can't tell him about Caroline, or that she is carrying my child. How can I convey the delicious joy I feel every time I hold her? Or look at her across a room?

"Happiness is a relative term, isn't it, Uncle?" he said at last.

The wily old man smiled knowingly. "I suppose so."

Having anticipated a large crowd, the family decided to hold Henry's funeral service at St. Mark's Episcopal Church. Philip escorted Ursula and Jessica, properly attired in their black veils, into the family pew. Ellen, regarding everyone contemptuously down her long nose, sat beside George in the front pew. At Julian's whispered urging, Elizabeth sat between Jessica and Ellen instead of with him and Benjamin's family in the second pew.

"Think how it will look," he pointed out, "especially before the reading of the will."

An august gathering that included Governor Curtin, Congressman and Miss Millicent Catlett, the senator and various other dignitaries of the Commonwealth of Pennsylvania and Creighton's Crossroads filled the church to capacity. Even Secretary of War Stanton sent his condolences.

Reverend Bates' eulogy extolled Henry's virtues as an example to all as a loving father and husband. He mentioned Henry's devoted service to his community and his country. "One son," he pointed out, "has left the battlefield to pay his last respects to his father and give consolation to his mother, while the other son was unable to travel across hazardous miles.

"It is during these trying times that a man's worth is measured. It is through your tribute to Henry, and his family, that bespeaks the quality of this man. He did his duty in life, quietly and modestly, with no expectation of notoriety or recompense. But a far greater reward awaits him. His struggle is over. As St. Paul tells us, to fight the good fight and to run to win the race is to win the everlasting crown. Our brother Henry has done just that. Let us pray."

By the time the congregation left the church, the wind had risen. Dark clouds dripped a mixture of snow and rain. Ursula hung onto Philip's arm as he held an umbrella over her and made small sobbing sounds, but he couldn't help noticing the conspicuous absence of tears. Jessica clung to his other arm, crying into his sleeve. Outside the family mausoleum, he stood, stoic and pale, listening to the sleet pelt his umbrella.

After the service, Denton Cobb took Philip aside and asked for a moment of his time.

"Certainly. I have a few things I need to discuss with you too. We will meet in Pa's library after the luncheon." Philip shook Denton's hand then helped Ursula into her carriage. Clutching Elizabeth by the arm until she winced, he said through his teeth, "Come, my dear, you can ride beside Mother." A dare twinkled in his hard eyes.

Left with no option but to comply, Elizabeth sat beside Ursula and, all the way home, she murmured condolences and patted Ursula's hand.

The luncheon guests scattered throughout the dining room and both parlors, finding seats wherever they could. As he circulated among the guests, Philip noticed the familiar signs of Ursula's classic headaches manifesting themselves, as she massaged her left temple or rubbed the bridge of her nose between her thumb and forefinger. He suppressed the perverse thought that the strain of carrying out the charade of the bereaved wife must be taking its toll, *while another lady in Baltimore truly mourns my father's passing.*

Presently, Ursula asked in a quavering voice to be excused, whereupon all the gentlemen rushed to assist her. Governor Curtin himself walked her to the bottom of the stairs.

What an actress, Philip snorted to himself. *Nearly as accomplished as Elizabeth.*

As the guests began their good-byes, Philip whispered into Elizabeth's ear, "Come with me."

Chapter 40

PUSHING ELIZABETH NONE too gently, Philip led her into the parlor where Henry had lain in state. He slid the doors closed and turned on her, his dark eyes flashing fire. "We need to talk."

"About what?" she asked, feigning innocence.

"I am in no mood for games, Elizabeth. You know damned well I mean the divorce." He crossed his arms and leaned against the locked door, watching her intently.

Backing away from his glaring eyes, she took refuge behind a sofa. "Your father isn't even cold in his grave and here you are, planning to disgrace his name with a divorce. What a heartless wretch you are."

"My father would have applauded me for ridding myself of you." Philip squinted at her. "Don't think for an instant that you fooled Henry Creighton with your artful female ways. Judging by the questions he asked before we were married, I suspect he saw through your little act. Besides, we are not here to speak of my disgraceful conduct, but yours."

"I still believe that the only reason you want this divorce is because of another woman. Well, if that's the case, I will not stand for it."

"Really?" His eyes followed her, piercing her, as she paced and twisted her handkerchief. "And am I expected to continue enduring your amorous misadventures?"

"Before I agree to this divorce, I expect you to settle a large sum on me."

"As I've told you many times before, I will not give you—or your damned paramour—one red cent. I will pay the legal expenses for the divorce, nothing more."

"How am I to live?" she blurted, panic now evident in her voice.

"Don't you think it is time that Julian assumed that responsibility? Everything has its price, does it not?" His face creased into a mirthless smile.

"You are unspeakable," she spat at him. "No gentleman would do such a thing to his wife."

"You are absolutely right. But then, you were never a wife to me and I have long since ceased being a gentleman where you are concerned. Consider yourself fortunate that I am willing to let you keep the house, all the doo-dads you bought in New York, as well as your jewelry."

"I—I can't think right now." Elizabeth gripped the back cushion on the sofa. "You have me too upset and confused. Let me give you my answer in a month or two."

"A month or two?" Philip made a menacing move toward her. "Damn you. But for your mindless procrastination and endless delays, this would have been settled last year."

"I need a large settlement so I can live properly, like a lady."

"Madam, there isn't enough money in the world to accomplish that."

"There is another woman," she countered. "Isn't there?"

Remaining silent in the face of her charge, he weighed his options against his needs. To achieve my goal, I may have to compromise and give her something. Time is of the essence.

"Very well," he said in a deliberate manner, "to show you that I am serious, I will give you ten thousand dollars and pay the legal expenses."

"Is that ten thousand dollars a year?"

Philip crossed his arms over his chest again and said, "That is ten thousand dollars, period."

Softening her voice, she lowered her eyes. "That is very generous of you to acknowledge that I need something to live on."

"Generosity has nothing to do with it."

She glared at him as she considered his offer. "All right," she agreed at last in a strangled voice.

"I expect you to stay here in Crossroads after I am gone and confer with your lawyer. Have him contact Denton to finalize the terms of the settlement. I am meeting with Denton shortly to give him the details." Philip slid the doors open to indicate that their interview had ended.

Elizabeth swept from the room, holding her skirts close against her. Philip grinned, knowing that she would immediately seek out Julian and give him the gory details of this meeting.

At Philip's sign, Denton moved unobtrusively toward the library. As soon as Philip closed the door, Denton said, "Let me say again, old friend, how sorry I am at the loss of your father. I held him in the highest regard, and enjoyed working with him."

"Thank you, Denton. I am going to miss him very much." Philip handed him a drink. "Here. But I doubt that you need this as badly as I do. It has been a hellish few days."

"I understand, so I'll be brief." Denton placed his wire spectacles on the bridge of his nose and consulted his notes. "It should come as no surprise that, under the terms of your father's will, you are the executor of his estate as well as his principal heir."

Philip dropped into a chair and stared at him. "All of it?"

Denton nodded. "Your father also made a few bequests of immediate cash to George, Matthew, your mother and Jessica. The bulk of the estate, including proceeds from rents on all properties, all investments and stocks, is to remain intact under your care. You own the newspaper building, the bank building, the tenant properties on the west side of town as well as some properties in Maryland. This home is also yours. It was your father's hope that your mother and sister will continue to reside here as long as they wish."

"Yes, yes. Of course," Philip agreed absently, still too stunned to speak. "However, until the war is over, necessity requires that I rely upon you to help me administer the estate."

"I will be happy to assist you. I will draw up a limited Power of Attorney for you to sign."

"Thank you. I will speak to the editor at the newspaper and the officers at the bank before I leave. They will have to carry on as they have been, and the bank officers can report to you."

"There's more." Denton sat behind Henry's desk and studied his notes again. "Your father turned over his oil stock shares to you, with two percent each going to George, Jessica and Matthew. That should represent a sizable income for them at the rate production has increased over the last four years."

Denton removed his glasses and massaged the bridge of his nose. "I believe that covers the main points of the will. I will provide you with a copy after the formal reading tomorrow. By the way, your father left an envelope for you. I will bring it tomorrow when I read the will."

"Before you go, Denton, I would, uh, like to ask one more favor of you." Philip stood but remained deep in thought. Finally, he turned and said, "Moments ago, I ordered Elizabeth to end these delays and have her attorney contact you about this divorce. I want this matter settled as quickly as possible.

"To force the issue, I have decided to settle a one-time payment of ten thousand dollars on her, give her the house and all the china and silver, plus her jewelry. Generally what I told you last March. The terms of my will when I left in sixty-one remain the same. Elizabeth gets nothing except what is provided for in the divorce settlement. If her attorney broaches the subject of alimony, I am not open to discussion on that issue. Once settlement is made, that will be the extent of any monetary transaction. I must also emphasize my wish that this action remain as quiet as possible. It is no one's business what I choose to do with my life."

"Of course," Denton said. "However, if I may be so bold, in spite all that is going on, I have noticed something different about you since I last saw you."

Philip smiled, recalling that Elizabeth had made that same comment last night. "That is because once I made the decision to divorce Elizabeth, a sense of peace settled over my spirit."

Then his aspect darkened. After a moment's reflection, he lifted his head and squared his shoulders. "If you will spare me a few minutes more, I would like to address another issue that is of great concern to me. Since July of last year, I have been romantically involved with a lady in Virginia."

Ignoring Denton's gaping jaw, he continued, "She lives on the property I confiscated outside of Petersburg. After I was wounded, she helped take care of me, but eventually it developed into much more. She means everything to me, Denton, and I intend to provide for her welfare."

Philip sat in the chair facing Denton across the desk. "In a month or two, the army will begin its spring offensive. Grant believes that Lee will abandon Petersburg as soon as the weather breaks. When that happens, I cannot assume anything about my own future, so it becomes even more imperative that I provide for her."

"Who is this lady who has affected this drastic change in you?"

A grin lit up Philip's face. "In a moment, but first, I want to talk about additional amendments to my will. Because of my involvement with this lady, if Matthew makes it through the war alive and I do not, I want my entire estate to go to my child born to Caroline Chandler Howard of Petersburg, Virginia. I appoint you and Matthew to act as co-executors until the child attains majority. Caroline will receive a generous monthly allowance to run her household in a manner befitting a Creighton."

Denton's head came up with a jerk from his note-taking. "Ch— Child?" he managed to say.

"Do you have a problem with that?" Philip asked, suddenly defensive.

"No, of course not. This news just took me by surprise, that's all."

"This child is to be treated as my legal heir, with all the rights of a Creighton. State it any way you wish, only make the will so binding that its terms can never be broken." *By my mother or my dear sister-in-law,* he thought with rancor.

"I will see to it," Denton assured him.

Philip exhaled a long sigh. "That relieves my mind. I hope I am not shocking you too much with these revelations of my wayward behavior."

Denton gave him a sheepish grin. "Yes, I must admit that I am shocked. In fact, my mind is reeling from all you have just told me. Its impact on so many other people is incalculable."

Philip waved his hand in dismissal. "I realize that, but I don't give a damn. I will move heaven and earth to have Caroline and today, Pa has given me the power to accomplish that. I've learned from past mistakes, so I won't let her get away as I did Samantha." He looked up to see Denton staring across the desk at him. "Why are you looking at me like that?"

"Sorry," Denton said, flustered. "I am astounded at the transformation in you. For the past few years, you have not been yourself. You'd grown moody and dark. Judging by what I had learned about your personal life, I understand why that was so. But now, when you speak of Caroline, your entire aspect brightens. I have never seen you like this before."

"I have never felt this way before. I can't wait to get back to her. I plan to marry Caroline as soon as I get this damned divorce out of the way. There is, however, one fly in the ointment," he said, his voice now hesitant. "She doesn't know if her husband is alive or not." He saw Denton's hand twitch at this latest bombshell.

"Caroline has not heard anything from him since Gettysburg," Philip continued. "I have tried locating him through our War Department and through Richmond, with no luck. There is no record of him. I don't know how we will handle that situation if it becomes an issue. I will just have to deal with whatever happens. But it won't affect my resolve to marry her."

Denton replaced Henry's pen in its brass and crystal holder. "Will you bring Caroline and the baby here to live after the war?"

"I have thought long and hard about that. Now that this mantle of responsibility has been draped around my shoulders, it appears that I have no other choice. I would prefer living elsewhere with her but what can I do?" His father's secret life came to mind but he rejected the thought of living that way. "I will make the necessary arrangements as the need arises."

As Denton slipped his spectacles into his pocket, Philip bolted from his chair, walked to the far corner of the room and back again. "All my life," he began in a tense voice, "I have been groomed to take over the family businesses. My father trusted me to do what was needed when the time came. Everyone will look to me now, especially George who cannot make a rational decision if his life depended on it.

"Now the Creighton fortune will consume even more of my life." He struck his fist on the corner of Henry's desk, causing Denton to flinch. "Damn it, it's time I look to my own happiness. And I intend to do just that with Caroline."

Chapter 41

ELLEN NUDGED A reluctant George ahead of her into the library. "Stop pushing," he protested. "I want to talk with Philip before Denton arrives."

"Never mind about Philip. He will get his come-uppance this day. Just you see if he doesn't." Ellen shivered with anticipation. "Just think, George, it is all within our grasp now. Hurry, let's sit here, close to the desk."

Ursula made her grand entrance in a black silk mourning dress, looking pale and properly aggrieved. Taking a seat on the sofa with a great affected sigh, she asked Jessica to place a cushion behind her back. "I have not been able to rest well since dear Henry's passing. What will I do without him?" she whimpered in a thin voice.

"I know," Ellen sympathized, and rushed to Ursula's side with a glass of water. "We all know how devoted you were to Father Creighton."

"Mother has been prostrate with grief," Jessica snapped. "I consider it barbaric that she is subjected to reading Papa's will so soon. However," she amended the tone of her outrage, "for everyone's sake, perhaps it is best that we get this settled right away. There is no point in causing her further stress by dragging this out."

Philip had slipped in unnoticed during Ursula's performance and stood by the bookcases to the far right of the desk, providing him a full view of the room, and his family's reactions. After witnessing the exchange between Ursula, Jessica, and Ellen, he rolled his eyes in disgust. Hypocrites. The only stress anyone might suffer is waiting one more day for their money.

Denton hurried in seconds later and shot Philip a wary glance. Seating himself behind Henry's desk, he put his spectacles on with judicious care before withdrawing Henry's will from his document case. "Good morning, everyone," he said in a solemn voice.

They all nodded silently, their barely concealed anticipation palpable in the air.

"Mrs. Creighton, I trust this is not too difficult for you. I can postpone this reading, if you wish."

Ursula shook her head slightly and waved her handkerchief in his general direction. "You are most considerate, Mr. Cobb, but that will not be necessary."

"Very well." Denton led them through the preliminaries before proceeding to the much-anticipated provisions of the will. After reading the individual bequests he'd outlined to Philip the day before that also included Matthew's portion, a stunned silence fell on the room.

Philip's gaze moved from one family member to the other, trying to gauge their reactions. George appeared too shocked and disheartened to react openly. Jessica stared straight ahead, her lips forming silent words of rage. Ursula remained motionless. Seeing her tightly compressed lips and the familiar red blotches on her neck and cheeks, he knew she was seething.

Ellen was the first to complain aloud in her most strident voice. "This is outrageous. As the eldest son, George is entitled to more consideration than this pittance. So what if he did not go off to war, like some folks." She turned her full-blown fury on Philip. "Someone had to remain at home. After all, George had his children to think of." Turning to Denton, she hissed, "You will just have to make other arrangements."

"That is beyond the scope of my powers," Denton informed her gently, but firmly.

"Two percent of the stocks and a monthly pittance? That is all I receive?" Jessica asked, finding her voice at last. She rose and whirled around to face Philip. "You put Papa up to this. Why else would he give us short shrift while you get everything?"

"Allow me to answer that, Jessica," Denton intervened. "Your father was bound by your grandfather Jasper's will, which stipulated that the estate remain intact under Philip's control. No one in this room, including myself, had anything to do with these terms."

"That can't be true! What about my dowry?" Jessica moaned. "Didn't Papa consider that? I can't go to a husband without a proper dowry. What will become of me?"

Philip frowned at her passionate outburst. *What has happened to my sister these past three years? In fact,* he realized with alarm, *to this whole family? How had this dichotomy of thought and values developed between them and me? Have they changed? Or have I been too close to see what was really there beneath the surface?*

Ursula lifted her head, slowly, deliberately, her eyes narrowed, all semblance of grief vanished in an instant. "That old man planned this to spite me. Well, I will have a talk with Solomon McMasters. He will rectify this travesty quick enough."

"Even Judge McMasters cannot violate the provisions of this will," Denton informed her.

"We will see about that," she said through clenched teeth. She rose and swept from the room, careful not to make eye contact with Philip.

Mother's must be the bitterest disappointment of all, Philip thought, and suppressed a smirk. *She is now dependent upon me for household expenses and her personal spending money to maintain appearances. Strange, that her treachery has come back to haunt her. You were right, Pa,* he thought. *Retribution needn't be swift, just fitting to the situation. But this is perfect.*

"Come, Ellen," Jessica was saying, "this calls for a family council." Pausing in front of Philip, she glared at him. "You got what you wanted, brother dear. I hope you are happy."

His eyes met hers evenly. "As a matter of fact, I am not happy about it. But I am sure you don't believe that."

"No, I don't. How is George supposed to live? What about his babies?"

George had not moved or made a comment. At the mention of his name, he looked around the room, confused, as though finding himself in an alien place. "What?"

"Let's go, George," Ellen ordered.

"All right," he nodded, and started for the door.

"George, wait," Philip said with urgency. "I need to speak to you."

"I will be along in a moment," George said to Ellen and Jessica, who were waiting impatiently in the foyer.

Before George closed the door, Philip overheard Jessica whine to Ellen, "Now that Leland is gone, there have to be other suitors. There just have to be!"

Philip stared at the closed door and thought, Even though your hopes of marrying Leland Myles were dashed, little sister, suitors may be mighty scarce, thanks to your bitterness and judgmental implacability.

"Philip," George began in an earnest tone, interrupting Philip's thoughts, "I assure you that I do not feel the way the others do. Besides, all that business is beyond me."

"That is precisely what I wanted to talk to you about. Denton warned me yesterday about the terms of Pa's will and, believe me, I was as stunned as anyone." Leaning closer so his voice wouldn't carry into the foyer, Philip continued, "Frankly, I don't want it either. I have seen what those responsibilities did to Pa. Despite what they think," he jerked his head toward the ladies on the other side of the door, "this inheritance is a burden. It will rule the life of whoever has it."

"I know," George agreed, "but I had expected to augment my income from some of the rental properties or a larger portion of oil stocks. The fifty thousand-dollar bequest is generous by anyone's standards, anyone's, that is, except Ellen's. There will be hell to pay for this," he groaned, "especially since she set about having children so quickly to ensure that this very thing would not happen. Oh, there will be hell to pay," he said again, and shook his head.

"I'm truly sorry," Philip said, moved by George's predicament. "But remember, not a word to anyone about what I told you in Baltimore."

George nodded, opened the library door and took a deep breath before facing the unhappy trio awaiting him.

Philip took a seat before the desk where Denton remained to avoid intruding upon the brothers. He expelled a long, slow breath to release his tension. "Well, that went as expected."

"I didn't know what to expect," Denton replied, and relaxed against the back of his chair. "Your mother worries me. She looks determined to overturn the will."

"Once she thinks about it, Mother will see exactly what Pa intended, and why. You are an astute man, Denton, so I'm sure you sensed over the years that the relationship between my parents was not what it appeared. Given his nature, Pa kept his own counsel where Mother's excesses and abuses were concerned. She may have perceived him as lacking the will to ever retaliate. If so, I'm afraid she seriously underestimated him.

"Pa once told me that there were ways to make people sorry they had abused your trust or benevolence. That is obviously what he intended here." Philip paused, thinking, now for the rest of her life, Mother will know that, even from his mausoleum, Pa has had the last laugh by inflicting the classic retribution upon her.

Denton sighed. "I can't say that I always understood your father, but I never underestimated him. Which reminds me," he reached into his document case and withdrew a sealed envelope, "here is a letter he wanted me to give you."

Philip eyed Henry's familiar bold handwriting before slipping the envelope into his pocket. "Thank you. I will read it on the way back to Virginia."

Chapter 42

THE WINTRY PENNSYLVANIA countryside slid by Philip's sooty train window unnoticed. The steady click of the wheels soothed his nerves. Shifting in his seat to get comfortable, he heard something crinkle in his pocket, and remembered his father's letter that Denton had given him yesterday. In his haste to conclude the legal matters and leave Crossroads, he'd forgotten about it. With unsteady fingers, he tore the envelope open.

> "My dear Philip,
>
> I must apologize for placing this great burden on your shoulders, but your grandfather left me no choice.
>
> Philip, you have always been a source of pride to me. My only advice to you now is to have the courage I lacked to take your happiness where you can and with whom you can. There is no substitute for happiness or love. I am sorry proof of that.

Be happy, son. Let nothing or no one stand in the way of your happiness.

With deepest affection,
Your loving father

Tears of gratitude blurred his vision. *Thank you, Pa. This is precisely what I need right now. I regret that you will never know Caroline. You would have loved her too.*

The dirty accommodations and bad food on the packet made the trip from Washington to Hampton Roads seem endless, heightening his exhaustion from the strain of the past few days. At the City Point wharf, he dragged his travel bag and packages up the slope and collected his mare at the stable.

Dusk had already fallen when he spurred his horse up the driveway at Howard Hill. Seeing the light in Caroline's bedroom window made his heart beat faster. At the back door, he threw the reins to his orderly and hurried into the house.

Lieutenant Hasselbeck came out of Philip's office just as he came through the back door. Startled, he said, "Hello, sir. I didn't expect to see you this late. Are you all right?"

"Yes, thank you," Philip nodded. "Just tired. If you left something on my desk, I will tend to it in the morning."

"That will be fine, sir. I don't believe there is anything urgent." Jesse cleared his throat. "Allow me to express my condolences again on the loss of your father."

"Thank you, Lieutenant. Good night."

Dropping his bag and packages in his room, Philip decided he could not go to Caroline covered with grime from that filthy boat. Removing his tunic, he scrubbed his hands and face, put on a clean blouse and headed upstairs.

At the top of the stairs, he saw her shadowy figure in the doorway. He dropped the packages and pulled her into his arms. "Come here, you enticing creature." He covered her face with kisses and whispered, "I have waited so long for this moment."

"Come in and tell me everything," she said between kisses. As he retrieved the packages, she asked, "What are those?"

"Later, little Miss Nosy. I have something much more urgent in mind."

He dozed immediately after their lovemaking, his arms still wrapped around Caroline. She waited a while before nudging him gently. "Philip, could you please move? You are smothering me."

Stretching long and leisurely, he grinned. "Sorry, sweetheart. Are you still curious about those packages?"

"Of course not. I'd forgotten all about them."

"Lovely liar." He kissed the tip of her nose. "Open them now."

"I will, but first I need to know—is something wrong? When you made love to me, it seemed so urgent. Almost desperate."

"It's because I was desperate to be with you again." He tightened his embrace. "Oh, sweetheart, when I learned that I needed to stay another day for those endless legalities, I nearly went out of my mind. You were never out of my thoughts. At times, I could even feel your presence."

He lay back on the pillow and stared at the ceiling. "This entire trip was a revelation from beginning to end. I went directly to Baltimore from here to meet with George. I also met Pa's lady friend, Mrs. Farley. I could see that she was genuinely distraught over his death. Unlike my mother," the tone of his voice changed subtly, "who made a great show of grief for the man she cared nothing about."

Caroline rose up from her pillows, her jaw agape. "Your father? And another woman?"

Nodding, he reached for her hand. "I hope you don't mind, but I told Mrs. Farley about us and that I am happier than I ever dreamed possible."

"So am I. For the first time, I feel truly loved." Twisting around on the bed, she situated herself to face him. "Do you feel like talking about the rest of it? If you don't, I'll understand."

"You have every right to know what happened. To my disgust, Elizabeth and Julian showed up at the wake. I threatened their lives if they did not behave while they were there. Later, I told her in no uncertain terms that if she did not agree to my conditions and expedite this divorce, I would cut her off without a cent."

His eyes grew serious as he related the details of his interview with Elizabeth, and his family's varied and violent reactions after the reading of the will.

"Since leaving Crossroads four years ago, I have come to see my family in a different light, as they truly are." He looked into her eyes gazing so intently at him. "I also learned something else. When I witnessed my family's reactions to my inheriting everything, I realized that I did not know them, truly know them. I feel that I am a stranger in my own family.

"Even though I have been engaged in business and have met all sorts of people, I saw for the first time that my view of the world had been narrow and limited. And very privileged. I have never known want and those who have never known want are prone to waste. I, blind stupid fool that I was, wasted opportunities.

"I also discovered that being the Creighton heir has made me a prisoner and Crossroads is the prison. I am not so sure I want to go back there. At least, not without you." Smiling, he caressed her cheek. "I don't want to do anything without you."

Abruptly changing moods, he gave her a gentle kiss. "Now, madam, enough of this self pity. I know you are burning with curiosity, so start opening those packages. As you can see, I did a great deal of shopping in Washington, and in some of the best shops on Seventh Street."

"I am curious," she admitted. Lifting the lid off the largest box, she peeled away the tissue paper to reveal a white silk and lace peignoir with teal satin ribbons at the throat and wrists. "Oh, Philip, it is the loveliest thing I have ever seen. You are so sweet to spoil me like this. Thank you." Kissing him lightly, she reached for the next box.

He propped himself up on the pillows, smiling at her enthusiasm. "These gifts can never convey how much I love you. I buy them to indulge myself because I love watching your face."

The lilac-scented soap with matching dusting powder and the latest edition of *Godey's Lady's Book* evoked squeals of delight. After dusting herself liberally with the powder, she modeled the peignoir for him, twirling about to give him a better view.

"Do I show very much in this?" she asked, eyeing her protruding belly in the mirror.

"Yes, and you look beautiful. Which reminds me. Here," he held up another package, "is something for my son."

She ripped the brown wrapping paper off a wooden toy horse and a red ball.

"I stopped by Stundt's Toy Shop on New York Avenue where President Lincoln himself used to buy toys for his son Tad. I figure if it is good enough for the president's son it is good enough for mine. Why are you looking at me like that?"

"Will you be very disappointed if it is not a boy?"

"Of course not. Whatever we have, I already love with all my heart. I am just afraid that if it is a girl and she is like you, I will be even more helpless against the two of you." Laughing, he pointed to a small canvas bag at the foot of the bed. "Don't forget that one. It may not be as glamorous as the peignoir but I thought you might enjoy them."

"What on earth?" She pulled an orange from the depths of the bag. "How wonderful. Fresh oranges and lemons. I will have an orange in the morning," she said, smiling, "and I will finally have lemon with my tea."

"That's why I bought them. On my way to the Navy Yard to catch that poor excuse for a boat, I saw a roadside vendor selling them and thought of you. By the way," he reached into the pocket of his blouse that he'd tossed onto the rocker, "I nearly forgot this little bauble." He placed a black velvet jeweler's box in the palm of her hand.

"Oh, Philip I really must protest. This is too much."

"I will let you know what is too much. Open it."

Lifting the lid, she gasped at the diamond ring glittering up at her.

"It's just a trifle," he said with a shrug. "I saw it in a jeweler's window and immediately thought of you. The jeweler told me it is a perfect, brilliant, Marquis cut diamond. Four carats, I believe he said, with four quarter-carats on each side."

"This is the most beautiful, extravagant ring I have ever seen. I can't think what it must have cost," she said, fighting back tears.

"To hell with the cost. I asked the jeweler to send the bill to Denton Cobb who takes care of my finances now." With great ceremony, he slipped the ring on the fourth finger of her right hand. "Now do you believe that I love you, and have no intention of ever leaving you?"

Unable to speak, she gave him a tearful embrace.

Smothered by her gratitude, he managed to say, "I find it difficult to comprehend why women feel the need to cry when they are happy. You are happy, aren't you? I will accept these tears as an affirmative response."

"I cannot begin to tell you how happy I am or how much I love you. Thank you for all these gifts." She sniffed and brushed away her tears. "But I—I have nothing to give you."

"How can you say that? You have given me the most precious gift of all—your unconditional love." He patted her belly. "You carry my life within you. Could any gift be more precious than that?"

Taking her into his arms, he held her close. "Oh, Carrie, sweetheart, I could not draw my next breath without you."

"I feel the same about you. Every time you leave, I go numb with fear."

"I know what you mean. When I joined the army, I didn't care if I lived or died. But, now that I have so much to live for, I am truly afraid. Not out of cowardice but. . ."

She pressed her fingers against his lips. "Hush, my love. Nothing or no one will ever separate us."

Chapter 43

"CAROLINE! CAROLINE, WHERE are you?" Philip ran up several steps, turned on the landing and looked up toward her room.

"I am here," she called, leaning over the railing. Seeing his excited expression, her hand went to her throat. "Has something happened?"

"Not yet." He ran the rest of the way up the stairs, dragged her into her room and shut the door. "I know we have never discussed the war or anything I do, but this is a momentous occasion." He paused to catch his breath. "This afternoon a delegation from Richmond will pass by here on their way to meet with President Lincoln to discuss an end to the war. Alexander Stephens is part of the delegation."

"The Vice-president is here? But he is so frail. How can he make such a trip?"

"He is here nonetheless, along with John Campbell and Mr. Hunter who, I believe, is the current Confederate Secretary of War. General Grant has provided an ambulance wagon for their transportation."

Caroline dropped into her rocking chair. "The possibilities sound too good to be true."

He knelt beside the rocker and grasped her hand. "At last, there is hope for an end to the war. That is why I came for you. Put on your shawl and gloves. We can go down to the main gate and watch as they go by. Troops from both sides are already lining the road."

"Philip, are you quite mad? I can't be seen on the road in my condition. I will watch from the window up here."

"You can't see anything from up here. It's nearly a quarter of a mile to the gate. I will put you in the buggy with a blanket over you. My men and I will stand on the other side of the road. Hurry, they will be along soon."

"Who's gonna be along soon?" Cassie asked from the doorway, hands on hips. "Why you want Miz Caroline to hurry along? Is she goin' somewhere?"

"The Confederate delegation is passing by on the main road to meet with President Lincoln," Philip replied. "I told Caroline to bundle up and I would take her down to the gate so she can wave as they drive by."

Cassie shook her finger at him. "Colonel Philip, ain't you got no sense? No, sir, Miss Caroline ain't goin' nowhere."

"Be reasonable, Cassie," Philip cajoled. "I will see that Caroline is carefully concealed so no one, not even Alexander Stephens himself, will notice her condition. With you and Mina there—"

"Now hold on one minute. Mina, she's bigger than Miz Caroline. She can't go showin' herself in public. No, sir, it can't be done."

When the proposition was put to Mina, she nearly swooned. "Me? I ain't goin' nowhere to see no Southern gentlemens. I'm staying right here and that's final."

Amused, Caroline sat in her rocker and watched as the three discussed the pros and cons of the issue, with logic obviously on the side of the two women. Philip poured on the charm, using all the powers of persuasion at his command, but Cassie and Mina would not budge.

So, on that chilly February 2nd, 1865, Philip and his officers, the picture of decorum and military courtesy, smartly saluted the Confederate Vice-president and the other two officials as they made their way eastward on City Point Road.

Caroline, sitting in her buggy at the gate across the road and covered with a carefully arranged blanket to conceal her pregnancy, waved her handkerchief. Cassie sat beside her, glowering across the road at Philip.

Late the next day, Philip stood outside Caroline's bedroom door, struggling with his emotions. Knocking lightly, he entered to find her on her knees in front of the fireplace. "Hello, sweetheart." Forcing a smile, he helped her to her feet and gave her a hug.

After several kisses, she whispered, "I missed you."

"I missed you too. Your hands are cold. And your nose," he said, putting the back of his hand against her nose.

"I have been freezing all day. I was trying to build up the fire when you came in."

"Let me do that." Kneeling before the fire, he threw on more wood then stoked it. "There, that should take the chill out." He sat on the floor, pulled off his boots and thrust his stocking feet up to the fire, wiggling his toes. "Come here and sit by me, Carrie, so I can warm you."

Settling beside him, Caroline backed up against his chest as he folded his arms around her. "Much better," she purred. After a moment, she asked, "Are you all right, love? I noticed when you came in that you seemed distracted."

"It pains me to say this, sweetheart, but the peace conference failed. All the issues, namely Lincoln's policy on Reconstruction, armistice, and maintaining slavery were discussed. Neither side liked the other's proposals so they rejected everything."

Caroline turned around to face him. "What is going to happen now?"

After several moments, her eyes filled with terror at what his silence implied.

Following the failure of the Hampton Roads peace conference, Grant ordered the Second and Sixth Corps, and their cavalry, to probe and stretch the Confederate western defenses. In heavy rain and muddy terrain, the Strickland Volunteers played their part in the action at

Hatcher's Run. The Confederates, already stretched to the limit, offered resistance but were unable to prevail against the overwhelming Union forces.

On Wednesday, February 8, the mud-splattered, fatigued Strickland Volunteers dismounted at the rear of Howard Hill. Philip loosened the cinch on his mare before leading her to the water trough. Once she was in the corral, he started toward the medical tent to see about Wes who had sustained a head wound during the action. Outside the tent, he overheard Dr. Cook instructing one of the corpsmen to clean and bind Wes' wound.

"My God, Major," Dr. Cook grumped, "your baseball injury was more impressive than this. How did it happen?"

"I'm not sure," Wes said with a sheepish grin. "I was unconscious."

"Take it easy for a few days," Dr. Cook ordered. "Also, you can tell that black-hearted Colonel standing behind me to give you another pass for a nice long furlough with your family. Let me know if your vision becomes blurred."

Smiling at the doctor's order, Wes nodded and promised compliance.

As Dr. Cook had prophesied, Philip was indeed outside the tent with a signed medical furlough, waiting until the corpsman finished dressing Wes' wound.

Wes' eyes misted when Philip handed him the pass. "Thanks, friend. As I recall, you did something like this once before." He folded the pass and secured it inside his tunic. "I need to see my wife again before this next offensive begins."

Yes, Philip thought, and which of us will be standing at the end of it all?

As February came to an end, events meant to end this bitter conflict were set into motion. In the Shenandoah Valley, General Philip Sheridan's army chased down and successfully captured the last of Jubal Early's cavalry at Waynesborough, Virginia.

Further south, Sherman's army moved slowly but decisively into South Carolina. Leaving Columbia in smoking ruins, his massive army moved on toward Wilmington. Skirmishes broke out all over the eastern theater of the war, including Fayetteville and Bentonville, North Carolina and Mobile, Alabama.

Along the Petersburg line, and with the return of Sheridan's cavalry forces, Federal troop movements were already under way, beginning what everyone hoped—prayed—would be the last major campaign.

Chapter 44

AT MID-AFTERNOON ON Tuesday, March 28, Philip scraped the mud from his boots on the metal brush outside the back door. A sickening knot pressed hard in his stomach. *Damn, now that life finally holds meaning for me, it may be snatched away—again.*

But my duty is clear. No longer can I warm myself by the fire with Caroline. Dear God, he thought with sudden panic, *what will happen to her if I don't return? What if Morgan is alive and comes home to find her in this condition?*

The knot in his stomach tightened.

He climbed the stairs. With hands trembling and throat constricting, he opened the door to Caroline's room. At the sight of her, with her hair tumbling about her shoulders and fear clouding her eyes, his tenuous control slipped a notch. "Carrie, honey," he muttered.

"You don't have to say a word. I have known for some time that this day would come." She took both his hands into hers. "When do you leave?"

Lowering his gaze to conceal his own torment, he toyed with the diamond ring on her finger. "Four o'clock tomorrow morning."

"Dear God," she whispered. Tears welled up in her eyes.

"Please, sweetheart, don't do that. It rips my heart out when you cry."

"I can't help it. Every time you leave—"

He pressed a finger to her lips to stifle the rest of her sentence. "Let's not think about that now. We will make the best of the time we have left. Cassie can bring our supper up here and we will spend the evening talking. We won't even waste time sleeping. I can sleep in the saddle."

She forced a smile. "All right. I'll go down and tell Cassie right now."

"While you are doing that, I have several things to finalize. I will be back as soon as I can."

Pacing and fretting, Caroline checked the mantle clock again. Eight-thirty. Where is Philip? Did he forget about his supper?

She slipped down the stairs to the landing window to see if he was in the back yard. Her eyes scanned the area, from the blacksmith's wagon on her left back to the medical tent directly opposite the house, all lit by waning campfires. No sign of him. She returned to the upstairs hall and peered through the front window into the darkness but could see nothing.

Disheartened, she slumped to the floor in front of the window.

"Carrie," Philip's breathless voice called from behind. "Did you think I had forgotten you?"

She ran into his open arms. "I didn't know what to think."

"I'm sorry, sweetheart. I had to write out my orders, meet with the staff to discuss scouting reports, and make final arrangements. I also checked on what has been done so far, such as rations for several days, ammunition, even travel arrangements for the laundry women. But let's not talk about that." Throwing his arm around her shoulders, he led her into her room. "I'm starving. Did you save me some supper?"

They shared a picnic-style meal on the floor before the fireplace after which they settled back to talk. Several times during their strained conversation, Philip glanced at the mantle clock.

"Why do you keep watching the clock?" she asked after the fourth time.

"Sorry, but I have more duties awaiting me, including a prayer service Father O'Boyle is conducting later. I must be present for that."

"Must you leave me so soon?"

He kissed her several times before whispering, "Believe me, it is the last thing I want to do. I know I promised that I would spend more time with you but I have so many things going on at once. I will make more time for us, I promise."

Taking the stairs two at a time just as the hall clock struck one o'clock, Philip threw her door open. "I'm so sorry. I tried for hours to get away but one thing after another required my attention."

Caroline stirred in her rocker and blinked the sleep away. "Sorry, I must have dozed off. What time is it?"

"Never mind about that." Pulling her into his arms, he kissed her repeatedly. "I have been thinking about this the whole time I was gone. And this." He scooped her up into his arms and carried her to the bed.

Quitting her bed an hour later, they sat before the fire, pointedly ignoring the clock each time it chimed the quarter hour.

She had just poured each of them another glass of wine when she exclaimed with a surprised expression, "Oh! Your daughter just made her presence known. Put your hand here."

Gently placing his hand on her belly, he waited. When the child moved, he jerked his hand away. "Doesn't that hurt?"

"No, it feels wonderful to know that your daughter is active and well."

"You mean my son," he corrected with a smile, and kissed the place where his child was growing.

"Remember, Colonel darling, you do not give the orders in situations like this."

"My dear, since falling in love with you, I have learned who is really in command here." Suddenly overwhelmed by the thought that he may not live to see his child born, he pulled Caroline closer.

At the sound of the clock striking three, fear overtook them both. Instinctively reaching for one another, they cried and whispered all sorts of promises.

"Damn," Philip said, reaching for a handkerchief, "I vowed I would not do this."

Caroline ran to the wash stand and splashed water on her face. "I must look a fright."

"You look wonderful," he said as he buckled on his saber belt.

"Where is your rain slicker?" she asked, slipping her arms around his waist.

"It's downstairs, hanging by the back door. As for you, my dear," he shook a finger at her, "you must take your naps, and do not go up and down the stairs too often. And remember to keep the doors locked. Do you still have the pistol I left for you?"

"Now who is fussing?" she asked, her eyes mocking him.

He ran his fingers over the curves of her face, committing every feature to memory. "I'm serious, sweetheart. You must take care of yourself."

The mantle clock chimed again.

As he bent to kiss her, he realized that once they kissed there would be no more delays, or frivolous distractions about rain slickers. The men, supplies and wagons are all packed and ready, and Caroline and I are left to face this terrible moment.

As he gazed into her teary eyes, unwilling to let her go, Caroline placed her hands on either side of his face and smothered him with desperate kisses. Their leave-taking was now beyond control, with each venting repressed emotions.

Philip finally broke free of her embrace and, against his anguished protests, she accompanied him as far as the landing. At the foot of the steps, he turned and looked up at her as she stood beside the lamp table. With the soft glow of the lamplight surrounding her, he thought how much she looked like an angel.

The mound that was his child protruded against the folds of her peignoir, reminding him that here was his whole world. Everything he lived for. Oh, Lord, how can I leave her? Will I see her again? Will I ever see my child? Paralyzed by the possibility that she would be left alone to face a difficult, uncertain future his control crumbled.

He rushed back up the steps into her waiting arms. In her tight embrace, he murmured no words of undying love. No promises to return. The only sounds were those of the dry sobs that rose in his throat.

After a few moments, he summoned the remnants of his strength and stepped away from her. He stumbled blindly down the stairs, his saber clanking against his boot tops, his spurs jingling with each step. I cannot look back, he kept telling himself. If I do, I will see the desperation in her eyes and I will never leave.

Gripping the hilt of his saber, he took a deep breath at the bottom step and turned toward the back door. Don't look back at her, he reminded himself. You must not look back.

At the door, he paused and fumbled inside his tunic for a handkerchief. Caroline's hesitant footsteps echoed overhead as she dragged herself up the stairs to her room. Feeling renewed tightness in his chest, he prayed, Dear God, please. . .

Once he regained some semblance of composure, he slipped on his rain slicker and stepped out into the darkness of that rainy March morning. The Strickland Volunteers were already mounted and waiting for the order to ride off toward the retreating rebel forces—and uncertainty.

Chapter 45

CAROLINE STOOD ON the landing where she and Philip said their tearful farewells earlier that morning. Staring through the sheets of rain streaming down the windowpane, she watched the corpsmen dismantle the last of the medical tents. The Union army encampment that occupied the plantation grounds since last June had all but disappeared, except for their unwanted debris and their log and mud huts.

She turned at the sound of shuffling footsteps in the downstairs hall. Dr. Franklin Cook stood at the bottom of the stairs, hat in hand, dripping rain in a puddle around him.

"Mrs. Howard, I came to say good-bye." He cleared his throat. "There are so many things I wanted to say to you but damned if I can think of them now. I would be remiss, however, if I did not thank you from the bottom of this cynical old heart for your generous assistance. You did not have to do all you have done for this army, or for me. Your kindness accomplished far more than my pitiful skills ever could."

Caroline descended the stairs during his speech and stood in awe, thinking, is this my dear, irascible Dr. Cook? Aloud, she said, "You make too much of my efforts, Doctor."

"No, madam, I do not. As you may have learned by now, I do not make mistakes." A grin showed through his white beard. "But I bow to your skills as a miracle worker."

"Miracle worker?"

"Yes, miracle worker, damn it. Who else could have taken that gloomy lost soul and given meaning to his life? I do not mean to say that I approve of, well, some things, but you accomplished something with the Colonel that I believed was beyond the realm of possibility."

Embarrassed, Caroline lowered her eyes.

"Well," he muttered, "I must be off. I'm sure the Colonel gave you all sorts of orders for your well-being. You mind him, hear?" He wagged a finger at her. "If you do not take care of yourself and that child, I will come back and deal with you myself." Again, the grin appeared.

"Yes, Doctor." Throwing her arms around his neck, she kissed his cheek. "You are such a sweet man, and I am grateful for your help through my many crises."

He backed away, blustering, "Now, see here, madam, we will have none of that. I have always made it my business never to be sweet."

Caroline gave him a disarming smile. "Then, sir, you have failed miserably."

He shook his head. "You certainly have a way of bringing a man down, Mrs. Howard. God bless you, and take care." Hesitating a moment, he huffed and fumed before opening his arms to her. "Oh, hell, come here and give this old man a hug."

"Hold Five Forks at all hazards" was General Lee's order to General George Pickett. In order to abandon Petersburg and join forces with General Johnston in North Carolina, Lee needed his western defense line to hold.

Riding toward the rear of the Union position at Five Forks, Philip's horse nearly collided with a bent figure slipping and sliding through the ankle-deep mud. "Watch where you're going, man," he shouted over the sounds of battle and the lashing rain.

The figure, hatless and clutching his greatcoat to his throat, looked up, squinting into the rain at Philip.

"Brendan," Philip said with alarm, "what are you doing in this god-awful torrent without a hat or rain slicker? Find some cover immediately."

"I can't, sir. Too many men need me," he replied before breaking into a coughing spasm.

Dismounting, Philip approached him and pressed a hand to his face. "My God, man, you are burning up with fever. You must think of yourself for a change or you won't be able to see to the needs of others. Father O'Boyle," he commanded in his formal military voice, "get out of this rain or I will order you back to City Point. And find yourself a hat. There are plenty of dead men lying about who won't be using theirs," he called as he swung onto his horse.

With the Confederate western defenses falling one by one, retreat across the Appomattox River was Lee's only recourse. Amelia Court House became his next objective, not only to ward off Grant's pursuing army but to provide his men with much needed food. The expected supplies, however, did not materialize.

After a valiant effort by the weary Army of Northern Virginia, Amelia Court House fell into Union hands on Sunday, April 2. A newspaper reporter wrote, "With that Sunday's sun the hope of the Rebels set, never to rise again."

President Lincoln, who had arrived in City Point for a March 27 conference with Generals Grant and Sherman, remained there to be near the action. In Richmond, Confederate President Davis attended Palm Sunday services at St. Paul's Church. During the service, a messenger delivered a telegraph message from General Lee advising, "I think it is absolutely necessary that we should abandon our position tonight. . ."

Order in the Confederate capitol disintegrated. Prisoners broke free from prison, looters stole everything in sight. All remaining government records or military stores were burned after Davis' hasty departure. Fires raged out of control throughout the city.

The sun broke through and shone on the retreating Rebels as they tore across the muddy countryside, turning only to repulse the ever-advancing Union army, with its endless source of men and food.

After the battle at Sayler's Creek on April 6, the victorious, fatigued Union troops enjoyed a much-needed rest. Mind-numb and butt-weary, Philip collapsed onto the soggy ground under a tree. He dozed a moment before being awakened by Lieutenant Warden.

"Sir, I must speak to you. It's the priest. He's awful sick but he won't let me call Dr. Cook. He said not to bother you, knowing how busy you are and all, but I felt you would want to know. You'd better—"

Hearing the word 'priest,' Philip forced his sleepy brain awake and was on his feet before Lieutenant Warden could finish his last sentence.

Fifteen minutes later, he found Brendan in the middle of a cornfield, lying on a straw pallet that had been covered with a musty-smelling blanket. His greatcoat had been thrown over him for warmth. His once bright, rusty hair was now dull and matted with rain and mud. The hands, always busy doing for others, lay inert on his greatcoat, wasted and bony.

Brendan, his eyes dulled by fever, smiled up at Philip. "Never mind about me, sir. I'm all right. Really, I am. Just a bit tired."

Philip knelt beside his friend and asked in a gentle voice, "Damn it, Brendan, why?"

"I could not neglect my duty, sir. I have seen you do your duty when you were worn down by exhaustion." Another coughing spasm racked his wasted body.

Philip called to a passing corpsman, "Get Dr. Cook over here right away. I want this man looked after, then sent back to City Point." Turning to Brendan again, he felt an overwhelming sense of loss, and of pity. "Ah, Brendan," he said with deep emotion, "don't you know that I can't lose you of all people? How can you have wasted yourself like this?"

"Wasted? Oh no, sir. I pledged my life to the service of others. I was called here to do my duty with all my heart and energy. If I have done that in some small measure then I am happy." Turning away from Philip, he stared off into the distance. "I remember how me mum used to sing so sweetly as she worked about the house back home in Ireland. Can you hear her? She's singing—just now."

"Yes, Brendan, I hear her," Philip answered in a voice crackling with emotion. My God, he thought, this good man is dying before my eyes and there isn't a damned thing I can do about it. "Is there anyone you want me to write to? A brother or sister, someone who would want to know where you are while you recover from your illness?"

The smile returned to Brendan's feverish eyes. "How kind you are, Colonel," he said, his brogue becoming more pronounced with each word. "Always thinking of others. No, there is no one. Me mum died during the famine. My father and brothers were hanged years ago. The Rebellion, you know. My only sister, Annie, died of consumption not long after we landed in Baltimore. No, sir, I am the last."

Philip stared in disbelief. He heard no trace of bitterness in Brendan's voice as he spoke of losing his entire family to injustice. No tirades against the God he served so faithfully. Never an unkind word about anyone. Only solicitude and prayers for those in need. And full support of the war effort to help throw off the shackles of bondage he knew all too well from his homeland.

And now, joy shone on his face, a joy Philip could not comprehend.

Helplessly, he watched as one of his own tears fell onto the back of Brendan's hand, and realized there was nothing he could do to ward off the inevitable. His friend would die out here in the mud and be buried in obscurity. No one would ever know or remember the greatness of this man's heart. No one but him, and Dr. Cook.

Brendan opened his eyes. "Colonel, I have never said anything about you and Mrs. Howard before now, but I could see that you were eaten up with guilt. I pray that everything goes well for you and that matters are resolved, for the sake of the wee one.

"I realize all has not been well in your past, even though I never let on. I remember those dark days in Washington when you stalked about, drinking yourself senseless. Only a man in great pain would do that to himself." He squeezed Philip's hand. "I understand, and I am sure the Lord does too."

Philip averted his eyes. This man who knows my soul so well speaks no words of judgment against my actions. There is something unique about him. I may never know what, but at this moment, I am looking upon the face of a happy, fulfilled man.

"Thank you," he whispered.

Abruptly, Brendan's countenance was transformed. The tired, haggard look fell away. His eyes became brighter as though some distant object had suddenly become clear. He took a deep breath. "Doesn't the earth smell sweet?"

"Yes," Philip replied. But he did not smell the pungency of a burgeoning land or the sweetness of flowering trees. He was aware only of the overpowering stench of dead animals, moldy mud, and the unwashed bodies of dying men. He gazed at the devastated landscape. "I'm afraid we have ruined this year's crop hereabouts. A small price to pay, considering that we captured five Confederate generals today, including Bob Lee's own son Custis."

No response.

"Brendan?" he called frantically, and touched his arm.

Overcome by grief, Philip backed away, teary-eyed and disbelieving.

Some 8,000 Confederates had surrendered that day and nearly 1,200 Union troops suffered casualties. But none of that touched him. Only this man's passing touched his heart.

"Take care of this man," he ordered Corpsman Dawson who was passing by at that moment. Pointing to Brendan, he said in a husky voice, "Take good care of him. Don't let them bury him here. Send him back to Baltimore to be buried with his sister. That's an order," he said, fighting his rising emotion. "Don't let them bury him alone out here!"

Like a dazed, wounded beast bleeding its last drop of blood and gasping its last breath, the Confederate army dragged on, turning only to repulse the never-ending tide of blue that now bounded them in on three sides.

Given the circumstances, General Grant corresponded with General Lee: "The result of the last week must convince you of the hopelessness of further resistance on the part of the Army of Northern Virginia in this struggle. I feel that it is so, and regard it as my duty to shift from myself the responsibility of any further effusion of blood, by asking of you the surrender of that portion of the C. S. Army known as the Army of Northern Virginia."

At Farmville, on Saturday, April 8, Grant received Lee's reply, disagreeing with ". . .the opinion you express of the hopelessness of further resistance on the part of the Army of Northern Virginia, I reciprocate your desire to avoid useless effusion of blood, and therefore, before considering your proposition, ask the terms you will offer on condition of its surrender."

The struggle continued around Farmville where the Confederates repulsed the Federals before crossing the Appomattox River to relative safety. The chase continued, with Lee trying desperately to reach Lynchburg by the old stagecoach route.

Behind the Army of Northern Virginia were the Second and the Sixth Corps. To the south, were the Fifth Corps, and Sheridan's cavalry, who later seized Confederate supply trains at Appomattox Station. Some of General Ord's Army of the James was in front of Lee, blocking the route to Lynchburg.

Grant responded to Lee's inquiry, "Peace being my great desire, there is but one condition I would insist upon, namely that the men and officers surrendered shall be disqualified from taking up arms again against the Government of the United States until properly exchanged." He offered to meet with General Lee to receive the surrender.

Lee's response was swift. "I did not intend to propose the surrender of the Army of Northern Virginia, but to ask the terms of your proposition."

Chapter 46

CAROLINE WRINKLED HER nose at the musty smell that pervaded the entire house. She paced around the upstairs hall, wringing her hands and worrying. Now great inside her body and very active, the child stirred, bringing into sharp focus the cause of her worry. What will become of you, my little one? You will have no true place in this world and I will be an outcast. I cannot remain here at Howard Hill after the war, whether Morgan returns or not. But where will I go? To whom can I turn?

An eerie, unsettling feeling suddenly enveloped her, as if an unknown presence was watching her, cursing her adultery.

Nonsense, she thought with a shudder, it's just my imagination. There is no one here, save for Mina and Cassie and me. . .

After days of endless rain, the sun peeked out tentatively that afternoon. Perhaps, she thought with hope, a little sunshine will go a long way toward lifting my sagging spirits.

Standing on the front porch, she could see the smoke rising from the military train taking more supplies to the army, and returning with the wounded bound for the medical ships at City Point. Is Philip on that train? Or is he lying in a cornfield somewhere out there to the west?

She shook her head. I must not think those awful thoughts or I will surely go mad. As she turned to go into the house, she heard the sound of hooves pounding up the drive. She turned with a start and, shading her eyes against the sun, watched as a blue-clad figure approached the house.

A goateed Yankee sergeant reined in his horse, swept off his filthy hat and asked in a strange accent, " Are you Mrs. Howard?"

Gripping the porch rail for support, she managed to reply, "Yes, I am Mrs. Howard." Dear God, what terrible news has this man brought me? Feeling suddenly faint, she slumped down onto the top step.

Alarmed, the sergeant jumped down from his horse and ran to assist her. "Are you all right, ma'am? By your leave, I bring a message from Colonel Creighton, with his compliments."

Looking at the paper in the sergeant's grimy glove, she managed to say, "A message from Colonel Creighton?" With trembling fingers, she reached for the crumpled scrap.

"Yes, ma'am. The Colonel sends his regards, and wants you to know that he is fit and we are givin' them Rebs hell, if you'll excuse the expression, ma'am." Blushing, he stammered, "By your leave, ma'am, I best be getting on to City Point."

"Wait," Caroline called. "When did he give you this message?"

"Well, let me see. I believe it was yesterday morning. That's right, it was yesterday after we gave them Rebs what for at Sayler's Creek."

Caroline's heart leapt. "Was he all right?"

"Yes, ma'am. He was fine, near as I could tell. Well, if you will excuse me, ma'am." He saluted, mounted his horse and hurried away.

At the sight of Philip's familiar handwriting, Caroline trembled from head to toe. Opening the note, she read through her tears:

> 'My dearest love, Forgive this method of delivery
> but I was frantic to let you know that I am well.
> Fighting fierce but we will prevail. Even in battle
> you are always in my thoughts. Keep this note and in
> the event something should happen to me, present it to
> my attorney Denton Cobb in Creighton's Crossroads

Pa. He has already been instructed to provide financial support for you and our child. I can find no relief of mind or spirit until I know you are cared for properly. Please know that I love you.

Yours always—Philip'

He'd also signed it parenthetically, Col. Philip J. Creighton, Strickland Pa. Vols. Cav. USA.

Crying tears of relief, she read the note again and kissed his words. She pressed the note to her heart and wondered if he was still alive at this very moment.

Even with this note, she thought, I cannot go to his family and say that this is his child. What proof can I offer? Philip's note? They could say it was a forgery, and the child has no legal claim to the Creighton name or money.

So, here I am, alone, and carrying the child of a Yankee colonel who is in the midst of a raging battle somewhere to the west. If he does not return—dear God, if he does not return!—I will be left alone to endure for the sake of our child.

Chapter 47

WHEN THE UNEXPECTED news of the surrender reached Caroline, she was too relieved to absorb its reality. Cassie related her conversation with a passing Yankee who'd stopped to rest his horse and get a drink of water. When she asked what the commotion was all about, he'd replied, "Ain't you heard, nigger? The war's over. You're free and we kin all go home."

"Imagine," she huffed, "him calling me a nigger and him nothin' but a Yankee."

"What else did he say?" Caroline interrupted, impatient with the name-calling portion of the story. "Will the Union soldiers be coming back this way?"

"He didn't say nothin 'bout that. All I know is the war's over and them Yankees can go on home." Cassie started toward the kitchen then paused. "Where's my head? Mina, she's feelin' poorly today. I fear she ain't gonna carry this chile to her time."

Concerned, Caroline said, "I will take some Borage tea and look in on her."

"Well, it won't cure what ails her but it won't hurt neither. I 'spect a little visit from you might cheer her up at that."

Later that afternoon, Caroline retrieved her straw hat from a peg by the kitchen door and set off down the path to Mina's cabin with a pot of Borage tea. The long-abandoned cabins, with missing doors and broken windows, were stark reminders of days gone by. Winded by the short walk, she paused on the porch to catch her breath. Knocking on the open door, she called, "Mina, are you awake?"

"Yes, Miz Caroline. 'Scuse me for not gettin up, but I ain't feelin so pert."

"I brought you some of Cassie's Borage tea." She retrieved two cups from the sideboard and placed them on the small second-hand kitchen table.

Mina rose from her bed with great difficulty and sat across from Caroline at the table. Small of stature, with thin arms and legs, she had expressive dark eyes. Always busy like a bird, Cassie once described her. "My," she said with a weak smile, "wouldn't ole Missy be put out if she seen you doin' for me?"

Pouring the tea, Caroline chuckled and thought, Yes, Mother Howard would surely suffer an apoplectic seizure if she saw us sharing a cup of tea. She wondered briefly if Philip's convictions about slavery had begun to rub off on her.

After a chat about Mina's condition, the end of the war, and Daniel's imminent return, Caroline stood up. "Well, I had better go along now. Would you like Cassie to stay with you tonight?"

"No, thank you, Miz Caroline. I'll be just fine."

Caroline started to object just as Mina's eyes widened and her back arched. "Miz Caroline," she said between quick breaths, "maybe you better get Cassie after all. I spect my time done come."

Alarmed, Caroline helped her to her bed. "You lie down and take it easy. I will be back shortly with Cassie."

Throughout the night, Mina's screams carried across the deserted plantation. She called for Daniel, and for her sweet Jesus to bring relief. She even prayed to die.

"Look to me like she in for a hard time," Cassie whispered to Caroline.

"While we are waiting," Caroline whispered back, "I will take this opportunity to get some rest." To herself, she thought, I don't want to explain any unforeseen problems to Philip—or to Dr. Cook.

Caroline slept until ten o'clock the next morning. Upon awaking, her growling stomach reminded her that she hadn't eaten since yesterday afternoon. Going down to the kitchen, she put on a pot of coffee and found a leftover biscuit in the warming oven. As she sipped her coffee, she noticed that Mina's screams no longer filled the air. Had she delivered the baby?

She hurried out the kitchen door to find out. Part way down the path to Mina's cabin, she saw Cassie approaching, her eyes downcast. "Has the baby come?" Caroline asked.

Cassie nodded. "A little girl, the poor little still-born thing."

"Oh, no. Poor Mina. When?"

"Couple of hours after dawn. I reckon the poor little thing been dead for days. I cleaned the baby up and buried her out back. Mina, she cry and cry all the time, and say, 'How'm I gonna tell Daniel when he comes home?' She restin' now, like I'm gonna do after I fix you some breakfast."

"I have already eaten. Get something for yourself then get some sleep. There is fresh coffee on the stove. I will stay with Mina."

Just after dark two days later, Caroline lit a lamp on the entry hall table. "Cassie, I am exhausted for some reason. I think I will go up to bed now. Would you mind helping me?"

"Yes, ma'am, right after I lock up. Maybe I'll give your hair a good brushin' too."

In her room, Caroline threw off her clothes and let them fall into a heap on the floor. She slipped into the peignoir Philip had brought her from Washington in January. When Cassie arrived, Caroline sat before her dressing table mirror while Cassie brushed her hair and chatted, just as they had in the old days when there was nothing to worry about. When there was plenty of help on the plantation and Morgan looked after everything.

"I'm glad Philip can't see me now. Look at me," Caroline complained into the mirror. "I am so big and ugly."

"No, you ain't. You just big with his chile." Cassie arranged Caroline's hair down on her shoulders. "You know, there's lots of folks gonna say bad things 'bout you and Colonel Philip."

"Yes, I know. I wish I could be more like Philip and say I don't care, but I do." Turning toward Cassie, she cried, "What will I do if he doesn't return?"

"Hush, chile. He gonna come back. I feel it in my bones." She patted Caroline's shoulders. "Lordy, I ain't never seen a man so crazy 'bout no woman the way Colonel Philip crazy 'bout you." She gave Caroline a wary look. "I ain't never said nothin' before, but Massah Morgan, he ain't never treat you right, what with all them other womens and all."

Caroline swung back around to face the mirror. "You must not speak so of Morgan. I know he didn't love me the way Philip does, but he took care of me and gave me a home."

"That's true, but he say mean things 'bout you not givin' him a son. Don't be looking at me that way. I know them things. Maybe Massah Morgan think the same thing I think—that it's his fault he can't have no chile. Seems like it's true, cause here you are, ready to drop that chile before long."

Caroline jerked her head away from the brush. "We must not talk about this any longer. It is unseemly for you to say such things."

"I can say what I want cause Father Abraham done set me free," Cassie reminded her with a defiant jerk of her head. "Can't you nor nobody do nothin' 'bout that neither."

Caroline patted Cassie's arm. "You're right. Oh, Cassie, I do appreciate your staying on to help me. You and Mina have been a Godsend. I will never be able to thank either of you. And I know Philip appreciates everything you have done for him."

"Did I hear my name spoken in vain?"

The hairbrush slipped from Cassie's grasp and clattered against the wood floor. Turning toward the door, she cried, "Praise Jesus. Welcome back, Colonel Philip."

"Thank you, Cassie." Philip entered the bedroom, filling it with his male presence. "Isn't anyone else going to welcome this weary traveler?"

Standing slowly, her knees threatening to fail her, Caroline uttered something that sounded like 'Oh!' and made several other incoherent sounds, but couldn't move. Weak with relief and shock, she gripped the bedpost for support. Can this filthy, smelly apparition truly be Philip, beckoning me into his arms?

"Oh, well," he shrugged, "I have come this far, I suppose I can walk a few more feet to collect the hug I have been dreaming of these last fifty miles. Come here, Caroline Chandler, and prepare to be hugged as you have never been hugged before."

"Oh, Philip, is it really you?" she asked between kisses.

"Yes, it is really me, and I am here to stay. Tell me, my love, did you miss me?"

"Miss you? Oh!" She tightened her embrace around him.

To Cassie, he said, "As you can see, I am sorely in need of a bath. Would you please fetch some hot water for the tub?"

"Be glad to, Colonel Philip. You two just go back to saying hello." Retrieving Caroline's clothing from the floor, Cassie slipped from the room.

He regarded Caroline with a crooked smile. "Are you just going to stand there gawking?"

She touched his face, his arms, held his hands. "I cannot believe you are really here. I prayed for you every minute of every day."

"Thank you, sweetheart. I prayed for you too. And for our child," he added with a kiss on each of her hands, before stripping off his filthy uniform and throwing it on top of his travel bag beside the door. "This mud must be at least two weeks old. I will have to scrape it off my face with the edge of my saber."

As he bent over the washstand, briskly scrubbing the mud and grime from his face and neck, she noticed the nearly-healed scar on his back, its ragged surface glistening in the lamplight. To her, it would always be a reminder of what had brought them together.

Still wet from washing his face and neck, he turned around to face her, drawing her as close as his child would allow. Looking intently into her eyes, he stammered, "I. . ."

"I know," she whispered.

They broke into tears and clung to one another, releasing the strain of more than a month of agonizing uncertainty.

Chapter 48

NOW CLEAN AND relaxed, Philip opened his eyes to find Caroline sitting next to him on the bed, gazing down at him, her hair falling around her face like a veil. He looked up into her eyes. They were so near that they filled his entire field of vision. "I don't know what I did to deserve it," he said softly, "but this has been the happiest year of my life."

She cocked her head at an angle, questioning him with her eyes. "I would have thought that with all your money. . ."

A brief frown darkened his mellow expression then quickly dissipated. "Damn the money. It means nothing. You love me. That's all that I need to make me happy."

"Yes, I do love you, Philip. I love you more than my life."

Moved to tears, he kissed her with great tenderness.

Propping the pillows up against the tall headboard of the bed, he wiped away a tear with the palm of his hand. "You were constantly in my thoughts, sweetheart. I could even feel your presence close to me. All the way back from Appomattox, I must have thanked the Good

Lord a thousand times for sparing me so I could come back to you. That reminds me, did you get my note?"

Caroline dried her own tears before answering, "Oh yes, darling. I keep it in my dressing table. I must have taken it out at least a dozen times a day to read it."

"When I saw so many men falling around me, it became imperative that I let you know about the financial provisions I had made for you and the baby when I went home for Pa's funeral." He stroked her hair. "Is there anything new here?"

"Yes." She lowered her gaze. "Mina had a stillborn baby girl several days ago. She had a difficult time with it. About fifteen hours of what must have been the most horrible pain. I must admit that it frightened me, but I kept telling myself that my labor will not be like that."

Gathering Caroline into his arms, he said, "No, sweetheart, it will not. You have been wonderfully healthy from the beginning."

"Philip," she said, her eyes searching his, "I was frantic for your safety, and for news from the front. Were you there at the surrender? And were our boys as bad off as they say?"

"There are no words to describe those poor devils, but they were valiant soldiers. As the troops from both sides mingled together, I met a Captain Jennings from Culpeper. He was so gaunt, and his uniform was nothing but tattered shreds. I invited him and his men to share a meal with us. He started to refuse out of pride but eventually, he consented out of consideration for his men who were sorely in need of provisions."

After a moment, Philip's expression changed, becoming grave.

Caroline placed her hand on his bare chest. "Philip, dear, what is it?"

"Brendan O'Boyle passed away," he said in a quiet voice. "I have not been so affected by anything since my father's death."

"I am so sorry. I know how fond you were of him."

"I held him in high regard. Also, it seems he knew about my past with Elizabeth but never gave a hint of it. He even wished us well."

"That was kind of him. He always treated me with great courtesy." After several moments of silence, she asked, "Did you witness the surrender?"

"Yes. It ended at a stagecoach stop called Appomattox Court House. As you can imagine, there was great jubilation on our part. Our artillery began a celebratory cannonade, but General Grant put a quick stop to that. He declared that it was unseemly to flaunt our victory in the face of the vanquished foe.

"On both sides, one word was on everyone's lips—Home. I cannot help wondering what some of those poor soldiers will find when they return home."

He shifted positions before continuing, "I was on the hillside across the road from Mr. McLean's house when General Grant's party arrived to sign the surrender. The military band serenaded him and General Lee with *Auld Lang Syne*. It was quite touching. From what I could learn, Grant's terms to Lee were generous.

"I didn't stay behind to watch General Chamberlain receive the arms and battle flags during the surrender ceremony. When I tore out of there at dawn this morning, the printing presses were turning out paroles for the Rebels faster than you could count."

Sliding down onto the pillow, he fell silent and stared at the ceiling. "I think what I found most amazing," he said in a faraway voice, "was the resiliency of the human spirit. These men, who had tried to kill one another the day before, were praying together, swapping tobacco and coffee, and sharing stories. Many a grown man cried that day. But will anyone remember what we did here? Will the courage and sacrifice of so many brave men on both sides be forgotten in a generation?"

"Let us pray it isn't. And let us pray that this is the last war anyone ever sees. Philip, now that it is over, will you try again to learn something about Morgan's status? I cannot leave here with you not knowing."

"You must not fret yourself, sweetheart. I intend to look into it as soon as possible. And you must think about nothing but our child." He placed his index finger on the frown line between her eyebrows. "I don't want to see worry on your face ever again. Hear?"

Pulling her onto the pillows with him, they resumed getting re-acquainted.

Chapter 49

THE FOLLOWING WEEK, Philip joined Caroline on the front porch to enjoy their coffee after supper, a daily ritual since his return. He had already tendered his resignation from the army, effective May 31. He had also prevailed upon Col. Austin Graves to secure a minimal position for him at the City Point headquarters until his resignation became effective.

"This will allow me to remain with Caroline in the last stages of her confinement," he had told Austin. "The Strickland Volunteers can join the rest of the army for the victory parades in Washington. Once the baby arrives and Caroline is able to travel, I will take her away from this place and never look back."

Leaning against the porch rail this evening, relaxed and smiling, Caroline breathed in the fragrant air. "I love this time of day. Isn't the sunset pretty with all those different shades of orange and pink and red?"

"Yes, it is." Kissing her cheek, he asked, "How is my son this today?"

"Are you sure. . .?"

The sound of footsteps on the porch steps halted their exchange. Shielding Caroline with his body, Philip whirled around to protect her from an intruder and came face to face with a skeletal ghost in gray.

The ragged stranger stopped on the top step. "Whoa, Colonel," he said, holding up his hands, palms outward. "I don't mean no harm. I just stopped by to visit my Howard kin and see if I can get a bite to eat."

Caroline peered around Philip's shoulder. "Troy? Troy, is that you?"

The soldier's eyes widened. "Laws, Caroline, I didn't expect to see any of the family here."

Running to Troy, she threw her arms around him. After tears and hugs, she fussed, "Gracious, where are my manners? I will have Cassie fix you something to eat. It won't be as grand as in the old days, but, well, you understand."

"That sounds good. I'm mighty hungry," Troy said, following her into the house. "Ain't had much to eat since way before Appomattox. And not much since."

Caroline glanced over her shoulder at Philip, who motioned her to take care of her hungry relative.

In the kitchen, Caroline asked Cassie to prepare a plate for Troy. "And he needs a change of clothes," she said, eyeing the sorry remnants of his uniform. "When you are finished here, fetch some of Mr. Morgan's clothes. I stored them in the back bedroom."

"Yes, ma'am," Cassie nodded.

Troy gave Caroline a grateful smile. "Thanks. Now I can go home looking decent."

Caroline joined him at one end of the kitchen table and patted his weathered hand. "Now, tell me everything."

He shrugged. "Ain't nothin' to tell. We lost and I'm goin' home. What about you? When's your baby due? If you'll pardon me," he said, smiling sheepishly, "I couldn't help noticing."

She swallowed hard. "Next month."

"It's good to see life again." Troy's eyes lit up when Cassie placed a dish of left-over roast chicken, greens and fresh bread before him. "My, don't that look good." He ate with gusto while asking more questions between bites. "Morgan and Justin? They due home soon?"

"Justin is buried out back," Caroline replied, her gaze cast down to her lap.

"Where?"

"Gettysburg."

"And Morgan?"

Near tears, she whispered, "I haven't heard a word about him since Gettysburg."

"Where's Aunt Dorothea, Aunt Emmaline, and them?"

"Gone."

Staring at her in disbelief, Troy swallowed hard. "All of them? It must have been hard for you, with Justin and Morgan both falling at Gettysburg." Pausing, he looked pointedly at her condition. "If it's been nearly two years, then how. . .?" His eyes grew hard. "Not that goddamned Yankee I saw all over you outside."

"Troy, please."

He stood up, overturning the chair and rattling the plates on the table. "I never thought I would see the day when my own kin would take up with some damned Yankee. They killed your husband." He flung his arm in an all-inclusive gesture. "Your whole family! Look at you. Why, you ain't nothing but a—"

"Don't say another word, soldier." Philip stood at the kitchen door, as furious as Caroline had ever seen him. "In fact, you can get the hell out of here right now."

Troy faced Philip and swore, "Damned right I'm leaving." He turned on Caroline, his eyes blazing. "I ain't staying under the same roof with no damned Yankee lovin' whore."

"By God," Philip growled, and bore down on him, "I ought to shoot you for that."

With Troy and Philip raving over her head, Caroline covered her face. *Dear God, is this what Philip and I have facing us?*

Cassie returned at that moment with the clothes for Troy, but he rejected them with a profane oath. "I don't want charity from the likes of you. I'm proud to wear what I got." He tossed the clothes onto the kitchen floor and flipped over the dish of his half-eaten meal. "And I ain't eating food provided by no goddamned Yankee. I don't even want to breathe the same air."

"Then you are more than welcome to take your leave right now," Philip said through clenched teeth.

Troy cast a final glowering look at Caroline before slamming out the kitchen door.

A prolonged and terrible silence ensued. Philip stood in the doorway, his back rigid, his fists clenched at his side. Caroline remained seated, her head resting on her arms crossed on the table, and gave vent to her tears. Neither spoke for a long time.

Presently, she raised her head and said, "It had to happen sooner or later."

Philip offered no response. Finally, he said in a hoarse voice, "He had no right to say those things to you."

"Troy is right about what I am."

Philip wheeled around to face her with a pained expression. "Don't even think such things. Once we are away from here, no one will dare speak to you like that."

Kneeling beside her chair, he dried her tears with great tenderness. "Carrie, honey, I am so sorry about all this. I swear to you here and now that no one will ever hurt you again."

Chapter 50

STILL OUT OF sorts from his confrontation with Troy, Philip reined in his horse at his City Point office. He'd made every effort these last two days to be especially thoughtful to Caroline but soon realized that nothing he did or said could erase the sting of Troy's words.

Leaving his horse at the stable near the Porter residence, he noticed unusual activity at the telegraph office behind the Eppes manor house. It seemed strange for a Saturday morning, the day before Easter Sunday. He stuck his head inside the door and asked the telegrapher what was going on.

"Sir," the telegraph operator replied, "I guess you haven't heard. We just got news over the wire. The actor J. Wilkes Booth shot President Lincoln at Ford's Theater last night."

Stunned, Philip slumped against the door frame. "Was he badly hurt?"

"The President died about seven o'clock this morning."

"Did they apprehend Booth?"

"No, sir. After he shot Mr. Lincoln, Booth jumped down from the President's box onto the stage and got away. The whole damned army is out looking for him right now."

"There goes the President's plan for peaceful reconciliation with the South," Philip said, shaking his head, and turned away toward his office.

"By the way, sir," the telegrapher called out, "this message came for you a few minutes ago. I was about to send it over when you showed up."

Glancing at the message, Philip was shocked to see that it was from Jessica. Something about Matthew. Raleigh, North Carolina. And a funeral. He stared at the paper, his mind numb. "Has there been activity in North Carolina since the surrender?" he asked a sergeant outside the message center.

"Yes, sir. I heard General Sherman and his men took Raleigh and some place called Morrisville on their way to catch Johnston at Greensborough. They suffered heavy casualties. Damn shame, ain't it? After the surrender too."

Tears filled Philip's eyes. Yes, he thought with a deep sense of loss, a damned shame. He walked away and wandered aimlessly until he ended up on one of the river wharves, mindless of the activity around him, his body wracked with sobs. "Why him, God?" he cried out. "When will the killing end?"

He stared at the river for what seemed an eternity before reading the rest of Jessica's message through blurred eyes: 'Matthew's body is being shipped home with Denton's help. Can you come home?'

Can I come home? If I don't go home to pay final tribute to my brother, will I ever know peace of mind? Tears welled up again in his eyes. All those wasted years of living together but not truly knowing one another. I didn't even know about Polly Hilling until Matt was serious about marrying her.

Dear God, what else don't I know about him?

As President Lincoln lay in state in the East Room of the White House, and Generals Sherman and Johnston signed their "Memorandum or basis of agreement" near Durham Station, North Carolina, Philip sat in his mother's parlor, suffocating from the overpowering aroma of flowers sent by relatives and friends. It only served as a reminder of his father's death four months earlier.

Oh, Caroline, he thought, how far I have come since then, and how far I have drifted from this family of mine. Without Matthew, I feel no connection to these strangers who cling to me, crying and seeking strength I no longer have. I pray I get through this ordeal without screaming at them. Or at the injustice of life.

His eyes drifted to his mother who pressed a black lace-trimmed handkerchief to her eyes, whimpering to a neighbor about how empty her life will be without her beloved youngest son.

Philip snorted to himself. Matthew had never been a part of her life. He simply dwelled on the fringes of family life, unseen, asking for nothing and receiving the same. Ursula continued making great sobbing sounds but, as Philip recalled from his father's funeral, her eyes remained suspiciously dry.

Turning away from her hypocrisy, he caught sight of Jessica standing beside the casket, stroking the sleeve of Matthew's uniform and explaining to a friend how close she and Matthew had been while growing up. Like Ursula, her eyes remained tearless.

Only George appeared genuinely aggrieved. He sat next to Philip, stunned and oblivious to the callers and mourners. "What's happening, Philip? Pa is gone. The war is finally over. And now Matthew. Everything is moving too fast for me. I cannot comprehend it."

Your secure little world is crumbling around you, Philip wanted to reply, and there isn't a damned thing you or I—or anyone—can do about it. Instead, he patted George's knee and murmured, "I know."

In answer to questions about Elizabeth's absence from the wake, Philip gave the same glib reply, "I was unable to reach her, what with the telegraph lines in and out of Washington being so jammed after the President's assassination. I feel fortunate to have gotten here myself."

During the funeral service five days after Easter, Reverend Bates extolled Matthew's virtues and heroism in the service of his country. "It is not for us to question Matthew's untimely death. It was God's will—"

At this point, Philip's mind rebelled. No, it was not God's will. A loving God would never wish this on someone He loves. Why does

Reverend Bates—and everyone else—insist upon perpetuating that myth? And why do they all nod in agreement with him? Can't they understand that it was a rebel Minie ball that took Matthew, not wrath from God?

Outside the Creighton family mausoleum in the church cemetery, Philip watched Jessica, stoic and white-faced, as the pallbearers lowered Matthew into the ground. Look at her, Philip thought with disgust, displaying for all to see that she has the breeding and strength to bear whatever comes her way. Are George and I the only ones truly grieving for our brother?

Late the following day, Philip leaned against a pillar on the front porch at Howard Hill and stared unseeing at the sunset. His coffee had long since gone cold, but he didn't notice or care. Eventually rousing himself from his thoughts, he pitched the remnants of the cup into the flower bed.

Caroline strolled onto the porch, coffee cup in hand. Running a hand up his back, she said, "You did not say much during supper. I suspect it is something more than grief. Tell me."

He draped his arm around her shoulder. "Some unfinished business." In answer to her questioning look, he added, "Matt's fiancée, Miss Polly Hilling. She has a right to know about his passing as they planned to marry after the war, but I cannot bring myself to inform her through a letter or telegraph message. That seems too cold and impersonal."

"It is only fitting that you see her personally. Maybe sharing his passing with someone who loved him as much as you did will help you both to deal with your grief."

"You are so wise, Carrie." He gave her a kiss. "Is it any wonder that I love you so much?"

Chapter 51

THE MORNING SUN had climbed high in the eastern sky, sending its shadows westward over the house. Polly Hilling and her father Adam rocked lazily in the shade of the front porch, gazing at the gently rolling James River.

"It isn't too late to start planting," Adam spoke out of the depths of his beard. "This is good, loamy land. Been in my family for thirteen generations, since not long after Berkeley Hundred was settled." He heaved a worried sigh. "What will happen to the land now that all three of my boys are gone?"

Polly had often heard the story about her ancestors' struggle to carve a home out of the wilderness a few years after the 1622 massacre of white settlers up and down the James River. But she had always listened with interest, making the effort to remember the facts for future generations. If, she thought with a lump in her throat, there are future generations.

She reached over and patted his bony hand. "The Lord will provide, Papa."

"I know, darlin', but," The approach of a stranger on horseback caught Adam's eye. Squinting into the distance, he sat up. "Who can that be? I can't make out who it is."

As the blue uniform drew closer, Adam gripped the arms of his rocker. "It's one of them goddamned Yankees. Imagine the nerve, coming here in broad daylight. A renegade most likely, looking to steal what little we have left, and do whatever he wants with our women." Jumping to his feet, he hurried into the house, muttering, "Well, by God, I can still protect my womenfolk."

Polly stood up, walked to the edge of the porch and watched without fear as the blue-clad stranger approached slowly on horseback.

Reappearing on the porch with his ancient squirrel gun, Adam ordered in a menacing voice, "Stop right there, young fella. You got no business here, so you can turn right around and go back the way you came." He motioned with his gun. "Git!"

The stranger raised his open hands. "If I may, sir."

"I said git!" He brought the gun level with the stranger's chest, his blue eyes bright with anger. "This here's Hilling land. You got no business here, you goddamned Yankee."

Polly pushed the gun barrel toward the ground and said in her gentlest voice, "Put the gun away, Papa. I am sure Colonel Creighton will not harm us."

Adam turned a sharp eye on her. "Did you say Creighton? Well, by God, I got shed of one Creighton I can surely get rid of another. Be on your way, damn you," he ordered, brandishing the weapon again.

Polly patted Adam's arm, all the while regarding Philip steadily. "It's all right, Papa. Why don't you go inside and see to Mother? I think it's time for her medicine." She nudged him toward the door. "You stay with her while I see to our visitor."

"All right, daughter," he said, the bluster gone from his voice. "But you call me if that damned Yankee tries anything. I will blow his fool head off."

"Yes, Papa, I will," she nodded, and urged him toward the door.

Dismounting, Philip approached the porch, looking relieved. Removing his hat, he said with a bow, "Good morning, Miss Hilling. I am Colonel Philip Creighton, your most humble servant. And I am deeply indebted to you for saving my life."

"Hello," she said with a shy smile. "You must not mind Papa too much, Colonel. He likes to intimidate, but that old gun hasn't been fired in ages." Staring into his dark eyes that seemed so familiar, she recognized the pain within. Cold fear traveled down her spine, making her shudder.

"Oh dear," she exclaimed, suddenly flustered, "where are my manners? May I offer you a glass of cool water? I'm afraid it is all we have."

"That would be nice, thank you. It's a long ride from City Point." He walked to the top step of the porch before asking, "May I?"

"Please, come onto the porch where it is still shady. You must be weary after your long hot ride. I will only be a moment."

"Thank you. The sun is quite warm." Philip seated himself in a high-backed rocker.

Presently, Polly returned with a tray, placed it on a small table between them and poured two glasses of water. "I'm sorry that we have nothing better to offer."

"This is perfect. And most welcome. Thank you." Philip drained the glass and held it out for a refill. "I don't mind admitting that I was shocked when you called me by name. How did you know who I was?"

"How could I not know? You are the image of Matthew. Your coloring is a bit darker, but the look is there. I knew right away that you were Philip. He spoke of you so often." Refilling his glass with a trembling hand, she asked in a whisper, "When did it happen?"

Lowering his gaze to the glass, he tried several times before he managed to say, "Near Raleigh, North Carolina. At some God-forsaken place called Moccasin Swamp. April tenth, I believe."

The pitcher slipped from her hand and shattered into a dozen pieces on the porch floor. "The day after the surrender?" she said, her hand at her throat.

"Yes, damn it. Pardon my language, Miss Polly, but I am still very bitter about it," he said, and struggled to regain his composure. "We are fortunate to have brought his. . ." His voice broke again. "He is buried in the family mausoleum."

Polly patted his hand. "That must be a comfort to your poor mother."

Philip did not respond.

She broke the ensuing silence by saying, "I had not heard from Matthew for so long that, deep down, I knew." As the reality struck her full force, she gave herself up to her grief and burst into heart-wrenching sobs.

After several moments, she dried her eyes on the handkerchief Philip offered her. "Forgive me, I never dreamed that losing Matthew would hurt this much. I am still numb from losing all three of my own brothers."

"I am so sorry to hear that. Your parents must be devastated."

Dabbing at her tears, she nodded. "Travis was killed at Harper's Ferry and was the only one sent home for burial. Luke and Jonas," she choked back rising sobs, "at—Sharpsburg. They were buried before we could claim their bodies. Poor Mama has never quite recovered from their loss."

Philip's eyes were fixed on a distant point toward the river. "This war has been devastating for both sides. Personally, I cannot see where it has solved anything. Feelings run just as deep, hatreds are as rampant as ever. With Lincoln gone, I shudder to think what life will be like in the South. Good men like Matt and your brothers are gone while. . ." He paused, his eyes hardening at thoughts of Julian's wastrel life.

Polly's eyes misted with remembering. "Luke used to sneak Matthew's letters to me when they were at the university. Now, I have nothing left but those precious letters."

"We will always have our memories of him," Philip said with great tenderness.

"Oh, Philip, why do greedy men always have to start wars? Those of us who are left behind have nothing but broken dreams and aching hearts." She turned tearful eyes toward him. "And so much emptiness. I pray we never see another war on this earth."

Philip could only shake his head as he fought back his own tears. "I wish I knew the answer. But I know from personal experience that war is man at his very worst. And killing is not the solution to any problem."

In the comfort of their common bond, they talked for a long time of Matthew and the difficult times ahead for everyone. Polly watched

Philip's countenance brighten as he spoke of Caroline and their expected baby. At least, she thought, he has a reason to go on.

"Of course, the baby will be a boy," he proclaimed with a silly grin.

"Now, Colonel," she chided good-naturedly, "we humans have no say in the matter."

"Caroline says the same thing. She out-ranks me, of course, so I have nothing to say about anything." He took Polly's hand into his. "With a smile as sweet as yours, Miss Polly, I see why Matt loved you. I would have loved having you as a sister.

"Well," he said, standing, "I must start back. It's a long ride back to the ferry."

She walked with him to the gate. Before he mounted, she said, "Thank you, Philip. It was considerate of you to come all this way to tell me."

"I felt it was better that you hear of his passing this way. Besides, I wanted to meet you while I was still in the area. Before I go, I would like to do something to help you. Now wait, before you object, I know times are hard. Besides, Matt had planned to take care of you. Here," he placed several twenty dollar gold pieces in her hand, "for Matt's sake, take these. Please. It's not much, but it will help."

"You don't understand. Papa will be furious if he ever found out. And it is not as if we are related or anything."

Philip reached out and touched her cheek. "We would have been. And if your father questions you about where you got the money, tell him it was something you saved from before the war."

Persuaded by his gentle insistence, Polly closed her fingers over the coins. "Thank you. I will think of something to tell Papa."

"If you ever need anything, anything at all, you can get in touch with me at my headquarters on the Eppes plantation upriver or through my bank in Creighton's Crossroads, Pennsylvania. They will see that I get your message. Before I go," he said, "let me kiss you good-bye."

They exchanged a warm embrace and kisses on the cheek. Lifting her chin, he said with deep feeling, "Good-bye, Polly. Be at peace."

"Good-bye, Philip. God bless you for your kindness." She stood by the gate and waved until he was out of sight, still clutching his twenty-dollar gold pieces to her heart.

Chapter 52

"DAMN!" PHILIP SWORE under his breath.

Caroline stopped brushing her hair and looked in her dressing table mirror at Philip who was standing behind her. "What's wrong now?"

He held two brass buttons in his palm. "These buttons came off my tunic."

"Calm down, Colonel," she chided with an indulgent smile. "Cassie has your other tunic brushed and pressed. Hang that one on the back of the door and leave the buttons on the bureau. I will sew them on before my nap."

Kissing the top of her head, he said to her reflection in the mirror, "Thank you, sweetheart. I love it when you spoil me."

Philip tossed the buttons onto the bureau, and hurried down the steps to retrieve his other tunic. Moments later, he called up the stair well, "Carrie, I'm ready to go."

Caroline labored down the stairs and, standing on the bottom step at eye level with him, put her arms around his neck and began what had become their morning ritual.

After exchanging kisses, he gave the usual instructions. "Take care of yourself and my son."

"You mean your daughter," she answered with a smile, and waved him on his way.

The tasks assigned to Philip for disposition of supplies at the depot required more of his time than he'd anticipated. He dealt with endless paperwork, usually requests for any remaining fodder, oversaw the inventory, settled disputes as they arose, and took the opportunity to send telegraph messages to the bank, the newspaper, and to Denton Cobb in Crossroads.

Also, in the weeks following Matthew's death, Ursula began writing to Philip, something he found annoying, given their strained relationship. Her letters were lengthy and full of questions: Why was it taking so long for him to leave the army now that the war was over? Had he ever considered running for public office? On and on she went, but never a word about Elizabeth, or the pending divorce.

Surely, he thought, Elizabeth has made her loving mother-in-law aware of my demand for a divorce. Poor Mother, he thought with a wry smile, she must be in a quandary about how to broach the subject to me. Or is she waiting for me to mention the divorce first? And is reconciliation truly motivating her sudden concern for my welfare?

With great deliberation, he wadded-up Ursula's latest letter and threw it into the fireplace.

Riding up the drive to Howard Hill after work that afternoon, he surveyed the plantation with a critical eye to see what work needed to be done. Out of necessity, he became financially responsible for the upkeep of the place. His first step was to hire two free darkies to help Daniel clear some of the fields so they could plant vegetables and goobers.

"After all," he'd explained to Caroline, "Mina and Daniel will need a source of income once you and I are gone. They have been so kind to both of us that I feel honor-bound to see to their welfare. Cassie can go with us to act as the baby's nanny."

He was dismounting when Mina came running out the back door, bursting with excitement. "Come quick, Colonel Philip. It's Miz Caroline. Her time done come."

Racing past Mina, he took the stairs two at a time. He paused in the doorway to Caroline's room, gripping the doorjamb to support his suddenly weak knees. Caroline lay in the center of her bed, her hair plastered to her scalp with perspiration. Her large eyes were sunken and frightened.

He walked to the edge of the bed and took her clammy hand. "Hello, sweetheart. Is there anything I can do?"

She forced a smile. "Thank you, Colonel darling, but you have already done your part. I think I can handle this." Suddenly, her eyes widened as another contraction struck her and she squeezed his hand.

Wincing at the strength in her hand, Philip turned fearful eyes to Cassie. "When did it start?"

Cassie, standing on the far side of the bed, dipped a cloth in a basin of water. "Right after you left this mornin'. Now don't you go worryin', Colonel Philip. Me and Mina delivered lots of babies, so you just go along. We don't need no help from you."

Before being ushered good-naturedly from the room, he kissed Caroline's damp forehead and assured her of his undying love. Unable to cope with the pain in her eyes, or her cries, he left willingly.

During the next two hours, he stood on the stoop outside the back door in an attempt to escape the sound of Caroline's screams. Even this far from her room, her cries tortured him. With a glass in his right hand and a bourbon bottle in his left, he took a long pull every time she cried out. "If she doesn't have that baby soon," he mumbled, pouring another drink, "I will be too damned drunk to know anything."

At ten minutes past seven o'clock on Friday, May 26, 1865, their baby was born.

Leaning out the landing window overlooking the back yard, Cassie called down, "Colonel Philip, you got a son. A little on the puny side, but a fine, healthy boy just the same."

Philip let out a war-whoop that would have put the rebel yell to shame and threw the bottle over the gazebo, a considerable distance from the back door.

Tearing headlong up the stairs, he burst into the room, pride—and bourbon—lighting his face. He knelt beside the bed and kissed Caroline's hand. "Are you all right, sweetheart?"

"Just tired." Caroline gave him a wan smile. "So, Colonel darling, you were right after all. You have a son, as ordered. Do you want to see him?"

"Now Miss Caroline," Mina admonished, carrying the new-born from the room, "you know Colonel Philip can't see this here chile till he's cleaned up proper."

Philip beamed at Caroline. "I will wait until my son is presentable," he said, his words slurred. "At the moment, sweetheart, I want to thank you from the bottom of my heart now that I have everything any man could ever want."

Caroline ran a hand over her hair. "I must look a fright, but I am too tired to care."

"You never looked more beautiful to me. Oh, Carrie, can you believe it? We have a son." He kissed her parched lips. "I can see you are exhausted. I will leave you for a while so you can rest. I love you, Carrie, but never more than at this moment."

Next morning, Philip entered Caroline's room carrying his newborn son. "Good morning, sweetheart. Look, a gentleman has come to call on you." He sat beside her on the bed, still beaming. "Isn't this the most beautiful baby you have ever seen?"

With a faint smile, Caroline watched as Philip removed the swaddling blanket. "He is a bit wrinkled and red. And his fingernails are still blue." She patted Philip's arm. "Perhaps, proud Papa, he will look better in a day or so."

"In a day or so? He's perfect right now." He gathered up the boy and walked around the room, alternately cooing to him and kissing his soft cheeks. "How are you feeling today?" he asked her, still gazing at his son.

"Exhausted," came the weak reply from the depths of her pillows.

He turned his attention to Caroline, concern creasing his brow. "Cassie is brewing you some tea," he said, barely concealing the sudden fear gnawing at him. "Personally, I think you deserve a huge breakfast after your ordeal yesterday."

"I don't want any tea. I don't want anything."

Her weak voice and extreme pallor brought Philip back to her bedside. "You must have nourishment to regain your strength. I will stay with you while you eat, just as you once did with me. Remember?"

Closing her eyes, she turned away from him. "I can't. I'm too tired."

He stood at the foot of the bed, clutching the baby close to his heart, and thought, this doesn't seem right. That shrew Ellen had her children with minimum effort and was up and about the next day, ignoring them. Why hasn't Caroline improved? She looks and sounds weaker this morning than she did last night. The circles under her eyes have grown even darker, more hollow. Perhaps she'll feel better after she has eaten something.

In the meantime, I had better send for a doctor..

By Sunday, Caroline's strength had diminished even more. Philip paced the hall outside her room, fighting his rising panic.

"I seen this before," Cassie said, closing the door to Caroline's room. "Poor thing, she so weak, she can't even nurse that chile."

"Yes, I know, and it distresses her. Until Caroline regains her strength, do you think Mina, that is, would you mind. . ." he sputtered.

"Don't you fret none, Colonel Philip. I already spoke to Mina."

"Thank you, Cassie. That relieves my mind. I sent Daniel into Petersburg to find a doctor at the Union garrison. Or even a civilian doctor. I've got to do something."

The military surgeon arrived early that evening. With Philip hovering outside the door, he checked Caroline over carefully and asked her several questions. Thanking her with a smile, he left her and motioned for Philip to follow him downstairs.

"There is nothing I can do, Colonel," the doctor said, his demeanor grave. "She has a high fever and an infection seems to have set in. I'm afraid it is child bed fever."

Hearing the devastating news, Philip stumbled back a step and asked in a panicky voice, "What about quinine? Or morphine? Laudanum?"

"I will give you what I have, but it won't do any good. Perhaps a bit of laudanum will relieve her distress." He fished in his bag, retrieved a small vial and gave it to Philip. "Give her just a few drops of this, but only if you feel it is needed."

Philip closed his fingers over the vial. "Thank you, Doctor."

The doctor patted Philip's shoulder. "Sorry, I wish there was more I could do, Colonel." Slowly, he descended the porch steps and climbed into his buggy.

Chapter 53

PHILIP SLIPPED INTO Caroline's room late on Monday morning, carrying the book of Elizabeth Browning's sonnets she loved so much. He kissed her burning cheek. "Would you like me to read to you?"

"Remember," she said in a thin, high voice, "how I would read sonnets to you when you were wounded? These lines," she struggled a moment to gather her strength, "keep going round in my head: 'Guess now who holds thee? – 'Death,' I said. But there, The silver answer rang... 'Not Death, but Love'."

Strangling on his emotions, he whispered, "Yes, it is love that holds you now. I love you so much, Carrie. I remember when you longed to hear those words. Now, I can't say them often enough." He stroked her damp, matted hair. "I need you so much. You are my very life."

Glassy-eyed, she licked her parched lips.

Sitting on the edge of the bed, Philip held the burning hand that lay inert in his and struggled with his growing fear at the red patches on her cheeks. Her skin appeared gray, unnerving him even more.

"Don't tax yourself further, sweetheart. You rest while I check on our son."

Downstairs, he stood at the dining room door and watched as Mina nursed the baby and cooed to him. Conflicting emotions churned within him. He was bursting with pride for his son, but his mounting despair over Caroline's worsening condition was ripping his heart to shreds. Dear God, he prayed, tell me what to do.

With Philip at her bedside, Caroline passed a restless night. Next morning, Philip told Cassie that he did not feel comfortable leaving her, so he sent Daniel to City Point with the message not to expect him for a few days.

He took up a bedside vigil, bathing her face and arms in cool water in an attempt to alleviate the fever. Just a year ago, he recalled, fighting back his tears, she had done the same for me. He read to her, whispered endearments in her ear, and spoke of his unutterable pride in their son, all the while unaware of his own distressed and haggard condition. He had not slept for three days and barely touched the food Cassie brought to him.

"You have made me so happy, my love," he said when Caroline opened her eyes to acknowledge his presence. "Have you decided on a name for our son?"

"Yes." Gathering her strength, she whispered, "Chandler—Matthew."

Nearly choking on his emotions, he kissed her. "You are so sweet to include Matthew. I'm sure he would have been proud to have his nephew carry his name. Thank you, Carrie, for making me so happy. In a few days, when you are stronger, I will carry you down to the stream where I first declared my love for you. We will talk about our plans. . ."

Her hand slipped from his and fell onto the sheet. Her lips were blue. Fear gripped his heart. Don't panic, his logical voice told him. He bent over her, whispering endearments as her breathing became more shallow.

"Cassie," he called out without taking his eyes off Caroline.

Cassie appeared in less than a minute. After looking Caroline over carefully, she shook her head, confirming his worst fears.

"You must be mistaken," he hissed at her. "I will send for that doctor again. I will send to Washington if I have to, but we must get her some help."

"It ain't no use," Cassie mouthed silently through her own tears.

He shook his head vehemently, unwilling to accept the inevitable.

"Take care—of our son," Caroline pleaded in a barely audible whisper. Tears glistened in her eyes. "And may God—have mercy on me."

Philip stared down at her. Dear God, she knows!

Taking her into his arms, he cried, "Don't say such things, my love. You are just exhausted. That's all. It is only a matter of time before your strength returns."

Unresponsive to his outcries, she fought for each breath. Philip lay on the bed beside her, praying, Please, God, let her live. Punish me if you must, not her.

She stirred, her eyes brightening. "Love you—Philip," she whispered in a voice so faint he could barely hear, even with his ear pressed against her lips.

"I know you do," he sobbed.

She tried to motion with her hand.

"What is it, sweetheart? What are you trying to say?" As he bent closer, he felt her body shudder and, in what was her last breath, he swore he heard her say his name.

Holding her close, he rocked back and forth, his face buried in the hollow of her neck, unmindful of the sour smell of perspiration and death. Instead, his senses were filled with the memory of her lilac scent that would remain with him until his last day.

"Please, Caroline, don't leave me. I cannot bear my life without you." Crying unashamedly over her still body, his tears dropped onto her face. After several moments, he placed her gently on the pillow and kissed her over and over, repeating in a strangled whisper, "No. No."

He stared at her a few minutes longer, committing every detail of her lovely face and form to memory. Standing with difficulty, he said to Cassie, "Call Mina to help you get her ready."

Nodding and sniffling, Cassie followed him into the hall.

Without warning, the dam of emotions broke within him. He pounded the wall with both fists and cried, "No! This can't happen. Not to her." After several moments of all-out war against the wall and ripping the curtains from the windows, he paused to catch his breath.

Pressing his battered palms against the wall, his head hung low, Philip sobbed, "Dear God, what have I done? I promised her that no harm would ever come to her. What have I done?"

Still panting from his outburst, he slowly raised his head and thought a moment, as though considering his options. "It's the only way," he said in a raspy voice, and ran down the stairs.

Muttering incoherently, he brushed past a startled Mina part way down the stairs, ran into his office and reached for his saddlebag. Inside, he found his side arm and yanked it out. Blinded by his tears, he fumbled with the cartridge belt in an attempt to load the gun.

Mina stood in the doorway, clutching the towels needed to wash Caroline's body. "What you gonna do with that gun, Colonel Philip?"

He turned on her like a man possessed, his eyes wild and unfocused. "What the hell do you think I'm going to do? I can't go on living. It's my fault that she's dead." He continued loading his gun.

Mina screamed for Cassie.

When Cassie leaned over the stair rail in answer to Mina's desperate cries, Mina pointed toward Philip's office and indicated with a twirling motion of her finger that he had lost his mind. She mouthed the words, 'He's got a gun.'

Alarmed, Cassie raced down the steps with the baby in her arms. She watched from the doorway as he stared at the gun with a smile of resignation. Then, very deliberately, he raised his arm. "You must understand," he told them in a trembling voice, "I'm nothing without her."

"What about this here boy?" Cassie blurted. "Who's gonna look after him?"

Philip paused, his arm in mid-air. Then, very slowly, he lowered the gun.

She held out the baby who squirmed and made small smacking sounds. "Ain't no turnin' your back on this here chile."

As Philip looked into his son's face, the consequences of his ill-considered actions struck him full force. What am I doing? What will become of him if Caroline and I are both gone? I cannot abandon him.

With that thought, a gush of air escaped his lips as though he'd been struck in the stomach. He tossed the gun onto his cot, took the boy into his arms and held him close. "My life isn't my own any more, is it?"

"No sir. That chile, he own you now. What you gonna call him?" Cassie asked, keeping his mind focused on the baby.

"Caroline named him—" After clearing his throat several times, he said in a husky voice, "Chandler Matthew." He gazed at the helpless bundle in his arms, kissed him and murmured, "It's all right, son. I will take care of you. I—I promised your mother I would."

Heaving a sigh of relief, Cassie turned to Mina, who'd slumped against the doorjamb, her lips moving in silent prayer.

Philip sat in a chair with Chandler on his lap and looked at the two women waiting patiently in the doorway. He spoke softly, in a voice suddenly devoid of emotion, "Cassie, get Caroline ready. Mina, tell Daniel to take my horse and hurry into town. Inform Reverend Parsons that he will be needed, even though I detest having that poltroon near Caroline. I would like the burial over as soon as possible, hopefully tomorrow. Do you know any of her relatives in Surrey County that we should notify?"

Cassie thought a moment, and shook her head. "There's still some Chandlers there, but they can't make it here in time anyhow. Massah Charles got cousins in Petersburg and Richmond. That's all I know about around here."

"In that case, tell that lecherous imitation of a minister to be here by noon tomorrow. I am sure word of Caroline's—" he swallowed hard, "her passing will spread quickly enough, once Miss Lucille learns of it."

My God, he realized with alarm, *I am talking about burying my Caroline.* He glanced quickly at the baby who had a firm grip on his forefinger. *I must focus on Chandler to remind me that someone still needs me.*

And to keep from losing my mind.

At the diminishing supply depot in City Point, Philip located a decent coffin and instructed the men in a halting voice to deliver it to

Howard Hill as soon as possible. He also offered to pay them extra if they'd serve as pallbearers.

Returning to Howard Hill, he dragged himself up the stairs, steeling himself for the ordeal he now faced. When he entered Caroline's room, he glanced around, glowering. The drapes were closed against the sun and fresh air, making the room dark and musty with the smell of death.

"Open those damned drapes and windows!" he ordered. "Get some light in here." He stormed from window to window, pulling back the drapes.

When the room was light again and fresh spring air poured in through the windows, he went to her bedside. Cassie and Mina had bathed and dressed her, but left cloths soaked in soda water on her face and hands to delay darkening of the skin. Removing the cloths carefully, he smiled down at her. She looked so lovely in the peignoir he had given her, as though she were asleep.

He sat in the same place on the bed he was sitting when she died in his arms. Holding her cold, rigid hand, he said in a conversational tone, "I have everything all arranged, sweetheart. Reverend Parsons will conduct the burial service. I hope you don't mind. I didn't know what else to do."

Cassie and Mina exchanged guarded looks.

"I will take care of our son, just as I promised." Teary-eyed, he pleaded with her. "I will do anything, anything, just please don't leave me, Carrie. How can I go on without you?"

In one last desperate gesture, he fell on her, his agonized sobs muffled against her pillow. "Please, please, don't leave me. Don't leave me, Carrie. Dear God, what will I do without you?"

Chapter 54

WEDNESDAY DAWNED COOL and overcast for late May, reflecting the somber mood at Howard Hill. Caroline's casket had been placed in the family parlor earlier that morning by several of the soldiers from City Point. Cassie and Mina, teary-eyed and silent, stood in the parlor and cast anxious glances across the hall at the door to Philip's office.

Presently, the door opened. Pale but composed, Philip stood in full dress uniform, saber belted at his waist, boots polished, his lips compressed into a tight line. His bearing might have been intimidating, except for his eyes, eyes that revealed unspeakable grief.

Reverend Parsons appeared at the front door just then, exuding indignation. Miss Lucille stood behind him, properly attired in black. "I will not perform a Christian burial for Miz Caroline," Parsons announced in a pompous voice. "She was a public sinner who has reaped the just reward for her sins."

Gasping in unison, Mina and Cassie looked toward Philip. With nostrils flaring, he stalked across the hall, grabbed Parsons by the throat and throttled him until his face turned crimson and he gasped for air. "You damned lecherous hypocrite. You dare to judge my Caroline!"

Cassie and Mina struggled to restrain him, pleading, "No, Colonel Philip, Miz Caroline wouldn't want you actin' this way."

At the mention of Caroline's name, Philip loosened his grip on Parsons, who was by now gasping desperately for air, and let him collapse to the floor like a rag doll. "Get out, damn you," he said through clenched teeth, "or I'll shoot you where you lay."

Miss Lucille rescued her wheezing brother from Philip's clutches. At the door, she turned and hissed, "You will rue the day you treated my brother this way. We will see that no one gives that Jezebel a Christian burial."

Philip's rage turned even darker but before he could reach her, she slammed the door in his face and ran with her brother to their buggy. Philip wheeled around and ran out the back door, claimed his horse and rode at breakneck speed into Petersburg to find another minister.

Unable to find anyone who was willing to help him, Philip was left with no recourse but to ask Union headquarters to wire Richmond for a chaplain. The answer came an hour later that a priest would arrive the next morning.

With that done, he bought a bottle of cheap whiskey and secured a room at Jarratt's Hotel for the night.

Next morning, the weather had improved considerably. The sun burned off the early morning fog, promising a beautiful early summer day. Baggy-eyed and haggard, Philip waited at the railway depot for the priest. He watched a few passengers alight from the train before catching sight of a tall priest with chestnut-colored hair, bag in hand, looking around the platform. Approaching the priest, Philip identified himself and offered his hand.

With a smile that lit up his gentle blue eyes, the priest introduced himself as Father Stephen Joyce, a classmate and friend of Brendan O'Boyle's. "I was sorely grieved to hear of Brendan's passing. He was a fine man and a good priest."

"Yes, he was," Philip agreed. "I was honored to call him my friend." Ignoring the raised eyebrows of local citizens, he handed Father Joyce the reins to his rented horse.

"Excuse me, Colonel," Father Joyce said hesitantly, "but headquarters was not clear about why you sent for me. Something about a funeral?"

"I apologize for the haste, but I need you to conduct funeral services for a deceased civilian lady who meant a great deal to me," he replied tersely as he mounted his horse.

Father Joyce nodded, mounted, and followed Philip out of town toward City Point Road.

"I suppose I should apprise you of the situation before we arrive at Howard Hill," Philip said after riding for several moments in silence. Slowing his horse's gait, he paused a moment and studied the priest, wondering if he had an understanding heart.

Drawing in a deep breath, he plunged into his explanation, "I might as well say it straight out. Caroline—that is the deceased's name—and I were not married. She died the day before yesterday after giving birth to my son. Her former minister refused to bury her. Said she was not fit for a Christian burial. I see it differently."

Removing his hat, Philip ran a trembling hand through his hair. "I may not be a very good Christian, but the way I understand scripture, God is the sole judge of our actions."

"You are right," Father Joyce replied with a wary glance in Philip's direction. "Whatever our personal feelings about a person only God knows another man's heart or has the right to judge. I certainly have no right to judge the other minister's actions, even though I disagree with them. That is not to say that I condone your actions with the deceased, but I cannot and will not judge you. You must have loved her very much to go to such lengths to see that she is laid to rest properly."

Philip didn't answer for several seconds for fear of breaking down again. After a short time, he continued, "Before I met Caroline, I was in the process of divorcing a woman who had never been a wife to me. She married me solely for my money," he added tersely. "I know you don't believe in divorce, but it was the only solution for me in light of her blatant adulterous actions after we were married."

Father Joyce raised an eyebrow but kept silent.

"As for Caroline's husband," Philip paused and swallowed hard, "she had no idea if he was alive or killed in action. For the past eight months, I have searched everywhere but I can find no mention of him either in Washington or Richmond.

"At the moment, there isn't anything harsh enough that you, or anyone, can say that I have not already said to myself." With a brush of his handkerchief under his nose, he added, "I hope you realize that the locals may be scandalized by your presence, given the circumstances, but I don't give a damn. Not any more."

"You harbor great bitterness, Colonel Creighton. The result, I imagine, of a great many things you consider unjust."

"I have witnessed many injustices in recent years, Father, as I'm sure you have. But I consider it obscene to deny a decent burial to a gentle lady who never hurt anyone in her life. All I want is kindness for Caroline."

Father Joyce reached over and patted Philip's shoulder. "I will do my best for you, sir."

Chapter 55

WHEN PHILIP AND Father Joyce arrived at Howard Hill, several neighbors were already gathered on the front porch. Philip observed a couple, apparently husband and wife, standing with another lady who, Philip guessed, was Alice Matheny, the cousin Caroline had spoken of, with her son. No doubt, he thought with a humorless smile, Miss Lucille has already regaled them with the juicy details of my attack on her sanctimonious brother.

The small assembly nodded coldly to Philip and the priest before following them into the house where they all crowded into the parlor. Philip stood at the head of the casket, his left hand resting on its edge. Alice Matheny and her son Willie joined the other couple across the room, Cassie stood in the parlor door. Mina remained in the dining room with the baby. During the brief prayer service, Philip could hear Chandler's whimpering, a much-needed reminder of his current purpose in life.

When the time came to close the casket, Philip gazed on Caroline one last time. Despite gasps and whispers from the hostile mourners, he kissed her cold cheek before turning away, stony-faced, to wait in the hall.

As the procession prepared to exit the back door, a buggy lurched to a halt in the back yard. Reverend Parsons alighted in haste and handed down Miss Lucille, who had her lips pursed in righteous disapproval. After curt nods all round and pointedly snubbing Philip and 'that priest,' they joined the procession to the burial ground.

Suppressing anger at their sudden appearance, Philip indicated that Father Joyce continue with the service. The soldiers who had agreed to act as pallbearers carried the casket out the back door and headed toward the distant line of trees. Walking directly behind the casket, Philip could hear the hushed murmuring going back and forth between the others trailing after him. Squaring his shoulders, he followed his heart to its resting place.

The family burial ground was situated on a knoll overlooking a sun-drenched meadow. The sound of twittering birds filled the air, hawks hovered high overhead. The approaching mourners disturbed bees that flitted from flower to flower.

At the graveside, Father Joyce led the mourners in the recitation of the Twenty-third Psalm, but Philip took no consolation from the psalmist's words today. When the time came to lower Caroline into the earth, his composure crumbled at the finality of the moment. He turned abruptly on his heel and, without a word, hurried away.

At the house, he ran into his office, poured bourbon into a water glass and downed it in one gulp. He heard the visitors several moments later, talking softly by their buggies parked in the front drive. "Howard Hill will not be dispensing hospitality this day," he muttered into his glass.

From behind the curtains, he watched Alice hesitate before getting into her buggy. Biting her lip, she glanced first toward the window then at the others talking among themselves. Her teen-aged son said something to her as he helped her into their buggy and drove away. Philip saw her glance over her shoulder one last time, making him wonder if she wanted to speak to him, or offer condolences.

A knock sounded at the door. Father Joyce walked in, folding his black stole. "May I intrude for a moment?"

Philip held out his glass. "Come in, Father. Have a drink with me. I'll wager you need it as badly as I do. Well, what do you think of the aggrieved who gathered to view the Yankee monster?" he asked, handing Father Joyce a glass. "What bothers me the most," he continued without waiting for a reply, "is that they came out of curiosity about me, not grief for Caroline, with the possible exception of a cousin and her son.

"Oh, hell," he said with a wave of his hand, "I don't give a damn any more. Nothing matters now except my son. It is my intention to bring him up to appreciate the differences in people. What a damned boring world this would be if we were all alike," Philip growled, and finished off his drink.

Regarding the amber liquid, Father Joyce said thoughtfully, "Those are admirable plans you have for your son, Colonel. I would like to take a peek at the wee lad, if you are agreeable."

Philip stirred from his thoughts and nodded. "I will have Cassie bring him down." Going into the hall, he called up the stairs to Cassie who appeared several moments later, cradling Chandler in her arms. She shot the priest an uneasy glance before handing the baby to Philip.

"Don't mind her," he explained after Cassie left the room. "She hadn't been exposed to Catholic priests before we arrived here."

Father Joyce smiled. "I understand. I had not met too many black people myself before coming to Virginia." He bent over the little form that cooed and waved his tiny fists after Philip removed the swaddling blanket. "I see why you are so proud of him. A fine looking lad he is."

"It grieves me to think what the future may hold for him. The names people will call him. There isn't a damned thing I can do about it except insulate him with so much money and power that no one will dare say anything."

"Is there that much money in the world, Colonel?"

Philip shrugged. "I intend to find out."

"I'm afraid you will find that you cannot keep your son from harm of any kind, no matter how hard you try."

"Yes, I suppose so. Is there no justice in life, Father?" Philip asked, his finger firmly gripped by the infant.

"No, not in this world. Only reward or punishment in the next."

"That doesn't seem like enough somehow. Not for some people."

"Perhaps not to our way of thinking, but whatever people may enjoy or suffer in this world is only for their lifetime. The punishments or rewards in the next life last forever."

"It would be infinitely more rewarding to see some folks get their just desserts in this life as well as the next."

A smile of understanding softened the priest's eyes. "Perhaps you worry too much about the Lord's business, Colonel. We must let Him take care of His own and things will work out just fine. You'll see."

Freeing himself of Chandler's grip, Philip stood and faced Father Joyce. "Do you think God is punishing me? I mean, if I hadn't loved her, this would not have happened." Overcome again by guilt, he slumped onto the sofa and covered his face.

Father Joyce sat in the chair across from him and said, "You must not be so hard on yourself, Colonel. You are guilty of a grievous sin, that is true, but sometimes we judge ourselves more harshly than the Lord does."

"There isn't a judgment harsh enough for what I did to her."

"We can't always understand God's plan for us, nor should we drive ourselves to distraction trying to understand. We must accept our lot and live as best we can."

Philip jumped up and turned on the priest. "Am I supposed to accept Caroline's death philosophically? Shrug my shoulders and say 'oh well' and go along as though nothing had happened? I loved her. I still do."

Father Joyce recoiled from the violence of Philip's reaction. "No, of course not. That is not what I intended. But at the rate you are going, this guilt will kill you in no time."

"That is precisely what I deserve. I should have been the one who died, not Caroline." He stared down at his infant son. "I cannot go on without her."

"Yes, you will," Father Joyce replied with gentle urgency. "I think the Lord has something in mind for you. What it is, I cannot say. No one can." He rose with a sigh and extended his hand. "Well, I had better be on my way. Allow me to offer my sincere condolences, Colonel Creighton. I am sure the Lord will comfort you in that fine son of yours."

Philip accepted the handshake and heartfelt sentiments. "Thank you for conducting the service, Stephen. Please, allow me." He reached into his pocket, withdrew several large bills and placed them in the priest's hand.

"This isn't necessary, Colonel, but I thank you for your kindness. I hope I gave you some consolation this day."

Philip nodded. "Also, I want to apologize for my rudeness a moment ago. I am not myself, and don't intend to be for the next few days." He indicated the waiting bottle.

Father Joyce paused at the door. "I realize it may seem impossible at the moment, Colonel, but you must find a way to forgive yourself. God bless," he added with a wave.

Stunned by the strange remark, Philip stood at the window and watched as Father Joyce rode away. I like this man. He makes no pretense at a holier-than-thou attitude, unlike that damned Parsons.

He turned back to Chandler. "Well, son, how will the world treat us?" he asked as he wrapped the blanket around the infant. "What the hell does it matter? You are a Creighton. No one will dare say a word against you. And heaven help anyone who tries."

After Cassie took Chandler upstairs, Philip wrote a note to Denton, instructing him to send a check for one hundred dollars a month to Father Stephen Joyce, in care of Union headquarters in Richmond, and to continue sending the checks until he was instructed otherwise.

With that done, he proceeded to get drunker than he had ever been in his life.

Chapter 56

PHILIP TOSSED RESTLESSLY on his cot, his painful memories crowding in on him. At times, he swore he could hear Caroline's footsteps in the room overhead. "No, not again," he'd mutter into his pillow, and willed himself to sleep. Before long, he felt someone touch his left ear.

He bolted upright in his cot, drenched in sweat. "Carrie? Are you there?" His eyes searched the room in the pre-dawn darkness. She must be here. I heard her whisper my name. The scent of lilacs is still in the room.

As tears welled in his eyes, he fell back onto his pillow. "I heard her. I smelled her scent." He drew in a deep breath, but no lilac water filled the air, only the musty odor of the ever-lasting, pervasive humidity.

Philip swung his legs over the edge of his cot and sat with his elbows on his knees, his head bent forward, resting in his hands. This is two nights in a row that I have felt her presence. I can't bear much more of this torment.

He rose unsteadily and walked to the east-facing window where the faint pre-dawn light streaked the sky. Staring blindly at the coming day, he came to a decision. *I must get away from here. It is pointless to subject myself to this anguish.* In the distance, he heard the far-away cry of an infant demanding to be fed, bringing his dilemma into sharp focus. *If I leave, who will take care of Chandler?*

Sudden dizziness and nausea overcame him. Using the furniture for support, he made his way back to his cot and lay still for several minutes, waiting for the room to stop spinning. *I know this nausea is from not eating or sleeping. I have got to do something. I cannot go on like this much longer.*

Later that same day, Cassie entered the gazebo and placed a cup of coffee on the bench beside Philip. He looked at the steaming cup as though considering an alien object. "Take it away."

"How long's it been since you ate somethin'?"

He turned away from her question, and the concern in her voice.

Cassie sat next to him. Hesitating a moment, she said, "Colonel Philip, I gotta say what's on my mind, so don't get mad if I overstep my place."

"I have never stopped you from speaking your mind. And don't call me Colonel. As of today, I am no longer in the army."

"Yes, sir," she nodded. "It's Mr. Philip from now on. Anyways, you got me and Mina real worried. I know you ain't eaten nothin' in days. And I heard you these last few nights walkin' around. I even heard you call Miz Caroline's name." Pausing, she bit her lip. "Don't be lookin' at me that way, Mr. Philip. You keep on this way, you'll get bad sick."

Shifting on the bench to face him directly, she added in a gentle tone, "I know how you feel. Now, before you go sayin' I don't know nothin', just listen to me. Back when I was a young girl, ole Mr. Justin, he took a shine to me. He kept after me, wantin' to breed me."

Philip raised his head, his interest piqued, and accepted the coffee she thrust at him. "What did you do?"

"You go on and drink that and I'll tell you." After Philip took his first sip, Cassie leaned back and crossed her arms. "In those days, my heart and my body belonged to my man Silas. We already jumped the broom, so I wasn't 'bout to let that ole man put his hands on me. No, sir, I made up my mind, he wasn't gonna touch me."

"Excuse me," Philip said, "I don't understand what you mean by jumping the broom."

Memories softened her proud countenance. "That means we was married African style but married just the same. Silas, he was the blacksmith here. Big and handsome, he was. We was crazy 'bout each other." Her eyes hardened. "But that ole man wouldn't leave me be. I tried every way I know to put him off, even though I knowed he could do whatever he want with me and there wasn't nothin' I could do about it. He could beat me, sell me off, or mess me up so bad no one'd want me ever again, and there wasn't a blessed thing I could do.

"Well, sir," she stood up and indicated her unblemished body, "you don't see no marks on me, do you?" Without waiting for a response, she sat down again, a smirk twitching at her lips. "I fixed him. I stayed mighty close to Ole Missy all the time. White ladies ain't supposed to say nothin' when their gentlemen want to stray with a nigger gal cause it don't mean nothin'. But for all that, ole Mr. Justin was afraid of her. He knew if ole Missy was ever to find out what he was up to with me, she'd come after him with a butcher knife. He knowed how she could be."

He suppressed a smile at the image of Dorothea depriving old Justin Howard of his manhood.

"I reckon he got mad cause a dumb nigger like me out-foxed him," Cassie went on, "so he hurt me worse than if he beat me senseless. He sold Silas south before ever I knew about it." She covered her face to stifle her sobs.

After a moment, she lowered her hands and lifted her chin. "But I never give him the satisfaction of seeing how bad I was hurtin'. Ain't him nor any other man touched me since."

Philip patted her shoulder. "I'm sorry for you, Cassie. And you are right. If anyone knows how I feel, you certainly do."

"Guess you and me wasn't meant to keep the ones we love most. Anyways," she sighed, "what I come to say is, why don't you go away from this place, least ways, till you feel like yourself again?"

Philip slumped against the latticed enclosure. "I have been considering it. There are too many painful memories here." He rubbed his burning eyes. "I can't sleep for hearing Caroline's voice. I feel her in the room with me. I know I must get away," he continued in a hoarse voice, "but because Chandler is still nursing, I cannot take him with me."

"Don't you worry none 'bout that. Me and Mina gonna take good care of that boy. You just get yourself well."

"Thank you. And when I can reason and feel again, I will come back for him." His voice quavered as he asked, "Oh, Cassie, what will I do without her?"

"I don't know, Mr. Philip. What are we all gonna do now?"

Philip lifted his eyes slowly, the implications of her remark becoming clear to him. I can take up my life any time I want, he realized. I have money. Resources. A place in life. While she and Mina face poverty and uncertainty. I cannot let that happen. Not after all they have done for me.

He gripped Cassie's arm. "Don't worry about your future. I will see to it."

Early the next morning, Philip, dressed in his civilian clothes, stood with Cassie, Mina and Daniel in the entry hall. "Do you have the money I gave you safely tucked away?" he asked Daniel.

"Yes, sir," Daniel nodded. "Thank you. We sure appreciate you takin' care of us like that."

"It should help until I return for my boy." After bidding a tearful farewell to Cassie and Mina, and shaking Daniel's hand, he took Chandler into his arms. Holding the boy close, he filled his senses with his baby smells, and kissed him repeatedly before returning him to Mina.

"Mr. Philip," Cassie asked, her manner hesitant, "do you want them pictures of you and Miz Caroline?"

"Pictures?" After a moment, he remembered Caroline's picture on his desk. "No, I can't look at anything that reminds me of her just now."

He picked up his travel bag and surveyed the room that had served as his office since last June. I will forever cherish the memories of

Caroline caring for me in this room. The night she came to me after the Smith shooting. The quiet evenings we spent in here reading to one another.

Renewed pain engulfed him, and the happy times and loving memories were over-run by waves of guilt and grief.

"Take good care of my boy," he said in a strangled voice, and hurried out the back door to his waiting horse.

THE END

Turn the page for a preview of

HARSH IS THE FATE

Book Three in

Betty Larosa's

Four-part Creighton Family Saga

**Coming soon to your favorite
bookstore or online.**

To live on still in love, and yet in vain, . . .

Elizabeth Barrett Browning
Sonnets from the Portuguese
Number XI

PHILIP

1865-1868

Chapter 1

FOR ATTORNEY DENTON Cobb, Cape Island, New Jersey, had always held the prospect of relaxation, fun, and socializing with friends. Today, however, as his train pulled into the Grant Street station of this popular seaside resort, it presented more of a mystery about why he had been summoned here this early in June. The summer season didn't usually begin until the first week of July.

Oh well, Denton thought with a shrug of resignation, only one person can answer that perplexing question—my client.

Managing his client's business affairs had always proven exciting at times and downright contentious at others, so Denton could not help wondering what hair-brained scheme his client had in mind this time.

First, there was the amended will when he joined the Union army five years ago, naming his younger brother Matthew as his sole heir, thereby preventing his wife Elizabeth from inheriting anything should he be killed in the war. Denton couldn't help noticing that something, or someone, had transformed Philip during his short but disastrous marriage to Elizabeth Stockton. Although just what had brought about that change he would never know for sure. Perhaps some day. . .

And then, Denton recalled with dismay, after Philip inherited the Creighton family fortune earlier this year, he announced that he was in love with a lady from Virginia and they were expecting a child.

A child!

Denton shook his head and thought, Philip never ceases to amaze me.

Alighting from the train, he smiled at a comely young lady in a yellow summer frock as he made his way through the crowd. He hailed one of the many hacks awaiting the new arrivals and gave the driver an address on Franklin Street, just off Washington.

At the address, Denton knocked on the front door of the modest boarding house. A moment later, a small, sturdy woman of middle age opened the door. Her iron gray hair was pulled back into a chignon, held in place by a tortoise shell comb. Her vivid blue eyes were alert, reminding Denton of his maternal grandmother.

As she dried her hands on her apron, she smiled up at him. "May I help you, young man?"

Removing his straw hat, he returned her smile. "Good afternoon, ma'am. Is Mr. Randolph staying here?"

"You must be Mr. Cobb. Come in, come in. I am Mrs. Willingham." She stood aside as an invitation for him to enter. "Mr. Randolph said you would be arriving today."

Denton entered the foyer of the prim little cottage and glanced around. To his left, he saw a small parlor with old-fashioned furniture. Judging by its worn appearance, the room had offered hospitality to a great many guests over the years. Dust motes danced in the sunlight slanting in from the south-facing window, but everything appeared immaculately clean and highly polished.

"Mr. Randolph is not here just now," Mrs. Willingham was saying. "About this time of day, he walks on the beach. If you want to find him, just follow your nose down this street. You will run right into the ocean. There aren't many vacationers yet, so he should be easy to spot."

Denton thanked her and followed the familiar salty smell of the sea air. Several residents working in their flower gardens stopped long enough to observe his passing and wave.

At the beach, he looked up and down in both directions. Presently, he spied his friend with his trouser legs rolled above his ankles, splashing along the surf in his bare feet. With his hands thrust into his pockets, he alternately stared out at the horizon then down at the water swirling about him. But his attire was scandalous. His shirt lay open at the throat, the shirttails hung loose outside his waist band. The wind ruffled his hair and whipped his shirt against his torso, revealing a startling weight loss. Why would he who was always so meticulous about his dress suddenly appear in public in that attire? Will wonders never cease?

As his friend drew near, Denton was stunned to see that his cheeks were sunken. His hollow eyes were ringed with dark circles. Flecks of gray hair glinted in the sun. My word, he thought, he's aged in the two months since I last saw him at his brother's funeral.

Collecting himself, Denton forced a smile as his friend approached.

"Hello, Denton," Philip said. "It's good to see you. I hope you did not have too much trouble finding me."

"No," he stammered, "but I can't help wondering why you instructed me to ask for Jonathan Randolph at the boarding house."

"I don't want anyone, not anyone," he repeated emphatically, "to know I am here. Did you bring the things I asked for?"

"Yes," Denton replied, still puzzled. "I brought several hundred dollars, and asked your housekeeper to pack as much of your wardrobe as I thought you would need at a resort. But with this sudden weight loss, I doubt that anything will fit you properly."

"I'm not here on vacation." Philip sat on a stone sea wall to retrieve his shoes and socks.

Denton sat beside him, questions swirling in his brain but, keenly aware that something was amiss in Philip's life, sensed that this was not the time to give voice to them.

"I have rented Mrs. Willingham's entire establishment for the duration of my stay," Philip said as he pulled on his shoes. "However long that may be. She has prepared a room for you, unless you prefer staying at the Congress or one of the other hotels. Since it is only mid-June, the regular crowds have not yet arrived."

"Mrs. Willingham's is just fine. Although," Denton said, scratching his head, "I am curious as to why you chose a boarding house instead of a luxury suite at one of the hotels."

"It suits my purpose," came the terse reply.

Seeing the all-too-familiar brooding look in Philip's eyes, Denton sensed that this was definitely not the time to press for answers to all his perplexing questions.

Standing, Philip brushed the sand from his trousers. "Come along. I imagine you will want to freshen up after your train ride."

At the boarding house, Philip showed Denton to his room. "I see Mrs. Willingham has already brought up your luggage. My rooms are just across the hall."

"It's very nice," Denton commented, looking around the neat, plainly furnished room, with its chintz bed cover and matching curtains that billowed in the ocean breeze.

"After you have freshened up and changed, I will meet you in the parlor. We can have a drink before dinner." Without further comment, Philip walked across the hall to his own room.

Denton stripped off his rumpled clothes and availed himself of the soap and water on the wash stand. Lying across the bed to collect his thoughts, he stared up at the ceiling webbed with tiny cracks in the plaster and wondered at the radical change in Philip's appearance. *What the hell has brought him to this sorry state? What could have aged him so?*

He sat up with a start. *Good grief, what about that lady in Virginia and the child that must have been born by now? Where are they?*

He swung his legs over the edge of the bed, stood up and reached for his white linen jacket. *Oh well, whatever the problem, Philip will tell me in his own good time. Which I hope is damned soon.*

Denton found Philip in the parlor standing before the window, drink in hand, staring straight ahead. "My," Denton said, as he strode into the parlor, "this house certainly is—cozy." He indicated the frilly room with its flowered chintz-covered sofa and chair and endless bric-a-brac.

"Yes, it is a bit small, but it's private."

"I suppose that is important to you just now," Denton probed.

Tight-lipped, Philip nodded, and handed Denton a glass of bourbon.

Taking his cue from Philip's reluctant response, Denton sipped his drink in silence. Mrs. Willingham appeared a moment later to announce that dinner was ready.

During the meal of roast chicken and homemade noodles, Denton noticed that Philip picked at his food but ate little. He did, however, keep up his end of the conversation, consisting of safe topics, such as the weather, Denton's train trip to Cape Island, and his own need for a wide-brimmed hat to protect his eyes from the sun.

His eyes, Denton realized with a start. Yes, that's what is different about him. His eyes lack their usual animation. Normally capable of thinking about several things at once, his concentration was absolute. But now, the light is gone. He goes through the motions of eating, talking, breathing in and out, but Philip Creighton no longer dwells within the ravaged shell I see before me. He appears bereft of all hope, as though the very life had been drained out of him.

He barely resembles the friend I grew up with. Why?

Very well, Denton thought, reaching for his coffee cup, I will wait. But, like it or not, Philip, you will eventually answer my questions.

"Our landlady," Philip was saying, "is the widow of a sea captain. She told me that Cape Island began as a whaling village. But after the hazards of that occupation had depleted the male population, the residents decided to turn their town into a resort for vacationers. For as long as my family has been coming here, I had no idea it had such an interesting past.

"Well," he continued, placing his napkin beside his plate, "shall we adjourn to the back yard before the sun goes down?

The two friends strolled about the garden screened in by a privacy hedge of boxwood and ancient forsythia bushes. Denton chose a wooden lawn chair under a shade tree and offered Philip a cheroot.

Raising his hand in a negative gesture, Philip demurred. "No, thanks."

Denton gave him a surprised look. "When did you give up smoking?"

"About seven or eight months ago."

What, Denton wondered as he puffed the tobacco to life, would make a former army officer stop smoking?

After blowing a few smoke rings, he said, "All right, Philip, I have been patient all afternoon but I cannot pretend any longer. Why all this secrecy? And why are you using a fictitious name? Are you in some sort of trouble?"

"No. I just needed some time alone."

"Would you care to expand on that?"

"Not yet."

"Very well," Denton sighed, and took a puff on his cheroot. "The flowers smell so fragrant with the evening dew on them. Too bad the lilacs aren't still in bloom. I love the scent of lilacs in the spring, don't you?"

Philip stood up abruptly. "If you will excuse me, I will be in my room, reading. Good night."

Denton sat in the garden long after dark, smoking, and pondering Philip's erratic behavior, and wondering what the hell had just happened.

Printed in the United States
115708LV00004B/18/P